DIGITAL SECRETS

Author:
ALAN D SCHMITZ

Black Hawk Publishing

Copyright @2022 by Alan D Schmitz/Black Hawk Publishing

Black   Hawk   Publishing
Alan@AlanDSchmitz.com

Ordering Information:
Quantity sales. Special discounts are available on quantity purchases by corporations, associations, and others. For details, contact the "Special Sales Department" at the web address above.

Digital Secrets/Alan D Schmitz – 1st. ed.
ISBN 978-0-9973573-2-5

As always, while I did a great deal of research for the writing of this book, it is a book of fiction. All characters in the story are strictly fictional and are not intended to portray any particular person. Any political or religious references are used only to create the story and do not necessarily reflect my opinion nor can they be construed by anybody as an accurate representation of any religious or political party or group. All geographic locations mentioned are accurate.

One side note for Digital Secrets: Upon my research, I thought it necessary to incorporate foot notes which are particular to *Digital Secrets*. Some of my discoveries I found very interesting to say the least. I footnoted some of these facts to help separate some facts from fiction.

Acknowledgments

I want to thank my readers, for it is you who keep me writing during the most tedious of times. *Digital Secrets* is the third of the Senator series, and it's here because in your reviews you were so supportive of Senator Steven Westcott in *DNA Never Lies & El Senador*. I hope you're as excited to see Steven in this new predicament as I was to write it. In *Digital Secrets* I have created some interesting new characters and brought back familiar faces from our last adventure. And don't forget *Memories Never Die*, if you haven't read it yet. It's the book that started it all.

As this book comes to print, I am already working on the fourth in the series, having retired to become a full-time novelist I hope to produce my next book much quicker, though as those before, besides editing, I am the sole creator so it takes me a bit more time. There are more stories waiting to be told, each packed with high-stakes political conflict and life-or-death struggle for the Senator and his friends. I'm glad you're along for the ride.

I have two requests. The first is, sit back, relax, and let my story take your mind away from whatever troubles you may have, large or small. Second, a simple review on Amazon.com is always greatly appreciated. With no further Ado, time to get on with the story. Enjoy!

Chapter 1

Reidsville, North Carolina:

Wade Sullivan smiled back at the shapely blond jogging up the hill towards him. He wasn't nearly as winded as he assumed he appeared to be as he stretched his legs out. From his position, he could clearly see in both directions that they were alone for the moment.

Her arrival wasn't a surprise. Weeks ago, he had hacked her phone, and synchronized her mapping app with his. In another hour, it wouldn't matter to either of them.

It wasn't lost on him that late mornings were the most private and peaceful time on the trail. And from his last two weeks of running the trail, not coincidentally the same days as Sue Witting, he knew that Mondays were particular quiet.

What was a bit unusual for a Monday was that a sailboat race was going on at the marina far below. The small boats were manned by two people each, though they were far enough away that he couldn't make out their faces. Wade reasoned that if he couldn't see them, they couldn't see him, and they certainly wouldn't be able to see what he was about to do.

He got ready to begin his jog back home in the direction the blond was running from. As he started to jog, he reached into his pocket with his gloved hand. He felt a sexual rush as his hand wrapped around the tool he kept there.

****

Sue Witting checked her pace on her athletic watch. She looked ahead and saw that she would have to push just a bit harder as the jogging path began a slow upward grade. She looked over her shoulder from the direction she had just come, and saw that the asphalt path was still absent of other joggers or bikers . Enjoying the serenity of the wooded area Sue had come to appreciate her late morning runs as a quiet time in the park.

She looked over her right shoulder at a peculiar sound. Had it not been for the quietness of the park she never would have heard the low-pitched whirring of a small drone as it hovered below her, rose, and shot out towards sail boats bobbing on the lake below. In an instant, it was just a small speck of black against the sky.

She saw another jogger stretching out his legs atop the next rise as she jogged on and looked over the countryside. She recognized him and his running leggings and top. She had seen him before and considered them as kindred spirits, as two of the few runners who managed to skip out of work mid-day to enjoy the stillness of the park. Sue turned her head for a moment to look behind her. From her rising perch, she could see a considerable distance. Nobody would be impinging on her inner serenity for a while, at least not from the direction she had come from.

Sue smiled as she reflected on the life she loved. Living in Reidsville, North Carolina was everything she had ever wanted from a sleepy town with only 14,000 residents. For Sue and her family, it was a perfect place to live and raise a family as had her mother and Father who lived only a mile away from their daughter.

She ran on Mondays, Tuesdays, and Fridays, and was fortunate to be a work from home mom. Her sister, who lived close by, didn't mind watching her three children for a couple of hours the three times a week. It was a mid-summer Monday; the weather was perfect, as was the forecast for the rest of the week.

The path went on for miles, intersecting with other paths along the way. Her husband Jack and she were both training to do a marathon in fall which was only months away. It would be her first try and she reminded herself that failure was not an option as she pushed on.

DIGITAL SECRETS

Her athletic watch was communicating with the smart phone tucked away in her fanny pack. It recorded her pace, distance, heart rate, and other statistics. The phone was linked in real time to her husband's computer at his office. He was probably following her pace and vitals on his computer at this very moment. They had a friendly competition going and he also played a part as her running coach.

Sue could feel the sweat running down her back and soaking the back of her powder blue sports bra. Her long blond hair was tied in a bunch, and she had weaved it through the back of her baseball cap, it bounced off her back rhythmically as she ran.

Ahead of her, on top the grade, she was much closer to the man with a bright red cooling towel draped around his neck. He had a white baseball hat protecting his eyes from the bright sun. She guessed his age to be about the same as hers. She smiled at him and he smiled back. As there had been nobody in front of her, she assumed he had jogged from the other direction and stopped for a break at the top of the hill. He looked a bit winded after running the steep embankment.

Sue smiled in understanding; she was tempted to stop on top of the crest herself. The view from it was spectacular as you looked down at the lake that a dam had created. She glanced again at the serenity of a dozen white sails billowed against the aqua blue color of the reservoir. She made a mental note that on her way back she too would reward herself with a short water break at the exact same spot.

As she approached the top of the ridge, she could see over it, there was nobody but the one other jogger around to break her runner's meditation and stride. Sue smiled again at the man dressed in running gear. He had on sunglasses so she couldn't see his eyes, though he smiled back at her as he stood tall and started a jog towards her.

****

Wade took from his pocket a brand-new bright orange plastic box cutter. He slid the blade out about two inches, tightened the small lever that locked the blade in place. Keeping it hidden, he continued a light jog down the hill.

The young blond was approaching on his left. There was plenty of room for the two of them on the asphalt path. As she passed, he shot out his left hand and ran the blade under the chin of the blond. He had no need to look back; he knew that the thin razor-sharp knife had done its job.

Wade looked at his hands; he had cut so fast that the latex gloves he wore didn't have a drop of blood on them. He let the box cutter slip out of his hand onto the grass and jogged down the path.

****

Sue stopped and wondered what the man had done to her as she turned to watch him continue down the path. She had felt nothing at first, but now there was a stinging across her throat. Blood started gushing onto her hands as she reached up to check her neck. She stared down the path at the man jogging away from her as her hands were sprayed with blood.

She suddenly felt weak and fell to the ground. Looking up, she saw bright white puffy clouds against a dark blue sky. Then the beautiful world around her became dark.

****

Wade jogged toward the marina, he kept a constant joggers pace to make his escape, and that was when he noticed the drone apparently filming the race. He glanced back at his victim about an eighth of a mile behind him. She was lying peacefully on the ground with nobody else in sight.

He jogged closer to the marina and the young man piloting the drone from his smart phone. Wade removed a small device from his fanny pack. When he turned it on, it acted as a Wi-Fi signal. If the young man had the Wi-Fi turned on his phone, there would be a good chance that it would lock onto his signal.

Wade had previously set up his Wi-Fi transmitter to clone the select few automatic joins smartphones typically employed. It didn't take long for the young man's phone to connect with the fake Wi-Fi signal.

Wade could have done much the same with a Bluetooth signal, but using the Wi-Fi protocol was preferable to him. He didn't even need the phone's password to connect, as the phone thought the signal friendly to it. The fake signal he was sending out looked to the phone to be one of the automatic join systems used by all phones.

Precious minutes were being used as his system downloaded the phone's information. Soon he would have a list of apps, contacts, emails, email configurations, and the phone's texting protocols, and in time would have a complete clone of the young man's phone and all the pertinent information that was on it. Much of it would undoubtedly be encrypted, but he could deal with that later.

Trying not to appear nervous, he glanced back up the hill and saw that the young woman's body hadn't been discovered yet. He glanced at the device, which was measuring the download. It was nearly done.

As he waited, he thought about a different technique he had used to acquire all the information he needed to kill the blond so effortlessly. The strange thing: it was her husband who provided the information.

Wade glanced around, eager to jog away. The precious minutes he was pretending to watch the sailboat race were much more than inconvenient. His heart was racing. The extra time meant that if the body was found, the park could be sealed down by the police before he could bike out.

With some relief, he heard his phone ding that the download was complete. The entire process had taken three minutes. Wade hoped it wasn't three minutes too long. With another quick glance, he saw that there were no other runners or bikers in sight. Hopefully he had time for one more action.

Wade was looking at an exact duplicate of the man's cell phone, right down to the application he was using to control the drone. He turned on the identical application now on his phone and with his even more powerful signal, took over the drone.

The drone shot out over the lake and mysteriously took a nosedive into the reservoir. Wade smiled. Even though the chances of the drone's camera recording the murder of the young woman were small, it was a chance he didn't want to take. The drone was undoubtedly now in a thousand pieces, with most of it sinking to the bottom of the reservoir.

The young man stood mystified and unbelievingly at the spot where his $500 drone had just disappeared. Wade chuckled, removed the battery from his phone again, and jogged away. It didn't take long before he found an even lesser-used side path and ran down it and around a bend. He walked into the woods and found the Trek bike he had hidden there.

****

Paul Whiting held a stack of papers. He was standing in an office doorway talking to a coworker. "Listen Jack, I've read through the report twice. I get it. There are risks involved, but we can do this, trust me."

"Ohh, I trust you. It's our competition I don't trust."

Paul laughed, "If it makes you feel better, I don't trust them either. I'll get right to work on this."

Paul left Jack's office and walked to his own office across a small hallway. He lazily slid into his chair while reading parts of the report. With a click of his mouse, he woke up his computer and clicked to life the fitness app he used to track his wife's progress.

He casually glanced at the reading and saw 0 mph on his wife's speed indication. He chuckled; he had caught her resting. He looked at her average speed and saw it was way behind her normal pace. That made him wonder about her current heart rate. His heart skipped a beat when it read zero.

Paul called his wife's phone to ask if she was having a problem with her wrist monitor. When she didn't answer and her position remained unchanged, he panicked.

DIGITAL SECRETS

****

Detective Denton Jones shouted in a disgusted voice, "Stop, no, no, don't you dare go over there!"

Senator Steven Westcott, his golfing partner for the day laughed then commented, "Being a big guy doesn't mean anything on a golf course if you can't hit straight."

"Tell me about it. That's the third ball I hit out of bounds today."

"Yeah, and we still have nine holes to go."

"I hope you have some extras, Cowboy, because at this rate I'll be out of golf balls long before we finish all eighteen."

"I've got you covered, big guy."

Detective Denton 'Jojo' Jones was one of the few people on the planet that could call the Senator by the nickname given to him while they served in the Special Forces together. And the Senator was one of the few people who could call him Jojo, a nickname he also picked up during their training.

"You told me you were taking lessons?"

"I am. I guess I need a few more."

"Yeah, just a few," Cowboy deadpanned.

Detective Jones reached into his golf bag for another ball. "Maybe I can't golf, but you have to admit I can cook ribs. This Black man could give you lessons on that. I can taste their smoky flavor already. And ooh, ooh, ooh, my special barbecue sauce. Well let's just say, it's one step away from being in heaven."

"I won't argue with you about that. Chelle has heard me brag about your ribs so often she has a pretty high expectation for tonight's dinner."

"They will not disappoint, I promise. Which leads me to ask, are you and that cute detective getting serious?"

"Serious yes, marriage not even close. Turns out we are good friends."

"Just good friends, yeah right."

Steven shook his head with a smile on his face and walked up to the tee box. It was a perfect day in North Carolina. A few puffy clouds floated non-threateningly in the distance. He set his ball on a tee and after a few practice swings, hit his ball straight down the middle of the fairway.

Jojo shook his head back and forth in disgust. "I gotta say, for a puny white guy, you sure can hit the ball."

"I resent that," Senator Steven Westcott said. "I'm not puny. I'm six foot and check out these biceps. I've been working out."

Jojo stooped down slightly and brought his massive bicep up against Steven's for an impromptu competition. "What were you saying?"

Steven laughed. "OK, OK, point taken. But at least I can hit a golf ball."

Jojo re-teed his ball and hit it again. Again, it zoomed out of bounds and into the woods.

"Point taken." Jojo said as he looked disgustedly in the direction of his miss-hit.

"Just cause I'm smaller than you doesn't make me puny, and yeah, it's all about timing, and club speed. I keep telling you, but you never listen. It's about tempo, tempo, tempo."

Jojo posed a striking figure with his broad shoulders, muscular build, and six-foot-four-inch height. He sported a thin mustache that sat well on his broad face that sat on a neck that seemed as thick as his head. His face was a bit fuller on his forty-five-year-old face than it had been at their fighting trim. But that was years ago, now Jojo wore glasses and his thin short hair was showing just a tinge of grey, though most of it was still coal black.

Unlike Jojo, Steven was clean-shaven with a welcoming smile and piercing hazel eyes. His neatly combed dark brown hair didn't have a hint of grey. Something that he managed to point out to Jojo at least two times already today.

"Ok got it, tempo, tempo, tempo. Hey, did I tell you about my new eighty-inch TV?"

"You mean the one with the ultra-digital display, the voice-controlled remote, and the app that connects to all of your movies. Yea, you mentioned it."

"It is so sweet. Wait till you see it."

Jojo was just about to tee up another ball when his cell phone rang.

"Yea, Detective Jones," he answered.

Steven watched Jojo's smile relax into a sad frown.

"Ok, I'll be there shortly. Tell them to not touch a thing until I get there. I mean it, you tell them not to touch a fucking thing."

Jojo slipped his phone into his pocket and tossed his ball back into his golf bag.

"Sorry Cowboy, I gotta run. There was a murder, a young woman. I need to get there before somebody screws up the crime scene."

"Hey big buddy, I get it. No problem. Let's go."

The two best friends headed towards the parking lot carrying their golf bags.

Jojo gave some last-minute instructions to Cowboy as he placed his bag into the trunk of his unmarked police cruiser.

"In exactly three hours, take the ribs out of the smoker. Put some more of the barbecue sauce that you will find in the refrigerator on them and cover with tin foil to keep them warm in the oven."

"Got it! Don't worry about dinner. Go do your thing."

"Tell the girls I'll be home as soon as I can."

"Good luck, buddy. Go get the bad guys."

"Oh I will, trust me, I will."

Jojo slid into the driver's seat and with his big hand he reached up through the window and popped a magnetic police light on top of his car. Seconds later, he exited the golf course parking lot and sped down the road with his siren screaming.

******

Tamara happened to be watching out the window when Jojo came home. It was later than she had expected. They lived in an older part of town, with huge mature oak trees lining the boulevard. The two-story, four-bedroom home they shared with their daughter still living at home dated back to the 1950s and was near the center of town. After an expensive remodel job undertaken five years ago, it was modern and comfortable.

Alan D Schmitz
DIGITAL SECRETS

Tamara walked into the kitchen as Jojo placed his holstered pistol into a small gun safe that he had installed inside a kitchen cabinet. He closed the safe door then closed the cabinet door over it. She watched, silently gauging his mood as her husband of twenty-three years opened the refrigerator door and withdrew a beer. With a quick twist from his wrist the top of the beer bottle was open. He tipped it up to his mouth and took a drink from the brown bottle.

She stepped up from behind and ran her hand around his thick waist as she came around in front of him and welcomed him home with a peck on the cheek. He gave her a small squeeze and a glance that told her it had been a rough day and he needed a few minutes to decompress from the unpleasantness that was his job.

Tamara, an ex-cop herself, understood and went back out to attend their guests on the back patio. Steven and Chelle, Steven's girlfriend, were sitting next to each other, also enjoying a cold beer. They were engrossed in a conversation ignoring the commercials on the outdoor television that was on as they waited for news about the local murder.

Tamara and Jojo had married young, and the years together had sped by. Her smooth ebony skin and wrinkle free face gave her a look much younger than the forty-three she actually was. Her hair was dark black and straight, and she now wore it at shoulder length, a bit shorter than she used to. She had also been able to maintain the trim figure on her five-foot, five-inch frame. At times she would be confused for the older sister of one of her daughters, something she delighted in and her daughters cringed at.

Steven looked up at Tamara as she came through the threshold of the door.

"How's Jojo doing? It's been a pretty rough day for him." Steven said.

"He'll be out shortly, but yeah, he just needs a bit of time to process what he saw today. He does his best to keep work from affecting our lives, but it's not always easy," Tamara said as she sat down on a plushy cushioned wicker chair opposite Steven and Chelle.

"As a former police detective I certainly understand. Do you think we should go?" Chelle asked.

FBI Special Agent Chelle Saltarie, formerly Police Detective Saltarie was in her mid-forties. She was a small woman, and her regular exercise program kept her shapely body trim. Her naturally curly brunette hair tucked inward just above her shoulder and brought out the color of her sparkling blue eyes.

However, any bad guy that tried to take advantage of her small size would soon find themselves at a huge disadvantage. Her weekly training in Krav Maga, a martial art developed for the Israel Defense Forces, would literally put them in their place on the ground.

Tamara protested, "My goodness no, he needs the distraction. Thank God, Reidsville is mostly a sleepy little town. When there is a murder here, we all take it personally, and none more than Denton."

Steven changed the subject, "Where's Kristal?"

"Her older sister came by and picked her up for a girl's day. They're on a mission to find a 'Dancing Chickens' sweatshirt for Kristal to wear to school."

"I've heard that they are the latest and greatest band," Chelle said.

Tamara nodded her head in agreement, "The group is on fire. I must admit, I like some of their music."

"I've heard 'Time to Reboot.' I kind of liked it. And how is Lorelei doing?" Chelle asked.

"First job after college, exciting time for her. Luckily for us she took a job in town."

The conversation came to an immediate halt when the commercial break ended and the television mounted outside and protected from the elements by the porch overhang mentioned the murder once again. They had been watching the news all afternoon as the local station reported on the murdered mother of three.

DIGITAL SECRETS

The male reporter looked seriously into the camera. "In our continuing coverage of this story, I want to remind the audience that there have been no arrests made yet in this gruesome murder. Here I am earlier in the day talking with the detective in charge of the investigation."

In an instant, Denton Jones's somber face came into view.

"Detective Jones, do you have any suspects in this grisly murder?" the reporter asked.

"None at this time. We are at the beginning stages of the investigation. However, I am confident we will find the perpetrator of this terrible crime."

"So, you believe it was only one person."

"At this time, I have no reason to suspect otherwise."

"Do you believe that this murder is related to the murder two months ago of Irving Duncan?"

"I have no reason to assume they are in any way connected."

"But if my memory serves me right, you never caught that suspect."

"As I said, it is still early in this investigation, and suicide is strongly suspected in the other death."

"But suicide was never proven?"

"No, the investigation is still open. That is all I have for you now, thank you."

Detective Jones turned his back and the screen cut back to real time as the reporter finished recapping things for his audience.

Jojo stepped out onto the outdoor patio and said, "Bullshit. I'll eat my gun if they're not related. It's just officially I was told not to connect the dots. Publicly announcing that we might have a serial killer running around Reidsville is not politically acceptable."

Chelle asked, "Do you want to talk about it?"

"It might be good for me to get some of what I'm thinking off my chest. Let me change into something more appropriate, then we'll talk."

Five minutes later, Jojo came back to the patio dressed in a pair of shorts and a t-shirt with a brightly colored parrot on it.

He had brought it back from a Bahamian vacation and to Tamara's regret it had become his official party shirt.

Jojo tossed an orange box cutter on the outside dining table; it slid to a stop in front of Chelle. "You tell me what you think. Both murders had an identical box cutter left at the scene and both people were killed with a deeply slashed throat cleanly sliced open by it."

"On television you said the first was suspicious of a suicide," Chelle asked.

"Yes, that's what I said. That is the official party line until I find the real killer. The first death was a businessman, a guy named Irving Duncan. His business was doing fine, so there doesn't appear to be a financial motive to kill himself. The autopsy didn't reveal any medical issues that might drive a suicide, but his wife of twenty years was divorcing him. Even though that could be considered motivation, I didn't buy suicide two months ago and I certainly don't buy it now."

"But you don't have a suspect for either murder, I'm guessing," Chelle added.

"Not a f'n clue. Just what you see on the table, that's all I got to go on. And I got that in a ten pack at the hardware store. Just like everybody else in the county.

"No fingerprints, no witnesses, no motives, nothing. And the cutters were both brand new, no forensic residue."

"Any cameras in the park?" Chelle asked.

"No, nothing. There are miles of recreational paths."

Chelle thought for a moment, "No fingerprints on either weapon?"

"No, both clean."

"You think somebody just picks random targets, slits their throats, and walks away?"

"That is one theory. He or she picks a spot, waits for the right time and victim."

"Scary," Steven interjected and asked, "Maybe they're not connected. What about the young woman's husband? Maybe a lover's quarrel?"

DIGITAL SECRETS

"Husband called it in, from his office. He was monitoring her jogging routine and noticed that she wasn't moving down the path and her heart rate was registering zero on their mutually shared athletic app. He was the one that insisted the police check on his wife. Shortly after his call, we got a call from the park by another jogger.

"The husband was at work all day, perfect alibi. I spoke with the husband, he was in shock, It wasn't him. Doubt she was having an affair, but we are still checking on it. My guess is still a random killing."

"And a random killer is hard to catch," Chelle reminded everyone. "No motive, no connection to the victims. The killer gets to pick the time and place."

Jojo took another drink of his beer. "A detective's worst nightmare. If we assume the attacks are connected, we can assume the attacker is a male. It would take some strength to cut that deep and fast."

Steven leaned forward and picked up the box cutter off the table and opened it. "Extremely sharp and thin and light. I wouldn't rule out a woman, though because of the savagery I agree it would be unlikely."

"Hell hath no fury like a woman scorned," Tamara remarked.

Jojo shook his head, "First thought I had. Positively not. The second victim was a very happily married woman and mother. And there is no motive that I can find for someone to kill the businessman. If someone killed him for money, staging a suicide negates any life insurance.

"The affair by his wife was already out in the open and a divorce pending. His wife or her boyfriend had little motive. I am of course still researching that angle, but they both have alibis for time of death. He was found in his car, in his garage by his wife. The knife was lying on the seat next to him. At this time, I believe the wife was not involved."

"But," Chelle interjected, "you said no prints on the knife."

"Which begs the question, how did he kill himself with it and not leave any prints on the suicide weapon?" Jojo finished.

Jojo answered his own question as he picked up a cheese snack and popped it into his mouth. "Apparently, he was a very conscientious suicide. He had on latex gloves. You know, the kind a dentist or doctor would wear."

Chelle didn't buy it, "He was killing himself and worried about his hands getting bloody?"

"It's a little hard for me to believe too, that's why I suspect foul play. And as far as I can tell, the two victims didn't know each other and had zero mutual connections."

Chelle came up with another scenario, "Maybe it's not entirely random. It could be somebody who knows the victims in one way or another and knows his or her habits. Thus, he knows where they will be and when. Based on that, they pick the murder spot."

"Plausible but again unlikely," Jojo argued. "That would imply some commonality. And maybe that is the needle in the haystack. I've got officers canvassing the area now looking for witnesses to anything unusual, we'll stop all the bikers and joggers in the park to see if maybe somebody saw something. As you can see, I have a right proper dilemma to solve. And assuming it is random killings, he or she could strike again at any time."

"One more unsolved murder and you will have a panicked community on your hands," Steven reminded him pensively.

"And panicked politicians with hands around my neck." Jojo looked into Tamara's eyes and added, "In the meantime, there is a family who lost a mother and wife today. God bless them."

Tamara hugged her big man and said, "I know you will find justice for them."

Steven tossed the box cutter back onto the table, Jojo picked it up again and turned it around in his hand, hoping it might trigger some answers. Looking up from it, he said, "OK, enough shop talk. I need to get my mind on something else. Tomorrow is going to be a long day."

Chelle took Steven's hand in hers and squeezed it as she said, "Officially the FBI can't get involved unless or until there are three or more connected murders. And even then, we have to be requested by the head of the law enforcement agency within the prosecutorial jurisdiction."

Chelle looked at Steven, caught his eye, looked back at Jojo and said. "If I can be of any help unofficially, let me know, even if it's just to bounce some ideas around."

"Thanks Chelle, I might take you up on that. We're a small town with small resources."

"Who is ready for another beer and the best ribs in the world? That is, if Cowboy didn't screw them up on me." Jojo joked

"Wow, did you guys see how fast he was willing the throw me under the bus. I just kept them warm. It's still your recipe, and I can't wait another minute to dig in."

Jojo toasted, "To friendship." Each raised their drink in salute. Jojo finished his beer before retreating back into the kitchen to finish preparing his special recipe ribs.

****

Wade looked over his shoulder as he pushed off with one foot and slipped his jogging shoes into the pedals of his Trek bike. He casually pedaled through the park and away from the lake, leaving the stunned drone pilot and lifeless woman behind in the silence of the wooded park path.

His application had again worked perfectly, and he now had everything he needed to know about Tony Reilly, the drone pilot. And what wasn't in the phone could be accessed from his computer, because now Wade had e-mail addresses, e-mail history, passwords, and much, much more.

The high-speed racing bike was easily a mile away four minutes later. He guessed that because he hadn't seen anybody but the racers. It would take at least ten minutes for somebody to come across the dead woman and another fifteen for the police to arrive. By that time, Wade calculated he would be back at his car five miles away and driving home.

DIGITAL SECRETS

Killing somebody with the right amount of information and planning seemed all too simple. Getting away with that murder seemed equally simple. Wade wondered if there wasn't a way to make the game a bit more exciting. He smiled at his own cleverness and about how his plan to kill the young woman had come about.

Two weeks ago, her husband Paul was having a beer with some friends at a local bar. While sitting alone at a corner table, Wade turned on his bluesnarfing software. That meant using his Bluetooth interceptor in his backpack to scan for signals.

Paul had his Bluetooth on his phone enabled to sync with his exercise band, which provided a back door into Paul's phone. While Paul joked with his buddies, Wade downloaded his phone's information from a corner booth while he ate a pulled pork sandwich and nibbled on some fries.

The easy part was fooling Paul's phone to think it was doing a backup, so all the information on it would be transferred. The hard part would be finding the right code to access the encrypted information on it. For that he would need Paul's six-digit numerical password.

Back home later that night, Wade had to make several attempts to unlock Paul's phone. He was prepared to have his home-made computer crunch it out if needed, but sometimes the old-fashioned way was still best and fastest.

It turned out that, Paul was like most people and used a simple code, something Paul and his wife would remember. The simple, six-digit numeric code was Paul's wedding date. That had been easy to find doing a short online search of Paul's name, which came up with all sorts of personal information that was also publicly available.

It wasn't the first set of numbers he had tried. Birthdays were always popular, your own, a spouse's, or children's. Street address, parts of your telephone number, or even Social Security numbers. In Paul's phone's case, it wasn't even a half-hour of attempts, when the clone phone gave up all its secrets.

The next day, Wade smirked in self appreciation as he recalled his exploits as he unlocked his bike from the bike rack mounted to his car. He hung it up on the two hooks in his garage. Inside his home, Wade gently set his backpack and all the contents in it onto the kitchen table. The old table was scratched and worn; it served as his office most of the time. He slipped out his laptop, connected the phone to it, and started to download all of Tony's info from his phone onto his computer. Tony didn't know it, of course, but he had just given Wade everything he needed to know to kill him. Just as he had used the information gleaned from Paul's phone to kill his wife.

While the download was going on, Wade showered and made a sandwich. Finishing the last of his sandwich and a glass of milk, he cracked his knuckles and started the timer on his watch. He wondered if he could crack into Tony's encrypted information even faster than he had Paul's.

Ten minutes later, Wade shouted excitedly, "Yes." He was looking at all the encrypted information. Tony thought his birthday had been a sufficient password. Maybe it was if you wanted to stop a casual acquaintance from using your phone without your permission. But it certainly wouldn't stop any dedicated hacker, as he had just proved.

Ten minutes was good, though not his fastest time. Wade also knew that time was relevant only to the challenge. Because it didn't really matter. He always cracked into a code, always. His most challenging had been days and that was before he had Mercury to help him.

After a few clicks, he was seeing exactly what the drone had seen. The flight had been recorded to Tony Reilly's phone. Wade watched his computer screen and relived the flight, wondering exactly what the drone might have recorded.

Chapter 2

Washington D.C.:

Senator Westcott entered his fifth-floor office inside the Philip A. Hart Senate Office Building just minutes from the United States Capitol building. He had just sat down at his desk and was set to read the Washington Post. It was still folded in half in his hand when his side office door opened.

"Hello Senator, good morning."

His scheduler, Shannon Johnston, greeted him and handed him a cup of hot coffee.

"Good morning, Shannon. And how are you today?"

"I'm great, I took your advice and took the weekend off. I visited Mom and Dad."

"How's my buddy Teddy doing?"

"Dad's doing great, and Mom too. Thanks for the time off and the advice. But this morning, things are off to a hectic start."

"Situation normal. Senate hearings?"

"Mostly. Half the senators want you to shut down the hearings and the other half want to know why you are dragging your feet and not pursuing leads faster."

"Yeah, and the press are just as divided. So how do I keep such a politically charged topic apolitical?"

"Probably can't, Senator. Nobody on either side would believe you are trying to do that anyways."

"I'm sure you're right, but that doesn't mean I can't try. I do want answers, but I want people to believe that they are honest answers so that our conclusion is also accepted as honest."

"I'm sorry, Senator, you are in Washington, D.C. Nobody is going to believe anybody here is honest, especially the chairman of the Senate Select Committee on Intelligence."

"I didn't expect a full inquiry to be easy, but I didn't think getting simple straight answers from our own agencies would be so difficult. Senate subpoenas mean nothing anymore. It's a joke. My God, in testimonies before us, our guest can't seem to 'recall' even their own names. The term stonewalling has risen to a whole new level.

Alan D Schmitz
DIGITAL SECRETS

"And worse, my own party is pressing me to close the hearings before elections. They're afraid it might reflect badly on their governance. If I don't come up with a compelling reason to keep this hearing open, and soon, I will be forced into closing it down.

"My committee's number one priority is specifically, to 'provide vigilant legislative oversight over the intelligence activities of the United States to assure that such activities are in conformity with the Constitution and laws of the United States.' How can the committee do that when everybody promises their full cooperation when talking to the press but as soon as they come before us, they all get sudden amnesia? And I'm sick of it. Hell, I would swear that half the people on my committee are in cahoots with them and ask softball inconsequential questions when given their chance to probe deeper."

"If you want my opinion...."

Steven smirked and gave a wide smile back at his scheduler, "Shannon, you and I both know that I am going to hear your opinion whether I want to or not. Besides, your opinion is worth more to me than all the other Senators' combined."

"That's because I tell it like it is. I'm not worried about a politically incorrect sound bite getting released on the evening news. And my advice is to keep digging, Senator. The more pushback you get, the closer you are to getting at the truth."

Steven couldn't agree more with the young woman's intuition. If he had learned nothing else over the last few years, it was that nothing in Washington was what it seemed on the outside. It was a lesson he had learned the hard way. Trust was not something Steven Westcott gave away easily these days.

"Well, I must be getting close. There is something fishy going on in the intelligence community and I am going to find out what it is. I'm going to start reminding them in some profoundly real terms that our committee can affect their purse strings. I want to know what the NSA is doing with ten billion dollars a year. Lord knows, our committee can't even find out how many employees they have. And we have top security clearances. If we can't know, who the hell does?"

DIGITAL SECRETS

"Keep squeezing them, Senator. On that note, I finally have some potential dates for the next hearing."

"Good, time to start working on more subpoenas or we will be sitting at that hearing with nobody to hear from, and that will be the end of it for sure."

Shannon glanced back at her list of notes.

"Just a reminder, this is your weekend with Tracy."

"Shannon!" Steven looked disappointed. "How could you think I would forget that my daughter is coming to town to visit me?"

"Because you left a note for me to try and get you in at Bistro on the River for Saturday night."

Steven felt his face turn flushed, something he was sure Shannon hadn't missed.

"Oh, that," Steven admitted sheepishly.

"I assumed you weren't taking your fifteen-year-old daughter to the swankiest new restaurant in town."

"I... I... just got my weekends mixed up."

"That's what I thought, so I made the reservations for a week from Saturday."

Shannon handed Steven a separate slip of paper with handwritten notes. "This is a list of possible things you and Tracy might want to do this weekend."

Steven looked down the list and smiled. "Shannon you're an angel."

"I know."

The Senator's cell phone rang. He glanced at the caller ID. He looked up at Shannon and said, "It's Chelle."

Shannon nodded that she understood, she said, "I'll be back in ten minutes, no longer. We have just started on this list."

Steven saluted Shannon crisply and said, "Aye, Aye sir!"

Shannon was just leaving the room when Steven answered and said, "Hi Chelle, glad you called. Say, about this Saturday..."

Reidsville, North Carolina:

Wade lifted an old rifle off his kitchen table. He had just oiled it, and with a few clicks checked that the action was smooth. The rifle had been handed down from his grandfather to his father. After his father passed, the rifle had become his.

It didn't have a scope, but Wade knew the sight was accurate. Besides, he wouldn't be shooting far. Knives were pure and clean when used right, but he had a date on a golf course and his victim would be amongst friends. After deliberating for days on the best way to commit his next perfect murder, he had decided that only a gun would do.

He had already scouted out the area on a morning jog. He had gone over the details in his mind repeatedly, writing anything down would be a mistake he wouldn't make. His plan was simple.

Wade looked at his phone and the intercepted text messages of a Mr. Bill Sanders. The weather looked beautiful and per the text messages between Bill and his golf buddies, they were all set on a tee-time for the morning. Guessing about fifteen minutes per hole, Wade had a good idea of when they would all be at the twelfth hole, the most secluded on the course.

****

Jojo was in his car, racing to the scene of yet another murder. Three weeks after the still unsolved murder of the woman in the park, he instinctively knew he was hunting for a serial killer.

He left his flashing blue police light on as he parked his otherwise unmarked black police cruiser along the side of a country road that paralleled a golf course. He knew the course. Three weeks before, he had played it with Senator Westcott.

In front of his police cruiser was an ambulance with its red lights flashing. Its job was now that of a hearse. He was told that the victim had died instantly.

The course had rolling hills and wooded seclusion. There were a few homes around it, though most were hidden from view. The particular hole he had parked next to was hole number twelve. It was well away from the clubhouse and about as secluded an area as the course offered, though there were others.

Jojo fought his way through a thicket between the country road and the golf course. When he emerged, he saw a group of people gathered on top of the raised putting green. Jojo silently walked up the small ridge onto the ultra-short, manicured grass of the putting surface. Only a few feet from him was the dead man. He was lying face down. The red pool of blood that surrounded him contrasted morbidly with the dark green grass.

Jojo, silently and intently focused, stared at the dead man for a moment. There was no doubt the man had died immediately. Half his head was gone, and blood, brains, and pieces of skull were splattered about.

He moved to his best guess at where the victim had been standing before getting shot. Jojo slowly turned his face around the course. He did this twice. With one more scan of the area he pointed.

"There. That's where the shooter took up position. If he was any kind of a marksman, he couldn't miss."

Jojo pointed to a uniformed officer. "You, come with me. But walk only where I walk. And if I tell you to freeze, you don't move a step. You understand?"

"Yes sir." Jojo could hear nervousness in the young officer's voice.

The two men slowly moved toward the spot he had pointed to. All eyes were on him since he had stood silently and calmly scanning the area. About twenty feet from the edge of a wooded area, he stopped and scanned each and every tree and branch. He made a choice and walked confidently towards it.

Just outside the woods he stopped and stooped down examining the ground before entering the area. He looked up and saw the branch he had spied earlier, and he took two steps into the woods towards it. It looked to be at the proper height, he examined it closely. Without touching it, he took a picture of a bare spot where the rifle had rubbed some of the bark off. He stepped back and took a photo of the tree and branch. He didn't think it his imagination; the smell of gunpowder was still around the tree.

He shouted out to the officer just feet from him, "Get some people up here and mark off a do not trespass line twenty feet either side of me. And nobody enters these woods until I say."

"Yes sir."

Jojo heard the officer talking into his radio and relaying the command. The street was not far, so he stepped out the woods towards it.

"Son of a bitch," he said out loud, though he was the only one to hear his voice.

The frontage road he and the ambulance and several squad cars were parked on was intersected by another road leading directly away from the golf course. That left the killer with three possible directions to escape.

Jojo stood still and let his senses absorb his surroundings. Besides the officer's radio, there were no sounds but a few birds chirping. The country road was still open to traffic but looking up and down the three directions he saw none.

No homes were in sight. He walked across the road and again searched up and down it. Apparently, the road was lightly traveled.

"Sir, sir." The officer shouted through the woods.

"What is it?" Jojo sounded angry, though he was just focused and didn't want to be disturbed.

"Sorry sir, they need you by the body. They want to know if they can wrap it and take it away. They have it chalked and photos taken."

"Yes, but tell them any witnesses need to stay."

Jojo spotted something down the road intersecting away from the course. He started walking towards it as the road started a downward grade. After a quarter-mile he saw just as he suspected. There was a small lake, more of a marsh. It had cattails growing along the edges.

"You son of a bitch," he said again. "I'll bet a day's pay you threw the gun in there and just drove away like nothing happened, didn't you? No, you didn't drive away, at least not from here. No car, too easy to track, somebody might have seen it parked nearby. That would give us color, make, and so on.

"I'll bet you dropped off the gun a day or two before and hid it in the woods. Later, you jogged up, killed a random golfer, and tossed the gun into the lake. And just like you jogged away from the young woman you killed, you jogged down the road like nothing happened. You bastard."

Jojo found his way back to the course. As soon as he was in hearing distance of the officer dutifully waiting for him, he said, "I need a patrol car guarding the lake a quarter mile down Miller Road from here."

Jojo was sure he knew what had happened. He would take the time to interview the dead man's buddies, even though he doubted they would have any idea who would want to kill their friend.

What he wouldn't share with them was that any one of them could have just as easily been killed. It was only the luck of the draw that the lifeless body of the man being taken away was just the easiest target at the time.

Jojo wondered why the shooter had stopped at only one victim. Certainly, he would have had time to shoot at least one other during the confusion.

****

Wade Sullivan hung his Trek bike upside down on the hooks in his garage. His electronic odometer said that he had ridden twenty miles that day. That checked with the time on his watch. It took about forty-five minutes to get to the golf course. He had to wait about fifteen minutes for the foursome to start putting on the twelfth hole.

He walked into his suburban home and checked the refrigerator for something to eat. With nothing of interest in the refrigerator, he found some frozen, pre-made hamburgers in the freezer. It was still a beautiful day out, so he decided to grill his next meal outside and enjoy it. Outside, the sun was warm against his face. He closed his eyes and looked towards it and let

Alan D Schmitz
DIGITAL SECRETS

it warm him. It had been a perfect day for a leisurely twenty-mile ride on his bike. Wade smiled, thinking about Bill Sanders. Only an hour ago he was enjoying a beautiful day and a round of golf. Shame he didn't get to enjoy the entire day.

Wade started a pile of charcoal on the fire, and soon it was white hot. He carried a plate with two burgers on it out to the grill. But before cooking his burgers, he tossed the pair of latex gloves he had worn in the woods onto the white-hot coals; they quickly shriveled up into nothing.

Replacing the grilling rack, he dropped his frozen burgers onto it as they sizzled and steamed. While watching his burgers cook, he contemplated what he had done with an empty satisfaction as he sipped on an ice-cold beer.

This morning's exercise had gone exactly as planned and he was sure he would never be associated with it in any way. How could he? But that made him feel a bit disappointed. The murders were feeling like hollow victories. Yes, he was successful, but if he planned and executed the murders properly, he would never be caught. But that would also mean he would never get the credit for perpetrating the perfect murders.

Bill Sanders was most certainly dead. The shot had been accurate. Getting into the right place and the right time had been ridiculously easy. Like everybody else, Bill had habits, habits that could be exploited. It was as simple as following Bill to the driving range. Bill used his golf watch to keep track of the distances he hit his various golf clubs. His watch was connected to his phone via Bluetooth. Again, Wade faked Bill's carrier's signal and cloned his phone. With that, Wade had all the information he needed to plan another death.

Wade chuckled at the philosophical dilemma. Of course, he didn't want to go to prison, or worse, be sentenced to death. But what was the point of committing the perfect murders if he didn't get some sort of recognition?

He carried his cooked burgers into the kitchen and finished them off with some ketchup, mustard, a couple of leaves of lettuce and a slab of cheese. Adding some chips and beans, he headed out the kitchen with a beer in hand towards to living area where the television was playing some sort of game show. He slid down into his recliner just as a commercial came on.

The commercials came to an end, and he continued to munch on his hamburger as the ongoing program was interrupted by a local news flash. A female reporter looked seriously at her audience inside the lens of the camera. "This is Cynthia Rosen reporting live from the Templeton golf course. Today, sometime around ten A.M., a man was fatally shot right here not far from where I am standing. So far, the police have no suspect, but Detective Jones is here, and I will see if I can get a word with him."

Wade sat up and set his plate on the nearby end table. He moved to the edge of his chair with his chin resting lightly on the fingertips of his interlaced fingers he spoke to the television.

"Yes, do tell us, Detective. How will you catch this terrible person? Why don't you tell them you don't have a fucking clue? Have you even put two and two together yet? This is a string of murders, dumbass."

Wade saw that the detective had almost managed to get his car door open before being jumped by the reporter. He could see the reluctance in his face as he stepped up to the reporter looking somber. Wade guessed it was no act.

The reporter talked hurriedly to convey the serious pace of the breaking news. "Detective, Detective Jones, please, please could you tell the citizens of Reidsville how this could happen here. What is being done to catch the murderer and how do you stop it from happening again?"

"This was a terrible tragedy and mine and the city's sympathies goes to the family of the deceased. The murder happened only hours ago so the investigation is just beginning."

"What investigation, dumbass? What are you looking for? Who are you looking for?" Wade said arrogantly at the television.

"We are withholding the victim's name until his next of kin can be properly notified."

Wade smiled at the TV and said, "I'll bet my life that you won't find the gun at the bottom of the marsh; you won't even look. And even if you did, so what? It was my gramp's old gun and he bought it at a gun show. It would tell you nothing. Admit it to your citizens, you have nothing. And there is nothing you can do to stop me," Wade said out loud with a bit of disgust in his voice.

Detective Jones continued, "And I promise that I am doing everything in my power to catch the killer of these victims."

Wade excitedly slapped his knees. "Holy crap, you did figure out part of it?"

Jojo's face, magnified on the television, immediately gave away the fact that he had misspoken. But it was too late, the reporter picked up on it too.

"Are you suggesting, detective, that the other murders are tied to the same killer? Does this mean there is a serial killer roaming the streets of Reidsville?"

"I have no proof of that, but I wouldn't be doing my job if I didn't consider the possibility."

Wade heard his cell phone ring. He looked at the caller ID and a questioning frown took over his face. "Hi, this is Wade."

"Wade, dude, it's me Red, you know, James McConally."

"Yeah, I got you, man, I just wasn't expecting to hear from you."

"I know, long time, dude. I have an invitation for you."

Wade glanced back at the television.

"Hold on for a sec, Red." Wade put his phone on mute and listened to the television. The reporter cupped her earpiece tight against her as she got a spin directive from her producer. She spoke with even more urgency in her voice. "Ok folks, you heard it here first. Reidsville possibly has a serial killer on the loose. He or she could literally be anywhere. As you know, there have been a string of murders all unsolved and all within the last two months."

Wade saw the detective in the background climb into his car. Soon the car was out of the scene. "You better flee. You have no answers, none. You are completely lost, aren't you Detective Jones?"

Wade realized the excitement had come back. He was smiling ear to ear and had got out of his chair and was pacing back and forth in front of the television feeling more alive than he had in a long time. Power seemed to be coursing through his blood. It was an excitement he hadn't expected. Even though Wade knew he had to stay anonymous, at least his actions were being noticed. Soon they would give him a name, they always did. He wondered if they would call him the 'Slasher', or 'The Reidsville killer', or maybe the 'Reidsville Slasher'.

Wade unmuted his phone just in time to hear.

"Wade, Wade, are you still there?"

Wade hit the mute button on the television.

"Sorry Red, I just was distracted for a moment by something on TV."

Wade fought to contain his excitement as he thought. *Finally, they notice. Finally. All right, now we're talking.*

"You were saying something about an invitation?"

"Freddy Farly is having a massive party during Blackhat USA in Vegas this August. You're going to Blackhat aren't you?"

"Of course. No self-respecting master hacker like myself would think of missing it and DEFCON too. What about you?"

"Nah, my boss wouldn't spring for DEFCON. They only take cash and if he can't write it off, it's a no-go. Anyways, Freddy said I should invite you to his place when you're in Vegas. He is sort of sorry for what happened and doesn't want any hard feelings between you guys."

"Fats wants to apologize to me?"

"I didn't say apologize, I mean he had no choice, he had to can you. But he isn't pissed at you or anything. He said he doesn't hold a grudge and still respects your work. In fact, he thinks you are one of the greatest hackers of all time."

"Fats said that about me?"

"Yeah man, but don't call him Fats, he doesn't like that."

"Is he still fat?"

"Oh yeah."

"Sure, I'll go, sounds like fun. I would like to say hi to Fats to let him know that I don't have any hard feelings either."

"Awesome man. I'll be in touch with the details. See you in Vegas."

Wade tossed his phone onto the end table in front of the TV. The invite was intriguing. Meeting up with Fats would be fun. Except he did hold a grudge against the man that fired him from the best job ever.

Wade crinkled his empty aluminum beer can together and tossed it into the garbage. With a wry smile on his face he thought, *I'll bet I can find a creative way to make my Vegas trip a bit more interesting.*

****

"Welcome back to D.C." Senator Westcott gave his daughter a big bear hug. "How was your flight?"

"The flight was great; I'm starting to know some of the flight attendants."

"I'm so sorry you must do so much traveling, sweetheart. But with everything going on..., well I'll be honest. It's so much easier on me if you come out here than if I go to Peabody."

"Dad, I didn't mean it as a bad thing. I love coming to D.C. It's only an hour-and-a-half flight, and everyone is so nice to me on the plane, which is all I meant. Besides, I get it, after the divorce you don't have much reason to come back to Peabody."

"It sure seems that way. My apartment back in Massachusetts doesn't seem to get much use, even though it's where my constituency is. This job is supposed to be part-time. That's how the founding fathers saw it. It's supposed to be about everyday folks taking time off from their everyday occupations to serve in Washington for a while, and returning to their homes and regular work after performing their duty to country.

"And I guess I have gotten caught up in the professional politician occupation like so many others. The fact is, nobody can do this job and keep their former occupation going too. And I don't know that is a good thing. I think the framers of the Constitution had it right. But enough shop talk. I have a wonderful weekend all planed. And tonight, we can have takeout at home or we can go out to wherever you want."

Tracy tugged her rolling bag behind her and suggested, "Pizza at your place sounds best to me. After that you can teach me some more about poker."

"Teach you? You mean you want to scam your dear old dad out of more of his hard-earned money?"

"You let me win last time; I know it."

"Don't be so sure."

Steven took Tracy's bag from her and pulled it to the taxi stand.

As they walked, Tracy asked, "How's Chelle? You're still seeing her, aren't you?"

Steven paused for a moment looking away and down the road for the next taxi. It was hard to think of his little girl as sounding so adult.

"I'm tempted to say none of your business, but I guess in a way it is. And yes, I'm still seeing her."

"I'll bet I can think of another reason you stay in Washington."

"And you are growing up way too fast."

Soon it was their turn for a taxi and Steven opened the door for Tracy, placed the rolling bag in the trunk, and ran to the other side and got in. Steven wrapped the safety belt around him and clicked it closed. With a side-glance he was happy to see that Tracy had already done the same.

"What about Shannon? Will we have time to visit her?" Tracy asked once the taxi was on its way to Steven's apartment.

"That could be arranged. I know she will be at the office tomorrow and I need to do a quick stop-in anyways."

"How's she doing?"

"She's fine, in fact she was back in Peabody last week visiting her family."

"I know that her dad is still mom's attorney on the financial stuff. I hear her talking to him sometimes."

"That isn't any of my business, but Teddy is a good guy and will treat your mother fine. In my opinion, she's in good hands."

Traffic was light and soon the taxi was on the 395 heading over the Potomac and back into Washington D.C. Steven's mind

drifted off to his married life. He carried no ill will towards
Tracy's mother. The affair she had was nothing short of
entrapment by evil doers. His wife an easy target after the loss of
their daughter to a drug overdose as their relation had suffered
as a result.

It was a bad time for the two of them and Tracy too. His wife
had found some comfort in another's arms. He didn't fault her
for that.

Steven was woken to the present when Tracy asked, "Will
we be back to the apartment by nine Saturday night?"

"I guess we could be. Why?"

"Dad, don't you read the news? The Dancing Chickens are
going to be on cable."

"The what?"

"You know, the band. It's their first television appearance.
It's a live concert and they're going to broadcast it. It's a pay-per-
view thing. Can we get it?"

"That's right, I have heard of them. I think they are a favorite
of Kristal Jones too."

"I know they are."

"And how would you know that?"

"Kristal and I are Facebook friends. And every now and then
we talk."

"I didn't know you two were such good friends."

"Dad, we practically grew up together."

"I guess you did."

"Anyhow, The Dancing Chickens are my favorite band in the
whole world and they're going to be live on cable Saturday."

"I see no reason we can't be back in plenty of time to watch
them."

"You could ask Chelle over. We can have a party."

Steven was taken aback and sat up a bit and turned toward
his daughter. "You want me to ask my girlfriend over?"

"Sure why not, we're all adults. I should get to know her,
don't you think?"

Steven slid back into his seat. "Young lady, let me remind you that you are not an adult yet, but you certainly are growing up."

Steven didn't know if it was a good idea or not. The taxi started off, he finally said, "I guess I could ask."

Chapter 3

Chelle was sitting at her desk inside FBI headquarters on Pennsylvania avenue just blocks from the White House. She was sorting through the FBI's version of the Post Office's dead letter files. It was her job to sort through the pile of request and determine which ones had true merit.

Her phone rang, "Hello."

"Hi Chelle, this is Steven."

"Hi, so nice to hear your voice. How are you today?"

"Doing great, Tracy's flight was right on time and we're doing fine. And on that note, I want to officially invite you over to my place tomorrow night to watch the pay per view début of The Dancing Chickens."

Chelle laughed. "I didn't know you liked them."

"This is Tracy's idea, and it was her idea to have you over. Get this, she suggested that it's time you two got to know each other better."

Chelle played with her hair, twirling a few locks around her finger. It was a strange habit that she seemed to do whenever she talked with Steven. "I just happen to be free Saturday night. It seems my boyfriend bailed out on a date we had for that night."

"I already told you I'm sorry about that. You'll come over?"

"You know the group is actually pretty good. Maybe even the beginning of another British Invasion."

"Really, a group called the Dancing Chickens?"

"Did you ever hear of a band called The Beatles' or The Monkeys? Or how about The Red Hot Chili Peppers? And I could go on."

"Touché."

"It's a date, tomorrow around eight. And thanks."

Chelle laughed, "Don't sound so apprehensive, you might find out you like them."

"The Dancing Chickens? I seriously doubt it."

"What are you guys up to tomorrow?" Chelle asked.

"I have a few options, depends on what Tracy is in the mood for. But one thing we might..."

Chelle's desk phone rang.

"Sorry, gotta go. I'll talk to you later."

"By, love you."

"Love you too, see you tomorrow." Chelle pressed a button on her desk phone. "Hello, this is Agent Chelle Saltarie."

"Chelle, this is Detective Jones."

"Excuse me, who?"

"Chelle, it's me, Jojo."

Chelle sat upright and un-twirled the hair from around her finger.

"Jojo, oh my God, I'm sorry. I just, well, nevermind. What's up?"

"I think I need your help."

"Do you have a lead in the murders?"

"No, not a f'n clue. And we had another one. Guy shot on a golf course. No motive, no weapon, no suspect. Not even a bullet casing."

"Three possible murders, are you going to get the FBI officially involved?"

"Unfortunately, not my call. My captain and the mayor are still counting the first death as a suicide. I'll be honest. I don't know what to do. This guy is going to strike again, I'm sure of it and feel so darn helpless. Chelle, I've only been a detective for a couple of years, in a sleepy town where I mostly do shoplift and burglaries. The murders I did see were crimes of passion and pretty obvious."

Chelle was already making notes on a large yellow pad.

"A guy?"

"Height. It could be a tall woman, but unlikely of course. I saw the rifle rub point on the tree he used to steady his gun. And he was shooting down. I make a guy at least six feet."

"Let's go over all three murders, leave out nothing. I want you to focus on every detail you can remember."

Chelle took copious notes as Jojo talked. She made him go over the crime scenes repeatedly.

"Let's not be distracted by a possible suicide motive for the first death. For the sake of our investigation let's assume it was murder one," Chelle surmised. "Or, maybe it wasn't murder one.

Did you check on all recent suicides? Maybe there were other murders made out to look like suicides, only not as obvious."

After a moment of silence, Jojo responded, "Damn, I never thought of that."

"Another angle," Chelle suggested, "maybe these are just the murders in your jurisdiction. One good thing about being tied to a desk, I have ready access to some pretty powerful computers. I'll do a search within a hundred-mile radius of Reidsville for unsolved murders and suspicious suicides see if any match our profile."

"What profile, A six-foot suspect? Sure, not many of them around."

"As you said, probably male based on height. You can't find any commonality, which means he kills unsuspecting strangers, which means these are not crimes of passion. Because of where the jogger was killed, we can assume the person is somewhat athletic, probably a runner or jogger, or bicycler. This would be based on crime location, time of discovery, and lack of witnesses during a relatively short time frame afterwards. Somebody moved quickly away from the crime scene."

Jojo said admirably, "Wow girl, you are good. Move over, Sherlock Holmes."

Chelle laughed, "Just simple deductions, Watson."

Chelle sat back in her chair and lifted her Garfield coffee mug towards her lips and then assumed the coffee in it was long time ago turned cold, so she sat it down again. She turned off the speakerphone and took the receiver into her hand and placed it against her right ear. She added, "I agree with you that he or she are smart enough not to take the chance of being identified by their vehicle. So only a bicycle would be logical to get them away from the crime scene speedily without raising any suspicion. Also with typical biking attire, such as a helmet and sunglasses on, they would be unidentifiable, and could ride away without suspicion."

Chelle pondered out loud, "So in the case of the shooting, how does one leave a crime scene and not be seen with a rifle in your hand? Or for that matter ride a bike?

"There is a small marsh pond nearby. He, she or they could've tossed the gun into it and jogged or biked away."

"Could you send in a diver to look for the weapon?"

"It's more a marsh than a pond. I'm afraid it would have to be dredged. With what little we have, I doubt my captain will spring for it on just a hunch."

"I agree it's not much, but we are building a profile. Or let me remind you, one possible profile. I will start a file going. If your killer strikes again, and if you can convince your captain to request FBI help, we'll be able to hit the ground running. Either way, please give me a call. Every small bit of information tells us something."

"That's assuming another murder, I hope we have seen the last of him or her."

"Don't bet on that, Jojo."

"Why not?"

"If you do have a serial killer on your hands, and I believe you do, the profile is for more killing until they are caught.

"Thanks Chelle, you have given me some hope. Please let me know if you dig up any more information or have any other ideas."

Washington D.C.:

Senator Westcott stormed into his office. Shannon Johnston wasn't surprised. She had been watching the hearings of the Senate Select Committee on Intelligence. Shannon was still listening to the news accounts of how the hearing had gone as she watched the senator rush through the workplace and closed the door to his private office with a bang.

The rest of the office staff stared at Shannon. It was an unspoken truth that she was the only one brave enough to let their boss vent to. The televised hearing left no doubt that the chairman of the committee was less than pleased with the answers given, or lack thereof.

Shannon stood and went slowly to the office coffee machine. Approaching the Senator in his foul mood wasn't something she was looking forward to, though she felt it necessary. She poured a mug of coffee and hoped it would be accepted as a peace offering.

She knocked lightly and didn't hear an order to not be disturbed, so she entered. Closing the door after her she offered the cup of coffee to Steven who was pacing back and forth in front of his desk.

Steven thanked her quietly and accepted the coffee and set it on his desk without tasting it.

"I assume you were watching," he construed.

"We all were. It must be frustrating."

"It is. I'm surprised the director remembered his name, and that it wasn't classified."

"At least this hearing proves your point that you and the committee need a closed-door hearing and will start pursuing one."

Shannon couldn't ignore the anger in his voice when he answered, "You're damn right I'm pursuing one. I am going to subpoena anyone and anything I can. Hell, I'm even going to subpoena the director's dog. I'll probably get more answers out of it than him, but if he thinks this is over, it's not.

Shannon watched as Steven slunk down in his desk chair. "They sure have a strange way of assuring us and the public that nothing illegal is going on when they can't answer simple questions about what they are or are not doing."

Shannon said, "He did say he could assure the committee that the agency is not doing anything illegal."

"By whose definition?" Steven sat back straight and looked her in the eyes. "I learned the hard way not to trust anybody, and I can tell you this, I don't trust him. But I do know this: somebody is going to talk. Somebody besides us was watching this, somebody who does know what is going on and wants the truth to come out. And when they do, I'll be listening."

"Senator, may I make a suggestion?"

Steven looked up with his face still tense with anger, "I'm all ears."

"Because the hearings are already wrapped up for the day you pretty much have the afternoon free, maybe a walk and some fresh air would be a good idea."

Shannon waited patiently when her boss broke eye contact with her and stared at a cherished memento on the credenza next to him for a moment, "You know what, you are right. I need some time to think about my next move. And a walk through the National Mall might be just the place to get some inspiration." Steven picked up his coffee and sipped on it. "Thanks, Shannon."

"No problem, Senator, it's a fresh pot."

"No, I mean thank you for listening and for, well... for being yourself, I guess. You always seem to know what's best for me."

"You're a good man, Senator Westcott. You will figure it out."

"I hope you're right, but I better do it quickly. I'm running out of time. I'm afraid that all the delay tactics are going to work. The entrenched bureaucrats know that. All they have to do is wait out until the next election. They know the game will change, it always does."

"But they never had to deal with you before, and that is a game changer too." Shannon walked out the office and left the senator alone.

Steven flicked his computer screen to life. Shannon was right; a walk would do him good. He glanced through his e-mails for anything that might require an immediate response. Seeing none, he was just about ready to close his computer down when he noticed a flashing message.

That was strange, never in his life had he seen an e-mail header flash on the screen. It read, "They lied to you today. Open immediately, this message will self-destruct in five minutes."

Steven was at once suspicious and curious. There was no sender address and that made him suspicious. The secured government computer and e-mail account shouldn't be able to be hacked. Yet the first line drew him in.

Steven clicked it open, ready to literally pull the plug on his computer if he had to.

Alan D Schmitz
DIGITAL SECRETS

"We were watching the hearings on TV. They are lying. NSA is collecting ALL information on EVERYONE! We have proof. If you are interested, we will meet you in Las Vegas at the buffet in the Paris Hotel. One o'clock, two Fridays from now. Come alone, we will know.

"P.S. keep your electronics home. You will be tracked."

Steven read the words over again, only slower, after his second reading the message started to shake. Slowly at first and then more and more erratically until it appeared to burn up from the center of it. The burning hole grew until it was gone.

Reidsville, North Carolina:

Wade had his laptop open and was going over old files and making sure that none of them could link him to any of the murders. He was using an enhanced version of 'The Terminator,' a file deletion software that used an advanced system to overwrite deleted files several times so that not even a portion of a deleted file remained.

It was a tedious process, but extremely effective. To help pass the time in between deletions, Wade was watching the Senate hearings. He had recorded it during the week when he was at work.

Wade wasn't typically interested in politics; in fact, listening to the ramblings of political idiots was the last thing he would waste time on. However, this committee and particularly the chairmen of it, were delving into something near and dear to his heart. Wade thought it interesting how the chairman, a Senator Westcott, kept circling back to trying to find out what the NSA was spending all the money on. Wade found the proceedings to be exceedingly entertaining as he saw how the director of the NSA aptly danced around each question.

Wade's computer dinged at him, announcing that the last sets of files were terminated. As he listened to more of the proceedings, he selected another series of files to be terminated.

Wade talked to himself at he selected files and glanced at the television more listening than watching. "I can see, Mr.

Chairman, that you suspect something isn't right, but you will never ever guess at what it is. And they sure as hell aren't going to tell you. Why don't you ask me? I'll share." Wade chuckled. "I know a lot more about it than that idiot, even though he's in charge of it. They fired me for being smarter than them. That was a huge mistake on their part."

Chapter 4

Reidsville, North Carolina:

Jojo was filling out paperwork in his small cubicle. He lifted his half-filled mug of coffee to his lips and was immediately aware that it was lukewarm at best. He got up and walked to the coffee maker, noticing that the carafe was empty. Whether he wanted to or not, the only way he was going to get a cup of coffee was to make it himself. He took the empty carafe, rinsed it out and filled it with fresh tap water from the bathroom.

When he came back, two other officers were already waiting for a new pot of coffee to be brewed. They continued their conversation as Jojo prepared the coffee maker.

"What a shame," said one uniformed officer. "A young person with so much going for them killing themselves, it just doesn't make sense."

"There are way too many nowadays, that's for sure. I guess they just feel overwhelmed by the demands placed on them by today's society and end it the only way they know how."

"That, or we as a society, and as parents, are not doing enough to prepare them for the challenges and disappointments in life."

Jojo asked, "What are you talking about?"

"Another suicide. Young man just starting college."

"How? Where?"

"In a park, took his father's gun and shot himself."

"Any suicide note?"

"Nothing yet, mother, father, girlfriend all emotionally shattered right now. All said they just can't believe it. But nobody ever does. Seems like family is the last to know if a young person is disturbed enough to do themselves in."

Coffee started to fill the carafe with a muted splashing sound. Jojo instructed. "Put a copy of your report on my desk. I want to take a look."

"It's a suicide, not a murder, detective. Case closed. Some young man named Tony Reilly shot himself in the head with his father's gun."

"Just curious," Jojo asked. "Did he happen to do it with latex gloves on?"

The officer looked up at Jojo. "Yeah, how did you know? Guess he didn't want to get his hands bloodied."

Jojo replaced the carafe with his mug and let it fill instead of waiting for the full pot to brew. "I want the report on my desk in ten minutes."

Jojo took his filled mug and replaced the carafe under the stream of fresh coffee.

"Yes, sir. No problem. You think he was murdered?"

"I'm leaving no stone unturned, that's all."

Jojo walked back to his desk and considered Chelle's suggestion. Maybe things weren't what they seem to be.

Jojo scanned his watch. The wake for Mr. Sanders was tonight. He had just enough time to wait for the report, drive home, catch a bite to eat before heading off to the funeral parlor on Richardson Drive.

At home, Jojo heard Tamara's voice as he was rummaging through the refrigerator.

"You're home a bit early."

"Just for a bit. The funeral for Bill Sanders is tonight. It's at Wilks funeral home."

"I can go with you if you give me a few minutes to change."

"You don't have to, hon. It's just something I think I need to do. I've talked with Mrs. Sanders and her children about the murder. I guess I just think I should be there tonight too, just to show I care."

"We are a small town. In a bigger city, I might even say it would be inappropriate. But we all feel so connected to each other here, I want to go."

"Tell you what, let's go and grab a bite after."

"I'll change and be right down. It won't take me long."

Jojo closed the refrigerator door and took Tamara into his big arms and hugged her gently. "I love it when you keep reminding me of why I love you so."

After a lingering kiss, Tamara ran upstairs.

Jojo unfastened his holster to put his gun away. He rolled up the worn black leather belt that held his holster, his gun neatly tucked into its pocket. As he was about to lock it away for the night, he stared at it for a moment.

With a murderer on the loose, being prepared for anything seemed like the better plan. He unwrapped the holster and cinched it back on; soon his nine-millimeter pistol nestled inside the small of his back once again.

He reasoned that after he slipped his sport coat on, it would, as usual, be easily concealed. He was well aware that someone seeing a gun and not knowing he was an officer of the law could be suspicious at best or exceedingly distressed. The last thing he wanted to do was further upset those grieving, but there was a killer on the loose. Best for their safety that he was prepared.

****

Jojo was driving his unmarked, black police cruiser. Tamara watched out the window as they turned into the funeral home. She saw a black hearse and a small procession of cars parked under the wood canopy of the funeral home. The parking lot was only half full, but cars were starting to stream in.

After parking, Tamara and Jojo walked silently through the pillars of the main entrance and Jojo opened one of the double doors nestled between the red brick façade. Tamara signed the visitor book on both their behalf as Jojo scanned the line of visitors that was starting to approach the doorway.

"Looks like Bill was a popular guy," Jojo whispered as he took Tamara's hand and approached the end of the line of mourners.

Big screen televisions on both sides of the viewing room showed reminders of Bill's life. It showed a constantly changing view of photographed highlights; all, of course, in one way or another, featured Bill.

Along the wall they followed were life boards set up. They celebrated Bill's full life of family and friends and better times with the many photos taken during his life, from childhood to the most recent. Tamara felt Jojo's hand tense around hers. She looked up and saw the color change in Jojo's face. He was staring at a large photo of Bill's smiling face as he proudly held up one of his grandsons to the camera.

"Sweetheart, are you OK?"

She saw a bead of sweat was forming on Jojo's. brow.

"I, I just had a flash back to the murder scene. I wasn't prepared."

"Ok honey, keep talking to me. It'll take your mind off it."

Jojo took his handkerchief and wiped his face. "I try not to make it personal when I'm out in the field. But his face, it was gone last time I saw him. It just hit me hard when I saw his smiling face, I was caught off guard. I think I'm going to be sick."

Tamara could see that her husband was having a hard time staying steady on his feet.

"Look." Tamara pointed to a picture board they were approaching. "Here is Bill and Jeanine at a wedding, that must be Sam their oldest. Oh, and look at this. Bill liked to fish, that's a big one. Do you know what kind of fish it is?"

"That's a striped bass, I'm sure. Nice size."

He understood what his wife was doing, and it was working. The unsettledness of his stomach was slowly going away. He continued to scan the pictures and laughed with Tamara as she pointed to some of the sweeter or funnier ones.

"Thanks honey, I think I can control things a bit better now. You're an angel; the distraction helped."

A moment later Jojo saw something on one of the pictures that piqued his interest. Though it wasn't a something, it was more like a someone.

Jojo whispered to Tamara, "Does this person look familiar to you?"

Tamara whispered back, "Oh my God, it looks like the woman who was killed on the jogging path. A bit younger, but it certainly looks like her."

Jojo looked to his left then his right and when he suspected nobody was looking, he removed the small tack holding the photo and slipped the photo into his pocket.

"They might have known each other."

Tamara glanced towards the waiting family to see if they were being watched. They weren't. She saw that the casket was surrounded by flowers, and as expected, closed. Propped up on top of it was an oversized portrait of Bill.

"It's possible," Tamara agreed, "but you can't ask Bill's wife now. This is not the place."

Jojo was about to argue the point when he realized his wife was right. Time was of the utmost importance. But she did deserve her moment of peace.

The next day:

Wade Sullivan scanned his computer, going over everything he knew about his next victim. It was Friday night, and he was busy meticulously planning the next murder. He knew the police, especially Detective Denton Jones, were certain the victims were a matter of a random picking. They couldn't be more wrong, but the illusion of random victims was important, and the death of Tony Reilly would add to that illusion.

Wade also knew, the detective wouldn't find any information to connect the murders. The ambiguity of the project would have demanded that level of security. Nobody knew exactly what they were working on or who else was also working on it.

There were of course a few exceptions. And he was one of them. His job had been to coordinate between certain contractors. He had used that information to learn even more about the project. He was one of the few that had the knowledge and resources to connect the dots. At least he had the resources. Along with his previous job, they had evaporated too.

The fools running the project didn't realize that as one of the creators, he couldn't be compartmentalized. The same skills he was recruited for, he used clandestinely to gather the forbidden knowledge. And it was that knowledge that had brought him to the sleepy little town of Reidsville, North Carolina. Bill Sanders had thought he was clever to hire the girl to help him. It was all off the books, Bill didn't believe anyone else would ever know. But Wade could read computer code like others could read handwriting. And just like handwriting, he could tell when code was written by different people.

Her name was one of the last he had gathered before he was fired from the project, and that knowledge had caused Sue her life. The fools thought they didn't need him anymore. He would prove them wrong one more time.

But now, as strange as it sounded, what was frustrating Wade was the ease of killing. He already knew exactly how his next victim would die. And he already knew he wouldn't get caught. In fact, he wouldn't even be a suspect. It was all too easy. The thrill of murder wasn't fun for him if there wasn't risk. It was like playing a game of chicken on an empty road. What was the point?

Wade closed his eyes and tried to bring back the excitement of his latest murder. He saw himself entering the Reillys' home. As per the text he had intercepted, nobody was home nor would there be for over an hour. He tilted the large flowerpot by the side door and slid out the key to the house that was left under the pot just as mom promised.

Wade relived the aroma of the beef stew cooking in the slow cooker. He tried to imagine the small taste he had taken with the oversized kitchen spoon. It was unfortunate for Tony that the drone had captured a silhouette of him murdering the blond jogger.

Wade found the young man's bedroom and his computer. With gloved hands he woke up the screen, he made sure all the video of the drone flight had been properly erased. He was meticulous to leave everything else in the room untouched.

Next was the search for the gun safe. Tony's dad had just bought a new gun safe. In a text to his son, he'd said it was best if somebody besides him knew the combination. His father told Tony that the combination was his birthday, something they could both remember.

Wade saw himself move from room to room as his mind replayed the memories. He remembered his heart starting to pound harder the moment he found the safe.

"Click, click, click," the safe opened. Wade could even see his latex gloved hands turning the handle firmly.

In real time, Wade felt his heart pounding. The excitement was coming back. His eyes were closed as he imagined how the 9mm pistol felt in his hand. The clip of ammunition was out of it, but the clip and bullets were on a shelf next to the gun. Wade loaded the clip and snapped it into place, carefully relocked the safe door and exited the home.

In an instant, Wade could see himself standing in a secluded wooded area. He had transported himself to the jogging path. It was ironic that it was the same trail that the blond had used though a different location a mile away. Tony had a jogging routine and kept his route, pace, and miles ran on his phone, just as the blond had.

The movie in his mind was a combination of fast and slow motion of his actions. First, a glimpse at the phone in his hand. The yellow dot was Tony's phone, and it was moving closer to him. Wade's heart pounded even harder in real time as he relived the moment. He confused the young man by stepping in front of him with a wave and a smile. Wade remembered the surprised look on Tony's face when he lifted the gun to below his chin and pulled the trigger.

Wades heart was thumping now. His mind saw the instantly limp body fall back. He fast-forwarded to the placing of latex gloves on Tony's limp hand to explain the lack of fingerprints on the gun.

In real time, he could feel the adrenaline surging through his veins. It was a type of high that had been unknown to him only months before. It sexually aroused him; he knew it was strange, but the feeling of control and power was a turn on.

The problem with the memory was that he knew he would only be able to replay the last murder in his mind a few more times before the memories no longer provided the desired effect.

DIGITAL SECRETS

A new victim was needed, and that person was Professor Patrick Cox. What Wade knew of the professor was just basic information that could be attained by surfing the Internet. Not that the information wasn't informative and substantial. In fact, Wade was sure that the information in front of him would ultimately help him crack into the professor's computer.

The professor and his wife had been married for over 40 years. Pictures on Facebook showed their 40th anniversary party. They had three grown children, two boys and one girl, though the two boys had moved away. The daughter was still living in Pittsburgh, the same city as Patrick. She was married and had three children of her own. Wade could tell by the photos in front of him on his computer that they still stopped by often to visit Papa, as Patrick called himself in texts to his grandchildren.

Patrick was planning on retiring in two years, though as a tenured professor he would forever be associated with Carnegie Mellon University. Wade typed furiously on his keyboard. His connection to Patrick's computer seemed tenuous. Picking Patrick as his next victim was the challenge he had needed.

The challenge was to see if he could commit a long-distance murder. The planning and effort going into the next murder was full of highs and lows. Wade found the chase exhilarating and almost as exciting as committing the murders themselves.

Chapter 5

Jojo stood respectfully next to a large oak tree. He was on a slight rise and could see the much smaller group of people gathered below him today for the funeral of Bill Sanders. It was a nice day for a funeral, if there was such a thing.

The sun was out, birds fluttered from tree to tree, often singing to each other oblivious to the sorrow of the family below them. Mom was doing her best to be strong and brave and pulled her small children to her as the casket of their husband and father was lowered into the earth and blessings were made.

An abundance of relatives was on hand to help Mrs. Sanders and the children cope as best as possible. An older, stately gentleman helped to usher the children back to the car he was driving. Jojo assumed it was their grandfather.

Before Mrs. Sanders could join them in the car, Jojo approached her as respectfully as he could.

"Detective," Mrs. Sanders said as she saw him approach.

"Mrs. Sanders," Jojo acknowledged, and he took off his hat and held it in front of him with both hands.

"Again, my condolences. And I want to assure you that I am doing everything I can to catch this monster."

Mrs. Sanders reached out her hand that still held a white lace handkerchief that was damp from drying tears. She gently touched his hands and held them lightly, "I know you are. Your support has been most comforting."

"I have another reason to be here. I'm afraid I have another favor to ask."

"Will it help you catch this person?"

"It may. I saw this photo last night at the wake."

Jojo produced the photo that was hidden behind his hat until now. "Forgive me, I took this off one of the photo boards last night. I noticed a familiar face. Maybe you could help identify her for me?"

Jojo pointed to the small face in the background.

With red in her eyes Mrs. Sanders looked up at Jojo and asked incredulously, "You took one of my pictures?"

"I'm sorry. It's important."

Mrs. Sanders looked back down at the picture and took it in her hand.

"This is from years ago. Bill looks so young."

Jojo pointed at the woman in the photo again. "Do you know her?"

"I think it was some sort of work photo. I mean from before he went out on his own. I know some of the people. Not her, but now that you mention it, she does look familiar."

"I think she might be the young woman murdered in the park, Sue Witting."

Jojo was watching Mrs. Sanders face closely; he saw the sudden realization of the coincidence. "They knew each other?"

"If it's her, this could be an important clue. Could you help me find someone who might know who she is?"

Mrs. Sanders pointed to another person on the photo. "That's Mitchell Plat, he worked with Bill back then. I'm sure he would. His number is in Bill's phone which you still have."

"May I keep this photo for just a bit longer?"

Mrs. Sanders handed it back to him. "Yes, as long as you need. I would like it back, though."

"Certainly Mrs. Sanders. You've been a big help."

****

As an expert in computer engineering, Professor Cox was providing a challenge to Wade, a challenge Wade had accepted and was determined to win. Because CMU was known for its expertise in turning out the finest graduates in computer sciences, its local area network or LAN was a challenge to hack into, even for Wade.

Wade respected that, and as he had worked himself through various security protocols over the last weeks, each success had provided him with the needed rush to continue. He looked at CMU and Professor Cox as a direct challenge to his hacking abilities. With each win, Wade felt a particular gratification.

He was happy that CMU was only using 2FA authentication. That meant anyone trying to gain entry had to crack two different types of authentications. The bad news was that 2FA was exceedingly difficult to crack. The good news was it could have been multi-factored, meaning three or more types of authentications.

The first part of his hack was sending out a fake website login page to a list of CMU employees. That list was easy enough to attain from the 'Contact Us' area of the real website. All it took was one of the real employees to answer the security question from the fake log-in page Wade had built and send it back to him.

The second authentication was much harder; it was based on an algorithm, computed from a key fob number, furthered by another algorithm based on time of day. The time-of-day factor was intended to create a constantly changing second authentication login.

Wade had a theory on how to crack such an authentication procedure by using a combination of known algorithms and brute force, meaning using computing power to create thousands of attacks a minute.

He had an advantage, though; the same type of security was proposed and tested for the project he had been working on. All the methods of cracking into it had been thoroughly discussed by their group and tested by none other than him.

Wade looked at his computer screen, it was already eleven PM. Wade admitted to himself that he was tired and needed to sleep. Tomorrow was a workday, and even though he felt that he could do his work in his sleep, he still needed rest for the job that for now paid the daily bills.

Wade used his laptop to send parameters to Mercury, his mini supercomputer, which resided in his basement. It was easier to keep the power-hungry machine cool in a specially created room. Confident that Mercury would do the work while he slept, he got up for a glass of milk. As he walked to the refrigerator, his mind wondered back to his last job. He had heard that despite his objections, they'd opted for a biometric system combined with a multi-factored approach. Wade had an untested idea or two about how to crack that too.

DIGITAL SECRETS

Wade stopped what he was doing his mind already focusing on the solutions to the hack. Cracking into his previous bosses' precious computer would be the hack of hacks. In fact, after that, there wouldn't be a need to hack anything else. It would certainly be a dangerous game, but the thought excited him. If they found out that someone had hacked into it, they would come begging him to come back. With everyone dead and gone, their options would be limited.

From the kitchen, he heard his computer ding a notification bringing him back to his current task. Walking back to his computer he saw the hack was done much sooner than expected. Wade felt all-powerful knowing that he could now wander the wonderful computer world of CMU. He had been tired but now felt wide-awake.

He used another off-the-shelf hacking program to find all the registered IP addresses. This would list every computer, printer, scanner, and whatever else might be directly connected to the network. It also listed the names of the device.

Armed with that information, Wade was able to sort through probable computer names. Using the data he had collected on Professor Cox, Wade looked for personal information that might lead to the name of his computer. A computer's name wasn't considered a security wall. That meant anyone naming a device, including Professor Cox, would probably name their computer after something meaningful to them. Often using even their real name, as in 'Prof. Cox's laptop'.

Wade didn't find anything that obvious, but he did see a computer that had the same name as Professor Cox's dog. Scanning through the shared drive files left no doubt he had indeed found the Professor's computer.

Before he went to bed for the night, he left himself a note. It was a reminder to pick up a cheap burner phone before he left for Las Vegas, which was now only a week and a half away. What he needed more specifically was one that used the Mobile Virtual Network, making it untraceable, and to pay for it in cash. The minutes of use could be bought in Las Vegas from any drugstore chain. He would pay for the card in cash too.

Alan D Schmitz
DIGITAL SECRETS

The Las Vegas conference would be a company paid trip or at least the first part. In his current line of work, his bosses wanted him to be as informed as possible on the latest hacking techniques so he would be armed with the information he needed to keep their servers secure.

The second part of the program was called 'DEF CON', and it was even more important to him. Those programs were only paid for in cash. Hackers of his caliber weren't interested in being identified. And even though Wade considered himself one of the premier hackers on the planet, there were always new tricks to learn. And the people teaching those tricks would be in Vegas this coming week. That was why learning about the latest hacking software at the Black Hat Cybersecurity Conference was one of the highlights of his year.[1]

Washington D.C.:

It was Friday evening at the Capital Grill in Washington D.C., the week after Steven had dropped his daughter off at the

---

(Quote from Cyware.com RE: 2020 Black Hat)

"[1]Think of Black Hat as the commercial wing of DEF CON. Started (and then sold) by the same founder (Dark Tangent, aka Jeff Moss) Black Hat has global appeal and it functions throughout the world (Middle East, Asia, Europe, and the US). Think of the Black Hat attendees as being more corporate and the DEF CON crowd as being more "street" and stereotypically "hackerish". Here's a nice comparison between DEF CON and Black Hat that I read that I thought sums it up neatly: at DEF CON you can only pay cash, whilst at Black Hat you can pay with the company and personal credit cards. Why? Because the type of people that go to DEF CON simply don't want to be identified!"

airport with the promise of another get together real soon. Steven and Chelle followed the maître d to a table that was tucked neatly into a back corner. Steven had arrived earlier and was on his third drink. He carried it with him to their table.

Once seated and some wine was ordered, Chelle asked, "Are you going to tell me what's bothering you, or are you going to make me play detective?"

Steven smiled, "No, Agent Saltarie, I'll go along peacefully."

Chelle smiled, glad she didn't touch a nerve. "So, a penny for your thoughts."

Steven swirled the remaining cube of ice in his glass of scotch. He wasn't sure if he should say out loud what he had been contemplating all afternoon.

"Well?" Chelle coaxed.

Steven looked up from his glass and gave a bit of a smirk. "Just something I have been thinking about lately."

"Care to share? What are these deep thoughts of yours?"

"What if I went back to the private sector? The hell with this senator bullshit."

"Just how much have you been drinking?" Chelle joked.

Steven took a big sip from his glass, half emptying it.

"I'm serious. I'm always battling somebody. You in particular know what the last years have been like and the price I have paid. A price one of my daughters paid, a daughter I had just begun to know. I want to do what is right for the country and my constituency but I'm being stopped at each turn, often by my own party.

"And look at the danger my friends and I and family have been put in over and over again. You were permanently injured, and it could have been much worse. You could have been killed. And now you're not doing what you trained for because of me."

"I assume you are referring to me being desk bound."

Steven finished his drink with one last swallow. "Exactly, my fault."

"No it wasn't. You didn't cause what happened, and it was my call as far as my becoming involved in the first place. I was part of that decision-making process, Mr. Senator. I am responsible for my own actions."

"You didn't know what you were getting yourself into. You came down to Mexico to help me. But you never knew the kind of danger you would be in."

"Water under the bridge."

"But now you are desk bound. Unofficially, probably because you happen to be the girlfriend of a Senator."

The wine steward came with a semi-sweet Sauvignon blanc they had ordered to go with their dinner. Chelle used the interruption to contemplate what Steven had said. Officially, she was told that she was being taken out of the field for now to recoup from her physically and mentally harrowing experience in Mexico.

Chelle knew that physically she was healed, and she suspected psychologically she was also ready. But her request to be reinstated for fieldwork might have been turned down for exactly the reason Steven had suggested. His guess that their relationship might be behind it had some merit.

After a sip of her wine, she said sympathetically. "Destinee's death isn't on you, and neither was Rebecca's."

Steven picked at the shrimp scampi on his plate, he didn't look up when he said, "I can't stop feeling that if I was around more, I could have, or would have been able to save Rebecca from going down that dark path."

Chelle reached over and squeezed Steven's hand. "From what I've learned, is that you and Lucille did everything in your power to help her."

Steven's eyes were tearing up, he said,."Apparently it wasn't enough. And as for Destinee, a daughter I was just beginning to know. Her death was a direct result of her reaching out to a father she didn't know. She was killed, murdered, for no other reason than she was becoming associated with me."

Chelle stared into Steven's watering eyes and warmed his hand with hers, "Please Steven, don't torture yourself like that. We know that Destinee's murder was an attempt to get to you. But that doesn't make it your fault. There were bad people doing bad things I sympathize with you over the loss of two daughters, but their deaths were not your fault.

"I suppose it's possible I've been relegated to desk duty because you could be compromised by something I did, but we don't know that."

Steven added, "Or I could be targeted by somebody threatening to harm you if I don't do what they say."

"You mean exactly like what happened in Mexico."

Steven said, "Exactly, you became a pawn." Steven took a big taste of his wine.

Chelle interjected, "We both became pawns in somebody else's game."

"My point precisely. Look Chelle, think about it. I can quit being a senator. I can make more money starting up my investment company again. You can do whatever you want. Join me in the new company or stay with the FBI. Either way, you would no longer be high profile because I am no longer high profile."

Steven sat back in his chair as their hands broke. He took another big taste of his wine.

Chelle asked, "How long were you here before I arrived?"

"Long enough to do some serious thinking."

"It looks like you have an objective tonight," Chelle challenged.

"Meaning what?" Steven took another big drink emptying his glass.

"You are getting drunk."

"So? I can get drunk if I want. And don't change the subject. I'm right, aren't I?"

"You have a point yes. But that doesn't mean you are correct in thinking you should step down as a senator. You have worked so hard to become one. You have the name recognition, and the election machine all in place. Polls show you are a shoo-in for the next election."

The waiter saw Steven's empty glass and refilled it from the bottle on the table.

Steven took a small sip, realizing that Chelle was right. He was getting drunk. "I didn't say it was an easy decision. But when I think about it, what am I giving up? Nothing."

"Do you think drowning your sorrows is wise?"

"I'm not drowning my sorrows. I'm just trying to..." Steven danced his half-filled glass of wine around in front of him for a bit. "I'm just trying to free my thinking. I've been so focused on this senator thing that I think I haven't been seeing clearly."

"Well think about this. It's not just you who I'm thinking about. Do you have any idea how many people you have affected in a positive way since becoming a senator? Have you asked yourself why you became a politician in the first place?"

"Sure I have, many times. I started out thinking I could straighten things out. Get the people's house in order. But things that had been crystal clear to me are now murky. There are way too many grey areas.

"And what about IRENE? Once I'm not a Senator, they would leave me alone. They would leave us alone."

"I thought they were leaving you alone."

"For the time being, yes. But you and I know it is a dangerous organization, and for some reason I seem to be on their radar. Our paths have dangerously crossed far too often. We both know that if I wasn't a senator anymore, they would have no use for me.

Chelle, think about it, we could go anywhere in the world. Do anything we wanted. Buy a sailboat. Sail around the seven seas."

"I think it's the alcohol talking."

"Maybe a bit. Maybe it's helping me see things differently. Take this investigative committee I'm on. Why am I working so hard at it? Nobody seems to give a hoot what I find or don't find."

"Now we're sailing around the world. I didn't even know you were a sailor?"

"I'm not, but I could learn. We could learn together. No FBI, no IRENE, no bad guys to go after. Just us, lazily bobbing on the ocean, with a stiff breeze taking us where it may."

Chelle smiled as their dinner was served. The Maître d' asked if she wanted more wine with dinner. Chelle smiled and waved her hand no. She looked Steven in the eyes with a mischievous look and said, "I have a funny feeling sailor, that by tomorrow morning you will be thinking differently."

Steven finished the last of his drink and sat the empty glass down carefully. He looked up at Chelle and said, "I don't think so. I'm serious, honey. I am entirely fed up with trying to be the knight in shining armor to everybody. And you know what happens to the knight in shining armor."

"No, what?"

"Too many people have different ideas for them. It never ends well for the knight."

Chelle and Steven were both silent for a while as they enjoyed their meal. Chelle ordered some coffee for them both. When out of the blue Steven said. "I had an email burn up on me today."

"What!" Chelle laughed at the joke thinking it was the alcohol talking.

"I'm serious." Steven looked up and slurring his words just a bit said, "I had an email burn up, right on my computer screen. Poof! Gone in a puff of flames and smoke."

"How does an email burn up?"

Steven gave a sideways smirk and said, "This is top secret, my eyes-only type of thing."

"Your eyes only? Why tell me?"

"I have to tell somebody."

Chelle could tell that the alcohol was having a cumulative effect on Steven and knew it was time to leave the restaurant.

She asked, "Why don't you tell me at your place. I think it's time to leave."

Steven looked around the restaurant suspiciously, "You're right. We can't be too careful. But it did this 'Mission Impossible' thing. Poof...and it was gone. I couldn't find it back anywhere on my computer. It just disappeared."

Chelle signed for the meal and helped Steven out of the restaurant by pretending to be in his grasp when the reality was just the opposite.

They got in a cab and Chelle gave the directions for Steven's apartment.

Steven stared out the window of the cab immersing himself in the lights of the Capital saying nothing for the entire ride.

Chelle used her key to open the door to Steven's two-bedroom apartment and immediately proceeded to make some coffee as Steven tried unsuccessfully to gently sit down at a kitchen table chair.

"Want to know what the email said before it went poof?"

"You said it was for your eyes only?" Chelle mocked.

"Oh Chelle, what have I got myself into again?"

Steven looked up at Chelle's face and suddenly realized what he had said.

"Steven, this is so not like you. What is going on?" she said, concerned. "What did the message say?"

"They lied, they all lied. NSA is collecting everything on everybody, and we have proof."

"That's it?"

"I'm tired. I want to go to bed?"

"Not until you've had some coffee."

"OK, coffee sounds good. Should I make some?"

Chelle laughed a bit to herself as she poured a cup of coffee out of a carafe and set it down in front of Steven.

Steven looked up surprised. "Wow, you are good." He used both hands to steady the cup and took a slow, slurping sip. "That's hot, but good."

He looked back up at Chelle with a serious look on his face, "I love you. No really, I love you. I'm not afraid to say it. I love you."

"I love you too. Now drink more coffee."

Steven loudly slurped some more down. "I don't ever want anything bad to happen to you again."

"Steven, what did the email say?"

"They want to meet with me."

"To give you the proof?"

"I guess. In Vegas, two weeks from today."

"Who is they?"

"Don't know, poof!" Steven used his arms and hands to mimic the message disappearing.

"Are you going?"

Steven slurred out, "That's the problem with us knights in shining armor. We don't know when to go home and let someone else slay the dragon." He took another slow sip of his coffee.

Steven looked up from the chair at Chelle who was standing next to him. He realized he was seeing a bit blurry eyed when he looked at her eyes, and with a wag of his fingers he added, "And that is when our friends get hurt."

Chelle took Steven's head against her thigh and held it softly.

"I think I have to go to bed now. Thank you, sweetheart. I've had a wonderful time tonight. Maybe a bit too wonderful."

Steven dragged himself into the bedroom with Chelle's help to make sure he got to bed safely.

Chapter 6

Chelle was walking down the hall towards the FBI lunchroom. She saw the caller ID on her phone and answered.

"Hello."

"Chelle, I'm so sorry for last night. I don't know what came over me," Steven said meekly into his cell phone.

Chelle laughed as she walked to the lunchroom. "No need to apologize. You were, shall I say, entertaining."

"Ohhh..." Steven groaned. "What did I all say, or don't I want to know?"

"You told me you love me."

"I do love you."

"Several times."

"How many?"

"Didn't count. But you did say you weren't afraid to say so. I had no idea you were such a brave man."

"Oh boy, can you forgive me?"

"Nothing to forgive. I think even a senator needs to blow off a little steam every now and then."

"Is that what you're calling it?"

Chelle looked over the day's specials written on the chalkboard next to the counter.

"I want to make it up to you."

Chelle said, "Hold that thought for a moment."

Steven heard her order her lunch.

"No apology needed or expected. I know you have a lot on your mind, and you needed a night to let things slide."

Chelle took her food tray with one hand and found a table that was unoccupied.

Chelle kidded, "I know, you want to take me to a 'Dancing Chickens' concert?"

"Not exactly what I had in mind, but if that would do it. It's yours."

Chelle laughed, "I don't think even a senator can get a ticket to their concerts less than a year ahead of time."

Steven laughed, "I did have fun watching my daughter so enthused about their music. It wasn't terrible, I guess, but not my cup of tea. And you, you did a great job pretending you like them. You and Tracy bonded pretty well that night. That was fun to see."

"I did like them. And Tracy was so kind to me. You should be proud of her; she is turning into an impressive young lady."

"I am proud of her. And you. However, I do feel I have been neglecting our relationship a bit and I do want to make last night up to you."

"How about a short trip to Las Vegas, say in two weeks."

Steven groaned again, "I told you about that?"

"You did. And about the disappearing email."

"Chelle, I'm sure it'll be a wild goose chase."

"So you are going?"

"After a lot of soul searching."

"And a lot of scotch and wine," Chelle added.

"Ouch. At any rate, yes, I think I need to check it out. I've been waiting for a break, and this might be it. If this doesn't turn out to be something important, I think my committee is in a battle we will lose."

"I'm serious too. I've been cooped up behind a desk for far too long. I need to get out to preserve my sanity. And a short Vegas trip sounds perfect."

"I don't know, Chelle, they warned me to leave all electronics behind because I might be followed. They might be suspicious of you."

"Sounds dangerously clandestine, right up my alley."

"It certainly could be dangerous, Chelle."

"And as you said, "It could be a wild goose chase.""

"You're not going to let me off the hook, are you?"

"You said you wanted to make last night up to me."

"And you said I didn't have to."

"Are we going to Las Vegas, or aren't we? Because you are not going without me."

"I guess we are going to Las Vegas. I'll make the arrangements."

Chelle a bit surprised her ploy worked said, "Oh my God, seriously, we are going to Vegas? I'm not sure what I have to wear."

"It's just for a few days. Don't worry; we'll buy whatever you need when we get there. There are fantastic shops inside Caesars and the Venetian. Hell, we can take a gondola ride right through the Venetian."

"I can't believe it; we are going to Las Vegas. How many days?"

"I was planning on four."

Chelle was about to put a forkful of food in her mouth but replaced it onto her plate, her mind racing. "I know we'll only be gone four days, but I'll need a swimsuit, and casual clothes, and shoes. Oh my God, this is going to be so much fun."

"And best of all, leave your cell phone behind. I will too."

"I don't know if I can do that. I mean what if somebody needs me?"

"But that's the point. No distractions for four whole days, just us. Besides, if there is a chance that our phones scare off these people it's a chance I don't want to take. This could be a one-time opportunity."

"I guess, why not. After all, what did people do before cell phones?"

"That's the spirit."

The impromptu trip to Las Vegas made the conversation easy. Steven and Chelle came up with more ideas of things to do than they could possibly squeeze into four days.

Their conversation ended when Chelle said. "I still can't believe it. Two hours ago it was just another day. Now, in two weeks we'll be in Vegas."

Reidsville, North Carolina:

Jojo went over the file compiled on Tony Reilly's suicide. Just like the young mother who had been killed, the young man had gone out for a jog, except he decided to kill himself halfway through his run.

DIGITAL SECRETS

Jojo strummed his pencil eraser against the report. Who goes jogging for three miles with a pistol and then stops and bang, kills themselves with it while wearing latex gloves? It just didn't make sense to Jojo. Still, suicides never made sense to Jojo.

The report further stated that the only explanation the girlfriend could come up with was his recent distress over losing his expensive drone. He had spent money on it he knew he should have used for college, but he reasoned it was important to the photography and videography field he was going into. Only in an unexplainable instant it was gone, crashing into the lake.

Jojo certainly didn't see that as an excuse to kill oneself, but to a young person maybe they saw that as an insurmountable mistake. Jojo scanned the report once again. A date popped out at him in the testimony of the girlfriend. The drone was lost on the same day as the young mother had been murdered, and in the same park. In fact, the two incidents were only a half-mile apart while the young man filmed the boat race.

He remembered that race. It was going on at the same time the woman was murdered. That meant the drone was lost during the time of the murder. He sensed the connection and doubted the young man's suicide. Was the young man another victim? Did he see something? Did the drone? Jojo didn't believe in coincidences but how would the killer get the young man's father's pistol. How would he even know he had one? Did he follow the young man around for the right opportunity, or did he know exactly when and where that time would come? And not only was the young man in the same park on the same day as the woman killed, he was wearing latex gloves. It seems as if there is an epidemic of neat freaks committing suicides. Unfortunately, the drone was lost in the reservoir with any video evidence it might have had. Or was it?

****

Jojo rang the doorbell; he didn't have to wait long.

DIGITAL SECRETS

"Hello, detective."

"Hello Mrs. Sanders, I'm am sorry for the inconvenience, I assure you. I wouldn't be here if it weren't important."

"Bill's friend Mitchell confirmed the woman in the photo was Sue Witting. May I go through his office again?"

"Why?"

"I didn't know what I was looking for. I assumed Bill's murder was a random act of violence."

"And now?"

"I'm hoping to find a link between your husband and Sue Witting besides this photo."

"So, you believe the same person killed them both?"

"Yes, just a hunch right now. Would you mind?"

"Come in, I'll walk you to his office."

Mrs. Sanders looked tired and more aged than he remembered from his first visit. Her auburn hair was a bit disheveled, as if she started to comb it and quit half done. She had no makeup on, and her face appeared sickly. Though she was a bigger woman, Jojo could see the simple beauty she certainly had possessed in her younger days. But today, understandably, her blue eyes were red and dreary looking.

Jojo had already considered where he might start. He asked, "Can you tell me who did the invoicing and billing for your husband?"

"He did it all himself. It was all electronically managed somehow. I'm afraid I won't be of much help. He was the computer geek in the family."

"Well, there is one thing I've learned: even the most sophisticated computer system still uses paper, and sometimes lots of it."

At the office door, Mrs. Sanders opened it for the detective and said, "I'd rather not watch as you search through my husband's things." Then she admonished, "Please don't take any more pictures."

"Mrs. Sanders, I promise I won't take anything without your permission."

****

An hour later, Jojo had spread out on the desk a series of papers. Some invoices, work orders, receipts, phone records. He took pictures of every piece of information which could be remotely relevant. True to her statement Mrs. Sanders never interrupted. An hour and a half had passed since he had entered the office. He opened the door and questioned soft spoken, "Mrs. Sanders?"

"Yes detective, I'm still here. Care for a cup of coffee?"

Jojo was surprised at the offer, "That would be wonderful. I would like to share with you some of the things I found. I think you could find them useful."

"Please detective, forgive me for my earlier comment."

"No need. I intruded, and I shouldn't have."

"No detective, it is I who shouldn't have scolded you. I want you to, no, I need you to find out who and why they did this to my husband, to our family. I don't know how I can ever find any peace if I don't get those answers."

Mrs. Sanders offered a hot mug of coffee to Jojo. "Cream or sugar?"

"No, black is fine, smells good."

Jojo noticed that her hair was combed, the worn bathrobe she had on when she greeted him was replaced with a black blouse and a black skirt. But her eyes seemed just as red from crying.

Mrs. Sanders offered Jojo a chair next to a worn dining table.

She rubbed her hands across the rough surface. "This table is full of memories. It has certainly taken years of abuse. It's like an old friend now. I don't know if I will ever be able to replace it."

"I understand. We don't dare replace ours for a few more years. Until our youngest is grown, she still does all her craft projects on it." Jojo laughed. "I usually just scrape off the dried glue and such with a razor blade. Our table has a few memories scratched into it too."

Mrs. Sanders smiled; she was taking a liking to the detective.

"What have you found?"

"I saw some recent invoices. It appears that various companies owe you money yet. I can come back on my own time if you want and I could help you sort it out. It wouldn't be police business, but I would be happy to help you."

"That is a kind offer, I may take you up on it. I haven't felt much like doing anything lately. Did you find what you are looking for?"

"A link between your husband and Mrs. Witting? I did recognize her number in his phone records. He called her a few times, but it was months ago. I didn't find any other connection. If they were working together on a project, I found no evidence of it. I did find something else. Are you aware that your husband worked for the government?"

"Yes, he cursed the procurement process, but he liked the money. He said he always got paid and that was more than he could say about some of the startup firms he worked for. Do you still think the murder of Mrs. Witting and my Bill are connected?"

"I do, but at this time I have no clue as to how or why. It's just the coincidence is too, well, coincidental."

Jojo held up a stack of papers in his hand. "I would like to take his phone records with me. Do you mind?"

"By all means, take what you need."

"Oh, there is one more thing. I didn't see his computer, I assumed it would still be in his office. Last time I was here you said you would try to remember the passcode to open it."

"I tried every combination of passwords I could think of, but for the life of me I couldn't remember what it was. I gave it to Ann, my attorney. She said she might know somebody who could open it"

As Jojo was walking out the door he turned and said, "If she brings it back, could you let me know. Whatever is in it might be important to both of us."

"Yes, of course detective. I will."

****

Wade packed a small suitcase for his trip to Las Vegas. He looked at his watch; his flight was scheduled to leave in three hours. The plane had Wi-Fi on it, so on his flight to Las Vegas would be as good a time to kill Professor Cox as any.

He triple-checked that he hadn't forgotten the burner phone in his pocket. He would use it to call Detective Jones from Las Vegas. After that call, the game would be officially on. The excitement in the pit of his stomach churned deeply. Wade smiled and said to himself, "Damn," as he realized that his groin was feeling the excitement too. He was getting turned on just by the contemplation of what he was about to do. Weird, he thought as his pants tightened against him.

He started his car and backed it out the garage. He took a moment looking at his bike hanging on the wall of the garage. It was time to dispose of his bike. It was the most identifiable part of him.

Chapter 7

Las Vegas, Nevada:

It was still morning in Nevada when a commercial jet screeched its tires across the runway as it landed. Half an hour later the top was down on the red Mustang Steven and Chelle had rented. A slight breeze blew through their hair as they raced away from the airport.

Steven sported a wide grin as he looked at Chelle through the sporty sunglasses he was wearing. Chelle shouted over the wind as she held on to her wide brim hat with one hand and an ocean blue silk scarf wrapped around her neck blowing in the wind. "I feel like a teenager who skipped out of school."

"Steven laughed, "You look like a teenager who skipped out of school."

The sun was warm on their faces as Steven took a road out of town.

"Where are we going?" Chelle asked, not particularly concerned.

"Don't know, let's just drive and see where we end up," Steven said as they turned onto the freeway.

Chelle talked loudly over the noise of the wind and road. "Locking our phones away inside your car's glove box was hard. But now, I have to admit, it gives me a certain undeniable feeling of freedom."

"I know what you mean. I feel I have committed some crime against humanity because I can't be contacted, and I'm glad."

As they entered the freeway, Steven pointed to a large electronic sign on the side of the road. "Can you believe it? Look who's coming to town."

Chelle saw the sign and laughed. "The Dancing Chickens. I told you they were the latest hot band. I'll sure it's already sold out."

"You're kidding? Two months from now?"

"I wouldn't be surprised if it was sold out the day it was announced."

"How come I've never heard of them until three weeks ago?"

Chelle laughed, "Maybe you're getting old, senator?"

"Me? Old? Never." Steven stepped on the gas and the car took off down the freeway until it became chocked with traffic. Chelle pointed to an exit and suggested, "How about that-a-way?" Her hand pointed off to the mountains in the distance.

The red convertible slowed just a bit as Steven turned off the freeway and turned on to highway one-fifty-nine west. The wind blew through their hair again as the car picked up speed and headed away from the glut of neon lights of the city.

"Perfect, this should take us far, far away from school. And I have a great idea on where to go." Steven looked at Chelle, smiling.

"No school today," Chelle shouted out the convertible to some people walking along the road as they sped past. She giggled at her silliness as Steven laughed.

****

Wade Sullivan stepped outside the conference center of the Paris Hotel, Las Vegas. The air was starting to get hot, though the temperature for this August day wasn't expected to rise past ninety degrees and that was hours away. The long shadow of the Eiffel Tower pointed northwest up Las Vegas Boulevard. He walked under and through one of the massive legs of the half-size replica of the famous tower.

He found a secluded area near the road. Wade didn't want anyone to overhear his conversation. He was sure the background road noise would cover his voice from any pedestrian that might wonder too close.

Across the wide boulevard was the huge Bellagio Hotel that was reflected in the giant pool in front of it. Kitty-corner from him was Caesars Palace; it covered a city block all by itself. Just down from Caesars, on his side of the street, rose the five-hundred-foot High Roller Ferris wheel. Wade watched its individual gondola type party cars staying perfectly upright as the giant wheel moved ever so slowly.

He took out the small phone in his pocket and turned it on. After opening an application that would change his voice, he entered a number he had memorized. It rang a few times.

"Reidsville Police Department," a sweet-sounding woman's voice answered.

In a choppy, synthetic voice, Wade said, "Put me through to Detective Jones."

The woman's voice sounding a few octaves higher, tried to remain calm despite the obvious electronic voice disguise she heard, "May I say who is calling?"

"No, you may not. But trust me, he wants to talk to me."

Wade looked at his watch and marked the time. It was an analog watch, given to him as a graduation present from his parents. It was not at all like any one of the many different smart watches available to the masses. He knew the dangers of being constantly electronically connected to the Internet of things.

When his call was transferred, he recorded the various beeps and tones he could hear through the phone. The tones confirmed his guess that the police department still used an older system of using tones to identify a particular number. The series of beeps and tones should be the clues he would need to attain the detective's direct number for the next time he called.

It didn't take long before a man's deep voice answered.

"Is this Detective Jones?" Wade smiled when the person on the other end acknowledged it was. Wade made a note of how much time had already passed. "Hello, Detective, so nice to talk to you. I'm afraid I can't tell you who I am. Let me rephrase that. I mean to say, I can't tell you my name. However, I can tell you that I am the person behind the recent spate of murders in and around Reidsville.

"I can't talk long but I do want to help you a bit. You see I have another victim, Patrick Cox. I believe he will die from a heart attack. I'm afraid that is all the information I can give you at this time."

Across the boulevard, a music, water, and light show started up. There was a loud explosion as powerful jets of water screamed upwards. The blast of water danced to the accompanying music.

Wade looked annoyingly at the show. Wade admonished himself for not anticipating the hourly show. The jets of water were changing color and crisscrossing each other. There were powerful shots of water spraying straight up into the air. They sounded like cannons as compressed air forced the water hundreds of feet into the air.

He tried to ignore the distraction across the street. "At least as of this morning his death wasn't reported yet. Can't chat any longer. I just wanted you to know."

Wade turned off the throwaway phone and took out the battery. He wasn't necessarily afraid to use it again, but why take chances. He dropped the phone to the ground and crushed it under his heel.

He smiled as he imagined how the professor's already weak heart was doing after the good professor discovered he was a pedophile. Even worse, his wife, children, and faculty and students all discovered it at the same time.

It had only taken a few clicks of his mouse from thirty thousand feet to change the professor's life forever. It was unfortunate that the professor 'accidentally' emailed everybody on his contacts list links to videos of child pornography, which would immediately lead to a search of his personal hard drive, which the authorities would find also contained child pornographic content, lots of it. The professor would find it extraordinarily difficult to claim the photos and videos weren't his, with his reputation as a cyber security expert. Wade chuckled, thinking about the emails he had read where his doctor warned his patient that it was imperative for the professor to avoid stress. His heart condition was extremely tenuous. Besides, even if Professor Cox didn't die, his life would be over.

Wade could feel the unusual excitement take over his body. His room was across town and he considered going back to his hotel just to relieve the sexual tension in his groin. He glanced down at the program flyer for the Black Hat conference in his hand and made the decision to postpone his relief.

The next seminar was about hacking into networked home appliances. That sounded interesting, not necessarily deadly, but interesting. He easily could imagine some of his peers using the information to hack into somebody's refrigerator and using its re-order system to order gallons of ice cream from it as a prank. He could think of more sinister uses already.

Wade knew and understood what every Black Hat hacker knew. The greatest weakness of the internet was that even the most innocuous device could become a portal. And that portal could be used to unlock an entry into the world of the internet, and all anonymously. It was being called the 'Internet of Things,' a collection of everyday devices talking to each other through the internet.

As he walked, he continued to scan the program schedule in his hand. He examined Friday's schedule and noted two or three technical programs he might like that were going on tomorrow afternoon. One was titled 'Is Big Brother Watching You?'

He was in a hacker's paradise, but that meant decisions had to be made. There were more programs going on throughout the week than he could possibly attend. Wade had another burner phone in his backpack. If he hurried, he would have time to surf the internet looking for any traffic on a Professor Patrick Cox. It was possible that the professor was either arrested or dead by now.

Reidsville, NC police station

Jojo's face was white as a sheet; he could feel the blood draining from his head. He sat down on the nearest chair. Just then his captain walked by.

"Detective! Are you all right? You look like you just saw a ghost."

"I just got a call; the person's voice was disguised somehow but he said he was behind the spurt of murders around Reidsville."

The captain looked around to see if anyone else was listening. He didn't see anybody in sight but still suggested. "Let's go to my office and go over this phone call right away. I don't want any details to escape us."

"They won't. I been recording all my calls. If it worked like it's supposed to, I have it recorded."

"My office, let's give it a listen."

"We need to find somebody called Patrick Cox."

"Why?"

"If I heard right, he's taunting me with the next victim's name."

"Detective, I need to hear exactly what he said."

"Yes sir!"

The two men walked to the private office and closed the door behind them.

Red Rock Canyon, Nevada

Steven held Chelle's hand as they climbed around a series of giant red boulders. Steven looked into the sky. The sun was getting low. He said, "I hate to say it but it's time we went to town and checked into our hotel."

Chelle looked out into the distance at the red-faced canyon walls that seemed to glow all the more spectacular as the sun set. Mesmerized by the sight, she said, "The setting sun against the rocks is stunning."

Steven turned the same direction as Chelle and squeezed her gently with his strong arms wrapped around her shoulders. "It is. The mountains seem to glow with magic."

"Yes they do."

"But I have another surprise or two and unfortunately we need to be on our way."

"Another surprise or two? Now you have my attention."

Chelle and Steven held hands as they meandered around the rocks and took the narrow dirt path back to their car. With the push of a few switches, the soft top of the convertible had neatly tucked itself away.

DIGITAL SECRETS

There were three other cars in the small parking lot next to the trail. Two were empty, one of the vehicles was a black SUV, and it had two men in it. Steven felt a little unnerved as they watched them unabashedly.

Chelle asked, "Where are we staying? I never asked."

"That, my dear, is one of the surprises. You'll know when we get there."

"You are certainly a man of mystery, aren't you?"

Once Chelle was seated, Steven started up the car and it roared to life. They turned out the parking area and down the park road to pick up highway one-fifty-nine to Las Vegas. The heat of the sun was past its worst and the warm air was comfortable as they raced away.

As they took the winding road out of the park, Steven casually glanced back from an opportunistic bend in the road. It wasn't his imagination. The black SUV was following them.

At the main highway Steven turned east towards Vegas. The GPS said it should take them about a half-hour to reach their destination.

The red convertible headed east towards town, Steven glanced in the rear-view mirror and saw in the distance that the black SUV was still following them.

Chelle followed Steven's eyes, "You seem to be a bit preoccupied by something, want to share?"

"That black SUV from the parking lot left when we did and is following us."

"We are in the desert. There aren't that many ways to go. Anybody heading back to Vegas has to take this road."

"I know, but two guys at Red Rock Canyon, watching us, not the scenery? It's seems out of place. Still, it could just be me being paranoid."

"I would tease you about it, but I know better. I have learned to trust your instincts."

"And I yours. We'll know soon enough."

Steven turned north onto the freeway; the black SUV had closed the distance between them even though Steven had been driving a bit over the speed limit.

"They're still following, and they sped up."

"You know those desert roads; nobody does the speed limit." Chelle provided a calming voice.

"And they turned onto the freeway the same direction as us."

"A fifty-fifty proposition."

Steven sped up to seventy-five miles per hour.

"Seems to me, they're being precise in keeping us in sight. Let's see what happens if I slow down."

Steven watched Chelle reach into her purse.

"Now who's paranoid?"

"Better safe than sorry." Chelle said as she pulled out her handgun.

"Don't leave home without it?"

"You might have talked me out of my phone, but never my Glock."

Steven glanced in the rearview mirror as he slowed. "They are just keeping pace. I tried to make it seem like it was normal traffic slowing me down. I don't know if they bought it."

"What next?"

"Step two in the 'is someone following you playbook'. Is your seatbelt on tight?"

"I don't like the sound of this."

"I just want them to get a little closer. I have to time this just right. Hang on!"

Steven veered the convertible sharply to the right.

He cut off one vehicle that objected loudly to his erratic driving with a loud, long horn blast.

Steven concentrated on his driving as they just barely made the exit ramp in time.

Chelle turned to look at the black SUV

"Shit, they're trying to make the turn."

More horns blared and tires screeched. Steven turned his head just in time to see that the SUV, despite a dangerous effort had missed the exit. It gunned its engine and took off down the freeway.

"So much for paranoia." Steven rubbed his chin, his hand shaking just a bit.

"Great driving." Chelle slipped her pistol back into her purse. "Now what? Do you have any idea what that was all about?"

"Not a clue, but I do know that I saw government plates on the SUV."

"Secret Service shadowing their favorite senator?"

"Military plates. I don't know what branch."

Steven turned down a side road that would take them to their hotel.

"Why would the military be following you?"

"I don't know. All I do know is that I am not making any friends up on Capitol Hill. My committee is apparently being a bit too persistent."

"So much so that you are pissing off the military brass?"

"At least Shannon would be happy."

"I'll bite. Why would Shannon be happy we are being tailed by the military?"

"She told me that the more pushback I get, the closer I am to getting at the truth. I must be getting very, very close. And talking about close, we are getting close to our hotel." Steven said as they turned a corner onto Frank Sinatra Drive.

"Darn, wouldn't you know it? Road closed due to construction. We'll have to double back." Steven said as he found a place to turn around. "Probably for Caesars Palace, they're building another huge addition. This time they're adding a tower to house a new water show. It's already being advertised as the newest, state of the art, mind-blowing experience in Vegas. It should be done soon."

Chelle stretched her neck to look at one of the tall construction cranes. She said, "Just another reason to come back here."

Reidsville, NC police station

It was late afternoon in Reidsville, Jojo, along with other officers were frantically trying to find the right Patrick Cox. With the captain's blessing, Jojo had set up a mini task force. They had found many Patrick Coxs, one in Reidsville, others across the state and still more across the country.

Because the other murders happened in and around Reidsville, that Bill Cox was their first attempt to contact. An officer eventually made contact by phone and a police cruiser was sent out to his location at his office to assess his situation and protect him if needed.

Jojo said to his captain after ending another unsuccessful call. "He could have meant any of the Patrick Coxs we have found. We can't call them all up and tell them their lives might be in danger."

"Do you take this guy seriously?" The captain asked, knowing the answer.

"If I start making more calls, I'll be calling out of state."

"I know," The captain admitted, "I have already placed a call with the FBI. We are getting out of our jurisdiction and in over our heads."

A uniformed officer came over to Jojo and the captain with a computer printout in hand.

"I may have found the Patrick Cox we are looking for."

Both men looked up. Jojo got up out of his chair to look at the printout the sergeant gave to the captain.

"Son of a bitch." Jojo whispered.

The article stated, "Professor Patrick Cox was found dead in his hotel room this morning by the police who were there to arrest him. He was recently estranged from his wife of forty years over a recent scandal involving child pornography. Cause of death is unknown, foul play is not suspected at this time. The professor was known to have a weak heart."

That night inside the Eiffel Tower Restaurant:

"Your outfit looks stunning." Steven complimented.

"Thank you again. You didn't have to buy me this."

"Are you kidding? I get the pleasure of looking at you in it all evening. And besides, how often do you get to eat in the Eiffel Tower? And we never had to leave the USA."

"This is the kind of surprise I like. You are way too sweet. Maybe later you can help me out of it."

"Are you trying to rush me through dinner?"

Chelle gave a sly smile. "Slow down, tiger. I want this night to last forever. Just look at the view from here."

Their table inside the restaurant level of the Eiffel Tower was by a window looking west over the fountain and reflecting pool of the Bellagio Hotel on the other side of the wide Las Vegas Boulevard.

Steven turned just a bit to look in the same direction as Chelle.

Steven held Chelle's hand and smiling said, "You are right, it sure is."

"How high are we?" Chelle asked as she peered almost straight down.

"This restaurant is eleven stories. But later we can go even higher. As a half-sized replica of the real Eiffel Tower, the top observation deck is five hundred and forty feet above the Strip."

"Ohh, look," Chelle said excitedly.

Colorful lights came on across the boulevard, brightening the night. Jets of water an entire block long pounded toward the sky out of the artificial lagoon in front of the Bellagio Hotel. The various fountains danced to music that could even be heard slightly inside the restaurant. The stories high water fountains glistened through the multicolored lights shown on them.

"I wonder how big the reflecting pool is?" Chelle pondered out loud not realizing she was overheard.

"I hear that question all the time," The wine steward said as he topped off their wine glasses. "It is exactly eight and one-half acres, and thirteen feet deep at its deepest."

Chelle held up her glass in a salute to the wine steward. "Your timing is impeccable, sir."

"You are most welcome, Madame."

Chelle turned back towards the water show. To Steven she said wistfully, "That is one of the most beautiful things I have ever seen. Thank you so much for bringing me here. This is wonderful." Chelle took another taste of her wine with a wide smile as she enjoyed the water and light show.

Dreamily she added, "What a way to cap off an amazing day. Seeing Red Rock Canyon by convertible was magnificent. Who would have dreamed that the desert could be so beautiful?"

Steven took her hand and looking her in the eyes said, "It pales next to you."

"Senator Westcott, please. You embarrass me." Chelle accepted the compliment. "Now if we could just find out who was following us and why."

"I'm sure if I started poking around, I would be told it never happened, all in my imagination."

"I saw it too."

"We know what we saw, but we have no proof. But I might have an idea of why. I was warned."

Chelle was about to ask for an explanation when they were both distracted by a series of what sounded like explosions, there was a wall of water shooting high into the sky. When the water finally settled, the show was over, and the reflecting pond calmed.

Steven explained, "They use compressed air to blast the water that high. The higher the water goes, the more air pressure needed, thus the bigger the boom."

"What an unbelievable sight. Only in Vegas."

Steven casually looked around to make sure they were still having a private discussion. Softly he said, "As far as I can tell, my meeting is still on for tomorrow. Nobody has contacted me to say otherwise. After what we learned down in Mexico, you know I trust nobody, especially anybody in government, except you. And after being tailed today, my radar is on high. Even though I didn't want you to come down here in the first place, I may need your help."

"Are you afraid that whoever contacted you might be dangerous, and you want me to go along with you to the meeting?"

"Not them. I don't think they would have contacted me to hurt me. Besides, if they see you, they will run like scared rabbits. They might be watching us now and already got cold feet."

"If you're not afraid of the people who contacted you, who are you afraid of?"

"The same people they're afraid of. The e-mail warned me that I could be followed and to leave my electronics at home. I am sure that the people they want to expose are the same people my committee suspects are overreaching their authority of using electronic surveillance. Think about this. The NSA gets somewhere north of ten billion dollars a year. My God, that's ten thousand million dollars a year.

"Even the FBI doesn't spend that much money a year. They also employ more people than the FBI. Anywhere from forty thousand people to one hundred thousand. Of course, that's all classified too."

Chelle set her wine down and whispered, "You want an FBI agent to protect you from our own government?"

"Not an FBI agent, you. But..." Steven hesitated to finish his sentence.

"Now what?"

"The more I think about it, the more I'm thinking that getting you involved could be a mistake. You bring up a good point, you are a federal agent. If I accept classified information from them, they and I might be committing a federal crime. Possibly treason. If you know about it, you could become complicit." Steven took a moment to ponder about what he had said. After a few seconds more, he added, "I think I made a big mistake in asking you here. You shouldn't be here. This could be the real deal. At first, I thought what I didn't tell you couldn't hurt you, but just by being here you can become complicit. Hell, Chelle, I don't know what is right and wrong anymore."

Chelle sat back understanding the predicament. "But how can you know what they are going to give you?"

"Obviously I can't. The only thing I do know is that I'm not supposed to know what they say they are going to show me. But that is exactly why I need to see it. This is a no man's land, area of the law, the Wild West. A judge, if it even gets to one, could rule either way, and because we are dealing with national security it could all be hush hushed and swept under the rug and you and me with it.

"Hell, just by talking to you about it is dangerous to you and your career. Maybe you should go straight to the airport and jump on an airplane right now and head back to D.C."

There was a bit of silence as Chelle considered what Steven was suggesting.

Steven added to the equation, "And even though the president assured us he condemned the actions of IRENE and would undo them."

Chelle interrupted surprised at the suggestion, "IRENE? You think they are involved?"

"What if the president didn't or couldn't shut down IRENE?"

"So, the not-so-secret, secret organization raises its ugly head again," Chelle pondered.

"I wish I knew. The organization has been around since shortly after World War II. I doubt that one man, even the President of the United States, has the power or influence to change them. The International Resolution for the Establishment of Nations' Equality has proven they have tentacles everywhere. I'm not saying they are involved, but we can't take anything at face value. They were willing to blackmail me to get my cooperation as a Senator, and willing to kill me when I didn't.

This is the type of thing they could have their fingers in. The fact is, I don't trust anybody but you."

"The President assured us that Alfonso Lucas was a rogue agent of IRENE and would be 'dealt with'."

"Neither of us knows what that means. Chelle, I can't ask you to stay, I won't ask you to stay. In fact, my advice is for you to leave now and let me deal with this. If IRENE is involved, you know how dangerous that organization can be. They have already murdered to accomplish whatever their misguided intentions require. And for some reason, I seem to be on their radar screen over and over again."

"I do. And that is why I'm staying."

"Almost worse, it might not be IRENE we need to worry about, it could be our own government."

"I understand that too. All the more reason for me to stay."

"The rational part of my brain is saying you should leave right now. The selfish part of me wants you here because I feel I might need your help."

Chelle smiled mischievously, she said. "Ok it's settled, I guess we are both all in."

Steven didn't smile back but took both her hands in his and gave a gentle squeeze, and said, "I hope we don't both regret this decision."

Chelle knew that whether she liked it or not, their romantic getaway was over as she pushed her half-drunk wine away. "How do you get yourself into these situations?" Chelle shook her head and smiled a bit, "And me with you?

"Another no-win situation. If you don't check out the material they claim they have, you might never know the truth. But by looking at it, you might be breaking the law and helping what could be traitors."

"Possibly," Steven corrected. "Or it may be nothing but chili recipes."

"So how does a whistleblower receive protection from exposing national secrets that aren't supposed to be secrets? Who makes that call? Them? The country can't have every government employee thinking they are the last bastion of sanity in a world gone crazy."

"If I was lied to during the hearings, it might not be so grey. However, either way, they are taking a huge risk. I guess their hope is that by exposing the info to a Senator they will be exonerated if found out."

"You mean as opposed to throwing it out on the internet for the world to see."

"Exactly. And when you think about it. That makes them somewhat brave if they believe they are exposing criminal activity at great risk to themselves."

Chelle sat silently for a while, suddenly taking an interest in those sitting around them. "My bet is they are real, and a self-deleting e-mail shows some degree of computer sophistication. I have to believe they have a smoking gun, or at least what they believe is a smoking gun."

Steven finished his after-dinner drink, clinking the half-melted ice cubes together. He set down his glass though he held its coolness in his hand for a moment more. "My committee has oversight responsibilities over organizations that specializes in keeping secrets. In other words, we are responsible to watchdog over things we don't even know about and couldn't unless somebody tells us.

"The United States could have a program of building an army of Sasquatches and we wouldn't know about it because nobody on our committee asked the right question. Not that we would get an honest answer even if we did.

"My instincts smell a rat. Does the NSA need over forty thousand people just for the job of spying on foreigners?"

"And that's why we left our cell phones at home."

"Yes," Steven pointed to the analog watch on his wrist. "And my smart watch, so we couldn't be tracked or listened too. Chelle, I love you and I don't want you hurt in any way. But I don't know whom else to trust. I could be in way over my head, and I wouldn't want anyone else to have my back, 'cept Jojo of course."

"Of course, no offense taken, I think. But what exactly do you need me to do?"

"I wish I knew. I'm afraid that if you go with me to the meeting, it'll signal a no deal. They were quite specific. But, that doesn't mean you can't be gambling nearby while I grab a dinner."

Chelle glanced around the room once more. She was particularly interested in the couple closest to them who had stood as the gentleman helped his girl with her wrap. As they

Alan D Schmitz
DIGITAL SECRETS

waked away, Chelle said, "This evening sure turned one-eighty fast. Now you have me wishing I had my gun on me."

"Sorry for putting you on the spot. I,,,I shouldn't have gotten you involved, I'm so sorry." Steven stood; "Are you sure we shouldn't find you a plane ride back to D.C.?"

Chelle stood as Steven helped with her chair. She took her small, gold-sequined purse in one hand and grabbed Steven's hand with the other. "I'm sure. If we are going to gamble, we are in the right place. And as long as we're here, let's see about getting those chili recipes. "

Chapter 8

The next day, Steven found Chelle gambling on a quarter machine. She was busy playing a video game promising a big payout if five pictures of a four-leaf clover lined up. Proudly he held up two tickets.

"I got em. I can't believe it. Just as the concierge is telling me it's sold out. He says, 'two tickets just became available, good ones too.' I told him to grab them."

They were in the casino area of the Paris Hotel, the same hotel they were staying at. An evening sky was painted on the high arched ceilings around them, and the side walls had silhouettes of supposed French men and women drinking wine between the faux window frames of the buildings surrounding them. The effect was a feeling of being in the middle of a Parisian village, including streetlights that lined the walkway of well-worn cobblestone.

The sounds of slot machines enticing players and announcing payoff with loud ringing bells was a constant reminder that they were not on a Parisian Street. Chelle was nestled under one of the four remarkably real and huge arched iron legs for the Eiffel tower that rose from the base of the casino. She stared up at the tickets Steven was holding and asked, "Two tickets to the Dancing Chickens, for who? You don't even like them."

"These tickets will make me father of the year. Tracy and one lucky friend are in for a huge treat. I feel a bit neglectful lately with the congressional hearings going on and everything. These tickets should go a long way to making it up to her."

Chelle took the tickets in hand. "Wow, these aren't the cheap seats."

"Are you kidding? They are the only seats. How would you like to come back to Vegas with me to chaperone Tracy and her friend?"

"I think I would like that."

"Hold them up, I want a picture. I'm going to send it to Tracy. She won't believe that I have them. She'll think they are for us. After checking with her mother, I'll surprise her and tell her they're for her and a friend."

Steven snaped the picture then glanced at his watch. "Do you mind guarding those while I go to the meeting?"

Chelle carefully tucked the tickets into her purse. "What do you want me to do?"

"The buffet where I'm supposed to meet them is over by the elevators. I'm going to walk that way and back. If you spot a tail, scratch your ear. Otherwise, give your nose a slight squeeze if the way is clear."

Steven gave Chelle a kiss and walked away. Chelle pretended to be distracted by her video machine though she glanced in Steven's direction using her trained eye to spot any suspicious movements.

Steven stopped and examined the contents of a window display full of cigars. He glanced back at Chelle who smiled and rubbed her nose just a bit. Without so much as even a nod, he headed for the line that had formed of patrons waiting to enter the buffet.

Steven joined in the long line, jealous of the V.I.P. guests who flashed a card to the hostess and were seated immediately. In line with him were businessmen in suits and ties. Other visitors wore t-shirts and shorts, and others leather or lace. There were men and women of all ages, many with hair colored every color of the rainbow along with hairstyles that exceeded imagination. Others, like he, were dressed in khakis and sport shirts. Many of each variety wore ribbons around their necks, which supported oversized identification badges that were intentionally styled to look like nineteen-eighties vintage, five-inch-wide floppy disks.

Steven remembered seeing the real thing in use, though he doubted that most of the young visitors ever had the occasion or need to use the now antique method of transferring data between computers.

After fifteen minutes in line, a hostess ushered Steven in. He had not noticed anyone pay any more attention to him than anyone else. He walked past edible designs of French bread piled high. The décor was set to remind of the Parisian atmosphere, including framed pictures of French countryside and people living their lives out in vineyards, small towns, and farms. And of course, there were many photos of the real Eiffel Tower in France, during various stages of construction.

The food smelled delicious and was as varied as a supermarket. Steven took a seat at the table assigned to him, not sure of his next move. A hostess came by with a glass of water and carafe of coffee. She smiled politely as she set down dinning utensils wrapped inside a cloth napkin. Steven scanned the other tables, and nobody seemed to be taking notice of him. After five minutes, the various plates of food that continually marched past got the better of him.

He toured the food stations, filling a plate with an assortment of delicacies. When he got back to his table, he noticed there was something slipped under his napkin. It was a mock five-inch floppy disk, just like so many of the people in line had around their necks. Only this I.D. badge had his name on it.

Steven sat and tried not to act too suspiciously as he scanned for whoever may have planted it. He placed his napkin across his lap and read the rest of the badge. It was for a seminar in the Versailles Ballroom. Steven looked at his watch; the seminar would start in fifteen minutes. He read further; the seminar was titled 'Is Big Brother Watching You'. The Black Hat group was sponsoring it.

The Versailles Ballroom was just down the hall, but the pedestrian traffic was heavy, and he didn't want to be late. So, after a rushed meal he headed out the door and down the wide cobblestone indoor street to the Versailles Ballroom. He followed it past a jewelry store, street vendors, and a children's clothing store.

A sign pointed to the Versailles Ballroom. At the entrance, the line of attendees was a reproduction of the line of characters in front of the buffet. Each wore an I.D. Badge around their neck. Steven slipped his on and soon was inside the large hall.

Once inside, he followed a young woman, or at least he believed it was a young woman. Her sloppy dress and leather coat made her gender questionable as it did the young men who wore long hair and earrings and other piercings. Their dress screamed anti-establishment, which he assumed was exactly as intended.

Steven decided to assume she was a female as he observed long pink hair to one side of her face and when she turned her head, he saw that on the other side of her face it was green, short, and spiked.

The lights began to dim, and he found a row of seats largely not taken and slipped himself into one of them, trying to not appear out of place with his neatly trimmed short brown hair and sport shirt. Steven looked around at the participants still coming into the room, most dressed in t-shirts, making him feel a bit overdressed.

The introduction speaker began, "I hope nobody has their phones on."

The crowd laughed at the joke. Steven didn't understand the humor.

"At least this is one place we don't have to worry about phones ringing during the seminar. And if it is on, it will shortly be hacked and turned off for you."

The crowd laughed again.

A young girl with a jet-black Mohawk sat next to him to his right. The Mohawk was thick and flowed down the back of her neck. She wore a black leather jacket over a white t-shirt and various piercing protruded through the dark skin of her ear and a ring surrounded full lips that had been turned from red to green with lipstick.

The lights were turned down even more as the introduction continued. A man Steven guessed as being in his early forties dressed in a black tee shirt and jeans excused himself as he scooted past Steven's knees. He wore square eyeglasses that looked thick and heavy. His hair was light brown and hung down a bit unkempt into his right eye.

He kept walking past Steven and that was when Steven realized a small brown envelope had been slipped onto his lap. Steven looked down the aisle as the man took a far seat.

Steven was about to open the envelope when the young woman next to him warned. "Don't look at it now. To prove we are serious, we researched you, the FBI agent you came down to Vegas with, and your daughter. Don't share it with anyone or the deal will be off. Your girlfriend seems clean, but she could be one of them, so don't trust her either. We will contact you again if we think it is safe. Remember, big brother is always watching, and we'll be watching you too."

The young woman got up and disappeared into the crowd still filing into the lecture room. Steven decided leaving right away would be too obvious, so he stayed and the lecture began.

Reidsville, NC:

For Jojo, the weekend was anything but relaxing after the unnerving phone call from the killer. He was trying to take his mind off things by watching some television. His plan wasn't working.

He tossed his phone onto the table in front of him. Tamara walked into the room from the entry way behind him and could sense his frustration. She asked, "Who are you trying to get a hold of?"

Jojo twisted his head a bit to see his wife approach. "Oh, hi, doll. Didn't see you come in."

"I'm not surprised. You seem to be pretty preoccupied, and it's not with me," Tamara teased as she rubbed her big man's back.

"It's Cowboy, he doesn't answer his phone. And neither does Chelle."

"I'm sure it's nothing. Maybe they went up to the mountains to get away and they are out of cell range."

"You kidding, Cowboy without his phone? Same goes for Chelle. She's FBI, she doesn't go anywhere she can't be reached."

"Everybody deserves time off. In fact, that is exactly what we are going to do after you catch this guy. And we are turning our phones off too."

Tamara bent down just a bit and hugged him and gave Jojo a gentle kiss on his cheek.

"Lord knows you have been under enough pressure to cave in even your big shoulders."

Jojo reached up and patted the soft arms that were caressing his chest. "That call I got was unnerving, I need to talk to Chelle about it. At least now Captain Mitchem admits we need the FBI in on this thing."

Las Vegas – Versailles Ballroom:

The hour and a half of the lecture flew by. At first the envelope on his lap seemed to be screaming at him to open it up. But once the speaker caught his attention, he found the lecture riveting.

Steven realized the subject matter wasn't an accident. Whoever had contacted him had wanted him to hear this particular message. Months ago, he would have put the speaker on par with the conspirators who don't believe the moon landing ever happened. Now he wasn't so sure. The lecturer assured his audience that the NSA had much more information on average Americans that they let on. And they were using that information to spy on Americans. The only question was if it was illegally or legally?

One question in particular to the audience reverberated in Steven's mind. If you monitor what people are doing on Facebook, or Tinder, or Linkedin, etc.., are you doing anything illegal? If the government does it, are they doing anything illegal, even if they are doing it exponentially greater?

After the lecture Steven walked out of the hall sobered by the new reality of ever-present and never destroyed digital information. The Internet had changed everything. The flow of the crowd was moving past a sports bar a few stores up the indoor faux French street. Steven looked through the window, it didn't look too crowded and could be just the place to look at the files he was given. Walking past a light post and under a huge stained-glass dome towards the restaurant he glanced back towards where he had come from wondering if he was being followed. Steven caught the eye of a white male, dressed in a suit and tie, who glanced away and turned sharply into a shop selling children's clothing.

Steven decided to investigate and turned back. The crowd was thick and walking against it was difficult. He couldn't be sure, but the same man came out of the store and headed away from him. He seemed to be at an advantage, there was a break in the pedestrians and moved in the opposite direction. Steven tried to keep up, but the man soon became lost in the maze of the casino and rows of slot machines.

The files in his hand demanded attention so he gave up the pursuit and turned back toward the pub. Once there he was ushered to a table by a young woman whose gender was undeniable. She smiled at Steven as he sat. "What can I get for you?"

"A beer please," he said as he smiled back.

"I'm afraid you're going to have to be a bit more specific. We have twenty-five beers on tap." The waitress smiled broadly and handed a menu to Steven with the back of it displayed and a list of beers filling it.

"Wow! That is an impressive selection. How about the house amber ale?"

"Good choice, small or large?"

"Small, thank you."

"Any appetizers?"

"Not right now. Thanks."

"She smiled broadly at him again and assured, "I'll be right back."

The second she was gone he opened the sealed envelope and saw the three files. Each was thick and clearly labeled. There was one for Chelle, Tracy, and Senator Steven Westcott. Steven opened his and examined it.

It didn't take long to appreciate its thoroughness. The first page was a synopsis of his life from grade school on. It talked about his parents and how they died. Another two pages were about his brother Ernie and a short synopsis of his life, including things Steven didn't think were known by anyone but him.

Alan D Schmitz
DIGITAL SECRETS

He scanned more pages. He saw his report cards, from first grade through high school. On the next page were his college transcripts. After that his army records were all listed. Steven was amazed at the details of his life, including known associates.

Clearly the report was designed to give someone a quick overview of his life. The next section was titled 'Current Status'. It went from most recent on the first pages and proceeded backwards in time.

Steven noticed a beer had at some time been placed in front of him because the waitress was nowhere to be seen at the moment. He realized that he had been so absorbed by the file he had been oblivious to its delivery.

He took a long sip as he turned the page. He nearly spit out the beer in his mouth when he saw the photo of him and Chelle in a red convertible. Steven recognized the location immediately as being their ride from yesterday. The caption said the photo was taken on Las Vegas Boulevard, Las Vegas. Nevada. The photo was also time stamped.

It mentioned their room number at Paris and the fact that they ate inside the Eiffel Tower restaurant the night before. His flight and seat number were listed, as well as a copy of his driver's license, phone numbers including his private cell number, and all the e-mail addresses used the last ten years.

It listed him as a United States Senator and dates elected and terms served and committees assigned. A list of people who he currently associated with was included. Chelle's name was prominent and clearly reported as his sometimes-overnight girlfriend. There were more photos of him, him with friends, him with Chelle, him with Tracy. Another date and time stamped spreadsheet denoted his exact location throughout each day for the last two months.

In shock, Steven replaced his file into the manila envelope and opened the file on his daughter. Her file was equally detailed if not even more so. Even down to her high school friends and pets and like and dislikes. The file was truly scary; it appeared as if somebody had been stalking his daughter throughout her entire life. And not only was the file extremely detailed, it was accurate.

Absent-mindedly he drank his beer in-between turning pages. Steven knew enough about his daughter's high school life to know whom her friends were. The latest report card was something he didn't have access to yet and he saw a class or two that needed some more work. Steven was enthralled and studied the report realizing there was a lot about his daughter's life he didn't know, at least until now.

The waitress came by and asked, "That must be some pretty interesting reading?"

Steven didn't hear her at first and when he realized the interruption he looked up, "Ahhh.. yeah, it is." Steven slipped Chelle's report and Tracy's back into the large envelope.

"Another beer?"

"No thanks."

The waitress dropped a slip on the table with an amount. Steven tossed more than enough cash on the table to cover it and walked off. It was time to find Chelle and despite the warning he had received, she had to know he had been successful in finding the smoking gun that the NSA was collecting information on U.S. citizens it shouldn't be.

****

Steven found Chelle near where he had seen her last. He could see the relief on her face as he approached. She said, "Thank God you are all right. You were gone so long but I didn't know where to go to find you. Next time we don't go without out phones."

"Sorry, but it was worth it."

"Where were you and what is that around your neck?"

Steven held out the lanyard and glanced at the oversized floppy disk identification. "It's ID for the convention going on."

"Is that what they are, I saw more than a few unique characters with them on."

"Unique is putting it fairly mild." Steven grinned. "It's for a hackers convention, more specifically they call themselves White Hat hackers or Black Hat hackers."

"I was mysteriously invited to one of the seminars. This was left on my plate when I came back from a buffet line with instructions to attend the seminar. I guess I'm an honorary Black Hat hacker now."

Chelle added, "I have heard of it, just didn't know it was today. It is one of the biggest. You see Black Hat is the term for a person that illegally hacks for personal gain, as opposed to White Hat. Those are the people who try to stop them. Funning thing, both sides come to the same convention to learn the latest hacking techniques."

"How do you know about it?"

"The FBI sends people to this convention. As White Hats of course."

"You're kidding, the FBI?"

"And other law enforcement. Teaching somebody to hack isn't a crime. This is the place to go to learn the latest methods."

"Hacking does strange bedfellows make."

"Well-put."

Steven dropped the lanyard and asked. "How's your luck been?"

"Not so great." That's when her penny machine started spinning wildly and soon Chelle was richer by fifty dollars.

Steven laughed, "You were saying?"

"Another two hundred and I'll be even."

"Talk about hacking. After I show you what I have in my hand, you may never want to use your phone again. Come on, let's head up to the room to talk in private."

"It's about time. I've lost enough money for one day." Chelle cashed out and took her voucher slip for one hundred and ten dollars and slipped it into her purse.

"Your day isn't going to get any better. You know what, after what I just heard and saw, I don't trust our room isn't bugged. Let's walk the strip and find a corner bar someplace. And keep your eyes open for a tail. I'm sure I'm being followed."

"Any description of who I should be watching for?"

"A white male, grey pinstriped suit and tie. Older, sixty to seventy my guess. I could swear he was following me to a restaurant."

"I'll keep an eye out. But you just described ten percent of the people here. Do you think it has something to do with our tail yesterday?"

"No, I doubt it. Didn't seem military to me."

They walked out of the Paris Hotel turning north towards a row of small shops that sold everything from hot dogs to ice cream to fine watches and jewelry. Music started up across the street and it caught Chelle's attention.

"Look, it's the water show starting, let's watch." Music blared and the water sprang up from what had been a calm reflecting pond just moment before. Sprays of water twisted and danced to the music. After a while, there were loud blasts that sounded like cannon shots. Immediately after, enormous fountains of water were thrust hundreds of feet into the air.

The song came to an end, and so did the water show with a final thunderous explosion of water high into the air. Chelle couldn't help herself and clapped for the computer run show. She said, "That was fun. It was pretty last night, but seeing it up close is so much better."

They continued down Las Vegas Boulevard picking up an ice cream cone on the way. Eventually they found a bar called Margaritaville. It was a nice day; however, the afternoon heat was building so they decided to find a place out of the sun. They saw an open table along the raised patio facing the wide boulevard that was shaded and also being cooled by the water misters surrounding them. There was just the slightest of breezes as they climbed the few steps to the patio.

The raised perch gave Steven and Chelle the perfect spot to watch for any pedestrians that seemed to be loitering. A hostess offered them a table with an umbrella to shield them from the worst of the sun. When their waitress came by, Steven said, "When in Rome. I'll have a margarita."

Chelle said, "Just an iced tea please."

The waitress walked off and Chelle whispered. "So far, I'm not noticing a tail, unless you are concerned about that little old blue-haired lady sitting behind you. She just sat down; I'm sure she's following us."

Steven was about to turn to look when Chelle laughingly warned, "Don't turn around. The last thing we want to do is let her know we are on to her."

"Very funny. I'm telling you there is something strange going on. Let me tell you what happened after I left you."

Chelle giggled mischievously, "I'm just teasing. And just in case you are wondering, after what you told me last night, I decided to carry some insurance. I have my Glock 19 in my purse"

Their table gave them the perfect perch to people watch. Steven and Chelle watched an eclectic parade of people that kept a steady pace past them on the sidewalk below.

Steven explained what had happened and showed her the envelope and slipped out Chelle's report and handed it to her. "Just for the record, I was told not to trust you because you might be one of them. I think 'them' refer to NSA spies. Also, I didn't look at your file. There's so many private details in mine and Tracy's that I didn't think it would be right to read yours."

The drinks were delivered, and Steven paid for them in cash. Chelle began to read her report as Steven kept watch for suspicious characters around them. There were many unique individuals walking the strip, but none seemed a danger to them.

Chelle became as engrossed in her file as he had. She showed him a different picture of her and him in the red convertible. "This is amazing. My guess is it was taken by a traffic cam."

"There was a photo in my report just like it. I mean red convertible and all, but it was on a different street corner."

"At least we know whoever these people are they weren't lying to you. This report is exceptionally recent and detailed."

"Detailed? Are you kidding? Mine even had a shopping list included from my local grocery store. It even mentioned what kind of wine I like and buy most often."

Chelle took a taste of her iced tea and scanned her report once more.

"I'm afraid your whistleblowers might be right. I might be one of them."

Steven was shocked. "What do you mean?"

"This is all detailed stuff. But if I was after a bad guy and I knew his name, or at the very least had a photo of his face, the FBI could come up with a report just like this. And it would be one hundred percent legal."

"OK, I can understand that, but there would be FISA courts for a foreigner, applications for wire taps, subpoenas, you know, all the checks and balances. I understand that when we need to go after, for example, a terrorist, or a network of terrorist, we must go after them with everything we have. But not a US Senator, and an FBI agent, and a teenager."

Chelle was calculating everything she saw and read in the report, "Somebody has to have been tailing us for weeks, more like months, and had access to a team of investigators, and profilers to produce a document like this. This is frightening to see the extent somebody is willing to go to collect all this information."

Steven was shaking his head in anger. "I know I was pushing somebody's buttons in Washington, but why Tracy? Why would they be trailing her and building a profile on a teenager? What would be the value to them? I mean, what would a report like this cost? Per person, in time, cash, and personnel? A hundred thousand wouldn't be a bad guess."

Chelle came back with, "Remember, it's not their money. The budgets these people have would make it seem like pennies to them."

"These records are so private. There must be warrants issued. But who would issue a warrant against a teenager?"

Chelle took a deep breath. She looked at Steven and confessed, "I'm afraid everything I saw on you, me, and Tracy isn't so private. It could be done without subpoenas or warrants. Time-consuming, but not illegal to obtain. Let me explain."

Chapter 9

Las Vegas NV:

Wade stepped out into the hallway as the big ballroom emptied. He had just attended the first class of a two-day seminar entitled, 'ACHIEVING SECURITY AWARENESS THROUGH SOCIAL ENGINEERING ATTACKS'. During the first class, attendees received a copy of the newly tweaked hacking software, Rabbit Hole 7x. Tomorrow would be more hands-on practice on using it to hack into social accounts of all sorts.

Wade, like most attendees, paid in cash to remain anonymous, something most hackers coveted. His preliminary inspection of Rabbit Hole 7x left him impressed. Most importantly were two new features. The first allowed adding your own code. The second was a red flag to monitor if the hack was being hacked.

"Wade, Wade," he heard his name being called.

"Is that you, buddy?"

Wade turned towards the call of his name.

"Red, you old dog. Great to see you."

Wade held out his hand as the two pulled each others' hands in and they bumped shoulders in a warm greeting.

Wade asked, "Do you still follow the Tartans?"

"Only football and basketball. They almost made the NCAA playoffs last year."

"They had a hell of a season, didn't they?"

"Did you see that game winning layup by Thomasson, He looked like he could fly he was in the air so long."

"Didn't see the game but I saw the shot on the internet. I think it went viral for a week." Wade had to agree, he asked, "So what've you been up to? You're looking good."

"Doing OK, working on all the computer stuff is so sedentary that I took up running marathons. It's keeping me in shape."

Wade reach up and mussed up his friend's hair. "At least you still have your red hair."

"Must be the luck of the Irish," Red said as he smoothed his hair back into place with his hands.

"Still working on the Lake Lerna project?"

"Yeah, and it's still top secret. We could go to jail just for talking about it."

"Fuck them. We both have security clearance."

"Not the way I heard it. Yours was revoked."

"Yeah, but they can't erase my mind, the dumb fucks. Anyway, screw them. Never mind those assholes, what else is new? Did I hear right? Did you have another kid?"

"You bet, now two boys and girl." Red laughed. "And a fucking dog, living the dream in the burbs. You would never believe what I drive now." Red tapped a few times on his phone and showed Wade the picture on it.

"No way, you're kidding, a minivan?"

"I know, who'd have thought? Wife likes the red color, says it matches my hair. Just call me Mr. Mom."

"What happened to your BMW convertible?"

"What do you think happened? I traded it in for this."

Wade chuckled and slapped Red on the back lightly, "I feel sorry for you man, you're a lost cause."

"I sure as hell am. But the minivan is perfect for the kids, I love it, room for them and all their stuff. I wouldn't trade it for anything in the world. I don't have it today, the wife needed it. I'm driving the old Buick today. It's old but the air works, and it gets me to work and back."

"You know, your van is just like what my boss is looking for. Does it have room for seven?"

"You bet, with the back seat up."

"Would you mind sending that photo to my phone so I can show it to him?"

"No problem, I've got front, back, and side, I'll send them all."

"Sweet."

"What about you? You're look like you've been working out. What are you up to these days?"

"Same shit, different town. Moved out east. I ride my bike a lot, not dating anyone serious, working too hard."

"Are you doing computer stuff?"

"Yep, still a computer geek from good old CMU."

Red motioned to the lecture hall that had just left and asked, "What did you think of the program?"

"Nothing they didn't warn us about at CMU. We all knew big brother was coming. Only none of us could even begin to guess at the degree. I suppose the monster is alive."

"I told you, Wade; I can't talk about it. But what about the party tonight at Freddy's? You still planning on going?"

"Sure, wouldn't miss it. Looking forward to seeing old Fats." Wade chuckled to himself and smirked when he asked, "Do you remember when I locked him out of the frat house in nothing but his underwear?"

"Oh man, I forgot that. He had to sleep in the bushes all night. The mailman found him in the morning. He must have forgiven you, cause he has got an awesome spread just out of town and you and I are invited."

"Forgiven me? Don't know about that. I don't think old Fats even remembers that night. He was pretty fucking wasted."

"Your secret is safe with me. Where're you staying?"

"Where most the action is, at Paris."

"How bout I show up around four, we can get a beer and catch up. Around five we can head over to Fats Farly's. And like I told you before, don't call him that, he gets pissed."

"Whatever you say, Red buddy."

****

Chelle examined her file a bit more and agreed, "These files are extremely personal, but nothing I see here has been taken from illegal sources. The synopsis from your birth to yesterday is something that the FBI could put together using legal sources in a day or two. Nothing special.

"Everything is online. Even you or I, without the resources the bureau has, can do the research. As an example, if you want to reconnect with high school or college friends it's all online. You might have to pay a fee, but before you know it, they will come up with friends addresses and telephone numbers.

"At the bureau all we need is a name. With that, we can discern a birthdate and birthplace. With that we discover parents' names. The information just starts to bushel. It takes time and sleuthing. But we have some exceptionally smart people who do nothing but those things.

"What we can't get online, I usually can get just by flashing my FBI badge. People are usually cooperative.

"You were in the military, so any information you supplied them--any history, medical conditions, schools attended--we can get, all legally. You are a licensed pilot, that means medical records are available."

"What about the details of who I was with and when. You and I, the reference to sometimes-overnight girlfriend?"

"There are several ways to obtain that kind of detail. One way is to tail you. It is time-consuming, and expensive for sure, but a warrant isn't needed.

"Or we could follow your progress and mine through the city's traffic cam footage for our license plate. Which by the way, we have legal access to because it's public information, again, no privacy rights. The bank across the street from your apartment probably has a camera. It recorded our coming and going from your apartment on it. You know that nice little bistro down the street? I know it has an outside camera for the street side dining area. With a flash of my badge, I most likely would be given carte blanche to view whatever I wanted, no questions asked.

"Think about the video you often see on the nightly news after a murder or terrorist attack. We usually can follow somebody from corner to corner. We confiscate the video from banks, gas stations, whatever we want. It would be highly unusual for a business to deny us access to their recordings. Most people and businesses want to be good citizens and help us solve crimes.

"Right here, right now, we are on camera. Probably several of them."

"What about our tail. Is she still here?"

Chelle laughed, "Yep, still there, I don't like the looks of it, she looks mysterious and covert for sure. Her 1960s, beehive-styled blue hair is a clever disguise. She's making it obvious she is watching us, probably some sort of scare tactic. Do you think we should call the police?"

Steven laughed at Chelle's joke and finished his margarita, "Maybe I am being a bit paranoid."

"Now as far as the report, think about it. In your case, you work in a government building with security cameras, cameras we would have access to. Somebody with a badge could just flash it and ask people when was the last time they saw you and where. With timestamped video taken all over the city, including traffic cams, you can be followed.

"Another way to follow somebody's trail is to purchase their cell phone pings."

"Their what?"

"As you travel, your phone is constantly pinging cell phone towers. That's how it and they know how to communicate with each other. All the carriers save and compile this information and sell it."

"You're kidding."

"I'm afraid not. Retailers might want to know how many people walk by their store as opposed to how many stop in. In fact, there was a Supreme Court ruling that said the police must have a search warrant to get such information on a specific phone."

Steven asked, "You mean for a successful prosecution."

"That's right, but they could track a person without a warrant, though using it might lead to an unsuccessful prosecution. The ruling still leaves plenty of room for interpretation. At any rate, exactly where you have been and how long you have been there is readily available for anyone who wants to pay for it. That is as long as you had your cell phone with you."

"Such as every minute of every day. And these detailed reports on us don't upset you?" Steven sounded a bit incredulous. "This is exactly what the speaker in the program was talking about. It scares me to think he may not have been a looney toon. He may indeed be right about everything. That means big brother already knows everything we do and say."

"For the record, of course the details in these files upset me. I never looked at my life as such an open book. Somebody spent a lot of money, thousands of dollars, and had to have used human resources to build these files on us. But you asked me if it's your smoking gun on illegal activities by the NSA. I'm telling you no. I don't see anything that would be illegally obtained.

"And let's just say that for some reason, somebody, maybe our blue haired lady, is interested in you, and thus me and Tracy by association. It is Orwellian, but not illegal."

"It has to be illegal. Look at all of this private information."

"Steven, you or I as private citizens could pay somebody to build a report like this on anybody we want. They might have a harder time getting government records, but with the Freedom of Information Act, almost anything the government has on us is public record."

"No," Steven didn't accept it and shook his head to show it. "Tracy doesn't drive or work in a government office."

"Collecting her school records wouldn't be hard, getting her class schedule would be relatively easy. Heck, the bureau might be able to get direct access to the school's computer that would tell us her attendance records. Or like I said, a friendly call from the FBI and it would be given to us."

"But the report listed her friends' names. Her pet dog's name."

"Probably all found out scanning her social media. If we suspect someone of a crime, that is one of the first things we would do. Especially young people, that's all they do is post who they are with, what they are doing, and photos of them doing it. It's almost too easy. Everybody's connected to everybody, not hard to crack into those records either."

"Is that legal? I mean cracking into somebody's social media accounts."

"Usually, we don't have to. If you know how to search it and find it, it's all accessible. Even if somebody is doing a pretty good job of keeping their information private, that doesn't mean their friends aren't sharing information. Many of the applications even publish to your friends exactly where you are."

Steven fell back confused. "And all perfectly legal. It begs the question, why would the NSA take a chance on doing something illegal when so much information is waiting for the taking? I might be chasing a ghost. The NSA may be doing nothing improper. Still, why are they being so secretive and stonewalling the committee? Or I wonder if they....." Steven stopped midsentence and watched a group of characters walk past them.

"It's her, I'm sure of it. The hair, the piercings, it has to be her. I think the guy on the end is the one who dropped the files on my lap. Let's go. I need some answers."

****

Steven got the jump on Chelle and didn't take his eyes off the three targets. He followed them as close as he dared as the three continued to walk south at a leisurely pace.

Eventually Chelle caught up to Steven. "Was it something I said?"

"Funny girl. It's them, I'm sure of it."

It wasn't easy to keep up with the trio, due to the heavy pedestrian traffic going both ways down the not wide enough sidewalk. They scooted around a group of three drunken women wearing identical pink t-shirts. Each shirt had a picture of handcuffs stenciled on the back and the date of their friend's wedding.

In front of them were two men in dark suits holding coffees from a Starbucks somewhere. And in front of them was a family with two small children, both in strollers. The family were taking up most of the sidewalk and slowing everybody behind them down.

The men in suits seemed in a hurry to pass, but found it difficult to overtake the family because of the rush of oncoming pedestrian traffic. Two women dressed as showgirls, they had on identical skimpy string bikini bottoms, oversized colorful feathers fanned out from their mock diamond headdress and flowed down their backs They walked towards the men and offered to have their picture taken with them. They were naked from the waist up with nothing but small tassels covering their nipples.

The men tried to wave them off, but the girls were persistent. That gave Chelle and Steven time to pass them, and next they scooted past the family. Steven pointed to the girl. "There, I'm sure it's her. That hair job is pretty unique. I think they're going back to the conference at Paris."

Steven added, "Do you see her? She's walking with two others, both males."

"You mean the three that all have small backpacks."

"Yes, that's them."

"We need to corner them someplace they can't run." Chelle suggested.

"I'm guessing if we corner one of them the other two won't have a real good reason to run."

"A fair assumption. One should be all we need to get some answers," Chelle assured him. "We'll wait until they go into a casino. That should be our best chance to outmaneuver them."

"Agreed."

It didn't take long for the opportunity they were waiting for to present itself.

Steven whispered, "See, the fatter guy that looks a bit like Newman from Seinfeld."

Chelle scanned the area, "I see him. You mean the guy on the right hugging his computer bag?"

"That's him, my guess is he would be the easiest target."

Chelle and Steven followed the three from a distance. Steven was right; they were heading back into the Paris Hotel and Casino. They walked under one of the four huge arched legs supporting the erector set look of the Eiffel Tower. As they approached the entry, two glass doors automatically swung open greeting them to the inside of the casino. Chelle and Steven watched through the glass doors as a uniformed guard approached the trio. He searched through their backpacks. The three obliged and were shortly on their way.

DIGITAL SECRETS

Steven and Chelle walked into the casino as the same guard smiled at them. There was a noticeable change in the group's pace. It went from hurried to slow and deliberate. The black-haired girl and the man in the black t-shirt made eye contact as 'Newman' stood uneasily behind them.

Steven and Chelle had spread out a bit to better keep an eye on the trio. The three walked towards the back of the casino to a raised gambling area surrounded by a decorative glass enclosure. A sign over the entrance marked it as a 'High Limit' gambling area. Chelle noticed the girl take out something that looked like a weapon out of a pocket of her backpack. T-shirt guy did the same.

Chelle and Steven both merged near a Wheel of Fortune machine not far from the High Limit area. "What do you think?" Steven asked.

"I think it's perfect, only one way in and one way out, unless they jump the glass enclosure. And they don't seem like the athletic types. But keep watching; they are up to something."

Trying to look nonchalant, Chelle and Steven moved into the High Limit area for a better look. And although the characters seemed unlikely, Chelle thought she was witnessing a potentially dangerous situation. She clicked open her purse and put her hand on her nine-millimeter pistol.

Steven's eyes stayed on 'Newman' as his eyes scanned toward the ceiling. The red-headed male followed his gaze and nodded. Whatever was in his hand he pointed and aimed at the ceiling? Chelle got a better look at the weapon, and she couldn't believe what she saw.

'Newman', satisfied with one target down moved his stare to another direction. This time it was the girl that used a toy Star Trek phaser pistol and aimed it in the direction of 'Newman's' stare. She nodded when she was finished shooting her phaser.

The identical action was carried out several more times. When 'Newman' gave another nod of his head, the red head stepped up to a slot machine and placed something against it. Chelle guessed it was magnetic, because it snapped into place.

Immediately after, he put some money into the machine and hit the max bet button, spending twenty-five dollars. The redhead looked around nervously as he stood by the machine. They didn't see Chelle directly behind the row of slot machines.

Chelle moved to the machine next to the one the redheaded man was playing. She fed the machine some money and started playing.

Steven approached from the other side. As soon as they had the trio trapped between them, he said, "I need to talk to you three."

'Newman' looked like he was going to pee as he froze when he recognized Steven. The girl tried to run, but Chelle stood up in front of her and whispered. "You know I'm FBI, let's not make a scene. We are all on cameras. We just want to talk."

The redhead caught between 'Newman' and Chelle tried to decide what he should do. He reached up and nervously rubbed the back of his head. When he put his hand down his thumb caught on his thick-lensed glasses and they flew from his head to the floor.

"Oh no, not again." He said as he got down on his hands and knees and picked up the two halves that had broken right in front of Chelle.

'Newman' said, "Got tape, got tape."

The black-haired girl just rolled her eyes and helped 'Newman' get the tape out his backpack.

"Dammit Roger," she said, "we don't have time for this."

'Newman' said, "five minutes, five minutes."

"You know I need my glasses."

"Give them here," the dark-skinned girl demanded.

Chelle and Steven looked at each other with questioning looks on their faces. Chelle was instantly reminded of a show depicting stereotypical geeks as she read Rodger's t-shirt, which had a painted on pocket protector with an assortment of painted on pencils and pens. The t-shirt proudly proclaimed that 'nerds rule'.

The girl calmly wrapped a small section of white tape around the bridge of the two thick pieces of plastic that made up the frame of Roger's glasses and he slipped them on and completed the nerd look.

'Newman' who never looked at his watch said, 'four minutes, four minutes."

"We gotta go now!" The girl insisted to her friends.

Chelle discreetly showed the hilt of her weapon out the top of her purse. "Are you guys hacking these machines? You know you won't get away with it; there are camera's all over."

'Newman' spoke mechanically, "No cameras, I saw them all. Cameras disabled, I'm sure."

"Shut up, Marvin," the girl with the jet-black flowing Mohawk scolded.

"What's with the Star Trek phasers? They're not toys at all, are they? They disable the cameras somehow, don't they?" Chelle asked.

The red head took his finger and pushed up his glasses right where the tape now joined them. He said proudly, partially showing the phaser in his hand. "Pretty cool. Everybody thinks we are just nerds with Star Trek souvenirs, so nobody hassles us. I made these myself. I mean not the phaser but making them shoot out a high intensity white light. There is a red aiming laser you can see, than POW, like a flash of lightning the CCD imagers get overwhelmed with an invisible hot light and crash. The laser disables the CCD imagers, but we only have a five to ten minutes window before the cameras reset themselves."

"Shut the fuck up, Rodger," the girl admonished.

She looked at Steven and added, "You shouldn't have followed us. You can't be seen with us or us with you."

Chelle stepped closer to Rodger, and he backed away towards his friends. Chelle moved in front of the slot machine and scanned the reel as it continued to automatically spin and spend the money he had put into it. Only it was making more money than it was spending.

Steven gave a friendly smile. "If you know who we are, you know what we want. And one thing we don't want is a scene. I just want you to answer a few questions. Then you can go. No harm, no foul.

"The reports you gave me are interesting, and we don't know how you got it together so fast, but it doesn't seem like any of the information came from extraordinary sources. So why did you give it to me?"

The girl blurted out, "Don't say anything; you know what happened to Snowden."

Steven stepped a bit closer indicating he wasn't backing down.

Chelle sat down at the whirling slot machine. She found the electronic device magnetically attached to the machine and with a click removed it and handed it back to the redhead saying, "Whatever you're doing, I would strongly suggest you stop. We're not here to bust you for anything, but we need some answers. Answer our questions and we can all be on our way."

"She's FBI, she's one of them. Don't tell her anything," the dark-skinned girl warned again.

Steven sat down next to a lucky diamond machine hoping to defuse the situation by talking calmly. "I wouldn't start running towards the door. You'd be stopped before getting halfway down the hall if we make a scene."

Steven slipped a fifty-dollar voucher into the machine, and it came to life. He pressed the spin button but didn't watch the whirling images. Instead, he scanned the eyes of the three friends. "Look, I don't think you have done anything illegal, at least not yet. Maybe you abused a security clearance a bit to create the reports you showed us. But the information is hardly top secret. Why all the cloak and dagger stuff?"

Marvin was clearly agitated and repeated, "three minutes, three minutes".

The red-haired man put his hand on Marvin's shoulder and whispered. "It's OK, it's OK, everything will be just fine."

Marvin's legs started to quiver as he hugged his computer even tighter. "We gotta go, gotta go."

The redhead looked at Chelle, "You don't understand, that was just a test, and you failed it. We needed to know if we could trust you. I guess we can't. We didn't create those reports; they were already in the system. We just accessed them and printed them out to get your attention."

"It had photos of us driving down Las Vegas Boulevard from yesterday."

"The computer automatically updated the file by searching for recent photos and last known location. I can get a similar file on any American."

"Any American?" Steven questioned.

"Sure, since the day the computer was turned on it, has been crunching away day and night putting together a file on every American. But that's not what we're here to tell you."

"What computer? Every American? How?" Steven asked.

"NSA. A big f'n computer, quantum computing, artificial intelligence, and all of that. It searches all government and social networking sites for anything connected with the current subject of its search.

"Rodger, shut up!" The girl insisted.

"He's a senator, he has clearance to know these things."

"Not your job to tell him. You want to get locked up for the rest of your life? I'm out of here."

"Well do you think he is that dumb to believe that the NSA spends ten billion dollars a year just to monitor select foreign communications?"

The girl started to move away. Chelle stood and made a motion towards her gun. "I can get security's attention real quick. I'm sure the hotel security would be interested in all your toys. We have more questions."

The girl looked at her two friends clearly disgusted with what they had gotten her into.

Steven reminded, "You contacted me; the e-mail was very clever by the way. You said they lied, they all lied and they are collecting everything. I assume you don't like that, and it's obviously what I have been suspecting and trying to get to the bottom of. You have apparently been paying attention to my committee's hearings; you know I'm telling the truth. Now I need to know the truth from you, or I can't do anything about it."

Marvin repeated three times in a row, "Not right, not right, not right. Two minutes, two minutes."

The black-haired girl said again, "She's a cop and can't be trusted."

Rodger looked at both his friends, he didn't get their approval but continued anyway, "We don't work directly for the NSA. We work for a private firm that contracts with them. We all have high security clearance. If we tell you what we know, we will be called traitors."

Marvin whispered again, "Not traitors, not traitors."

"But we know what your security clearance is and what you and your committee's oversight job is, and you are being lied to. That puts us in a no-win situation. If we tell you what we know, we are traitors and breaking our security clearance. If we don't tell you, you might never know the right questions to ask or if you are being lied to or not."

Steven turned in his chair and asked Chelle, "You're the closest thing we have to a lawyer here. Wouldn't they be protected by the whistleblower law?"

"I'm afraid they are right. Best-case scenario is their security clearances would be revoked."

Marvin repeated, "No more work. No more work. One and a half minutes, one and a half minutes."

Chelle continued, "And that is best case. A judge could decide that there was no wrongdoing and that exposing the agency's spying tactics endangered our national security. They can't go to their bosses with the complaint because their bosses are probably complicit."

"No shit they're complicit," the girl with the Mohawk said with an attitude. "And if we expose the whole scheme on the Internet we will be hunted down and end up like Edward Snowden, best case. Guys, fuck 'em, we just go back to work Monday, do what we do and keep our mouths shut, not our fight."

"I don't want any of you to get into trouble for helping me. But there must be another way."

"The plan was, if you didn't know who we were, we could slip you information and it would stay confidential even though exposed to your committee. Now we can't do that. You can identify us."

"The reports, you said they were already done, why? Why were reports done on us? What can you tell us about them? My committee is trying to make sure that the NSA isn't doing anything illegal and that they're not spying on citizens they shouldn't be. And now you're telling me you have no information contradicting that."

Marvin said, "Time, it's time. No time, gotta go."

Marvin was becoming more and more agitated. He was squeezing the life out his computer bag and starting to shake.

The redhead looked at his watch; the girl with the jet-black Mohawk was backing away from Chelle.

Steven pressed for answers, sensing he had nothing to lose. "Am I wasting the committee's time? Are they just collecting publicly accessible records? What do they call it? You know what I mean, 'The Cloud', 'The Cloud', that's what they call it. Are they just sorting thorough stuff stored publicly in 'The Cloud'?"

Chelle was startled as the machine she was standing near started to ring a bell loudly signaling a major win.

The three used the distraction to head down the hallway towards the open-air exit back to the strip. Rodger pointed in a direction to his compatriots and shouted over his shoulder as they left. "Don't you get it? It's all legal cause they own the information. They are the cloud."

Chapter 10

Red parked his car about a block down the street. It was the closest parking spot he could find next to Freddy's home. They walked up the street; the sun was starting to set and the night air was still hot.

As they approached the home and entered through the open gate of the drive Wade said, "Wow, you weren't kidding. It looks like old Fats is doing OK for himself."

"Yeah, that latest government contract is big-time for him."

Wade said sullenly, "You mean the one I helped him get?"

Red mostly ignored the comment as they walked on the light red paving bricks that made the driveway. "He's not married; he has tons of dough. And the best part, he's still a party animal."

The front door was opened to the night air, they walked in and were immediately greeted by cool air and a smiling, clearly overweight man in his forties. His hair looked a bit greasy and was brushed to one side.

Wade wondered how his shorts stayed up as it didn't look like he had a waist. His Hawaiian shirt was half-tucked in and half-out.

"Sully, Red!" Freddy Farly came up and gave them both a grand high five. "This is awesome, just like the good old days at USC."

The three did the old buddy's 'special handshake'. They high fived each other and laughed at the silliness of it.

"Hey dudes, want a beer?" Freddy asked.

"Sure, Fats." Wade smiled back.

The smile on Freddy's face instantly faded. "Look, maybe I had that coming. But I invited you here so that there are no hard feelings. After all, you didn't give me much choice."

Wade looked at Freddy and smiled. "You're right, no hard feelings."

"We're cool?" Freddy asked

"Yeah, man, just f'n with you a bit, we're cool."

"In that case, check this out." Freddy started to smirk.

Freddy pulled out his smartphone, unfolded it, which made it twice as big. He opened an app that showed a video of people partying in the other room.

He manipulated the controls on it and soon the video started to move about the room.

"No way bro!" Wade exclaimed knowing exactly what was happening.

"Way man."

Freddy manipulated the drone as it flew through the ultra-high-ceiling, open concept home. "Check this out."

Soon the camera hovered over a cooler on the floor. The drone descended and a contraption on the end of a line that was connected to the drone gripped onto a beer in the cooler.

With a couple of thumb movements on the controller app the drone lifted the beer out the cooler.

"Did you invent that?" Wade was truly interested.

Freddy laughed. "Yeah man, it's like an arcade claw, only a lot stronger."

Wade looked up from the video the phone was displaying and saw the drone hovering above everybody as it crossed the room. It dropped down and Wade took the beer in hand and the claw opened.

"Red, need a beer?" Freddy laughed. "I call it Wonder Woman. She flies and gets me beers and doesn't complain. I even fitted her with a red, mini Wonder Woman bra."

Red laughed, "Doesn't sound anything like my wife. You bet I need a beer."

The drone took off towards the cooler once again.

Wade watched the drone hover across the room. "Is it controlled through Wi-Fi?"

"You got it," Freddy bragged. "When I'm in my loft bedroom, I can send it down to the kitchen to get me an old brewski. Not too shabby."

The drone came back with a beer. When Red had it in his grasp, the claw released and the drone hovered nearby.

Freddy looked at Wade, "Hey Wade, I'm way sorry I had to fire you from the project. I didn't have a choice. I hope you understand that."

"There are always choices, Freddy."

"Not for me, not that time. You pissed off the military bigwigs. I needed that contract."

Wade made a point of glancing around the huge home. He took his time staring at the marble tiled steps leading to the upstairs. "I guess the contract I helped you get paid off pretty well."

"Like I said dude, I had to fire you. I'm sorry but I had no choice."

Wade shook his head not buying it and explained for the hundredth time, "They were idiots. I told you what they wanted me to do. That was the stupidest thing I ever heard of. It would have set the project back months."

"It was stupid, and you are right, they are idiots, and it did set the project back. But you should have just gone along like I did. Shit man, I was compensated for those extra months. And paid good. The point is, dude, you just couldn't go with the flow could you? It didn't matter that you were right, and they were wrong. They were the ones with the checkbook. Besides, I heard you landed on your feet. I knew you would."

"If you call what I'm doing landing on my feet. After my security clearance was pulled, I had to go to nowheresville Massachusetts for a job I didn't want. I do computer security for a two-bit trucking company."

"Look, I'm sorry, dude, but not my fault. All you had to do was keep your big mouth shut, and you couldn't. So, no hard feelings, let's shake hands and be good."

Freddy held out his hand and Wade weakly accepted it.

Freddy smiled at Wade and added, "And I still think you are one of the best White hat/Black hat guys around. Listen, I'll be back in a bit, I gotta mingle. I'm having open house all week cause of all the guys in town for the tech convention. Come by anytime."

"Hey Freddy," Wade said meekly.

"Yeah?" Freddy was about to walk off.

"You are right. No hard feelings. In fact, if you want, I'll entertain your guest for a while with the drone while you make small talk."

Freddy looked at the control in his hand. "No funny stuff?" He asked.

"No funny stuff, I'm actually pretty good with these things."

"OK, Show me."

Freddy handed over the controls a bit suspiciously.

Wade gently played with the up and down control and the side to side. "I think I'm getting it."

Freddy seemed impressed. "OK, the tricky part is picking up a beer by the claw."

"Ok Freddy buddy, give me some tips."

Freddy enjoyed talking Wade through the first retrieval, they found a guest looking for another beer and flew it to him.

"Good job bro." Freddy congratulated.

"Care if I do some more?" Wade asked.

"Go for it. I have to take a piss anyways."

Wade wasn't in the mood to socialize. Flying the drone delivering beers kept him busy for the next hour.

The more he flew the drone, the more the strange erotic feeling started to come over him. It would be a challenge for sure, but that was what excited him. His mind was already churning with ideas. There was no reason his most recent hobby of killing for pleasure had to be confined to Reidsville.

****

Chelle and Steven watched the three disappear through the glass doors onto Las Vegas Boulevard. Chelle was about to suggest to Steven that they leave the high roller area when security guards surrounded them. She wasn't allowed to keep the money her machine had won. She didn't argue. Once the casino acknowledged that Steven was indeed who he said he was they decided that instead of arresting him they would welcome him to their casino.

The head of security explained, "All our cameras in this area of the casino went dark at the same time. The machine your friend the FBI agent was playing was hacked somehow. We couldn't see who did it, but it went off line even though we could tell it was still working."

Chelle insisted again for the tenth time, "I didn't hack into anything. I saw this machine spinning around and decided to sit by it. When it stopped spinning with three diamonds in a row, it said I won three thousand and eight hundred dollars."

Another guard came up with a printed-out photo. "We did get a few shots of who we think it was as they entered the casino. We think it might have been these three. Did you see them in this area?"

Steven took the photograph and said, "I can't make out any faces."

"It's the best we have right now. But what about her hair, or this guy in the black t-shirt?"

"There were some odd-looking characters here when we came by, but they left soon after. I didn't pay much attention."

The guard gave the picture to Chelle. "Can you identify them?"

Chelle glanced at Steven and noticed he was holding his breath wondering what she might say. Chelle felt conflicted as a law officer, then relented to what could be the greater good.

"The hair, definitely the hair looks familiar. But to be honest, I've been seeing a lot of unique people ever since we checked in."

"Damn." The head of security said. "Probably from the Black Hat group. We have problem with those people every year. They think we are all idiots, and they try different methods to steal from us. It's just a game to them."

Looking back at Steven he said, "Sorry to have bothered you and your friend, Senator. Please enjoy the rest of your visit."

A man in a suit walked up and introduced himself. "My name is Joe, and I am one of the casino hosts. I am going to have Margaret here set you up with a VIP pass to all the hotel's amenities."

A young woman in a black pants suit nodded with a smile and said, "I will be right back, Senator."

Joe added, "Please, Miss Saltarie and Senator Westcott, accept our apologies; we are so sorry for the inconvenience. Here is a voucher for dinner on us. Any restaurant in the casino is yours to enjoy. Just show the VIP pass and you will be escorted right in."

Steven and Chelle were left alone to enjoy their stay. The security guards and Joe the Host all disappeared into the casino again.

The lone other occupant of the High Limit area sat down at a hundred-dollar machine near them. "That was exciting," she said half watching her machine twirl around and half watching Steven and Chelle.

"It's not every day I get to see a United States Senator trying to explain he's not a crook. Although come to think of it, it does happen more often than one would think it should. I'm glad I caught back up with you. You sure took off in a hurry."

Steven and Chelle both realized at the same time the woman talking to them was the blue haired lady from Margaritaville.

"Mrs. Winston?" Senator Westcott asked.

"I'm so flattered you remembered me." Mrs. Winston kept playing the machine in front of her, putting another hundred-dollar bill into it.

She had two plastic coiled cords hanging around her neck. At the end of each cord was a players' card. One was already inserted into the machine, recording how much money she was gambling.

"I saw that they gave you a VIP card. I have one too."

Mrs. Winston showed them the card dangling from the cord. "I'm a Triple Diamond player. That means I'm what they call a whale. You know, a big fish. I spend a lot in their casino. If I can give you some advice it's to use the perks, that's where the money is. They'll do anything to keep me happy gambling in their casino."

"Mrs. Winston, I would like you to meet Chelle Saltarie. Chelle, this is Mrs. Winston. She and her husband are from California, and they have been generous donors to my campaigns."

"Please to meet you, Mrs. Winston."

"Ohh please.., call me Winnie. I'm sorry, I couldn't help but overhear what the three odd looking young people told you."

Chelle, a bit startled, looked at Steven, who in turn looked like he was thinking of a way to explain. While Mrs. Winston who never stopped her play added, "Don't worry, your secret is safe with me. I'm on your side. Remember? I support what you are doing in the Senate. I think the hearings are exceedingly interesting and so does Melbourne. He wants you to know that you need to keep pushing, the truth is near."

"What does Melbourne know? Is he here too?" Steven asked, looking around a bit.

"He is. In fact, he saw you after one of the programs was over. He didn't think it wise for you to be seen with him, so he told me to follow you."

Winnie looked at Chelle and explained, "Melbourne is my husband." She took out another hundred out of her purse and fed it into the machine. Looking around and not seeing anybody near them, she said, "Those young people are on to something; you should listen to them."

"Please Mrs. Winston. If you know something that can help me, please tell me. Why is Melbourne here?"

"He is here on official government business. The information here is state of the art. What better place to come to learn how to stop hackers, than a hackers' convention."

"Mrs. Winston, you said Melbourne wanted you to follow us. Why?" Steven asked.

"He wanted me to relay a few messages, but he told me to be careful who you were with when I gave it."

Mrs. Winston pressed the spin button. It didn't take long before her most recent hundred dollars was also gone. She said loud enough for Chelle and Steven to hear over the noise of the casino. "Did you know there are people following you?"

"Steven leaned in towards Mrs. Winston and pointed at something on her machine as a distraction. He asked softly, "No, where?"

"When I followed you from Margaritaville, two men in suits saw you walk past them and immediately followed you. When security came by, they took off."

Chelle walked to the other side of Mrs. Winston, and they all pretended they were discussing the top payout of the machine.

Chelle said to Steven, "I saw them too, they were suspicious."

Mrs. Winston said, "I'm sure they're right around the corner. I've learned to keep a watchful eye. I've been robbed, right in this casino. One person distracts you and the other cashes out your machine when you're not looking. Happens in an instant. They take off with your voucher and are gone.

"I've learned not to get too distracted by all the lights and noises. I am constantly on the watch for suspicious characters. Just like those three you were talking to. Anyone could see in an instant that they didn't belong in the high limits area."

Winnie took her players card from the machine and let it drop on its lanyard. "I have an idea. Let's go for a walk and see if those two follow."

Winnie stood and took Chelle by the hand and asked. "How is it that after nearly arresting Senator Westcott you ended up his girl?"

Chelle was taken aback a bit by the woman's bluntness. She glanced at Steven, who just shrugged his shoulders.

"Of course, you know it was just an elaborate scheme to catch a killer," Chelle answered.

"Oh, of course. Whatever you say, my dear."

Chelle had the feeling that Mrs. Winston wasn't a believer in their explanation to the public, Chelle changed the subject. "Where are we going?"

"To the high rollers' club." Mrs. Winston pointed to two large oak doors. "With my Triple Diamond card, we can get into this private club. If those two are following us, they will be stopped before going in."

Chelle scanned the casino as they waited in a small line to enter the exclusive clubroom.

Winnie flashed her triple diamond card at a hostess and they were escorted to a much less crowded room with a long bar at one end and expensive woodwork surrounding them. It reminded Steven a bit of the Capital Grill.

Immediately the noise of the casino, the activity, and the crowds disappeared. The calm of the private club was not lost on Chelle.

As they were escorted to a table, Chelle whispered. "I saw them. They were still following us. Both with short hair, muscular build, dark suits. Fairly obvious, surprised they didn't have sunglasses on."

A waiter with a white apron came by. His nametag identified him as Lowell. Lowell asked if they wanted a drink and an appetizer. "I'll have a Bloody Mary and tell Marty to make it spicy. He knows how I like it."

Steven ordered a scotch and Lowell made a few suggestions of brands available. Steven settled on the Macallan, eighteen yr., Sherry Oak. "Over one cube," he added.

Chelle ordered a Coke.

When Lowell left, Mrs. Winston asked, "Not friends of yours?"

"Not ours, yours?" Chelle asked.

"No, and I doubt they are casino security. The casino is more discreet and can watch us with cameras like that one." Mrs. Winston let her eyes linger for a moment on a camera that was neatly tucked into a corner of the lounge.

'I guess we have drawn some attention from somebody," Steven agreed.

"Without a Triple Diamond card, they are not getting in here. So, for now, I wouldn't worry."

Steven asked, "You said you have a message for me from Melbourne?"

"It's about the hearings. He becomes a bit upset while watching them, he keeps yelling at the television. At you actually."

"Me?"

"Yes, he keeps saying over and over again, 'You are not asking the right questions.'"

"I feel his irritation. I don't think I'm asking the right questions either. But I don't know what the right questions are."

"You want to know how much information the NSA is collecting on non-foreign agents."

"Yes I do. I'm trying to find out if they are using illegal means to collect information on U.S. citizens. They are supposed to get FISA warrants to investigate citizens, and only as it relates to foreign activities. I'm afraid they are overstepping their bounds."

"What are their bounds, Senator?"

The drinks came and Steven pulled out his wallet to pay for them. Winnie laughed. "This is the Triple Diamond Club honey, it's all comped, it's on the house."

"Melbourne says I'm not asking the right questions. Do you know what he means?"

"Remember what that young man said: 'They are the Cloud.'"

"I heard him, but I'm not sure what that means."

"I don't either, but I think Melbourne does. He keeps ranting, 'They have it all. Damn the fourth amendment. They just don't give a shit about it'."

Chelle asked, "Who's they?"

"You! The FBI, CIA, NSA."

"But that's simply not true," Chelle protested.

"No offense, honey, but you have no more say in it than anybody else. The fourth amendment was adopted back in Thomas Jefferson's time, around 1792. Of course, it granted U.S. citizens the right to be secure in their persons, houses, papers, and effects, against unreasonable searches and seizures. Only through a warrant can our homes or bodies be searched, and our papers and things be seized. That was two hundred years ago. Things have changed a bit since."

Chelle nodded in agreement unimpressed. "And that doctrine has been expanded for the digital age."

Steven interrupted, "Unfortunately, it hasn't kept up at all,"

DIGITAL SECRETS

He tasted his eighteen-year-old Macallan, made a small swallow, "As a Senator, we hear arguments for expanded protections all the time. But the truth is, we haven't kept up. Not even close. There have been a few tries to tackle the issue such as HR 699 of 2016.[2]

"I think you know that I supported that bill, Mrs. Winston."

"Please Senator, please call me Winnie. And, yes we do, and that is one reason we support you. But that bill hasn't been signed into law yet and doesn't look like it will be in the foreseeable future."

"No, probably not," Steven said, "and that's my point. Technology changes so fast that Congress doesn't have time to react. By the time we all agree to do something the problem has changed already."

Chelle said curiously, "I am unfamiliar with that bill."

Steven continued. "Under current law, the government may use administrative subpoenas instead of warrants when forcing companies to turn over customers' electronic communications, including emails, when those messages are more than 180 days old. While warrants require 'probable cause,' subpoenas don't, and they allow much more information to be collected."

Chelle added, "As a law enforcement officer, I am familiar with the difference. Subpoenas are much easier to obtain."

"I'll say," Mrs. Winston said sounding a bit indignant. "Miss Saltarie, as a federal agent you can issue one anytime you want."

---

[2] The **Email Privacy Act** is a bill introduced in the United States Congress. The bipartisan proposed federal law is sponsored by Representative Kevin Yoder, a Republican from Kansas, and Representative Jared Polis, a Democrat of Colorado. The law is designed to update and reform existing online communications law, specifically the Electronic Communications Privacy Act (ECPA) of 1986.[1][2][3]

(As of January 2022, still unpassed)

"That's not true; only if it is relevant to an investigation. And it has to be an administrative subpoena.[3]"

"Pretty broad, don't you think, Agent Saltarie? What is the definition of investigation? Anybody you are curious about? What would prevent you from going back to Washington and doing an investigation of me and have the department issue an Administrative subpoena requesting all my old emails?"

Steven finished his explanation, "That is part of the reason for the new bill. It would change the 180-day rule, which is from an era in which it would have been largely impractical for an email service provider to store emails for more than six months and cloud storage was not yet available or even invented. It is universally accepted that the law has not kept up with current technology. Hell, it was enacted way back in 1986. Lifetimes ago in the digital age."

Steven asked, "Melbourne said, 'They have it all.' What did Melbourne mean?"

Mrs. Winston continued, "Melbourne is a genius, and a bit eccentric. Some days I'm surprised he can tie his own shoes and when he starts talking computer stuff and things I just nod my head because I can't even begin to understand what he is talking about. But we love each other and that's all I need to know."

"But the messages?"

"That's what I'm trying to tell you. They don't make sense to me. And I have to be honest. I don't always pay attention to the things he says because, well, he is a bit erratic. Though I thought he was being paranoid when he said he was being followed. Now I'm not so certain."

---

[3] An **administrative subpoena** under U.S. law is a subpoena issued by a federal agency without prior judicial oversight. Critics say that administrative subpoena authority is a violation of the Fourth Amendment to the United States Constitution, while proponents say that it provides a valuable investigative tool.[1][2]

Steven and Chelle looked at each other. Chelle added, "We know the feeling. But what Melbourne said sounds a lot like what we just heard. 'They are the cloud.'"

Mrs. Winston proceeded, "I'm just putting two and two together, but think about this. With cloud storage, everybody's emails are sitting in servers somewhere outside their home and will be literally forever. HR 699 would end this loophole and require government agencies to seek warrants for digital communications older than 180 days just as they need to for younger data."

Chelle defended herself and the FBI, "We are not interested in everybody's e-mail, but there are a lot of bad guys out there whose communications could be vital to saving lives, many lives. And getting to those emails in a timely matter is critical."

Steven agreed, "I have carefully studied both sides. It isn't as cut and dried as it sounds. There are checks and balances."

"Checks and balances?" Mrs. Winston said with a huff. "Where have we heard that before. "In court, when asked how many administrative warrants it has issued, the FBI testified that it didn't know. Doesn't matter anyway," Mrs. Winston said as she threw her hand back dismissing the entire conversation. "It's much worse than that anyway. According to Melbourne, the right to expect privacy of your digital life is nearly dead anyway, the courts have said so.

Mrs. Winston held up her empty glass as Lowell serviced a table nearby. "I'll have another, please."

Lowell nodded and scooted away for another drink.

"Have you heard of the 'Third Party Doctrine'?"[4]

---

[4] The **third-party doctrine** is a United States legal doctrine that holds that people who voluntarily give information to third parties—such as banks, phone companies, internet service providers (ISPs), and e-mail servers—have "no reasonable expectation of privacy." A lack of privacy protection allows the United States government to obtain information from third parties without a legal warrant and without

"Not familiar," Steven said.

Chelle explained, "Part of law enforcement training is knowing what you can and can't do. Mrs. Winston is referring to a 1979 decision in Smith v. Maryland. The Supreme Court ruled in favor of the government and concluded that a person has no legitimate expectation of privacy for information they voluntarily turn over to third parties."

Chelle explained further, "What that means is that a federal agent, such as me, can get third party records from a bank, telephone company, cell phone provider, and so on, without a warrant."

Mrs. Winston smirked, "Yeah, and in todays world, tell me what isn't turned over to a third party to hold in a server some where. The cloud they call it. Including your emails, facebook pages, linkedin, twitter, financial records. If you back up your phone to the cloud everything on it is on a third party server, my god, the list goes on and on."

Lowell came over with one more drink in hand for Mrs. Winston. Mrs. Winston didn't hesitate to point to Chelle before accepting it, saying, "And as a federal agent, she can access it all."

Lowell looked at Chelle, clearly hearing the accusation and looking at her with a bit of suspicion in his eyes.

Chelle caught the glare from the waiter and argued back, "It's not that simple, or easy. Trust me."

Lowell asked, "Anybody else need a drink?"

Steven ordered himself another scotch and Chelle ordered another Coke. Steven interjected, "This is all interesting and certainly I have heard debates on the floor of the Senate. But nobody has come up with a definitive answer on how to deal with going after the bad guys versus protecting our citizens' privacy."

"And that is the problem and something you will have to start taking more seriously."

---

otherwise complying with the <u>Fourth Amendment</u> prohibition against <u>search and seizure</u> without <u>probable cause</u> and a judicial <u>search warrant</u>.[1]

"I agree, Winnie, but what about those three characters, and what they said?"

"I can only tell you what Melbourne tells me. And what I pick up through his rants is just incidental. I have been using Agent Saltarie as an example because she is with the FBI, the most controlled of the intelligence gathering agencies because it is in charge of domestic crimes. The rest of the intelligence community is much less restrained. The NSA is controlled by the Department of Defense. The CIA is an independent agency.

"There are seventeen various agencies in charge of collecting diverse types of intelligence, plus the FBI.[5] Congress can't possibly keep their eye on all of them. And as you have found out Senator, you can't get a straight answer out of even one of them."

Lowell brought over to the table some more nachos and an exact duplicate of Steven's first drink, right down to the single cube of ice.

"Thanks, Lowell," Mrs. Winston said.

Lowell asked, "Are you really a United States Senator?"

Steven stood and apologized, "Yes I am." Steven reached out and shook Lowell's hand. "Sorry for not introducing myself. I am Senator Steven Westcott from Massachusetts."

Lowell was all smiles, and duly impressed that he had shook hands with a Senator. "No sir, no problem at all. If I can be of any more help, just call me over."

"Thanks, Lowell."

Lowell left and started clearing and cleaning unoccupied cocktail tables.

5

Central Intelligence Agency, Defense Intelligence Agency, National Security Agency, National Geospatial-Intelligence Agency, National Reconnaissance Office, Army Intelligence, Marine Corps Intelligence, Navy Intelligence, Air Force Intelligence, Space Force Intelligence, Surveillance, and Reconnaissance Enterprise, Office of Intelligence and Counterintelligence, Office of Intelligence and Analysis, Coast Guard Intelligence, Federal Bureau of Investigation, Office of National Security Intelligence, Bureau of Intelligence and Research, Office of Terrorism and Financial Intelligence.

Mrs. Winston touched Chelle's hand lightly and said, "Honey, please don't take our discussion personal. If it was my job to defend the country and I could do whatever I wanted to do, I would push every envelope there is too. In fact, that is what Melbourne is so worried about. Well-meaning people with unlimited money are doing unthinkable things under the guise of protecting us from a never-ending war on terror."

"But does he have evidence of that?" Steven asked. "Or is this all just some grand conspiracy theory talk? You could be one hundred percent right, or not. What can be proved?"

Mrs. Winston lifted the skewered olives from her drink and pulled one into her mouth. "I can't prove a thing. Melbourne is under a strict confidentiality agreement with the government. He's afraid that just talking to you could put him in jail. But he wants me to tell you a few things off the record of course.

Steven urged gently, "You know I can be trusted. What kind of things?"

"One thing he said I should tell you is that he hopes you know what you are up against."

Chelle asked, "What did he mean?

Mrs. Winston said, "I apologize, Senator, but I quote, 'Tell that damn fool Senator to be careful, or he won't be around much longer.'"

With concern, Chelle asked, "Why Steven? Who wants to hurt him?"

"Why, the other side." Mrs. Winston seemed surprised at the question. "There are people who believe taking the right to privacy to the very edge is their patriotic duty. If you are not with them, you are against them. And anybody against them must be a traitor and needs to be stopped."

"Even a United States Senator?" Chelle asked.

"Especially a U.S. Senator."

"And you think those guys following us are out to harm Steven?"

"I don't know who or what they are. But my Melbourne is seldom wrong. How do you think he made his millions?"

"You're not the first to warn me to be careful, and I'm starting to become a believer."

"He also wondered why you never ask about the Lake Lerna project?"

Steven stared at the half empty glass in his hand for a moment. "Strange, the name does sound familiar, but I can't place it." Steven repeated out loud, "Lake Lerna project. No, nothing, but the nagging feeling I've heard of it before."

"Doesn't mean anything to me either. At any rate, Melbourne wanted me to make sure you heard the name if you hadn't before."

Something is scaring my Melbourne, and he has seen just about everything in his life. It must be something big to be getting his attention.

"Oh, and one other thing. He doesn't want you to contact him in any way. He said it would be dangerous for you and him."

"You can tell your husband I will respect his wishes. However, if he could somehow help me in any way, I would be grateful." Steven looked at his watch, "It's time for us to go, but I was wondering if you think your friend Joe the casino host might do us a favor?"

"I'm sure of it. Just name it; it's his job to keep me happy."

Steven talked softly about his plan as they finished off the nachos and their drinks.

Chapter 11

Steven, Chelle, and Mrs. Winston walked out of the Triple Diamond Club, pretending to be laughing about a recent joke. Chelle spotted the two suits almost immediately, though she was careful to not lock her eyes on them. They were watching the private doorway intently and looked away as soon as the three exited.

The trio continued down the cobblestone path towards the exit. Without looking back, they exited the casino and walked to the taxi stand. When the two men followed out the door, four big men dressed in the hotel security colors stepped in front of them and escorted them to a secluded area outside the casino.

Steven, Chelle, and Mrs. Winston watched as the four security guards from the Paris hotel asked for the men's identification. There seemed to be some resistance, but when it was apparent the hotel security was prepared to call in the local police the men relented.

It didn't take long before the four security guards went back into the hotel, leaving the two suits standing alone. Steven, Chelle, and Mrs. Winston stepped out of the taxi line. Chelle said, "I've had enough of this hide and seek."

She approached the two men with Steven and Mrs. Winston just steps behind of her.

"All right, enough games, who are you guys? Why are you following us?"

One of the suits stepped into Chelle's face looking down at her. "None of your fucking business."

Chelle didn't take kindly to the threat. "I'm a federal agent, show me your identification right now."

"Fuck off!" The man closest to her said as he took his finger and jammed it against her collarbone.

Before Steven had time to react, Chelle grabbed the man's finger and twisted it. Soon he was on his knees. Chelle pulled out her gun and pointed it at the other man who was moving towards them. "Stand down," she shouted. "Let me see your identification, now!"

By this time, uniformed officers patrolling Las Vegas Boulevard became curious about the commotion and ran towards the situation. Steven intercepted them and said, "I'm Senator Westcott. These men were suspiciously following us."

One of the cops said, "Yeah, I recognize you. Who's the little terror with the gun?"

"My bodyguard. She has a license for the gun."

"Hands up, where I can see 'em." One of the cops shouted as he drew his weapon and pointed to the man still standing.

The man complied; raising his hands while his partner cringed on his knees in front of Chelle.

"We can take it from here."

"I would like to see their identification first," Chelle said as one of the cops were preparing to hand cuff the man still standing while his partner kept his gun aimed at him.

"You heard the lady."

Reluctantly he pulled out his wallet and handed his identification over to Chelle.

"Office of Naval Intelligence?"

"What?" The officer was shocked. "Let me see."

After a moment staring at the ID he asked, "What about the guy on the ground?"

The man on the ground slowly took out his ID as Chelle slightly let up the pressure on his finger.

Chelle looked over it first and handed it to the officer as she released the man from her grip.

Chelle still angry said, "How come you were following us?"

"Orders, and that's all we're saying."

The officer with the gun, holstered it as Chelle did the same.

"This looks like some sort of a spook standoff. We're not getting involved. Come on Pete, let them sort it out. Senator, nice to meet you. Hope you enjoy your stay."

Steven stepped up and confronted the military agents, "Who gave you the order?"

"Our captain, sir."

"And exactly what were your orders?"

Reluctantly the two glanced at each other and weren't sure any more about the chain of command. Did a US Senator outrank their captain?

DIGITAL SECRETS

One divulged, "We were instructed to monitor and observe, nothing more."

Let me see your identification please. Steven wanted to memorize their names because he intended to learn more about why they were following him.

"What is your captain's name? I might want a word with him."

"We meant no disrespect, sir. We were just following orders."

"You were spying on me. I don't give a crap if you were following orders. I want to know who ordered them."

"Captain Brian Volk."

"Stationed where?"

"Norfolk, sir."

Steven handed the ID's back. "I don't want to see you or anybody else following us. Those are my orders. Understand?"

"Yes sir."

The two men walked away down the boulevard.

"Naval Intelligence?" Chelle said unbelievingly.

Mrs. Winston stepped forward, "Don't say I didn't warn you. I hate it when Melbourne is right all the time. Ready for another drink at the Triple Diamond lounge?"

"Not a drink, but I am hungry. Winnie, how would you like to join us for dinner?" Steven asked.

"That would be wonderful. I do enjoy your company."

"And we yours." Chelle smiled.

Mrs. Winston used her Triple Diamond card to get them immediate seating at a restaurant that had outside dining. They were ushered to a table that was on a platform raised a few feet above the sidewalk. They were separated from the pedestrians by an iron railing; above them, water misters kept the air cool.

They ordered drinks, unsweetened ice tea for all.

Mrs. Melbourne was beaming, "This is the most fun I've had in Las Vegas since I won fifty-thousand dollars. That was exciting."

Chelle laughed, "I don't know if it was fifty-thousand dollars worth of entertainment, but I have to admit it got my adrenalin flowing."

Mrs. Melbourne took a long sip of her ice tea through a straw. When she was done she asked, "Have either of you heard the term in law called 'Broken Shade' theory? It's something Melbourne kept ranting about. He would say to you when he saw you on television, they're using 'Broken Shade' you fool. Sorry Senator"

Steven laughed, "No apology needed, I felt a fool after those hearings."

Chelle said, "Come to think of it, I have heard the term 'Broken Shade'. Let me explain the theory of 'Broken Shade' as it applies to law enforcement. Maybe it will shed some light on the subject of surveillance.

"Our homes are our castles; the right to privacy within our homes is strictly enforced. However, if I or anyone else should walk up your front walk, which I remind you is by definition, a public access way, and I see criminal activity going on inside the home through, say, a broken shade, all bets are off. I can proceed as if the individuals inside the home were doing their illegal activities in a public park."

Steven asked, "So how does a broken blind relate to privacy in our electronic communications?"

"There was a group using a supposedly untraceable software to locate and display illegal pornography. The FBI hacked into their computers to discover the illegal materials and where it came from. The judge ruled that because they used a third-party server and because nobody could reasonably believe that their home computer was safe from prying eyes, they had no reasonable expectation of privacy on their home computer."[6]

Mrs. Winston gave a smirk, "So, in effect, their computer had a broken blind, thus no privacy should be expected."

---

[6] USA VS Edward joseph Matish, III

"Exactly. That doesn't mean it will hold up if challenged further, but the logic that is being used is evident."

Steven whistled, "Wow! That would mean every computer in the U.S. is subject to inspection by the government. Because nobody in the U.S. has the right to expect their computer doesn't have a broken blind, i.e.: an open access point."

Chelle admitted, "If someone wanted to take it to an ultimate conclusion, yes."

Mrs. Winston added, "I don't know of any law that specifically forbids the FBI or anybody else from taking such measures, do you, Senator?"

"I'm afraid I don't."

Dinner was served and the three ate mostly in silence, contemplating the ramifications of their discussion.

****

The Sunday night flight back to Washington, D.C. had been uneventful. It was late enough that Dulles International wasn't its normal hectic self. Steven slipped their roll-on bags into the trunk and unlocked his car doors. Chelle slid into her seat and the first thing they both did was withdraw their phones from the glove box.

Chelle breathed a sigh of relief as she powered hers on. "Boy does that feel good. I feel like a kid on Christmas morning."

Steven was already accessing the internet. "I had no idea how many emails I get in a day, and now I have three days' worth."

Steven was driving them back home. The first stop was Chelle's apartment. Chelle, who was studying her phone said, "Detective Jones has been trying to reach me."

"Who?"

Chelle laughed, "Jojo. He's been trying to find us."

Steven said, "It's too late to call now, I'll call in the morning and explain our escape. I never thought that he might start worrying about us. I'm probably going to get a tongue-lashing."

Chelle typed a few words into her phone to do an Internet search. After a minute she had her results.

"I did a search on Lake Lerna. I think I know why it rang a bell."

"Enlighten me"

"It's the mythical Greek portal to Hades."

"I'm a little rusty on my Greek mythology; please fill me in."

"It says, 'It is the fathomless lake where the monster Hydra guarded the entrance into Hades.'"

"I remember, it was in the movie, The Legend of Hercules. It was a multi headed monster."

Chelle read more of the myth. "It had nine heads and killing it was one of the twelve labors of Hercules."

"Hmmm," Chelle pondered. "The home of a multi-headed monster. Maybe it's more than myth. And guarding the path to hell, I wonder if what the government might be doing isn't exactly that."

Steven added, "The three geeks said that the 'NSA is the cloud'. To me that would mean or imply that the government is collecting data."

"I agree. It certainly seems to imply some sort of digital storage effort."

"Then Mrs. Winston's husband, a computer genius, wants to know if I heard of the Lake Lerna project."

Chelle surmised out loud, "A mythical lake."

"If it's true, it would undoubtedly represent a top-secret government project."

"Don't forget about a quantum computer," Chelle added. "Which by the way, I thought were just in the experimental mode, residing mostly in the minds of academics."

Steven turned his head momentarily towards Chelle. "No, they're real. Although the technology is in its infancy, IBM, Google, Honeywell and more all have working quantum computers. But to work they need to be serviced by a team of PH.D. researchers."

"It would be the type of thing Melbourne would be involved in. If we put it all together, we have massive quantities of data that are being stored, which would do no good if you couldn't sort through it all. Which a quantum computer would be able to do."

After a period of silence in the car, Steven said, "I think it's time to start poking the bear with a few pointed questions about a Lake Lerna project and quantum computing."

"Usually poking the bear is not a good idea."

"I agree, and this is a terribly big mean bear. But I don't see this bear being cooperative on its own. I desperately want to contact Melbourne Winston and ask him about what 'Lake Lerna' means and what he knows about it. Only I don't know how to make my emails burn up on screen like those three characters did to theirs. Because if there is a 'Lake Lerna' project, it would obviously be top secret. Which would automatically mean that Melbourne could not talk about it, even to a Senator. Even if that senator is by definition in charge of watching over the agencies in charge of top-secret projects."

Chelle laid her head back leaning it lazily against the headrest; she closed her eyes to rest them. After a moment she tiredly said, "So if you can't go to the source. You need to poke the bear and see what stirs."

"Something like that. Or..."

"Or what?"

"Or maybe this senator should just sit this one out. Not my problem. Go back to private life, no campaigns, no fundraising, get out of Washington. Hell, I could make a lot more money in the private sector. I did it before. And no, I haven't been drinking. I'm stone cold sober. Lord knows, and you know from personal experience, that this job has already taken a terrible toll on me, and on you for that matter."

"Don't get me in the middle of this."

"Sorry, you already are. And that's the point. Your association with me, seems to constantly expose you to my dilemmas."

"Isn't that what relationships are all about."

"Ours seems a little one-sided to me. You didn't ask for nor do you need the extra drama in your life. Hell, you even compromised your professional life over lying about those three characters we ran across."

"Oh that, I was on vacation. Even a cop gets time off from the bad guys. Nobody expects me to nor wants me to arrest every citizen I suspect is doing something illegal or whom I think is going to do something illegal."

"I guess I'm just tired of it all. If it's not IRENE after me, it's my political enemies, if not them, it's the press. Half upset over what I did, the other half upset over what I didn't do."

Chelle sighed a bit, "You know what I think."

"Please do tell me."

"Vacations are tiring." Chelle yawned. "If it wasn't for IRENE trying to frame you for murder, I never would have met you. So, there is always a bright side."

Steven pulled to the side of the road. Chelle was home.

Chelle lazily turned her head towards her apartment.

Steven reached over and took Chelle's hand and squeezed it lightly. Deep in thought he stared at a street light in the distance, the picture in his mind blocking everything else out.

Steven agreed contemplatively, "Yes, they killed Destinee, a daughter I never knew. Lucky for me, in the end, you trusted me."

"I was just following the facts, and maybe a bit of intuition. In the end, you did get to know Destinee, at least a little bit. IRENE didn't know she was your daughter, she was simply a pawn in their game. Her life was a difficult one, I think you brought some sunshine into it for a brief time."

Steven still staring at the street light said, "You're right, she had a painfully difficult life until it was taken away from her. To them she was some sort of throw away hooker. To me, that makes their crime even worse. They killed an innocent woman to get at me."

Chelle agreed, "They did, but still, it wasn't your fault, it's all on them."

Steven smiled and looked at Chelle, "I like imagining her smiling face, she was a beautiful woman. And so are you, you are something else, you know that."

"Something else? I guess I'll take that as a compliment. And you know what else I think?"

"Please share."

"You're tired too. Tomorrow you will wake up ready to fight for your country. Because that's what you do. If people are overstepping their bounds somebody must stop them. That somebody is you, my knight in shining armor." Chelle winked and smiled at Steven.

Steven gave Chelle's hand another gentle squeeze.

"What have I done to deserve you?"

"Exactly what you are doing. Suck it up cowboy, time to get back in the saddle."

"Cowboy? I kind of like the way that sounds."

Chelle laughed at the inside joke.

"And now it's back to the real world for me too. I can't help but wonder how Jojo is doing with his investigation. Lord, it seems like I have been on a desert island for a year.

"I don't know if I have the energy to walk up to my apartment."

"Suck it up cowgirl."

Chelle chuckled. "I did have fun, thank you."

Steven took her hand in his. "Only you would say that being followed, chased down a freeway, having an altercation, and drawing your weapon in self-defense was fun."

"Chelle laughed, "I 've been on worse dates with you."

"Indeed you have. Indeed you have."

Steven helped Chelle with her small bag up the first outside flight of stairs. After a short kiss goodnight inside the lobby, they parted ways.

Back in his car Steven looked over his voice messages and listened to one in particular. Soon he realized he had made a huge mistake.

He immediately made a call, "Hi honey, it's dad."

"Dad, are you OK, I was so worried."

"I'm so sorry honey, I'm fine. I was gone on a short vacation and forgot my phone."

"How could you forget your phone?"

"I made a big mistake; I should have told you I would be gone for a few days. I'm sorry, I'll never do it again."

"Where were you?"

"I was with Chelle; we went to Las Vegas for a few days. Just got back."

"I think even mom was worried."

"Tell her I'm fine. In fact, I have a huge surprise for you if it's OK with your mother."

That same time in Las Vegas:

Wade was sitting in the car that he had borrowed from his friend Red, who had told him he was crashing early that night and wouldn't need it if Wade promised to drop him off and pick him up again in the morning.

Freddy Farly's home was just on the other side of the privacy wall he was parked near. Wade opened his computer and had it scan for nearby Wi-Fi signals. Right after that, he turned on his radio interceptor. If he could catch Freddy arming his security system wirelessly, he could capture the arming and disarming code. Almost immediately Wade saw the same Wi-Fi name as Fats had used to control the drone.

The question was, did Fats have some way to secure his signal that was much more secure than the average user? All the more challenge, Wade started his hack. It didn't take long for Wade to discover his suspicions were correct.

Fats must have had his own installers from within the company because his Wi-Fi system was much more secured than that of an average homeowner. This hack could take half the night. Wade had his laptop connected directly with Hercules back in Reidsville; he was sure it would be critical to this hack.

Wade had named his computer Mercury, or Hermes if you preferred Greek mythology over Roman. Just like Mercury, his computer was fast, real, real fast. While working for the government, he had stolen spare parts, processors mainly, lots of them. With those, he had built his own home supercomputer. If a regular computer was compared to a single machine gun spewing out bullets of information rapidly one calculation at a time, Mercury was like a thousand machine guns, all disseminating information at the same time.

The government project he was working on was so massive that an entire boxload of processors were never missed. His current employer had supplied some of the multiple power supplies, and various computer parts, though they didn't know it. Other parts he needed were easily and relatively cheaply bought off eBay.

To crack into Fat's Wi-Fi system, Wade needed the help of Mercury. Routing only specific answers through his laptop, he went about using Mercury to go through its huge database of rainbow tables to crack security codes. And it could do in minutes what might otherwise take hours or days, or even weeks.

Building the computer was rather straightforward. He just duplicated over and over again connecting processors. The hardest part was keeping the big machine in his basement cool. That took a containment system and a dedicated air conditioner. Liquid cooled was another solution, but Mercury, as sophisticated as it was, still wasn't of the capacity to need that type of structure.

Mercury continued humming in his basement back home. Eventually, by combining a few tricks, and a few educated guesses from being a former employee, and an hour and a half of repeated attempts, he was now into the system. Just as important, about an hour ago, Freddy must have gone to bed because he intercepted a code being sent at 400 Mhz.

Wade talked out loud to himself as he typed on his laptop. "Once you are asleep, a good old fashioned gas leak should be enough to blow up that big, beautiful house of yours. Hmmm, how about that. No special surprises. Freddy, Freddy, did you actually believe that nobody would ever hack into your network? Did you believe it was so secure that no more precautions needed to be taken? Shame, shame."

Wade was surprised that once into the system, Freddy's security wasn't any different from the rest of the world. Wade found his way into Freddy's digital virtual assistant systems.

From his two visits, Wade knew that Freddy had several scattered around the house, all interconnected, of course.

Wade hacked into the system and listened. First, he listened to the assistant marked kitchen. There was only the sound of an appliance. He clicked on another, he listened to the one called media room. It was silent.

There were two more, but he took a guess that the one marked bedroom would be his best bet. Wade clicked it active and immediately he heard snoring. Wade laughed, "In bed already Fats?"

Of course, Freddy being the tech nut he was, everything was interconnected, including his smart TV's. It didn't take long for Wade to find the bedroom television. Using hacking software, he soon had control of its camera and microphone.

The microphone on the remote gave him the same sound of snoring. Wade tried to activate the camera; it was either turned off or taped over. Not an unusual precaution for somebody as tech-savvy as Freddy.

Wade knew Freddy was safely tucked into his bed; what he didn't know was if he was alone. Wade scanned the list of connected devices, that was when he found something interesting. It would take another hack, but he was confident that between him and Mercury it wouldn't be a problem.

Wade knew he couldn't just kick the security system off-line. A good system would be hardened against such an attack. Fortunately for Wade, the security system was open sourced so third-party application developers could interface with it.

He had already downloaded the same application that Freddy would be using to control his system. With the open-source code, Wade could delve into its operation. With the captured code, even though it was encrypted, he could now find the 'hash' created by the passcode. All he had to do was have Hercules create series of numbers until one set created an identical 'hash'. That would be the code to disarm Freddy's security system.

With only four digits to work with, Hercules only needed to come up with ten-thousand variations. The law of averages meant only half that many in all probability. It hadn't taken Hercules long at all, within minutes he had a matching 'hash'.

Once the alarm was disarmed, it would be easy to electronically unlock the front door. He could sneak in, loosen the natural gas fitting going to the hot water heater, light a candle in the next room, and leave before all hell broke loose.

Wade had already devised the plan to keep the door to the equipment room mostly closed to contain the gas while he made his escape. A slight push from the drone when he was safe outside should open the door and let the gas escape causing a massive accidental explosion.

But with what Wade had just discovered, Plan A had just become Plan B, but for plan B to work Freddy needed to be sleeping alone. Wade, knowing Fat Freddy's lack of success with women, that was an extremely good probability.

The best hack was next. Wade opened software that would talk to and control Fredy's drone from his laptop. That software was free online from the drone manufacturer. It didn't take long to find the machine listed as a connected device in the Wi-Fi portal list.

Wade felt the excitement building inside of him. If the rest of his plan worked, his old boss would never wake up again and unfortunately would never know what happened to his life.

Wade opened the drone application. The software asked for a password. Wade was a bit surprised, because the Wi-Fi would be considered impenetrable, passwords would not be needed once in the system. Wade stopped typing for a moment and tried to think like Freddy would about some of his favorite movies and his favorite characters.

Once again, he fed potential words into Mercury's system and let it do its magic. Minutes went by when Wade came up with a better than average guess, Fat's favorite superhero. Wade typed in "Wonder Woman" Wade said it to himself. "It has to be. It's a she, gets him beers, and it flies."

Mercury crunched through variations of 'Wonder Woman'. It only took seconds for Mercury to process thousands of variables. Wade had instructed it to add dates to the main words.

When the finial variation was a success, Wade slapped his knee. He should have known it was the year Wonder Woman was created, 1941.

None the less, instantly he was permitted into the controlling application. Soon he had Wonder Woman out of its charging cradle and up in the air.

Wade set the drone into hover mode. He searched his backpack full of electronic equipment and found what he was looking for. He flipped open the cheap burner phone and turned it on.

As it was booting up, he connected a sound synthesizer to it to conceal his voice. "Hello, Detective. I have a name for you. Freddy Farly: he will be dead soon. He lives, I mean did live, in Las Vegas."

Jojo had to listen hard to understand the synthesized voice. "Why?" he asked, "Why are you killing these people?"

"Detective, that is obvious. Because I can."

"Why are you telling me?"

"That's simple, too. If I wouldn't have told you who I killed, nobody would suspect that they were even murdered. A couple were obviously murdered by somebody. But others I made to look like accidents or suicides."

"You mean like the young man who was flying a drone in the park."

"Detective, you surprise me. Yes, exactly like him."

"Why him?"

"Telling that would be cheating. I must go, can't talk much longer. But I think it's time that you had a little skin in the game too. After all, up until now, I have been taking all the risk. Welcome to the game, Detective."

Wade smiled; he felt an erotic sense of energy flow through him. "Wow, what a rush." He said to himself, surprised by the effect the call had on him. He opened the back case of the cheap burner phone and removed the battery.

Wade turned on the drone's lights and that gave him enough light to navigate by. Wade could hear the noise of the buzzing drone over its built-in microphone.

Alan D Schmitz
DIGITAL SECRETS

Wade felt excitement crawl through him. He was virtually inside Freddy's home. Carefully he flew it to the stairs. He watched the screen on his computer and could see the drone going up the flight of stairs towards Freddy's bedroom. Wade paused the drone by the door for a moment as he contemplated his next move.

It looked like Freddy was sound asleep, He piloted the drone further into the room. He needed to know Freddy was alone. Wade knew that Freddy was a diabetic. What he didn't know until an hour ago was that he used an electronic insulin injector.

It was the latest technology that monitored his glucose and injected only as much insulin as his body needed. It was connected to the Wi-Fi system to transmit the data to his doctor and to communicate with his smart phone which was used to control the pump.

Wade smiled, and spoke to his computer as he typed, "I knew a big fat slob like you would be sleeping alone. Nobody around to hear your glucose alarm go off, is there?"

Wade flew the drone back towards the open doorway to the hall and placed it in hoover mode.

"No need to screw with your alarm system, I can kill you from here with just a few clicks of my keyboard," Wade said as he grinned.

"What the hell!" Freddy mumbled as he turned his head towards the sound of the drone. He fumbled a bit in the darkness and turned on the light next to his bed.

With the light on, he could see the drone in the doorway for a moment.

"What the fuck?"

Wade giggled, "Uh-oh, did I wake up the slobbering fool? Want to play, Freddy?"

Freddy got up and, wearing nothing but his underwear, walked towards the drone, ready to snatch it from the air.

As he got closer it moved just out of reach. Freddy followed. The drone inched itself closer and closer to the stairs.

Freddy lunged at it several times, but the craft managed to stay just out of reach taunting him.

"I don't know what son-of-a-bitch is hijacking my drone, but when I find out, there will be hell to pay."

Wade had to concentrate on piloting the drone. It was unfortunate that he couldn't manipulate the software to turn on the insulin pump at the same time, at least not right now, though he was sure an opportunity would present itself.

The drone moved over the steps. Freddy carefully followed it down one step, then another. Outside the bedroom the stairs were lit only by the lights of the drone flying around him casting weird shadows around him as it danced in the air.

"Whoever you are, stop fucking with me." Freddy threatened, now fully awake and getting angrier by the second. Wade, you son-of-bitch I know it's you. No wonder you wanted to learn to fly the drone. Damn it, I should have known."

The drone flew up over Freddy's head. Freddy looked straight up, following it.

"Come here, you little son-of-a-bitch."

The drone shot to the top of the stairs. In a burst of speed it went directly at the head of the big man on the steps.

Wade watched as the light on the drone shone directly into Freddy's eyes and temporarily blinded him. Freddy put his hands up in a defensive position as the drone went for his face.

The drone hit him hard. That was all it took for him to lose his balance.

Freddy tumbled backward, he fell hard and tumbled repeatedly all the way down the sharp and hard, marble tiled stairs.

The drone which was still flying, casually flew down to where a lifeless body laid. It looked like Freddy had hit his head hard. There was an obvious gash and blood was pouring out. A leg was bent in an unnatural and curious way.

"Ouch" Wade said. "Looks like that would hurt, that is, if you could feel it."

With perverse pleasure, he let the drone linger around the body as he viewed it from every angle. "God damn!" Wade exclaimed giddily as he carefully he flew the drone back to its charging cradle. "I guess plan C worked." Wade laughed at his cleverness.

"Poor Fat Freddy lost his balance and fell. woo-hoo, now that was fun."

He drove off casually. The next morning, he picked up his buddy Red from his home. It was a forty-five-minute drive each way. Wade didn't mind one bit; having the car overnight was priceless. Today was the last day of the Black Hat convention. Today's program promised a few of the latest hacking tools and what the white hat people were doing as new countermeasures, and as always, new ways around the new countermeasures.

At the end of the day, Red and Wade said their goodbyes with the same silly handshake. Tomorrow he was leaving Las Vegas for California but right now he felt excited and invigorated and exceptionally horny

Walking back to his room, a street vendor handed him a card. 'Girls right to your room' the card said over a picture of a full-breasted naked woman. Wade took out his burner phone and reset the battery. After some negotiations and preferences, a girl was promised to him. In another hour, his guest arrived. Wade graciously invited her into his room and offered her anything she wanted from the fully stocked mini bar.

She accepted a vodka and poured it over a glass full of ice. "By the way, my name is Chardonnay."

Wade smiled a bit sideways and said, "I'm sure it is. At least at night."

"Chardonnay Houston."

"Well, Miss Houston, let's get acquainted."

An hour later, Wade was naked as he stood up and gazed at the equally naked girl on his bed. The flashing lights from the neon lights of the strip illuminated her with interesting colors.

There was a large cash tip lying out on top of the bedroom bureau that he made sure the girl on the bed saw him leave for her before they had sex. Wade didn't believe for a second that her name was Chardonnay Houston and didn't care what she wanted to call herself. However, she certainly was pretty as she smiled wickedly at him, trying to tease him back to bed.

The idea of killing Freddy with his own drone in his own home without even entering the home, using only technology was an unbelievable turn on. He congratulated himself on being one of the few people on the planet who could do what he did and could hardly contain his excitement throughout the day. The sexual tension inside of him was building to a pressure he could no longer ignore. It turned out that Chardonnay was undeniably good at her job. Wade looked at Chardonnay and smiled and closed his eyes.

He envisioned Fat Freddy tumbling down the stairs. He thought about the old man whose heart gave out after realizing he was going to be arrested for collecting child pornography. Wade was feeling the now familiar stirrings take over him again and enjoyed it as even another plan came into mind. He opened his eyes and saw Chardonnay smile seductively at him thinking it was her naked form that was physically changing him in front of her.

Wade envisioned how he would soon be dueling with the FBI instead of the country bumpkin cop. This could soon escalate into a real battle of wits. It would be him against a team of crime specialist. He wished his opponents well and hoped they were up to the task.

He was now fully hard and smiled back at Chardonnay and she offered herself to him again. Wade didn't know how anybody, including the FBI could connect dots that weren't there. But he tried to remember not to become too sure of himself. After all, that's how criminals and killers are caught. He promised himself that wasn't going to happen to him. When he got back home, another call to the country bumpkin cop would be in order then the game would start anew.

He laid down on the bed next to her and smiled wickedly at the naked woman. He pulled her around roughly as he turned onto his back. She accepted the invite and lowered herself over his hard cock.

Wade smiled again and closed his eyes. He let her do her job as he planned his future. As a professional, he would limit himself to four more kills. If he won the game, he would stop, never to kill again and retire the victor. He felt that giving the FBI four opportunities to stop him was sporting enough. Even the best gambler can't beat the odds if they play too long.

With his mind racing through the next four deaths, he knew he wouldn't last long as Chardonnay slowly squeezed and released his cock with her vagina.

Wade looked up at her and reached up and held her thin waist between his hands. He guided her into a specific rhythm. He closed his eyes and reflected about how his victims would choose how they died.

It was all fate. Their deaths were preordained. Because after he intercepted their electronic lives, the information he obtained dictated how they would die. It had been all too easy, but now, now it was to become a cunning game.

Wade laughed out loud as he pressed against Chardonnay's waist tightly and increased her rhythm. His release didn't take long after that.

Chardonnay kissed his cheek and said, "That was amazing, you were marvelous."

Wade looked up and said, "I know. Your tip is on the dresser. My wallet is locked up, no sense in looking for it."

Chardonnay got up, Wade laid in bed and watched as she got dressed with the neon lights flashing on her.

As she walked out the door, she said, "Bye, maybe see you again sometime. You know my name, just ask for me."

"Don't count on it. And make sure the door locks behind you."

Chardonnay left and closed the door. Wade heard the door click closed. He got up, secured the dead bolt, exhausted, he climbed back into the warm bed that smelled of sex and Chardonnay, closed his eyes, and soon was asleep.

Washington D.C.:

It was Monday morning and Chelle was about to tackle the pile of work that had somehow tripled in size after a few days of vacation. Her cell phone rang. She smiled. It felt good to hear its sound.

She glanced at the name. It was Jojo. Anxious to hear the latest she said, "Hello Detective Jones."

"Thank God you're OK. I was afraid something happened to you."

"Steven and I went to Vegas for a long weekend. We didn't take our phones. His idea."

"Next time tell me. I tried to get a hold of him too. Obviously couldn't, so I worried about both of you. What a dumb idea. I'm going to pound some sense into him next time I see him."

Chelle laughed, "Sorry for worrying you. How are the investigations going?"

"That's why I'm calling. He called me."

Chelle's back reflexively straightened. "Who called you?"

"The killer, he called me, twice. The first was to warn me about somebody named Patrick Cox. He said, and I quote: 'Patrick Cox's life is about to be over.' By the time we found the right Patrick Cox, he was already dead. Cause of death appears to be a suicide; foul play is not suspected. At least not by anyone but me. He had a weak heart, and it looks like he took a handful of his heart meds."

"The guy had a thing for child pornography. His life was turned upside down overnight when he accidentally emailed just about everybody he knew some of the pornography in his collection."

Chelle whistled, "It certainly would make a suicide look unsuspicious."

"Yep, he was headed to jail big time, his name trash, wife leaving him, family not talking to him. What I don't understand is how could that even happen to a guy that is like some computer guru professor from Carnegie Mellon University."

"From where?"

"Pittsburgh. He taught at Carnegie Mellon University."

"Don't they have a big computer science department?"

"Yep, one of the biggest and best in the world, and this guy was its head. The FBI has already been notified; told them you already had a file going on a possible serial killer profile. The guy I talked to didn't sound impressed."

"It's an FBI thing, we don't believe anybody but ourselves."

"Chelle, it gets worse, when he calls me the second time last night. He tells me somebody named Freddy Farly of Las Vegas is about to die. By the time I got the Las Vegas police to believe me and look for a Freddy Farly, it was too late."

"Another murder?"

"Not yet. The victim is in intensive care in critical condition the last I heard. If it was our killer, and I have to believe it was, he made this one look like an accident too. The Vegas Police want to know how I knew the guy was going to fall down the stairs. No sign of struggle or home entry. In fact, the guy has a sophisticated alarm system, it was never touched. They said if I hadn't called them, in another hour or two he would have bled out, and as a diabetic he was in diabetic shock on top of it. Because of my tip, they peaked through the window shades and saw him on the floor.

"Then there was another suspicious death in Reidsville a few weeks ago. On your advice I checked it out. A young man, it was meant to look like a suicide. Only I don't think it was. I think it was our killer trying to cover his tracks. When I asked him why he killed the young man, the killer said, and I quote, 'Saying that would be cheating'."

"So, this is some sort of game to him."

"Sounds that way. The son of a bitch even had the bravado to threaten me."

"He threatened you? How?"

"He said I need to have some skin in the game too. Chelle, my captain has thrown in the towel. We need your help and he's officially asking for it."

"I'll get the paperwork going. In the meantime, do you happen to have a recording of his calls."

"You bet I do. I also think I have a thread to pull on. It's not much but it might be a beginning."

"Jojo, I think I can talk my supervisor into assigning this case to me. Just hold on for a few hours. I'll get back to you one way or another. And be careful, we don't know what 'you having skin in the game' means. Until we know differently, I think you should take this guy at his word. Jojo, as a fellow officer, I have a suggestion."

"I'm all ears."

"Between the guy in Pittsburgh and the Vegas killing, this is now interstate crime. That, combined with a potential serial killer makes it FBI territory. You just have to convince your captain that the two murders in Reidsville and all these seemingly accidental deaths are connected.

"Your recorded call threatening a law enforcement officer should be all I need to make my case. Regardless, I suggest that in the spirit of taking abundant caution, you, your wife, and daughters could go on a little vacation."

"What? No way. The hell if I'm going anywhere. I've been threatened plenty of times, and I'm still here. Besides, you know that I am your best chance of catching this guy. No ma'am, not interested. I'm staying right where I am in this. The FBI needs me. He's made me his contact person."

"Jojo. don't underestimate this guy. If your guesses are right, he has already killed five or more people. And he did it cleverly."

"I'm not running, Chelle. Not my style."

"You might not be the target. Your family could be his target. Remember, he said he wants you to have skin in the game. He might be talking about your family."

Chelle could tell that Jojo was considering her suggestion, because the phone became silent.

"Dammit, Chelle, you just raised my alert level from yellow to red."

"I think that's a good thing. Take precautions; we don't want to underestimate him. I'm going to talk to my supervisor about our immediate involvement.

Chapter 12

Tamara was in the back yard washing the kitchen windows when Jojo found her. He opened the sliding patio door, she looked at her watch and smiled. It was early afternoon, Jojo was home early.

Jojo saw Tamara standing on a step ladder and wearing blue rubber gloves that nearly went up to her elbows. "Honey, I said I would wash them next weekend."

"I know, but it was such a nice day out. And if you have enough time to wash the windows, I think you should go golfing instead. You need a break."

Jojo helped to hold the stepladder still as she stepped down with a bucket in her hand. She gave her husband a peck on the cheek and asked, "What's up?"

"I need to talk to you about something. Where is Kristal?"

"Kristal is at Mckenzie's, swimming. Why?"

"This concerns her too, and Lorelei?"

Tamara tossed the sponge in hand into the water bucket.

"What's going on, you look worried."

Jojo sat down on the concrete stoop that lead to the back door. Tamara sat next to him tugging on the gloves to take them off.

Jojo waited until he had his wife's full attention. Tamara tossed the gloves onto the concrete walk.

Jojo looked at his wife and caught her eyes. "I was threatened by the killer."

"When?"

"A few days ago."

"What, why didn't you tell me?"

"Oh, come on. You used to be an MP at Fort Benning; you know that threats come with the territory."

"Not from a killer."

"I didn't want to alarm you."

"So, why now, what's changed?"

"I talked to Chelle; the FBI is going to be getting involved. It looks like he's gone interstate. Makes it FBI territory."

"Sorry to hear about more murders but thank God the FBI is getting involved. You have been under too much pressure trying to catch this guy all by yourself."

"It wasn't just me. Everybody at the department wants this guy."

"You know what I mean. And how does this effect Kristal and Lorelei?"

"Chelle thinks I should take this guy's threat a bit more seriously. And as an added precaution, she thinks we should all head out on a vacation for a few weeks until the FBI gets this guy."

"You mean just like that, pack up and leave?"

"If it was just me, I would say screw him. But Chelle has a theory that he might be targeting my family. If she's right, that's a chance I don't want to take."

Tamara picked up the water bucket and dumped it out on the lawn. She asked, "What did he say exactly."

"Up until now he has taken all the risk. He said, it was time I had some skin in the game."

"And Chelle thinks we might be that skin."

"It's a possibility, yes. Or he might be just toying with me. If it's him, and I think it is, he is a sophisticated killer not to be taken lightly."

Tamara looked out over their small fenced in back yard for a moment. she said, "Let's go get Krystal, come back here and pack some things up."

Jojo asked, "What about Lorelei?"

"We'll call, explain the situation. I'm sure she'll understand."

Tamara picked up the gloves and slung them over the edge of the water bucket to dry.

They both hurried to the car. He tossed his wife his phone, "Call Lorelei, get her on the phone and explain things."

Tamara buckled in; Jojo was already backing out the drive as she dialed the number.

The phone up to Tamara's ear continued ringing.

"She's not answering."

"Shit, keep trying."

They were getting close to Mckenzie Thomas's home. Tamara, with the phone still pressing up to her ear she said to Jojo, "She's not answering."

Eventually the phone stopped ringing and went to voice mail. "Can't take your call, please leave a message."

"Honey, this is mom. Call me or dad back as soon as you get this message."

They pulled into the Thomas's driveway. A few moments later they were at the front door ringing the bell.

Mrs. Thomas smiled as she answered the door. "Tamara, how nice. Hi, Denton, I certainly wasn't expecting to see you two today."

Mrs. Thomas expression on her face changed when she glanced at Tamara and saw the worried look on her face.

"Is something wrong?"

Jojo smiled back not wanting to make a scene. "A little family emergency. We need to take Kristal home."

"Oh my, is there anything I can do to help? I hope it's not too serious."

Tamara who knew that Mrs. Thomas had a reputation as the local gossip added, "My mother took ill, though it doesn't seem too serious. I would feel better if I went to see her and Denton thought we should all go and make a vacation out of it."

"My, my, things certainly can change quickly can't they? I hope your mother gets well real soon. Detective Jones, what about the killer running around. Aren't you the one who is supposed to catch him? It's so frightening knowing he's on the loose somewhere."

"Mrs. Thomas, I'm sorry, I can't comment on an ongoing investigation. But let me reassure you that there are a great deal of people working on this besides me."

Thankfully, Kristal came to the door with her friend McKenzie. "Mom, Dad? Why are you guys here?"

"We'll explain in the car." Tamara said, "Please get your things, we need to go."

Mrs. Thomas chimed in, "Your grandmother is sick, and your mother wants to go visit for a while until she is better."

"Grandma is sick? You were just talking to her last night. You didn't say she was sick."

"It came on suddenly. Please Kristal, we need to go right now." Tamara gave Kristal a look that she hoped conveyed the seriousness of the situation.

"Sure, Mom, I'll get my stuff."

Jojo added, "We'll be waiting in the car, we have to make some calls."

"You're welcome to come in and wait," Mrs. Thomas said.

"I'm sure it won't take Kristal long. We'll wait in the car." Jojo ended the discussion.

As they waited in the car, Tamara tried to call Lorelei again.

The phone rang and rang until it went to voice mail. Tamara didn't leave a message this time.

Jojo suggested, "She's working and must have her phone off. Use my phone and send her an email. She'll probably get that first."

Kristal came to the car and jumped in the back seat. "Ugh, I hate riding in a police car."

Tamara said, "I'll try, but she always has her cell phone with her."

"Who mom, who are you trying to call?"

"Your sister."

"She turns her phone off at work; she said it distracts her."

Tamara typed a short message telling her daughter to call her father's phone immediately. She pressed send.

"I hope that works."

Kristal asked, "How sick is grandma? Is she going to be OK?"

"Grandma is not sick, we just said that for Mrs. Thomas's benefit," Jojo said.

Jojo's phone rang. Tamara looked at the caller ID and immediately breathed a sigh of relief and said, "It's Lorelei."

"Hi honey, it's Mom. I need you to listen to me carefully, very carefully. As you are aware, there have been a series of

Alan D Schmitz
DIGITAL SECRETS

murders in and around Reidsville. A person who may have been the killer, called your father and threatened him. We suspect that the threat was aimed towards our family. We need you to get someplace safe right away."

Jojo interrupted, "Tell her to come home. Until we get a better plan we stay together."

"Come home right away. No, do not wait until after work. You need to come home right now. If Dad thinks it's that serious, it must be. Please no more arguing. Just come home."

Tamara gave a glance at Jojo. They were almost home. She spoke into the phone, "I'm sure they won't fire you for leaving early."

Tamara was having a hard time convincing Lorelei to leave work. Jojo took the phone.

"Lorelei, if you don't want me to come down there with the siren blaring and arrest you, you had better leave this instant. See you at home, half-hour or I am coming to get you, and you won't like it."

Jojo pressed end call and slid the phone into his top shirt pocket.

"So much for diplomacy." Tamara winced at the gruff message.

"We don't have time for bull crap."

Kristal asked, "How come you told Mrs. Thomas that grandma is sick if she isn't?"

Tamara placed her hand gently on Jojo's thigh to let him know that she would field their daughter's question, she could see that many things were on his mind and his patience was wearing thin.

"We didn't want to worry Mrs. Thomas or McKenzie. Somebody called your father and threatened him."

"It's the serial killer, isn't it?"

"How do you know about a serial killer?" Jojo asked.

"Everybody at school is talking about it."

"How do they know this person is a serial killer?" he asked again.

"Nobody even ever dies in Reidsville. I mean nothing ever happens here. And now there are killings and suicides. There was the old married guy who killed himself, the woman in the park with her neck slashed, and the guy on the golf course. BANG!" Kristal made a shooting motion with her fingers. "Mrs. Thomas was telling us all about it. She said she doesn't believe that Tony Reilly killed himself either. He was the boyfriend of Mrs. Thomas's friend's sister's daughter.

"Anyway, Mrs. Thomas said he hated guns and was excited to start college and his girlfriend just agreed to go steady with him while he was gone to school. She said no way would he kill himself, especially with a gun. No way!"

Jojo had to agree and realized that he had way underestimated Mrs. Thomas and her information pipeline.

Jojo said, "We don't know who made the threat; he disguised his voice."

"But it is the killer guy, isn't it?"

"It might be, it could be anyone, which is why we must be careful. The FBI is getting involved and a person I know at the FBI suggested that my family might be the target, not me. That is why your mother and you and Lorelei are going away for a few weeks."

"The FBI, cool. Is the person Chelle?"

"How do you know Chelle?"

"Duh...Tracy and I are like best friends. Her dad totally likes Chelle, and so does she. Tracy thinks she's cool, they watched the Dancing Chickens together. Anyway, I can't go by grandma's, I have to go to school. My entire science grade is dependent on our project. I have to help McKenzie finish it; she's counting on me."

Tamara looked over at Jojo. "I thought you were going too."

"I can't. The sooner I catch that guy, we catch that guy, the sooner you and the girls can come home. And what are Dancing Chickens?"

Tamara laughed as she looked back at her daughter who just rolled her eyes in her head.

Tamara asked, "Home from where? Where are we supposed to go?"

Alan D Schmitz
DIGITAL SECRETS

He looked into her eyes and replied, "Working on it."

"Mom, I told you I can't go."

Jojo and Tamara looked at each other, knowing a fight with their youngest daughter was brewing. Tamara considered her other daughter's mind set and made a mental correction: make that two fights.

Reidsville, North Carolina:

Wade's side trip from Las Vegas to California had cost him a day but had been well worth it. Now it was time to make the detective feel like he was part of the game. Wade didn't exactly know how he was going to do that yet, that was why he was sitting in a red rental mini-van outside a building that housed an accounting office.

Using his computer's extended Wi-Fi, he had cracked into the office's computer system. His computer had been in the process of downloading the last bits of information he had hacked into when it suddenly lost its connection to a particular computer.

When he saw Lorelei come out the office building he understood why. She had a laptop computer in a protective case, and it was slung around her shoulder. He recognized her because of the many Facebook postings she had shared with her younger sister and the rest of the world. Minutes ago, it had been plugged into the same local network he had hacked into, that explained the sudden lost connection.

However, he already had more than enough information to put together a profile on the young woman. He noted that she was prettier in person. Even prettier than Chardonnay.

He typed a few commands on his laptop computer, which was nestled into the passenger seat of his car. It had downloaded most of the information off the young woman's computer. And because her computer was synched with her phone, he had most of that information also.

Wade drove through the parking lot slowly, letting his computer do one more little hack for him. He drove past

Lorelei's car just as she unlocked it with her key FOB and climbed behind the steering wheel.

Wade checked his computer and smiled. It had successfully downloaded the FOB code. Now he could access her car anytime he wanted. But that wasn't the challenge. Using it to control her car would take some real creativity.

Hacking into a car was new to him, though he didn't anticipate it to be too difficult. There had been an entire two-hour forum with sample hacking software included at the Black Hat seminar. The idea of commandeering a vehicle had intrigued him and he had taken copious notes.

The process was rather straight forward, at least to him. It was all conceptually the same. Armed with the year, make, and model he would use the same system the car used to communicate with the driver's cell phone, such as blue tooth, or it's built in Wi-Fi system, or the built-in cell and satellite communication system.

Whatever the car used to communicate with the outside world, he could use to gain access to it. Each auto company had their own proprietary software running the car. Searching the internet would find him the right code to hack. Thus, time would be needed to discover the most accessible way to control the car's systems.

Wade found a parking spot and pulled in just as Lorelei backed out and drove off. He was using a rental as an added security measure just in case somebody believed him suspicious. Wade knew there were cameras everywhere; the odds of being filmed was near certain. If someone did try to identify him, he hoped that the rental and the fake driver license he used to rent it would throw them off the track. But plan number one was not to be suspicious looking.

Lorelei was well beyond his sight. There was no need to follow, he knew exactly where she would be from now on. Tracking her cell phone, car, or even her laptop computer if it was on would be simple.

Wade assumed that Lorelei's father had taken his threat seriously and summoned his oldest daughter home. That meant the detective was planning to protect his family.

An hour later, Wade knew his assumptions were correct when he saw Lorelei's car parked out front of her parent's home. At a normal speed, he continued past and turned the block. He drove directly opposite the detective's house on a separate road paralleling it and parked.

He could see the backside of their home from his car. Learning the address of the detective was just some of the bounty he had harvested from Lorelei's laptop.

He opened his laptop and after typing in a few commands, he could see Lorelei's face. He looked at the linked version of her computer on his. Through the camera on Lorelei's laptop, he could see that she was dutifully completing her work assignments while her parents cleaned off the kitchen table around her.

The close-up of her face showed light blue eye shadow blended into her light dark skin. Her hair was dark black, done up in tight coils; today she had it pulled tight into a band at the back of her head.

In the background he couldn't help but notice that both mom and dad had on holstered weapons. He listened to the conversation in the background as well, though little of consequence was said.

Wade turned up the volume as loud he could when the conversation turned to something a bit more interesting. He heard the detective say, "I think I know where you all can go for a little vacation until I get this sorted out."

"A vacation, without you? Doesn't sound like much fun," Tamara smirked.

"Let me explain my plan. It's getting too late. I don't want you driving at night, too easy to be followed. Everyone should be safe here for now. But tomorrow morning first thing, you three leave."

"Fine!" Lorelei huffed. "But if you think I am going to make this pleasant for everybody, you are badly mistaken." She closed her laptop with a hard click. I'm going up to my OLD room."

Wade recorded the conversation. Knowing the future made killing too easy. He envisioned how he might commit his next crime which in turn made his mind wander towards Chardonnay Houston. He was suddenly especially missing her, the discomfort stirring inside of him felt good.

He had seen and heard enough. With a few more clicks he hacked into what appeared to be a shared family computer. He did a high-speed transfer of the data to let Mercury deal with any encrypted files later.

Then for the fun of it he did another search for Lorelei's IP address. It immediately appeared. Wade whispered to himself, "Let's hope she opened that laptop. Oh yeah, it looks like the show is about to begin ladies and gentlemen."

Wade loved the role of voyeur as he watched the young woman undress. She was down to her bra and underwear when a text came through on her computer. She bent over to read the screen and type a reply.

Wade laughed, "Oh that's perfect honey, why don't you bend down just a little more for daddy. Oh yeah honey, that's perfect."

He saw Lorelei laugh at whatever she saw on her computer. Wade opened her texting app and read the small joke between her and one of her friends. It was apparently about something that happened at the office that day. He didn't think it that funny.

"No, no, sweetheart. No don't do that. Aw crap." Wade said as Lorelei ended his peep show by closing her laptop lid.

Wade took a screen shot of Lorelei's ample cleavage and made it his screen saver. He started up his car and drove off. During the drive home, he conceded that planning a murder was almost as fun as doing it.

Chapter 13

Washington D.C.:

It was early Tuesday morning at his office in the Hart Senate Office Building. Senator Wescott looked out the window of his fifth-floor office. The busy streets of Washington were just coming to life, the many people driving and walking the Capitol grounds seemed to him as mere actors in a play somebody else was orchestrating.

As he stared at the Supreme Court building to the south, he furthered his resolve to find justice for the people he served, even if he had to take that justice to the Supreme Court itself.

Yesterday, Monday, he had taken the day off. If you could call it that. He had worked out of his apartment answering the emails that had busheled up while he was gone. In his small apartment he had found solace from the self-important, ego-enhancing Washington experience. It was hard to not feel important, with the monuments of so many that had gone before surrounding him every day. But if he gave up this fight against what he felt was a wrong to the people, the real people that had elected him, he was nothing more than a place holder for the Senator that was sure to take his place in the near or distant future.

It had been a day of sober reflection. Chelle, as usual, had been right about him. He couldn't walk away from this battle and live with himself. That didn't mean he wasn't frustrated with Washington D.C. and the inherent dishonesty of what he guessed from experience was commonplace. But he had resolved that he had one more fight in him and he didn't lose easily.

Steven realized what had been bothering him the last few months. It was simple. The one thing he always had since he could remember, he had now lost. Whether it was completing high school with high honors, or graduating magna cum laude from college, or the Green Beret he had earned, and winning the fight to become one of the few people in the world that could call themselves a United States Senator.

It was strange to think it took a trip to Las Vegas, Nevada, to force the realization that he had lost his resolve. You can't win a fight if you don't want to fight it in the first place. His latest entanglement with the forces of IRENE, the disenchantment with Washington itself, the divorce he never imagined he would have, and sadly, probably most sadly, he felt he had lost the opportunity to be the father he always wanted to be. It all had worn him down.

Chelle was the bright spot. Along with his daughter Tracy, who never lost faith in him, they were all that was keeping him going. He realized he was only putting one foot in front of the other every single day, moving on, only because it was expected of him by others, not himself.

Today, that would change. Today he would reincarnate Steven Westcott the fighter. And today, with that newfound resolve, he knew how he would fight the next battle and how he would win it.

Stepping away from the window, thinking Washington be damned, he went to his desk feeling reborn. He found himself with a few minutes with nothing to do. He strummed a pencil against his desk. Then he found a heavy pen and started drumming it. Soon he had a two-handed rhythm going.

Shannon Johnston walked in the back door. Steven noticed the sound of the door creak but didn't stop his strumming on the bare wood of his desk, switching to a stack of papers and on top a book. As he moved, his improvised drumsticks across the different surfaces, they each added a different sound to his beat.

Shannon listened for a moment, "You're in early, and it sounds like somebody had a good time in Vegas. Are you thinking of becoming a street performer?"

"I think I could make it. I have a pretty good beat."

Steven finished up with a small drum roll.

"I'd toss you a quarter if I had one."

"That's what all the tourists say."

"You do remember that the closed-door hearing is later this week."

Steven tossed his improvised drumsticks onto his desk. "I do, and I'm expecting some fireworks, because at this hearing they will have no excuse to not answer my questions. I will insist on either a yes or no answer, no more 'I can't answer because of security concerns.' I will either get them for perjury before Congress or I will get some answers.

"And that is the reason for the good mood?"

"Sort of, I guess I had to do some soul searching first, but now I know what direction I must take. Not knowing, is the devil to contend with, knowing is a freeing feeling, isn't it?"

"Yes it is Senator, yes it is."

Shannon dropped a stack of papers on Steven's desk. "Sorry it is I who must ruin your musical reawaking. But there are several bills that need voting on, and this is the summary of each."

"I read them on the plane on my way back to Washington. Today I'm focusing on the Senate Select Committee on Intelligence, specifically the closed hearing."

Steven held up another stack of papers. "These are spending reports. Money in, money out, that sort of thing, and I'm good at that sort of thing. Nobody ever examines these because a.) They are boring. b.) They're privileged documents due to security concerns, so they don't get into too many peoples' hands. But I can and will comb through them with a fine-tooth comb. Did you know that there are seventeen various security agencies in this country, Shannon?"

"No, Senator. I only know about the CIA, FBI, Secret Service, oh.., and the NSA."

Steven held up a list, "Sorry, Secret Service doesn't qualify, they are separate from this list." Steven read off the list, "How about Naval Intelligence, Coast Guard, Marines, Air Force, they each have an intelligence unit. Here's a good one, National Geospatial-Intelligence agency, or how about Bureau of Intelligence and Research. Obviously, I could go on.

"The point is, our committee is charged with watching over these guys, all seventeen of them. Each of these agencies have their own operating budget. And as chairman I'm supposed to do it with a bi-partisan group of senators who can't even agree on lunch. I'm convinced these agencies can and do get away with murder. And you can take that literally.

"Watching over them all is not even possible. But," Steven held up the stack of spending reports again. "Even they can't avoid a money trail. And I know how to follow a money trail. And that is exactly what I'm going to do."

"Take as much time as you need, Senator. To me you are not even here today."

"Nor to anyone else," Steven added as he picked up his pencil and pen again and started strumming across his desk again.

"I wish I could tell you more. But I am on to something. I just haven't been able to connect all the dots yet." After a final drum roll, he added, "But I will."

****

Steven was pouring over another stack of papers in front of him on his desk. Across every tabletop, and counter, and even on the floor, he had documents spread out. He needed more space; his apartment would give him the privacy and room he would need, so he proceeded to carefully mark and pack them all.

He was filling what had been an empty box when his cell phone rang. Prepared to let it ring out he saw the caller I.D. on his cell phone.

"Hey Jojo, what's up?

"Senator Cowboy, I need a favor."

Steven laughed at the reference only a buddy would or could use, "Anything you need, just name it buddy."

"Are you planning on using your residence in Peabody the next couple of weeks?"

"Not with what I have going on here. Why?"

"That killer I've been after threatened me."

"What?"

"Well, more like he threatened my family. Said he wanted me to have some skin in the game."

"So, you want to disappear to Peabody. No problem, buddy. It's yours."

"Thanks, I knew I could count on you. The girls are just getting up, and I want to get them on the road pronto. Just Tamara and the girls are staying there. I'm going to hang back. I gotta find this guy before he can make good on his threats. I'm sure they'll be safe at your place. Nobody could ever guess that is where they are."

"Jojo, this sounds serious. I could leave Washington right now. I could meet them on the road north. You know, kind of watch over them in your absence."

"Tamara would kill me if she thought for a second I didn't trust her to take care of things herself. Besides, I'm sure she can. I wouldn't want to be the guy that messes with her."

"Knowing Tamara, I don't disagree, but still, maybe I should be there if you can't be."

"Thanks buddy, but letting the gals shack up at your place will do the trick. Like I said, nobody but us will know where they are."

"OK if you say so. Have you told Chelle? Did you finally get the FBI involved?"

"Officially yes, and Chelle has already been a great help, in fact her supervisor put her in charge as she used to be a detective in D.C."

Steven laughed, "So I remember, didn't know, haven't talked to her yet today, though I doubt she would share official FBI business with me. Nonetheless, good to know.

If there is anything else you or the girls need, just call, I mean it, please call. There is a lock box with an extra key for the maid. It's hidden by the eve by the front window. I'll text you the code"

"Thanks, Cowboy."

"Get them up there ASAP."

"Will do."

"I mean it, promise."

"I'm on it, but they're not liking it. By the way, Chelle is amazing, she hit the floor running. I recorded my calls, and she has copies of them. The guy used some sort of voice disrupter, but Chelle thinks her people can reverse engineer it away."

"I can tell you this from experience, don't underestimate her Jojo. If you and her can't catch this guy, nobody can."

"That's what I'm afraid of."

"What?"

"That nobody can. Thanks again, Cowboy, I owe you."

****

Wade couldn't contain his excitement. He pumped his fist in the air a few times to release some of the exhilaration. The Jones family wasn't the only ones starting out early. He had been parked on the road on the other side of the block from the Jones' home since daybreak. He still had the red minivan from yesterday. He felt a level of security in that the car make and color couldn't be used to identify him. Entirely to the contrary; if his plan worked, it would throw them off his scent completely.

He couldn't get Lorelei out of his head all night. He hoped for but was not rewarded with another show. For that he was disillusioned. However, he was just rewarded for his early rise regardless.

Wade needed to know where the family was going to be protected from him, and now he did. Watching the detective pacing back and forth nervously in the family's living room as he talked to his friend was voyeuristically rewarding. Wade's heart was pumping hard.

With the hacking software he had picked up at the Black Hat conference, he had turned on the FaceTime video conferencing feature of their smart television that was also connected to the Wi-Fi system. Now he could see and hear whatever was going on in the Joneses' living room.

He had also hacked into their voice-activated intelligent personal assistant he had seen yesterday on the countertop.

With that he could listen in on their conversations in the kitchen. But that hadn't been necessary.

Lorelei was back on her laptop, which was again in the kitchen. She was catching up on emails as she ate breakfast. He watched the detective walk towards the kitchen so he started to listen to the conversation from that device.

Interesting. Wade realized. Senator Westcott is the detective's friend. The same senator that is chairman of the Senate Select Committee on Intelligence. The man in charge of the recent investigation of the country's intelligence communities, small world.

Even more interesting is that he is leaving his wife and daughters alone in the Senator's home in Peabody, Massachusetts. And what was that about his girlfriend being an FBI agent? The agent in charge of capturing me. Now that is interesting. Suddenly we are all one big happy family. That was all about to change.

****

"I talked to Cowboy. I explained the situation and he said you can stay at his home in Peabody. He will be in Washington for a while, so he won't be using it. I want you all to be ready in a half-hour."

"Dad I know you are worried about us, but I can take care of myself." Wade saw Lorelei talking.

"Lorelei, honey, this guy is a complete kook. If the guy who threatened me is in fact the same guy, he has already killed several people. I don't take him as a bluffer."

Wade took some offense at the comment. He didn't consider himself a kook. In fact, Wade knew others, besides himself, considered him to be a sort of genius. Though the detective was perfectly right when he said he didn't bluff.

"I get it, Dad; he could be dangerous. But he could also be just some idiot getting his rocks off by scaring the local cop."

"That's a chance I'm not ready to take with your lives."

"What if it's a chance I am willing to take with MY life? I have a job I am diligently trying not to get fired from."

Denton looked at his wife for some help.

"Sweetie, I think in this case, your father is right. He can explain the situation to your boss. I'm sure she will understand."

"Really? In this case I'm right?" Denton protested.

Wade saw Tamara give her husband a look of 'not now honey.' Wade chuckled.

"I mean, I was a cop too. This guy scares me. That's why I'm keeping my pistol close and handy. And worse, your father can't catch him if he is worried about us. We owe it to the community to not be a distraction to him."

Wade smiled slyly and talking to the computer in front of him, he said, "Yes, isn't that right detective. You are so worried about your little precious daughters that you can't catch me. Sorry, Detective Jones," Wade sneered, "it's not going to be that easy for you. And thank you Lorelei for your dad's telephone number stored in your computer. I was having a bit of trouble pinning it down."

"Look," Jojo said, "this isn't up for debate. I don't care if you do lose your job, it's better than losing your life."

"Ok, I'll go, but I don't like it. I'm an adult. I don't even live here anymore. And if we are going to be gone for any period of time, I have to go to my apartment first. All I have left here are the clothes that I don't wear anymore."

"You're not going anyplace by yourself, and time is of the essence. We can't give that jerk one extra second to plan whatever it is he's planning. You can buy clothes up in Massachusetts."

"Dad, you're kidding."

"No, I'm not. Tamara, buy them whatever they need. Collect what you do have. In a half-hour, you all leave. It's a twelve-hour trip to Peabody and daylight is already burning, you need to get going."

Kristal looked at her sister with shock in her eyes and commented, "Who are you, and where is our father, you know the cheapskate who makes us wait for Christmas to get something for nothing guy."

Jojo laughed, appreciating the humor under the circumstances. Wade watched as Jojo took his younger daughter's hands in his. Wade foresaw the young teen was blossoming quite well. She would in short time rival her older sister.

The detective said, "Very funny. But I couldn't be more serious. I want you out of Reidsville as soon as possible. Keep your eyes open, be wary even though he can't possibly know you are all the way up in Massachusetts. If I didn't think you would be safe, I wouldn't send you away. Go to the art fair, see the shops. It'll be fun."

Lorelei closed her computer. "Fun, yeah right. I still have lots of work to do. Just because I'm gone doesn't make it a vacation."

Wade felt a moment of panic as he tapped a few keys on his computer to turn on the electronic personal assistant. By the time he had it eavesdropping for him, the room seemed oddly quiet.

From time to time he heard muted conversations throughout the house but nothing he could understand until the conversation came back into the kitchen.

"We can take my car," Lorelei suggested.

"Perfect," Wade smiled.

"The SUV has more room," Wade heard the detective suggest. "And it has Wi-Fi so you can continue to use your laptop to keep working on the drive up.

Lorelei negotiated, "OK, but my car goes in the garage."

"This is so unfair," the young teen complained.

"Tell me about it," her sister agreed.

Wade said, "Damn it!" He heard doors opening and closing. The family was preparing to leave, and Wade had an idea but needed to work fast. He started his car. A risk would have to be taken. But if his plan worked, it would be worth it.

He drove around the corner and parked his car three houses away from the detective's home. Wade watched them park

Lorelei's car in the garage and move Tamara's behind it on the driveway right next to the detective's police cruiser.

Suitcases and backpacks were loaded into the back of the SUV.

"You must be reading my mind." Wade said smirking to himself. Tamara's SUV was more like a computer on wheels, vs Lorelei's older model. Tamara's car was fully electric, everything computer controlled. He would use the same hacking software he used to intercept a cell phone for the SUV, because it did basically the same thing.

The SUV used the same cell system to keep its GPS guidance and OnStar systems updated and available. It also used it to provide a rolling 'hot spot' for not only the car's computers and entertainment system but also for any portable connected equipment its passengers used.

The Wi-Fi hotspot could be exploited. He activated his scanning software and soon was looking at a long list of Wi-Fi connections. His scanner was picking up every Wi-Fi signal in the neighborhood, and there was an expansive list. Most houses had at least one or more and the list had them all.

He sorted through the list as best he could. First, he ignored any that ran through a cable system. He narrowed it down further to only those that used one of the major cell tower systems.

Wade was feverishly tapping on his keyboard, trying to complete the hack in time. He looked up again and saw the detective wave goodbye to his family as they backed out the drive.

Wade wasn't ready yet. The SUV turned down the road and drove off away from his direction. Feeling a tinge of excitement, the chase was on. He didn't dare follow the SUV, which he needed to be within range of his computer to complete the hack. The detective would undoubtedly be watching if anyone was tailing his family.

He saw the detective follow the SUV with his eyes as it went up the street. Wade watched him turn his gaze down the street towards him. Just in time, Wade ducked down hoping an empty car down the road wouldn't draw any suspicion.

After a few minutes, he peeked his head up and saw that the detective had apparently gone back inside. Wade scanned the contact list from the information he had hacked from the detective's cell phone. It didn't take long for him to find his buddy the Senator's name. Two addresses presented themselves. One in Washington D.C., an apartment. Another in Peabody, Massachusetts.

Wade asked his computer the best route to that address and within seconds he had a pretty good idea of the route the SUV would be taking. Catching up with it shouldn't be too hard.

He started his car and casually drove off. Time was on his side, literally. All he had to do now was reestablish a link with the SUV's Wi-Fi signal, compare it with the list he had time stamped, and the right signal would be the only signal that was in both places.

****

Jojo locked up his home and jumped in his police cruiser and made a call.

"Hi Chelle, any word?"

"I've got the ball rolling on this side. My boss has given me one week to produce evidence that all these murders are connected."

"What does that mean exactly?"

"If I can't prove these murders are all connected, we don't have interstate killings and no serial killer. That would mean it's not in the FBI's jurisdiction.

"The good news is, my boss believes as I do that there's a nut out there that needs to be caught. The threat against you was a critical mistake. The boss doesn't take threatening an officer lightly. He's put our case on the top of the considerably big pile."

"On that subject, where are you and Tamara and the girls?"

"Cowboy gave us the use of his home up in Peabody. As of fifteen minutes ago, the girls are on their way. I'm on my way to the office. Let's get to it, the clock's running."

"They are already working on reversing the voice scrambling."

"They can do that?"

"Depends on how it was done. The old term that you can't un-ring a bell might apply."

"How's that?"

"If the voice was scrambled using a device that merely electronically scrambled it, it could be reversed. But if the scrambled voice was transcribed as an independent audio file, it is what it is. We should know soon.

"We have to connect the murders. You said you had a string to pull, mind sharing?"

"I discovered that Irving Duncan, the businessman who committed suicide in the car by slitting his throat, Susan Witting, the young mother in the park, and Bill Sanders all worked in one way or another with computers. They had different fields of expertise, and all worked independently of one another.

"Jojo, that sounds like not much of a string to be pulled on."

"It's more than I had a couple of days ago. I have no idea how they are connected, but I do know that Mrs. Witting at one time worked with Bill Sanders. I don't think it's a coincidence that Professor Patrick Cox was a professor of computer science and, get this. Doing a simple internet search, I discovered that Freddy Farly of Las Vegas works in the Information Technology field."

"You know I don't believe in coincidences."

"Neither do I, Chelle, neither do I. Now we must find the dots and connect them."

"Jojo, you have some of the best dot connectors on your team now. Send me what you have, and we'll get to work. You would be amazed at our database of information."

"I've got the file on my computer at the department. As soon as I get in, it'll be coming your way."

****

Wade was traveling on highway 29 going north out of Reidsville. The two-lane divided highway had a speed limit of seventy miles per hour and he was pushing eighty-miles-per-hour to gain on the women. Wade didn't have to guess at which route the women were taking; all he had to do was follow the blue dot on his phone that was Lorelei's computer.

It had just been a matter of time and after about a half-hour of driving, every now and then his computer would ping the SUV's Wi-Fi. He guessed he was within a half mile of the women and if he kept up his pace, in a few miles he would soon be in range of the SUV.

Soon he had a solid signal and it kept getting stronger and stronger with each mile. His computer locked onto the IP address the SUV was using. Now that he had the IP address, he could hack into the vehicle's computer system.

It was clear he wasn't going to make work again today. If his boss wasn't bluffing, that meant he was fired. Oh well, his loss. Wade reasoned.

With a solid Wi-Fi signal, he locked onto the only IP address that made sense. He drove with one hand and one eye on the road as he typed in commands with the other. It didn't take him too long and after a few close calls with his car to realize he needed two hands and total concentration for at least ten minutes to successfully complete the hack.

Wade could see the dark blue SUV in front of him. He could even see the three women. Unfortunately, he would have to be content with following them until they decided to take a rest stop.

****

Jojo looked at his phone and could see that his family was making good time. He was using his wife's phone as a tracking device. They had agreed that under the circumstances they would share locations with each other. Jojo also had Kristal's password to her phone, meaning he could track its position whenever he wanted, too. It was over three hours into the ride and they were well past Charlottesville, Virginia. He was starting to breathe easier, his family meant everything to him. Seeing them safe made him feel stronger and more determined than ever. He felt sorry for all the other families that hadn't been so fortunate.

****

Chelle had a series of files on her desk. She was sitting down, finishing her third cup of coffee.

"Chelle," a voice called from behind her.

"I have something."

Chelle swiveled her chair around. "Hi Jeff, what do you have?"

"We were able to filter out some of the electronic audio scrambling. I have better equipment in the lab but thought you might want to hear it pronto."

Jeff placed a portable speaker on Chelle's desk, he had his phone paired with it. "Listen to the background. I haven't placed it yet but it's distinctive. It's like gun shots going off in the background as well as music."

The speaker played. He was right, the voice was more distinctive but still not natural. But the sound in the background was her focus. "Is that Celine Dion?"

"That's what I thought. From the movie Titanic"

"Specifically, 'My Heart Will Go On'."

Jeff asked puzzled, "But why gun shots, or more like cannons going off?"

Chelle grinned with a knowing smile, "I was there, I know it. It's from the Bellagio's water show in Las Vegas. Listen, it's going to come again. A series of cannons going off."

"I'll be damned." Jeff said.

"What you are hearing are powerful air cannon's shooting water into the sky at the Bellagio hotel complex. Good work, we know the date and time of the call. We can verify with Bellagio the show being played at that exact time. But I'm sure I'm right. Try to clean it up some more, thanks."

As soon as Jeff left her office, she made a call.

"Hi Jojo, how is your family doing?"

"They're making good time, all most west of Washington, just north of Charlottesville; I've been monitoring their progress on my cell phone. I would imagine they will be needing to get lunch and take a bathroom break soon."

"It's good to know they are out of harm's way. I have good news; we've got something that links your guy to the murder in Las Vegas."

"Doesn't surprise me. Did you trace the phone call to Vegas?"

"Not directly, but he did call from Vegas. The call was made outside of the Bellagio Hotel. I could hear the Bellagio water show going on in the background. We are confirming it, but I'm sure of it."

"That would mean he was in the area and could have been responsible for Freddy Farley's accident."

"Certainly seems that way. And another dot to connect to the other deaths."

"What's that?"

"There was a conference going on in Vegas during that time. It was the same time Steven and I were there. It was a computer conference, specifically a conference on hacking.

"Now we can look into attendance information and flights from Reidsville to Las Vegas."

Jojo gave a slight laugh, "Good luck with that. You can't get from Reidsville to anywhere. Not easily anyway. The problem is that you must drive from Reidsville to any number of airports all within one to two hours away."

"It's what we do, Jojo. Assuming our killer lives in the Reidsville area, we can maybe narrow it down. We know when he was in Vegas, and we know when his last murder in the Reidsville area was."

"If you include the death of the professor, which would mean he was in Pittsburgh at that time. Maybe he flew out of an airport there."

"Good thinking, it's certainly another possibility. Stay safe. If you find out any more let us know. Right now, you are our boots on the ground in Reidsville."

"There is one death that doesn't fit the pattern. My theory is that the young man who committed suicide was killed by the same killer but for a different reason. I have an idea to pursue. It's for sure a long shot that I need to get working on. Talk soon."

"Good luck." Chelle hung up. It only took her a few moments to collate a plan. After confirmation the killer had indeed made the call from Vegas, she would ask for more help from her boss.

Checking flight manifests from many airports and many airlines would be daunting, but it was a start.

****

Wade was typing furiously while his computer kept trying different codes to crack into the SUV's computer. He had already managed the hack into the auto's Wi-Fi. The family had finally stopped for lunch and to find a power terminal to recharge the car's batteries. He had literally only a moment to collect whatever data he could before Mrs. Jones turned off the SUV. When she did, the Wi-Fi also would turn off and any chance to hack into the SUV's computer died with it.

Wade felt his stomach grumble. He was hungry too, but he had to make sure he cracked into the SUV's computer before they started out again. If he didn't hack into it before then, his entire day would be wasted. He had no intention of following them all the way to Peabody, Massachusetts. He had more work to do in Reidsville.

All three women stepped out the SUV. Mom plugged in the charging cord for the electric SUV. The family went into the small dinner and truck stop. Wade pulled up to a gas pump and filled his tank. He needed a bathroom stop as much as he assumed the women did. He could see through a window that the three had found a table. A waitress was filling their water glasses.

Wade went into the small store and after a quick bathroom break, he bought a pre-made sub and a Coke. Immediately, he went back out to his car. He would have to work with whatever information he had collected. If he was lucky, he would have a minute or two to finish the hack as soon as the car was started up again.

The software on his computer had managed to pick the internal coding of the SUV's satellite radio. It also had found the internal Bluetooth connection code. He had tried the software only once before on his car. It had worked as advertised, but his car was nowhere near as sophisticated as the SUV. Theoretically, that would give him more opportunities to disrupt the ladies' lives.

They came out the restaurant, it was show time. Wade had everything as ready as possible. Everybody climbed in. Mom was alone in front like a chauffeur. The modern family. The girls undoubtedly wanted the extra room in the back seat to work on their connected devices.

With the Wi-Fi found, Wade typed furiously. Waiting the interminable seconds for the software to find the right path was torture. The SUV's back up lights went on. It was too soon; he wasn't ready yet.

Chapter 14

Suddenly the backup lights went back off. The car pulled ahead a few feet and parked again. A door opened; the youngest daughter ran into the store. Mom left the car running, the Wi-Fi signal still strong. Wade typed and waited, typed, and waited. He was almost there, Wade felt excited his hack was almost done.

The young woman ran out again, proudly waving the magazine she had bought. The car once again started backing. It left the parking lot and reentered the highway, speeding away.

"Shit!" Wade cursed as he started up his red mini-van. He was so close; he was sure of it. Wade kept several cars between him and the SUV. Then it happened, the software made the handshake; the indicator turned green.

"Yes," Wade congratulated himself. "Let's see how this works?"

They were all heading down the highway at over 70 miles per hour. Wade dropped back a bit more. Whatever disaster happened he wanted to watch but certainly didn't want to be a part of.

Lorelei's computer was his eyes and ears. The first test was simple. He could hear the satellite radio playing the latest hit by the Dancing Chickens, 'Time to Reboot'. Wade pressed a radio icon on his computer.

A Frank Sinatra song blared loudly, replacing 'Time to Reboot'.

"Mom, why did you change the station? Turn it down. I was listening to that song." It was the youngest daughter's voice.

"I didn't." Tamara yelled back over the sound of the loud radio as she fumbled to find the volume control.

Wade laughed hysterically.

"That's weird," Tamara said as she turned the sound down.

Just like that, the windshield wipers turned on and the window was sprayed with wiper fluid.

"Oh my God!" Tamara screamed; it had taken her by surprise as she worked the radio.

Next, the air conditioning blower went on high.

Laughing, Wade saw the SUV swerve. The car behind it suddenly braked, wondering what was wrong in the car in front. Wade braked a bit too, not wanting to get in front of the women's SUV.

He pressed the button on his keyboard that represented the cruise control and kept tapping the arrow to speed the car up. Every time he saw the brake lights come on, he would set the cruise control even faster. Wade pressed a key which activated the ABS braking system. Instead of the brakes turning on he used it to override the manual foot brakes.

The split screen on his laptop showed a frightened Lorelei screaming, she shouted. "Mom, mom, what's wrong?"

"The car won't stop, it's speeding up. The brakes don't work."

Wade speeded up too. He needed to keep up with the SUV. He watched as the mother started weaving the car through the traffic in front of her at high speed.

The youngest daughter started to cry. "Stop it Mom, slow down, we're going to crash."

The mother shouted out. "Tighten your seat belts as tight as you can. I can't stop and I can't turn off the freeway."

Tamara remembered the parking brake. It might work. She lifted the button on the console. Nothing happened. The electric car was gaining speed. The heads-up display showed she was doing over eighty-five miles per hour.

She kept tapping the brakes with no effect. Her foot was nowhere near the accelerator, yet the car kept accelerating.

Wade watched the SUV swerve around car after car. Horns were honking all around him as he speeded up too. The cars in front of him were braking mostly out of reflex because by the time they noticed the SUV, it was already past. He weaved his way around the slower vehicles too, but the path ahead looked like it was getting more congested by the minute as cars cautiously slowed.

Wade glanced at the computer screen next to him. It looked like Lorelei's computer had been dropped to the floor. He saw two hands reach for each other. The car was eerily quiet.

"Aww, are the sisters afraid they're going to die," Wade said calmly as he tried to speed up though the slowing cars were making it difficult.

The SUV was headed for a tunnel. Cars were converging from the four lanes to two. The mother had somehow managed to avoid all the cars so far, but inside the tunnel she would have no place to turn. Eventually she would crash into a slower vehicle.

Between the distraction of the speeding and reckless driver passing them and the reduction in lanes, the traffic was bunching in front of him. Reluctantly, he had no choice but to slow down and merge with traffic. That was a shame because he was sure to miss seeing the accident about to happen.

Glancing back at his computer, the tunnel had darkened the screen and he could see nothing, but he heard the echo of none ending horns blaring.

****

Tamara saw no way to avoid an accident. Only luck and a bit of driving skill had saved them so far as she took necessary and extreme risks to avoid other cars. Glancing back at her daughters to see them one last time was a risk she dared not take. The end of the tunnel was still a half-mile away.

The car was now doing one-hundred miles per hour. The dashboard in front of her lit up like a Christmas tree with every warning light and safety system screaming for attention.

At a hundred miles per hour, she was rapidly gaining on the cars in front of them. Within the next thirty seconds they would most likely all die in a horrific crash inside this tunnel. She tried the brakes once again.

This time they worked; the car slowed down just a bit. She dared to slow it down some more without losing control. Slowing down bought precious seconds but she had to decide between crashing into the cars in front or if she stopped too fast risking a rear end collision and a pile up from behind.

Traffic outside the tunnel was opening again into the four lanes offered. They had a chance. Tamara narrowly avoided two cars nearly neck and neck in front of her as they moved to different lanes outside the tunnel. She somehow sped through and around them.

Daylight shown into the car. Tamara continued to slow the SUV until they came to a stop off the furthest right lane.

"Out of the car," she screamed. "It might decide to go again. Get out, get out,"

Kristal and Lorelei unlocked their seat belts and jumped out the car and found safety at the side of the road. The three women hugged and cried. Each was shaking from the experience, none more than Tamara when she realized what tragedy they had narrowly avoided.

Car after car came out of the tunnel. Most of the riders stared at the women and vehicle that so recklessly passed them that was now stalled off the side of the road.

****

Wade didn't understand what had happened. He had entered the tunnel cautiously, expecting to see fire or a crash scene. Traffic seemed to be approaching normal speed though it was evident that something had caused a slowdown. He exited the tunnel in the right lane and to his amazement a half mile ahead he saw the three women huddled out of the car, clearly upset.

"Damn. Good driving, woman. I'll have to let hubby know how good you did." Wade said to himself as he unconsciously slowed to relish the moment. "The tunnel, the tunnel broke the signal, didn't it?" Wade guessed as he slowed as much as he dared in the right-most lane.

As he passed the parked car and huddled women, he glanced over and couldn't help but to smirk. He looked directly at the youngest and laughed a bit when his eye caught hers and he saw her tears.

Soon the detective would be on notice that his wife and daughters were not exactly out of harm's way. Game on.

****

"Chelle!" Jojo said breathlessly as soon as the phone answered.

Chelle who was on her cell phone asked, "Jojo, what's the matter?"

"That son of bitch almost killed Tamara and the girls."

"Where, how?"

"He somehow turned off the SUV's brakes while Tamara was going down the road, He accelerated the car to a hundred miles per hour. Can you imagine? With the girls in the back seat, Tamara had to drive a car at one hundred miles per hour through traffic and no way to slow it down."

"Jojo, that doesn't make sense. Slow down tell me what happened."

"Tamara said they had just left a restaurant and gas station. She was back on twenty-nine heading north. First the radio changes stations all by itself. Next the washer sprays the windshield and the wipers turn on. She's distracted by all of that when suddenly the car speeds up and she has no brakes. It's only by God's grace that nobody was hurt.

"When the tow truck came for the SUV, he said nothing was wrong with it. The police are ticketing Tamara for reckless driving."

"Jojo, hold on, I'm with our computer specialist right now. Let me ask him a question."

Chelle pressed a button on her phone and immediately it switched to speaker mode. "I have Detective Jones on the line with me. He said somebody took over his wife's car and made it speed up and turned off the brakes. Is that possible?"

Jeff didn't have to think on it, "Sure it's possible. In fact, when I was at the Black Hat convention, they even gave away software to help you do it. What kind of car? Did it have Wi-Fi?"

"Yes, it was an all-electric Starlite SUV."

"That is one of the known vehicles, but almost any car with a Wi-Fi hot spot connection could theoretically be attacked. It can be done through Bluetooth also, it's a little different, but sure, it can be done. It's the same as hacking into a home computer through its Wi-Fi."

"And they can manipulate its controls?" Chelle asked incredulously.

"Anything that is computer driven. Anti-lock braking, collision avoidance systems, certainly radio, clock, air conditioning, whatever, it's all connected somehow."

Jojo asked over the speaker, "Could you tell if a car has been hacked into?"

"There might be some remaining code, though a good hacker wouldn't leave a trail." "Thanks Jeff."

Jojo asked, "One more question, Jeff. You said you were at the Black Hat convention in Las Vegas. Why?"

"Same reason as the bad guys. Technically, I'm a white hat, a good guy. The black hat guys hack for bad reasons, stealing information, credit card stuff, or just to cause havoc. Some claim they are more like Robin Hood, doing good work, finding weak spots in systems, and reporting them."

"But why were you there?"

"FBI sends a group of the IT team every year. Talk about good times, it's the highlight of my year. Company-paid trip to Vegas, it's awesome. It's the only way to stay one step ahead of the hackers. We must learn what they learn and do them one better. It's a constant struggle. The black hatters like to call it 'The Game'. It's no game to us."

Jojo asked, "Is everything that vulnerable?"

"I'm afraid so. I keep my phone off unless I'm using it. That's how paranoid I am. I don't even trust airplane mode anymore."

Ominously Chelle said, "Thanks."

"Jojo, did you hear that?"

"I did. I'm on my way north to get my family."

"Jojo, we must assume you are compromised. Your phone, your family's, maybe your house. Don't tell me where you are going. Turn off your phones, your computers, watches, you need to go off grid if you want to protect your family."

"Chelle, find this guy."

"I will, Jojo, I will."

****

Steven was sorting through papers in his apartment. Nearly every open area had stacks of files on them. Propped up on his couch was a white board with hand drawn arrows and boxes and circles on it. Most of it was in black marker, but some of the connected circles were blue and some green others red.

There was a knock at the door. He heard the word, "Delivery," and chuckled as he answered it.

"Come on in. I'm not going to apologize for the mess. It's intentional."

"You have been busy," Chelle said. "But you're going to have to make room, I have to set this stuff down somewhere."

"Smells like Chinese."

"It is, all your favorites."

"Give me a minute."

Steven studied a pile of documents on the kitchen table. He took a blue post-it-note and stuck it to the top page of the pile. He moved it to another blue pile. He Came back and marked one with a yellow post-it-note. He moved that.

"One more and we should be good."

With a pink Post-it, the last pile was moved.

"Chelle dropped the food on the table. It was starting to get heavy."

"Sorry! How was your day?"

"I didn't want to talk over the phone, but wow, what a day. And your friend Jojo's wasn't any better."

Steven checked his watch, "At least his wife and daughters should be safe at my place by now."

"They're not going to your place anymore. We are pretty sure that whoever this monster is, he tried to kill Tamara and the girls."

"What? How? Are they OK?"

"Physically fine, but Jojo said mentally they're a mess. Jojo's on his way to get them. The local police are protecting them until he gets there."

"Can you share?"

"I can. The guy we think is the killer of multiple victims somehow took over their SUV."

"Took it over? Not sure I understand. Did he break into it?"

"In a manner of speaking he did just that. He hacked into it, probably using its Wi-Fi hot spot feature. Doing that he used the radio and wipers to distract Tamara, He disabled the braking system and accelerated the car to a hundred in the middle of a freeway, with everyone around them doing seventy miles an hour."

After a few quiet seconds, a stunned Steven asked, "People can do that?"

"It's been documented as possible. The FBI top tech guys confirmed it is doable. I also found out that the killer was in Vegas the same time we were. I'm working on a theory that he was at the Black Hat conference. It's the type of thing that is not just talked about but discussed with top hackers on exactly how it can be done."

"The Internet of THINGS." Steven said softly. "Everything is connected, so everything is hackable."

"Unfortunately, for all the good that can be, this is the underbelly of the beast."

Without another word Steven pulled out his phone and said, "I gotta call Jojo; he might need me."

Chelle put her hand gently on Steven's arm. "Don't bother, you can't call him. We assumed his phone, emails, anything electronic has been compromised. Tamara, the girls have been warned. They have gone dark. I told him to not tell me where they are or are going."

"Wow, remember what I was told before Vegas. 'Keep your electronics home. You will be tracked'."

DIGITAL SECRETS

Chelle and Steven unpacked the Chinese take-out, both lost in their own thoughts. Steven set out plates and knives and forks. Chelle pulled out two set of chopsticks.

"When in Rome?"

Steven chuckled. "If I have to." He placed the silverware back into the drawer.

Steven said as he came back to the table, "There seems to be a common theme with those in the know. It's scary that the people who understand all the electronic stuff best are the most suspicious of its capabilities."

"We are slowly building a profile on this guy. Now we know this guy is a hacker."

Chelle expertly picked up some sweet/sour chicken with her chopsticks and popped a piece into her mouth.

"I tried to get show attendance records, names, address, things like that. Guess what?"

"I'm sure I haven't a clue."

"These people are so suspicious, they only deal in cash. There is no list."

Steven tried to wrap some noodles around his pair of chop sticks. He finally had enough to make it worth the attempt to get it into his mouth. He raised the long, dangling noodles gingerly and brought his mouth to the start of the noodles and lowered the rest into his mouth. The technique wasn't graceful, but it worked.

After he chewed and swallowed and washed it down with some wine he said, "Talk about scary, think about it, the electronic gurus go back to the Stone Age and use cash because they know the dangers of the alternative. And we saw in a notably personal way exactly what they are aware of."

"It is a brave new world. Which leads to another anomaly. Remember those extremely detailed and personal reports we were given?"

"How could I forget them, and by the way, I shredded them."

Steven twisted and turned his chop sticks around a pile of noodles to no avail.

"There is surprisingly little information on each of the people we suspect as being murdered. That is, except for the young man who supposedly killed himself with his father's gun. It's like their files were scrubbed. We have established that all of the people that we suspect were murdered by this guy are connected in one way or another to the IT world. What we can't find, is how are they connected to each other and thus to the killer.

"I sure could use the help of your young friends that created those reports on us, to build the profile on all our victims."

Steven dropped his chop sticks next to his plate and got up, "Unfortunately, they didn't leave their calling cards." As he walked back to the silverware drawer he said, "I'm sorry, I just can't get the hang of those things." He held up his prize in his hand. "If I want to eat my food while it's still hot, I'm going to have to do it my way."

Chelle laughed and expertly dropped some sweet-and-sour chicken into her mouth using the chopsticks.

"Showoff." Steven grinned.

Chelle finished her mouthful and asked, "Speaking about doing it your way. Are you learning anything from your research?"

"I've been finding a lot of suspect transactions. Tomorrow for the closed-door hearing, I think I know the right questions to ask now. At least enough to get the ball rolling in my direction. I haven't found any mention of a 'Lake Lerna' project. Or anything about quantum computers, that is suspicious. I did find an army sponsored grant to Mellon University. It's a start, I've subpoenaed the Director of Army Intelligence to address it."

"Strange, one of our suspected murder suspects was a professor from Carnegie Mellon University's computer science department."

Steven twirled a big mouthful of noodles around his fork. "Now we're talking," he said as he held up his accomplishment before stuffing it into his mouth.

"Not surprising, if your guy is into computers, he might have gone to that university. It has the best computer science program in the country. And even if he didn't go there, he undoubtedly knows people who did."

"How did the killer kill him?" Steven asked as he washed down his dinner with another sip of wine.

"He didn't, not directly at least. The professor died from an overdose of heart medication. He accidently sent out photos of some child pornography to everyone on his e-mail list, including his wife and children. He had a weak heart; it was common knowledge around campus."

"I'm not following. You said you suspected he was another victim of Jojo's serial killer?"

"Whoever the killer is called Jojo and told him a Patrick Cox was going to be his next victim. They didn't find the right Patrick Cox until it was too late. Jojo did his best, but he just didn't have enough information to go on to find him in time.

"I'm still not understanding. Do you think that the killer somehow made the professor commit suicide?"

"In a way, yes. We are negotiating with the school to have our experts examine his computer. I'm thinking that the guy we are after placed the pornography on his computer, sent out the mass email using the professor's email address." Chelle sat back and closed her eyes for a moment. "Imagine this, the professor suddenly became estranged from his wife and children. He now disgusted them; he was kicked out of his own home. He also knew the police would be coming for him. And if convicted, he would be spending the rest of his life behind bars as a convicted pedophile. Saying he didn't do it when the information came from the computer of a computer expert, well, that would be a hard sell."

"I guess you're right. And he knew it. That would be enough to make somebody contemplate that their life was already over."

"It might be what the killer was counting on, that the stress of the situation would give him a heart attack."

Chelle and Steven worked at cleaning up the table. They worked mostly in silence as they contemplated themselves being put in the same predicament as Professor Cox.

Chelle stopped working, starred at the wall for a long moment.

Steven said, "I know that look. What did you just come up with?"

"Jojo said the killer told him Patrick Cox's life was over."

"It's what you just said, whether he died or not, his life was over. Maybe he didn't care if he literally died. He just wanted his life to be over. The pornography dump would do that. If we find the computer was tampered with, we can clear the professor's name. And there would be no doubt the guy is a hacker. And that would explain him being in Las Vegas during a hacker's convention, learning all the newest tricks of the trade."

Steven pulled Chelle close to him and gave her a kiss on the forehead and a hug. Maybe this will get your mind off your killer for a moment. Thanks for bringing over dinner."

"I should get a better kiss than that for such a gourmet meal."

Steven was happy to oblige and soon they were in a long and passionate kiss. "Chelle, my love. I don't know how to tell you this."

"But!" Chelle said as she looked up into Steven eyes.

"But I have a lot to do tonight. And you would be a huge distraction."

"I think that is the nicest rejection I have ever had."

"Rejecting you would be impossible." Steven gave Chelle another long kiss on the lips.

He broke it off and said, "And that is exactly why I must ask you to leave. Besides," Steven winked at Chelle, "You are surrounded by classified documents."

"I understand, and I have my own problem to work on. I'm sure the killer isn't finished yet. He has a mission of some sort. He's playing a game with us, but he's up to something besides that. And that is how we are going to catch him."

Chelle picked up her purse and gave Steven one more kiss and left. Steven looked over the stacks of paper scattered around his apartment and realized that he would look like a conspiracy theorist to anyone not Chelle.

Chapter 15

Steven banged the gavel against the wood block. He said, "This calls to order the closed door hearing of the United States Senate Select Committee on Intelligence," Steven announced boldly into the microphone.

The meeting was being held in room H219 on the second floor of the Hart Senate building. This wasn't the most handsome meeting room in Washington, but it was one of the most secure. It also wasn't that large, as the meetings were usually smaller than anyone outside of Washington would imagine.

It was a room inside of a room, with special soundproofing material surrounding it. The idea was to keep its secrets, secret. He was told that it was impervious from any type of listening device. The exact construction was itself a secret.

At the center table there was room for the fifteen Senators whose duties it was to preside over the entirety of the United States intelligence communities of which there were many. It was the duty of the various intelligence communities to keep the committee informed of important and relevant tasks they were undertaking. The exception was if the President of the United States deemed it too sensitive for the committee to know or hear.

Steven started the meeting, "I want to thank the Senators for your time today and I also want to thank our guest here today for their time. I hope we can all agree that we are here in closed session so we can honestly and discreetly discuss the questions before this committee.

"I also would like to remind our guest that it is our job, this committee's job, to have oversight of all intelligence functions. We are here as representatives of the same people we all ultimately work for, the American people.

"I am particularly pleased to see James Mitchell, Director of National Intelligence here with us to provide us with his insights, though his presence was not requested. Henceforth, I will refer to him as DNI."

Steven was surprised though not necessarily pleased. James Mitchell was in effect the boss of the entire intelligence community. His being here signaled something out of the ordinary was happening.

"Also with us is Vice Admiral Matthew Cramer, Director of Naval Intelligence, Peter Gonzalas, Director of the National Security Agency, and Susan Carter, Director of the Defense Intelligence Agency."

All the Senators and all the guest directors were dressed in various bland design of the same civilian dark suits. Most wore white shits; only the ties and slight differences in the shade of their suits set them apart.

Steven continued, "To start, I would like to address the DNI. Are there any new surveillance operations or new surveillance tools that you would like to brief the committee on?"

James Mitchell straightened up. His suit was a dark gray with thin pinstripes and white shirt. The collar was stiff and a red tie with thin blue strips that ran diagonally across it finished it off. He was a big man and time had made his fit body a bit round.

Steven envisaged as he addressed the DNI, you couldn't be more red, white, and blue unless you wore Lincoln's stovepipe hat.

The DNI pressed the microphone closer to him, "Thank you Mr. Chairman, but as you mentioned, I was not requested by the committee to be here to give a prepared report. I am merely here as an observer."

Steven sounding a little perplexed asked, "Am I to understand that you will not address any questions referred to you today?"

"That is correct, Mr. Chairman."

The members of the committee exchanged glances; it was clear that everyone was a bit baffled by the exchange.

"I would like to ask the same question to each of the directors present today. Are there any new surveillance operations or new surveillance tools that you would like to brief the committee on? We can start with the Director of Naval Intelligence."

Vice Admiral Matthew Cramer turned on his microphone and blew on it lightly to make sure it was on and working. "The Navy has no new activity to report."

They went down the list of Directors present and each had the same non report to report.

In the silence after the last non report by the Director of the NSA, Steven looked at his other committee members and angrily said. "I'm curious, because the last time we had a committee meeting such as this, the intelligence communities had nothing to report. And I remind the directors, it is your obligation to willingly share the details of current and ongoing operations with this committee."

Steven was met by more silence. Looking to his right and to his left at the committee members seated on either side of him he asked, "Any further questions from the committee?"

Senator Sherman, of the opposite party from Steven, spoke up, "It has come to my attention and thus to the committee that we may need to ask the chairman a question in kind."

Steven even more confused said, "Excuse me. You want to question me?"

"I do Mr. Chairman. Have you been meeting clandestinely with members of the Intelligence Community to illegally obtain classified information on current confidential investigations?"

Steven immediately knew that he had been found out. There was no sense in denying he had, as no doubt proof had already passed through the committee. Today it was in fact himself that was on trial.

Steven glared at the DNI. "You are perhaps referring to recently when I was surveilled in Las Vegas. I identified the two Navy agents who were following myself and my girlfriend as we went on a short vacation to Las Vegas."

Steven looked at Vice Admiral Matthew Cramer. He aimed his question directly at him. "It was going to be my question at this meeting to the Director of Naval Intelligence as to why I was being followed. Maybe now would be a good time to explain that, Vice Admiral."

The Admiral adjusted his microphone and spoke bluntly into it. "I cannot comment on an ongoing investigation, particularly if it involves a member of this committee."

Steven's anger was building. "You, or somebody subordinate to you, was tracking and following a United States citizen. Your agents nearly got us killed on the highway into Las Vegas."

"I saw the report, Mr. Chairman. You were driving erratically. Were you impaired in some way, sir?"

Steven snarled back, "No, I wasn't impaired. I was trying to escape what I deemed was a dangerous situation as I was obviously being followed by people suspect to us."

The Vice Admiral asked back, "Why were you concerned for your safety? Were you doing something that would be deemed suspicious?"

Steven had been a politician long enough to know a smear campaign. He was on the wrong side of the Intelligence Community and they were going to make him pay. And the other party would be more than happy to help.

"As I'm sure your report would show, my girlfriend and I were returning from a hike through Red Rock Canyon area. I didn't know that constituted a national threat. I would like to remind the committee that I am not the subject of today's meeting."

Senator Sherman chimed in, "Maybe you should be."

Steven looked to his left and right, even his friends on the committee seemed in shock and tongue tied. He decided to go all in. Steven continued to address the Director of Naval Intelligence. "Vice Admiral, I would like you to address a discrepancy that I noticed as I went through some financial documents."

On a big screen on a side wall a photo of a spreadsheet popped up when Steven pressed an automatic control next to his desk.

"As you can see on line fourteen, there is a line-item deduction for two billion dollars. The funny thing is I couldn't find exactly where it went. Would you please explain it to the committee?"

"I object," said Senator Sherman. "This has not been discussed with the committee."

"I'm sorry, Senator; I first discovered the discrepancy last night. There was no time to preview this to the committee. However, as chairman, my question stands."

The Vice Admiral studied the enlarged spreadsheet. "There is no discrepancy, I can assure you that every dollar is accounted for."

Steven knew that Senator Sherman's objection was meant to give the Vice Admiral time to think about his answer, as there was no cause for an objection.

"Director, I assure you that as an accountant, I realize it went somewhere. That is my question. To where did it go?"

"Mr. Chairman, I must remind you that I don't personally keep track of all expenditures."

"I know that the entire spending of all military intelligence programs is about twenty-five billion.[7] The Navy only gets a piece of that. I would think that as the Director you might be curious where two billion dollars went."

Steven could tell on his fellow committee members' faces that he now had their attention.

The Vice Admiral said, "I'm certain that I can find out and report back to the committee in the near future."

---

[7] Funding associated with the 17 components of the IC is significant. In FY2019 alone, the aggregate amount of appropriations *requested* for these two programs is $81.1 billion, including $59.9 billion for the NIP and $21.2 billion for the MIP. For FY2020 the aggregate amount requested for the NIP and MIP is $85.75 billion—$62.8 billion for the NIP and $22.95 billion for the MIP. (For the mathematically challenged, 1 billion dollars is equal to 1,000 million dollars.)

"That's OK, Director," Steven said. "Maybe the NSA Director could help you."

Steven flashed to another screen shot. "Funny thing, I notice that the NSA had an equal amount of their fifteen-billion-dollar budget with the same line item. Director Gonzalas, do you happen to remember where over ten percent of your budget went?"

The Director of the NSA remained silent. Steven saw him glance at the DNI for a bit of guidance, The DNI was stone faced.

"Director, you must answer my question."

"I will have to investigate the matter. I can't remember offhand."

Steven clicked another page.

"Director Carter, I noticed the Defense Intelligence Agency has the same line item. It was better buried than the others. But I did find it. Can you explain where this money went?"

She didn't need to look at the DNI, she knew her answer already. "I'm sorry, Senator, I will also have to look into the matter."

Steven looked at his fellow senators. Some, he noted, all in the opposite party, seemed ready to attack him. He wondered the reason. He continued.

"I found other agencies all within the intelligence community that also had this same discrepancy. Guess what, I do know where it went."

He was watching the DNI. He sat expressionless. Steven gave the man credit; he was the best poker player ever.

"It all went to one place. It all went back to where it came from. That is what has me truly confused. Why would the DNI distribute all this money just to claim it back?"

Steven knew the last bit could be called a bluff, or even better, an educated guess. But he went with it. He was all in now.

Looking at James Mitchell he said, "Perhaps the DNI could shed light on the Lake Lerna Project? This is where all that money went."

The DNI sat quietly with no attempt to explain.

"Does the DNI deny the existence of the Lake Lerna Project?" Steven repeated.

The DNI sat emotionless at his chair.

"Vice Admiral," Steven asked, "Do you deny the existence of the Lake Lerna Project? And I remind you, Admiral, you are under oath. Lying to this committee would be a serious offense."

Steven could see in his peripheral vision that the senators on the committee were suddenly at the edges of their seats.

The Director of Naval Intelligence sat quiet, not responding.

"Director it is a simple yes or no answer. Either you have heard of it or you haven't."

James Mitchell sat forward, without using a microphone he boomed through the room. "We are done here today."

Steven said, "It does seem like there are secrets being kept from this committee. Perhaps the Director of the National Security Agency would care to answer the question."

James Mitchell stood. "As I said senators, we are done here today."

"Sir," Steven said so forcefully that he also didn't need a microphone. This committee is still in session. Your subordinates are obliged to answer my question and the questions of this committee."

James Mitchell, responded casually, "You will have to take that up with the President of the United States. There are certain state secrets that even this committee is not privy to. Especially if we suspect a traitor amongst the group."

"That is an exceedingly grave charge, Jim, I hope you are prepared to back it up." Steven threatened back. "I will get to the bottom of this. I am a member of the Gang of Eight. You might be able to run from this committee, but you can't run from me."[8]

---

[8] The **Gang of Eight** is a colloquial term for a set of eight leaders within the United States Congress who are briefed on classified intelligence matters by the executive branch. Specifically, the Gang of Eight includes the leaders of each of the two parties from both

Washington D.C.:

Jojo walked into the lobby of the J. Edgar Hoover Building. It looked welcoming; he was not fooled. He knew it was highly protected, including being bomb proof with an actual moat around it. Located at 935 Pennsylvania Avenue NW in Washington, D.C., it wasn't one of the prettiest structures in Washington.

Jojo went up to the lobby, identified himself as a police officer, and said he was here to see a certain agent.

"And what agent is that?" The guard asked.

"Agent Chelle Saltarie."

He flipped through his hand-held list, Not seeing a detective Jones on it he went to his computer. "Is she expecting you?"

"No sir. But she will see me. We are working on a case together."

Looking suspicious, the guard gave a nod to another guard to watch the big man while he did some checking behind a closed door.

Jojo smiled at the guard who simply stared back at him stone face.

It only took a minute when the first guard came back and with a small amount of friendliness said, "Agent Saltarie will be down for you. You'll need a guest pass. I'll make one up for you."

Ten minutes later, Chelle was taking Jojo into the bowels of the giant FBI building. She explained as they walked to an elevator. "With all the concrete around us, you would think this building would last forever. Unfortunately, it is already past its useful life. Even though it has nearly three million square feet, FBI agents are scattered across the city. To put it bluntly, the heating and air-conditioning systems are antiquated.

---

the Senate and House of Representatives, and the chairs and ranking minority members of both the Senate Committee and House Committee for intelligence

"It took ten years to build, mostly because of lack of adequate funding and it wasn't finished until 1975. The problem is it hasn't been maintained properly. The exterior has netting wrapped around it to catch falling concrete as it literally keeps falling apart."

Jojo stepped hesitantly into the elevator as Chelle pressed the button for the second floor.

Chelle laughed, "I think the elevators are safe. Obviously, the FBI wants a new building. But with government being what government is, I doubt that I will see it during my career. They don't even have a site picked yet. And even if they did, you are probably looking at another fifteen years between design build and move in.

Jojo watched Chelle almost lovingly touch the bare concrete walls as they stepped off the elevator. She said, "I don't know how the old girl will make another twenty. But she'll have to, I guess."

Chelle led Jojo into her office and once they were in private, she asked, "I assume your family is safe."

"They're safe. I'm the one who is in trouble when I told them they couldn't use their phones or computers. We found a bed and breakfast type place. I got Tamara a burner phone and gave her your number. My guess is mine is compromised.

"The only good news, if you want to call it that, is that after their close call on the freeway, the girls took my precautions a bit more seriously. I gave strict instructions, no computers, no phones, and I wrapped theirs in foil, too. They think I'm nuts."

"The more I learn, the more I can say you are not paranoid. I'm not too surprised to see you here. I didn't know how you would contact me; I just knew that you eventually would."

"I still have my phone, but it is off, and I have it wrapped in aluminum foil. Please tell me that actually works?"

Chelle shrugged her shoulders. "Can't hurt."

"I check it every now and then to see if a message from the killer was left on it. So far, he's been quiet."

Chelle pressed a few buttons on her desk phone. It only took a few minutes and there was a knock on her door.

"Come in, Jeff."

A young man with dark skin came in. "Jeff, this is Detective Jones."

Jeff was small and short with intense eyes looking through small round wire rimmed glasses. His hair dark, short and curly. He looked up and extended his hand to shake Jojo's.

"Detective Jones, this is Agent Jeff Planter."

"Nice to meet you in person. I heard your family had a near accident."

"They did. All are safe now. But they don't trust the SUV anymore. We switched cars; I drove it here to be gone over by your tech people."

"I looked into the incident. Going over the SUV might give us some clue as to what happened, but most likely there would be no lingering evidence of a hack."

"Do you believe my car was hacked into?"

"It's a good possibility. I mean it is the only thing that explains the radio, wipers, sudden acceleration and losing the brakes at the same time. It sounds far-fetched, but I'm afraid it's plausible with the right person and the right equipment.

"In fact, after your encounter I got curious, and I hacked into my own car. It took me a day to do it. But with the right training and equipment, it can be done faster. My guess is the hacker was following close enough to hijack the SUV's Wi-Fi signal. Using special hacking software, he could take control of the car's system."

"It's that easy?" Jojo asked a bit surprised.

"Not easy, but certainly doable if you're determined. In fact, I picked up the software to do it at the Def Con conference in Vegas. I'm guessing your guy was there too. Def Con is held right after and sometimes a bit concurrent with the Black Hat conference."

Jojo asked, "Say, isn't that the thing you and Steven went to?"

"No, I mean we didn't go to it, but it was going on apparently while we were there. In fact, after we took out some of the electronic distortion in that recording you sent me, we confirmed that the killer was in Las Vegas during that call."

"Jeff," Chelle said, "can you see if the detective's phone has any implanted software? We are guessing it's been compromised."

"Sure. I'll get right on it." He looked at Jojo. "Do you ever use your home Wi-Fi connection on this phone?"

"Sure, all the time." The look on Jeff's face told him that was a mistake. Jojo further explained, "My cell phone reception isn't that dependable from my home."

Jeff took the aluminum foil wrapped phone from Jojo. He said, "Nice try, some phones, even when turned off, still ping for cell towers nearby so it knows where it is when turned on. But the foil idea might even increase the antenna range. What you need is a Faraday bag."

"A what?" Jojo asked.

"A special bag designed to disrupt and protect electronic devices such as phones, computers, electronic car keys. Anything that uses a radio signal to communicate is hackable. A Faraday bag protects that signal from getting in or out."

Jeff looked over the phone. "This one is OK. When it's off, its battery is electronically disconnected. Of course, if it has been compromised, that feature could have been turned off and the hacker could be using your phone as a microphone to listen to everything you say."

"You mean my own phone can be used to spy on me?"

"Entirely possible: your phone, your television, computer, your home smart assistant or even a baby monitor." Jeff smiled slightly, "Even your smart refrigerator. You know, the kind that you talk to tell it to remind you to buy milk? Anything connected through your Wi-Fi to the internet or even through Bluetooth can be used as a listing device if it has a microphone."

"Damn!" Jojo whispered. "And people can learn how to do it in Las Vegas?"

"It's one of the bigger shows but there are others around the world. That's why I go every year. It's the only way to know what the hackers are learning."

Alan D Schmitz
DIGITAL SECRETS

Jeff held up Jojo's phone. "Well, I better get going and check this thing out."

As soon as the door closed behind Jeff, Jojo said "Please tell me you have made some progress."

Chelle looked up at Jojo and said, "A lot has happened since you left. Let's start with a cup of coffee. We will be here a while."

Back inside Chelle's sparse office, the two of them got right down to business.

"Well, what do you have?" Jojo asked. He was sitting on an uncomfortable aluminum chair across from Chelle who was sitting at her desk and punching buttons on her computer.

"The most exciting thing is after you told me what happened to Tamara and the girls, we canvased your neighborhood for potential security videos. Your neighbors were cooperative and helpful. The same car that you captured on your security camera driving past your house on the day your family left was seen on the road on the opposite side of your block that morning and the night before.

"I believe he was hacking into your home system the night before from the other side of the block. He would have been unseen by you, but close enough to pick up your household Wi-Fi system."

"You mean he was trying to hack into my Wi-Fi?"

"And once in your Wi-Fi system, he could gain access to any device connected to that system. And it is a he, voice analysis confirms it.

"So, this is how he knows so much about me."

"It certainly looks that way. He probably knew exactly where your wife and daughter were going as soon as you told them. He followed them and hacked into your wife's SUV. The computer guys here were able to reverse some of the electronic voice scrambling. Doesn't help much, but we have confirmed he was in Vegas the same time as Freddy Farly's accident. That helps our case a lot.

We also identified exactly where he was in Las Vegas. He was near the Bellagio Hotel. The hacking convention was going on at Paris across the street. It's somewhat circumstantial, but my team believes the killer is a master hacker and that would explain a lot. And you are right, all his victims, except one, were related to the computer industry. I've investigated as much history as I could find on all the suspected murder victims."

"Any dots to start connecting?"

"One dot. They all went to Carnegie Mellon University and all had Professor Patrick Cox as an instructor at one time or another. We are spanning many years, but that is a common thread."

"What about more recent activity between them all?"

"Aside from that, I can't find any commonality between them. In fact, their files seem to be more and more incomplete the closer to the present I get. It's like in each case they were slowly dissolving from society.

"Professor Cox gave a speech two years ago widely panned by his contemporaries."

"I guess that would explain why he kept a low profile after."

"I guess, funny thing is, Steven and I were just talking about the topic of his speech. Its title was, 'Quantum Computing, Closer than We Think'."

"Didn't realize you and Steven had such an academic relationship. In fact, I didn't think Steven even knew the term quantum computing."

"Chelle laughed, "Trust me, we don't know anything much more than that. Steven did say that he heard in his circle, the government was sponsoring some universities as they explored the concept.

"I will keep looking. I do have some good news. We believe we can get a plate number off the vehicle we suspect the hacker was using. It's indistinct, we lifted it off a video from one of your neighbor's security cameras. But with enhancement software my people believe they can sharpen it enough to read."

Jeff came back in with Jojo's phone in one hand and the battery in another. "Just as you suspected, it was hacked. I'm familiar with the software. Probably uploaded while you were sleeping. You can also assume he has everything on it."

Jojo said, "What? Everything?"

"I'm afraid so. All your contacts, notes, calendar, e-mails, even your sleeping habits, I saw you use your phone to monitor your sleep patterns."

Jojo still a bit stunned said, "It's an automatic feature with the wrist band I wear at night. Wait, are you telling me he has my wife's and daughters phone numbers?"

"Detective, like I said. You must assume he has every bit of information on your phone. And not only that, you must assume he can get access to even more information by using the passwords and details stored on your phone."

"You mean my bank accounts?"

"And more. You must change everything, and I mean right now."

"How can I do that? Like you said, everything is on my phone and I can't use it."

Jeff held up another phone. "I cloned your phone to this one. It has a different number. Use this one to call us, but do not let it connect to the internet in any way. I have the Wi-Fi and Bluetooth turned off. Keep it that way."

"Jojo," Chelle interrupted and she put her hand gently on his wrist. "I'll get you set up in a private side room. Let's hope he's been too busy to access your accounts. I guess you'll have to do this the old-fashioned way on a landline. And we know that if your family stays off their electronics, they are safe."

Jojo looked over the new phone Jeff had given him. "Can you send me the pictures of the car the guy was driving? I want to send it to Tamara to see if she recognizes it."

"Good idea, it was a red minivan."

After hours of time locking down his bank accounts and charge cards, he left the FBI office in Washington and headed back to Reidsville more determined than ever to find the person threatening his family. He had an idea, it was a long shot, but he had hope.

Chapter 16

Reidsville, North Carolina:

Wade was busy at his latest hack. This time it was a doctor, a doctor of science. Getting access to the good doctor's computer wasn't a problem. Whoever had set up the computer security for the laboratory was good. Good being average at best. Wade didn't consider this latest hack as an accomplishment. He sat back and enjoyed the fruits of his labor.

He was watching Dr. L.H. Langston working in his lab using the doctor's own laptop's camera. He turned on the speaker. Because the doctor was working alone, the only sounds he heard were of glass beakers being mixed and cabinet drawers being opened and closed.

Wade already knew that Dr. Langston was one of the leading experts in Cryogenics. However, that was not why Dr. Langston's lab was on the outskirts of Detroit. Wade understood the doctor's true passion. Wade knew that the doctor was in Detroit to be near to the Cryonics institute.

Dr. Langston was making notes the old-fashioned way, with a paper notebook and a pencil. Wade recognized the equipment that had the doctor's attention, it was a D-Wave refrigerator, capable of producing temperatures as cold as minus-450 degrees Fahrenheit. At that temperature, even helium turned into a liquid.

Cryonics was not to be confused with cryogenics, though it often was. The Cryonics Institute was in the business of freezing entire bodies. Wade didn't know much about Cryonics, only that the freezing process itself probably killed all the cells in the body. The frozen person's hope was somebody in the future would invent a way to undo that damage and a way to cure them of whatever disease killed them in the first place.

Cryogenics was what Dr. Langston had his doctorate in. It was the study of how supercooled materials behaved. Most often the material involved were gasses such as helium, nitrogen, oxygen and even mixed gases like air. Because at temperatures below −180 °C (93 K; −292 °F), these gases become liquid.

Alan D Schmitz
DIGITAL SECRETS

Wade was slouched back on his couch drinking a beer and watching the doctor work. His stocking feet were up on a table, and he watched his laptop. He watched the professor doing his work like others would watch football. When he saw the doctor take a live frog and inject it with something. Wade sat up and watched the computer screen intently.

The professor took a probe to the frog and tested the elasticity of the frog's muscles and skin. He placed the now limp or dead frog--Wade didn't know which--but the frog was placed on a plate and placed carefully into a smaller side box that look something like a microwave. Wade's assumption was that it was exactly the opposite. His guess was that it was a mini freezer.

The doctor busied himself turning dials, adjusting electronic digital displays, and when he was finished, he paused for a moment before he pressed an electronic on-off switch. Wade heard a small hissing sound and the glass viewing panel of the side box instantly fogged up. Ten minutes later the doctor took out the plate and using a fine probe he again pushed on and pulled on the skin and muscles of the frog. The muscles were still pliable.

The doctor made some quick notes and seemed pleased. He took a point and shoot thermometer and aimed it at the main mass of the frog. Wade could see its electronic read-out say minus-fifty.

The doctor excitedly made more notes. Wade didn't understand. The frog was obviously very, very cold. Yet it wasn't a frozen mass. Carefully the doctor took a small eyedropper and held it over the frog.

A drop of something fell from the dropper. In an instant, the frog was frosty white. Wade watched the professor use the same tool as before to poke and pull at the frog. Only this time it was clear the frog was frozen solid. It was one solid mass of ice. The freezing process had happened nearly instantly.

"Pretty impressive, doctor. You froze something but kept it from crystalizing. I hope you kept good notes."

Wade slugged down the last of his beer as Dr. Langston's face grew big on Wade's computer. The doctor looked down at his notes and typed them into his computer. Wade watched the doctor's eyes travel the page in front of him. With a couple of keystrokes, he had a mirror of the program on his computer and could watch what the doctor was typing.

Wade continued to type on his own computer as he spoke to the doctor, though unheard by him. "Pretty impressive, doctor. I will make sure your work is not lost after your death. In fact, Doctor Langston, I might go into Cryogenics myself. With my smarts and your notes to guide me, I could become one of the greats in the field in no time."

Wade copied all the doctor's notes and files onto his own computer. He even found the design and use directions for the D-Wave refrigerator.

****

Jojo was bobbing up and down slightly on a small eighteen-foot fishing boat. He was pulling on the second of his diving fins. Strapped on his back was a single air tank. He looked at the skipper of the small craft as he took a few breaths through the regulator to test it.

Lucious cut the engine to an idle. "Not much going on this early; the lake looks calm. According to a couple of the sailboat racers I tracked down, this is close to the spot they saw the drone crash. It should be accurate, because the race buoys are always set up in the same places."

"Good job, Lucious old buddy." Jojo looked out over the 750-acre reservoir lake. The lake wasn't deep, which was the good news. The other good news was, as a relatively shallow lake he didn't expect the water to be too cold, even though it was the middle of September. Certainly nothing his body couldn't handle. The bad news was, as a shallow lake, visibility through the water wouldn't be optimal. The sun had been up an hour; sunlight and the calm waters of the early morning were his best hope.

"Once in the water, I might not be able to see much. Drop the anchor, I'll use a jonline attached to it to keep me close so I don't drift off."

"Do you actually believe you have a good chance of locating a small drone that crashed over a month ago?"

"A good chance? No. But if it came down as hard as they say, it would have broken apart and the heavier pieces, including the main body that held the memory card, may not have drifted far. That's my hope at least."

It had been a while since the last time Jojo used scuba equipment. The hours of scuba training while a Green Beret made the exercise seem normal to him. As he was adjusting his buoyancy belt, he kidded, "You sure this equipment still works?"

"As the only official underwater salvage guy in Reidsville, I can assure you it worked last week."

Jojo adjusted the glass diving mask over his nose and eyes. He flipped himself over the edge of the boat. Under the water Jojo did a quick check of his equipment. He found the anchor line and snapped his jonline onto it. The lake only had an average depth of six feet. The area he was searching in was just a bit deeper and he looked at that as an advantage. The deeper it was, the less disturbed the water, was his hope.

It didn't take him long to reach the weedy bottom. He guessed he could see about ten feet. Using markers on his jonline, he would form an ever-expanding search pattern. A half hour later he found what he had been looking for. The blue and white wreckage of the small drone was caught in some weeds. The drone had hit the water hard enough to have fragmented.

He examined the main body; it was somewhat intact. He could see the memory card, it was exposed and bent.

Washington D.C.:

Chelle was in her office peering over photos lifted from grainy security videos. The residential security cameras weren't meant for street surveillance. The videos had only accidently captured traffic passing by the homes. The movement of the vehicle combined with the low-resolution cameras had made it impossible from stop footage to read the license plate.

With her team's help, she now had a readable plate number. At least it was mostly readable. Chelle was making a list of possible letters and numbers it might be reading. She could only be sure at times of what letters or numbers they weren't. Once she compiled the list, she would run it against the full database of license numbers.

What they had been able to give a positive identification to, was the make and model of the minivan. It would only be a small chore to use the process of elimination to match up a plate number with a red minivan. Then, she would have the owner's name. For the first time she felt encouraged that they were closing in on the killer.

****

Steven was sitting in his reclining office chair. He had it turned away from his desk as he gazed out the window toward the puffy clouds intermittently floating past the background of blue sky.

There was a light knock on his private side door.

"Yes!" he said loud enough for anyone on the other side of the door to hear.

Shannon entered with a handful of papers.

"Meditating?" she asked.

"Sort of. On the other hand, it seems hard to focus on anything."

Shannon sat down on one of the guest chairs not waiting to or expecting an invitation to stay.

"Being accused of being some sort of spy can sort of ruin your day." Shannon offered an excuse for his melancholy.

"Or week, month, or life. I get it that the intelligence community doesn't want me interfering in their business. But that even some of my own party would believe I am doing it as a spy is truly disappointing."

"Your formal request for a gathering of the 'Gang of Eight' has been out for a week now. Have you heard anything because I haven't?"

"Nope not a word. I think now that the spy bell has been rung, it can't be unrung. The ploy worked. Nobody knows what to do if a U.S. Senator is a spy. Especially if that senator is one of the 'Gang of Eight'."

"Can the President help?"

"That's what I've been thinking about. He could. The executive branch can call the meeting. But would he want to? It's possible that the President knows exactly what is going on. He may very well like the pickle I'm in."

Steven stared at another puffy cloud going across the sky.

"I guess I will never know unless I try. The President owes me a favor or two. I think it's time for me to call in my markers. But I need to do it in person. I need to see his face when we talk. That'll be the hard part, him making time to see me."

"And if he refuses to meet with you?"

"Based on past history, the President knows I am not a traitor. Anything but. He knows the narrative is false. So, if he flat-out refuses to meet with me, that tells me he's OK with the narrative because he's vested in whatever is going on."

Their discussion was interrupted by Steven's cell phone ringing. Steven assumed it was Chelle, but when he looked at the screen, he couldn't hide the shock on his face from Shannon. The look on her face told him she had witnessed his look of shock.

Shannon stood to let the senator take the call in private, whoever it was. Steven motioned for her to stay.

He answered, "Yes, Mr. President. How can I help you today?"

"Meet me tomorrow, same time and place as last time, leave any and all electronics behind. You may be followed, be careful."

The phone clicked off. "Damn!" Was all he could muster.

"Can you share?" Shannon asked.

"Nothing to share, Shannon. In fact, I never got that call. You understand?"

"What call?"

"I want you to go back to Peabody the fastest way possible. Stay with your dad and tell him why, but nobody else."

"Yes, Senator. Do you think I might be in danger?"

"This is getting more serious, real fast. As my personal assistant, somebody might want you to tell them what I know. Shannon, it's important, trust me. You can't tell anybody but your dad what just happened. As my lawyer, your father might need to know."

Shannon nodded. "You know I trust you. And with what I've seen and heard around Washington, I don't trust many others. You can count on me."

"I'm sure I can. I'll call you or Teddy as soon as I can decipher what is going on."

Shannon stood and walked out. Steven, alone in his thoughts, wasn't sure how he was going to survive the next twenty-four hours knowing that the President of the United States wanted a clandestine meeting with him.

Chelle was out of town on FBI business. She had said that she might know who the killer was and was on his trail. That solved one problem for now, it kept her away from Washington D.C. for at least another day. He had learned that keeping secrets from Chelle usually didn't work out well for her or him. But until he talked with the President, he had to trust his instincts that the less she knew, the better for her.

Las Vegas, Nevada:

Chelle looked at her watch. The first hour had been pleasantly cool. But now the morning sun was already burning brightly and rapidly heating up the Nevada air. It was seven a.m. and she had been staking out a house in a suburb of Las Vegas for the last hour-and-a-half.

The house looked medium-sized, at least for the subdivision it was in. All one level, with a colored gravel yard with no grass, it did have an abundance of cacti growing about it. A room she guessed was a bedroom had lit up about an hour ago. When that light went out, others came on. It looked to her like somebody was getting ready for work. From a blurry photo that was lifted off a low-definition video from a security camera, they had guessed at what the license plate had said.

Running the plate did produce an address and a vehicle type, make, and color. The licensing clearly stated that it belonged to a red minivan the same color as the one in the photo. If the information was correct, the vehicle should be just behind the white closed garage door.

Because they had no definitive proof of anything, even if they had the right license plate number, a search warrant was off the table. Chelle waited patiently, she was sure she would have her answer soon. Another fifteen minutes had passed, she sat up. The wide two car garage door opened. The white back-up lights of a small blue Buick lit up. The DMV information she had said it was a Mr. James McConally who owned an eight-year-old blue Buick in addition to the red minivan. The paint was faded; the car had been aged by the Nevada sun.

"Gotcha," Chelle said.

Next to the Buick was a red minivan. She used a pair of binoculars to read the license plate of the minivan and it checked. Even though the license number had been an educated guess, the odds that the red minivan they had seen on the video from Reidsville and this one wasn't the same, was marginal.

Still, Chelle needed to learn more about Mr. McConally before arresting him for murder. The strange thing was there was unusually little information about Mr. James McConally inside the system. He apparently was squeaky clean. It was just that nobody was that perfect. With a press of a button, her blue VW Jetta started up. After a few snaking turns inside the subdivision, they both turned onto a wide boulevard, and onto the freeway.

If Mr. McConally was aware he was being tailed, he certainly didn't show it in his driving. Keeping up with him was not at all difficult. Chelle picked up her phone and gave it a command to call back to her office in D.C.

"Hi Mike, it looks like we guessed right. I saw the red minivan with the same plate number in his garage. He's driving a blue Buick right now; its license plate also checks. I would bet a thousand dollars that this is our guy."

Chelle listened to the phone for a while, after a minute she said, "I agree, but first I want to see where he's going."

Chelle was still on the phone when she noticed the Buick signaling for a turn. "No, I promise you, I won't approach him alone. If and when it comes time for an arrest, I'll bring in the local police. He's turning onto the freeway, gotta go. I promise I'll stay in touch."

They turned onto I-15 going north. Soon they would be right in the heart of the main strip of high-end hotels.

Chelle talked to herself as both cars turned off northbound interstate fifteen turning east down Flamingo Road. "It's certainly strange that your employment records are missing. I assume you are doing something to support your family. Care to show me what it is?"

There was a strange sense of déjà vu for Chelle, because she and Steven had driven these same streets just a month ago. If the suspect was onto Chelle following him, he still didn't show it. His driving was neither erratic nor defensive in any way.

Chelle nearly missed the turn when the driver she assumed was James McConally turned sharply left into the south side of Caesars Palace. It wasn't the main entrance, and if McConally hadn't turned into it she would have driven by without so much as a glance.

The seconds she lost waiting for cross traffic to clear was enough for McConally to drive behind a decorative wall and disappear from her view. She pulled her car into a small parking area and saw the old Buick go past a gate of some sort. Chelle proceeded to follow him.

The gate had closed behind McConally's car as he turned another corner and disappeared. Chelle examined the gate and saw no call button. There was some sort of scanner, so she assumed it was for employee parking.

"At least I know where you work now. It's time to do a little digging into your life, Mister McConally."

DIGITAL SECRETS

Washington D.C.:

Steven paid the taxi driver stepped out into hot and humid air that felt too heavy to breath. The hot humid air was unusual for September in D.C. It was just past one in the afternoon and luckily for him, the entrance into the Eisenhower Executive Office wasn't far. It wouldn't take long on a day like this to develop a sweat, and meeting the President of the United States dripping wet with sweat wasn't proper etiquette, he was sure. He took off his grey, pin-striped suit coat and loosened the blue tie that had been snug inside the collar of his white shirt.

The President had said, "same time, place as last time, leave any and all electronics behind. You may be followed, be careful." Ever since Vegas, Steven had learned his lesson on the dangers of being tracked by electronics. His phone was left back on his desk. Though he also knew, if someone was determined enough, he could be found. There was no way he could hide from all the cameras that had undoubtedly captured his face between his office and here.

The President had picked the huge Eisenhower building for a reason. It was built on land originally used for the White House stables. Hence, it wasn't far from the office and residence of the presidents of the United States.

Steven knew from his hobby of Washington lore that the Eisenhower Executive Office had over ten acres of office space, enough area that even the President could find an unused corner to sneak into. Also, it was a fact that there was a vast network of tunnels around the White House and Capitol building, many secret and unpublished. The tunnel connecting the White House to the Eisenhower Building was not well known, though certainly not a secret to anyone who searched it out.

Apparently, the President had learned he could somehow navigate to it undetected because this was not the first clandestine meeting the president and he had there. After a half-block walk, cool air of the air-conditioned building greeted him. The problem for Steven now was remembering which of the identical doors and two miles of hallways he had traveled before.

The last time he had been guided to the President by a Secret Service agent. He didn't see anyone to greet him, so he took his best guess and walked confidently on pretending he belonged and knew exactly where he was going.

He decided to carry his coat a bit longer to let his body cool down a bit. Before he knew it, he came to an intersection of hallways and realized that the particular office he had been taken to last time did not have a number on its door. All of the doors he had past so far were all lettered and numbered. The maze of hallways had him confused. He paused at the intersection searching his mind for a clue as to which way he needed to turn.

"Senator."

He heard a woman's voice say softly.

"Turn right. He's waiting."

A slight woman in a dark pant suit with a white blouse stepped out of the shadows from behind a support.

Steven took the few steps towards her as he slipped on his coat and straightened his tie.

"Please follow me."

In silence he followed his guide down one hallway and up another and into an elevator. The doors closed and with a key she locked and stopped the elevator and said, "Excuse me, Senator but I need to search you."

"I left my phone at the office, I only have my wallet, some keys, and a hanky and comb in my pockets"

"Please remove them and raise your hands."

He knew better than to argue, he reached into his pockets and removed the items, he even slid his pockets inside out so she could see they were empty.

Steven raised his hands slightly.

She searched his wallet and keys, satisfied they were what he claimed. She checked his wrists.

"I left my watch at the office too."

Satisfied he wasn't wearing a smart watch, unabashedly she searched inside his suitcoat and patted down his chest and down his legs.

"You're being thorough. I didn't have to go through this the last time I met the President."

Unapologetically she tuned the key and the elevator started back up. When the doors opened, she stepped out and said, "Please follow me. He just got here and doesn't have much time."

Down another hall they turned, and the woman Steven guessed to be physically toned and in her late thirties to early forties opened a door and held it open for Steven to enter first. She followed, closed the door behind her. Inside, the room was empty, except for the male Secret Service agent, dressed in the male equivalent black suit and tie. The male agent rapped on another door lightly.

"Come in."

The male agent standing guard opened the door slightly and said, "Senator Westcott is here sir, should I let him in now?"

"Yea Mitch, please show the Senator in. And then I must ask you and Samantha to wait outside the outer room. The second Senator Westcott leaves, we leave. I must not be gone long."

"Yes sir."

Mitch looked at the Senator and said, "He will see you now."

Mitch left the office door open and the two agents went out into the hallway closing the main door behind them.

"Steven, come in, come in." The President, who was seated, got up and shook Steven's hand warmly.

"Mr. President, it is nice to see you again."

"We don't have much time so let's get to the chase. The intelligence community is up to something and you're on to it. What is it?"

"Sir?"

"I know scared rabbits when I see them. You know something you're not supposed to. I'm not supposed to. I knew it. I knew something was up."

"Who sir, who are the scared rabbits?"

The President was pacing, he wasn't the usually calm, calculating man Steven knew.

"All of them, all of them in the Justice Department, and the military brass. They are making, building, a case against you.

They are intent on proving you a traitor or spy or something. I have sources they don't know about, at least not yet. I can't help you if you don't share what you know."

"I'm not a spy or traitor sir."

"Hell, I know that. I know what you did for your country, the risks you took with your life. And all for no personal benefit. I get it. But that won't help you. These guys are rough players. If they start a grand jury investigation against you, I won't be able to stop it."

"A grand jury? For what?"

"You know the game. Doesn't matter for what. They'll think of something, and while they have the full resources of the federal government to use against you, you will go broke defending yourself. I call it financial torture. And they will keep it up until you agree to something criminal. Probably drag that cute FBI agent you're dating into it. Maybe even your ex-wife. Who knows who? And all will need lawyers. It'll cost everybody a bundle of money and a bundle of stress. And don't forget, they have the press on their side. They can't possibly lose a thing, and you will lose everything, including your reputations. And that's a best case. They'll keep throwing shit at the wall until something sticks. If they do find or create something that sticks, you're off to jail."

Steven didn't doubt the President, but that didn't mean he wasn't in on the game. He had poked the bear. The bear was certainly awake, and apparently coming after him. The one thing Steven did know was that he needed an ally, a powerful one.

"I don't know much Mr. President. In fact, I was bluffing during the hearing."

"Bullshit! I know you Steven, you don't bluff. You have the Director of the National Security Agency nervous, and nothing makes him nervous."

Steven added, "James Mitchell sat in on the closed-door hearing, I considered that strange."

The President took his right hand and pushed up the sleeves of his left to reveal his watch. He looked at his watch. "I'm running out of time."

Keeping his watch exposed he tapped it and asked, "By the way, do you know when I got this watch?"

Steven was surprised at the odd question. "No sir!"

"From my wife, thirty-years ago. Look at it, not even a battery, it winds itself with my wrist movement. Or, of course, I can wind it the old-fashioned way."

"That's sounds convenient sir. It certainly looks like a lovely watch."

"Relax, I haven't gone batty. The point is, it's not electronic, they can't use it to follow me. I know they are spying on people; I just don't know how. You do."

"Mind if I sit, sir?"

"Sorry, of course not. I need to sit for a while too. Dammit, Steven! Help me, help you."

The President pulled a wooden, bare-bone chair across from Steven and sat down. He motioned to Steven to take the only remaining chair in the room.

Steven took it and slid it across from the President. He sat down and looked President Julius Walker in the eye. "I don't know who to trust?"

"I'm sure you don't. Take it from me, don't trust anybody in Washington. But you need my help. So even if you don't trust me, I don't see anyone else with their hand out."

"I don't know much, sir. Apparently, there is a secret operation called the Lake Lerna Project."

"I know, I read it in the report of your meeting. They tried to redact it from me. Can you imagine that? I had to sue my own government to let me see what it said. What is it?" The President demanded.

"That's just it, I don't know."

"You do know."

"I was bluffing sir. I don't know. A lot of money has been channeled into it. I believe it is being master-run by the NSA. Every one of the seventeen intelligence agencies contributed to it, maybe others."

"You must have an idea or two?"

Steven went all in, "I think it's some sort of supercomputer. Possibly a quantum computer. Somehow it is collecting all information about everybody. I mean everything, who their friends are, where they eat, what they eat, where they shop, what they buy, how and when they travel, even down to exactly where they are at any given time of the day or night."

"How do you know this?"

"I don't for sure. But I saw a report on me, exceptionally detailed, I mean meticulous. And it had to have been compiled hastily."

"By whom?" the President asked.

"I don't know. It was given to me in secret. But I was told, and I quote, 'They are the cloud'."

"The cloud? You mean as in cloud computing?"

"I imagine yes, cloud storage, basically anything that goes over the internet."

"As in everything." The President stood up and dried his sweaty palms on the front of his pants. "Oh shit! And this is happening on my watch."

"I have no proof. That's what the closed-door hearing was all about. But everybody declined to know or remember anything."

"You poked the hornets' nest, and they aren't happy."

"That's one way of saying it. Probably not the best of plans."

The president looked at his watch again. "I have to go; I've been here too long already. What next?"

Steven shrugged his shoulders. "I was thinking maybe you should call a meeting of the Gang of Eight."

"That would paint them into a corner you don't want them in right now. Remember, they are trying to paint you as a traitor. Some on the other side would be more than willing to help them. Hell, as far as they are concerned, anyone not agreeing with them is a traitor. If you had proof that they are doing something highly suspicious and possibly illegal then and only then would we attempt it, and only after we have all our own bases covered."

"What are we to do, Mr. President?"

"Don't know, how do you settle down a bunch of angry hornets?"

"Walk away?" Steven asked.

The President looked Steven in the eye, "Sometimes retreat is a good strategy. Samantha will escort you out of here. If I'm asked, this meeting never happened, and you can't prove it did."

The President and the male agent were ready to go when the President turned once more toward Steven and said, "Might be too late to retreat. And I'm sorry, I don't know how I can help you on this one. I will promise you this, I will try to find a way."

The President turned away and disappeared around a corner. Samantha pointed down another hall and led Steven out the way they had come.

Las Vegas, Nevada:

Chelle drove around the maze that was Caesars Palace and found the parking structure. She parked and followed the signs that pointed to the main lobby and check in desk. Turning from the elevator bank from the parking structure she stepped into the huge opulent oval main lobby. Julius Caesar himself couldn't have built a more lavish memorial to himself.

Marble columns rose from the marble floor, all of which supported painted domes of gold, suspended from the majestic ceiling were huge chandeliers. Chelle stopped for a moment to admire the large fountain that graced the center of the oval.

From her college studies of fine art, she immediately recognized the twice life-sized marble sculpture of the Three Graces. If she remembered correctly, the sculpture was of the mythological three Charites. The three women were holding vases that were spilling water into the fountain below them. Each was a daughter of Zeus, who were said to represent youth/beauty, mirth, and elegance. What better way to welcome visitors to a fun time at Caesars Palace. The blended noise of hundreds of slot machines rang in the background, enticing the visitors to join in the fun, reminded her she wasn't in an art museum.

Duty called and she proceeded to find the right person in the huge hotel that could possibly help her. Looking at her watch she roughly calculated that if she was directed to the right person within a half hour, she would be doing pretty good. Her first stop was to wait in line to attract the attention of the next check-in host. Within minutes she was being helped and she flashed her FBI badge. That led to another floor manager, who directed her to security.

It seemed to her that at each stop along the stations, each higher-up couldn't pass her along to the next person fast enough. Chelle looked at her watch again. Forty-five minutes had passed as she waited for yet another step in the ladder to appear.

A full hour had passed until she was ushered inside a private office. When she saw the title on the frosted glass door, 'Director of Personnel', she had a bit of hope that this would be her last stop.

Chelle walked in with a wide disarming smile. A middle-aged woman, stately looking, dressed in a conservative powder blue dress smiled back. She was behind her desk and stood as she looked at the business card that at this point had been passed on by numerous people. All of whom now knew an FBI agent was looking for somebody who worked at the casino.

"Hi, welcome to Caesar's Palace, Agent Saltarie, I am the Director of Personnel, Emma Jones."

Chelle reached out to shake the welcoming hand.

"I'm sorry for interrupting you. I am on official business, and I need your help."

"May I see your credentials please? I'm sure you have shown them a dozen times by now but..."

"I understand." Chelle pulled out her badge and I.D. once again.

Emma scrutinized it carefully. "We can't be too careful; you would be surprised at what various characters try to pull around here."

"I'm sure I would."

Emma handed the badge and I.D. back. "What can I help you with."

"I followed one of your employees here. I need to speak with him. Could you help me do that?"

"You did say official business?"

"Yes, I did."

"And do you have some sort of authorization, or warrant?"

"I do not; this is a preliminary investigation. However, it is important. I guess I could have the local police accompany me if that would make you more comfortable."

Emma smiled, "Let's first see what it is you need. Maybe I can help you without causing a fuss."

"I need to know where I could find a Mr. James McConally."

"And you are sure he works here?"

"I saw him go through the security gate. He must have an employee I.D. badge of some sort, but besides his name, that is all I know."

"Let me check our database. Please sit and make yourself comfortable. Not knowing what department to look in, this might take me some time."

"I understand, it is important, I don't mind waiting."

"Would you like a cup of coffee while you wait?"

"Thank you for the offer, but not right now."

"Not at all, as I said, this may take a while."

Emma busied herself behind her computer. Chelle took her phone and skimmed through a list of emails for anything that might need her immediate attention.

It didn't take long for her to notice an email from the new address they had set Jojo up with. The encrypted email was from the FBI-supplied phone. Chelle opened it.

"Chelle, I have the memory card from the drone. I don't want to take the chance of ruining whatever is on it. It was underwater for weeks. I'm afraid of just popping it into a computer to see if it still works, any advice is appreciated."

Chelle looked up at Emma who was studying her computer and interrupted softly, "Emma, I need to step out into the hall to make a private call, is that OK?"

"Yes please, be my guest. There is a coffee maker and a small break room down the hall a bit. Feel free to use it if you want."

"Thanks, I might take you up on that. This won't take me long."

"I hope to have found your elusive employee by then. So far, no luck."

Chelle stepped into the hall and soon found privacy. "Jojo, I just got your email, you have the drone memory stick?"

Chelle listened as Jojo explained how he had found it. she said, "We must assume that the information on it is of critical importance. It needs to be handled with care. I hate to ask you to do this, but we can't trust the mail and time is of the essence. Could you drive it personally to FBI headquarters?"

"I was hoping you would say that, because I'm not letting this thing out of my sight. I want to get my family back home and to do that we need to catch this guy pronto."

"It might be sooner than you think. I'm in Las Vegas tracking the guy we think was spying on your family. I need to check on a few more things before I bring him in. If the drone did capture the murder in the park, it might be the evidence we need to hold him."

"I'm on my way."

Chelle stepped back into the office after giving a light knock on the door.

"Agent Saltarie, you are back just in time. But I have some bad news for you. Nobody with that name works for us here at Caesars Palace, Las Vegas. We have many other properties, are you sure he works here?"

"I saw him go through the employee gate with his car."

"Exactly which gate, there are several."

The entrance off Flamingo Rd. The South entrance. He turned and went down a ramp going west.

"I'm afraid that could be anyone. I mean that entrance is used for construction of our new aqua show theater. The construction manager's office might be able to help you. I'm so sorry you wasted your time here."

"Emma, you have been of great help. I'm sorry I wasted your time. I just assumed he would be one of your employees."

"I can understand the confusion. Let me find out who the construction managing company is. It's such a big project and so exciting, I mean the new show, we hope to be open in a few more months."

Emma whispered as if someone else could hear her, "I just came from a management meeting, they just told us the theme for the show. It'll have monsters, and fire, and Hercules."

Chelle was intrigued by the inside information, eager to share it with Steven when she got back home. "Hercules? In a water show?"

"We are Caesars Palace, after all, so we bring in a Roman god to wrestle and kill the Hydra guarding the way to the underworld, one of Hercules' twelve labors. The huge magical lake we created for the event is called Lake Lerna, also from Greek and Roman mythology. I've been told the lake is a technical marvel. I can't wait to see it."

Chelle's eyes widened, "Did you say the lake is to be called Lake Lerna?"

"Yes, all the action happens in, on top of, around and over the Lake. It will be spectacular. I'm going to make a few calls and get you that name and a contact person."

Chapter 17

Detroit, Michigan:

Dr. L.H. Langston was busy in his laboratory as usual. In fact, he was a bit busier than usual. Dr. Langston didn't know why his laboratory equipment was behaving so erratically. No sooner did he troubleshoot one piece of equipment than another would indicate an error.

Wade had been enjoying playing his small pranks on the good doctor this week. But the time had run out for Dr. Langston. Today he would die.

Wade picked up his phone he turned on the voice changing software. The phone rang a few times before the Detective answered. "Hello Detective. You know I can't talk long. I'll get right to the point. Dr. Langston will be my next victim. Let me be a bit more precise, a Dr. L.H. Langston.

"I'm going to give you four hours to find him. I think that most generous, especially since you have the FBI helping you. By the way, I hope I didn't scare your beautiful family too bad the other day. I just wanted to wake you up a bit. I hope you are having fun? I know I am."

Wade clicked his phone off. And even though he used a VPN (Virtual Private Network) and was sure his call was untraceable, he powered down the burner phone and took out its battery.

Somewhere between Reidsville and Washington D.C.:

Jojo walked out of the gas station. He needed gas and a bathroom stop. In hand he had a fresh cup of coffee and a microwave-heated breakfast sandwich, even though it was past noon.

Alan D Schmitz
DIGITAL SECRETS

He heard his former personal phone ring. It was in his left pocket, the FBI-issued phone in his right. It had been a nuisance to carry two phones with him everywhere, but he couldn't afford to miss a call from the killer, if and when he decided to call.

He felt his left pocket vibrate. His hands were full, but he couldn't miss the call. Jojo knew he had to answer, and he needed both hands. "Damn it!" He swore, as he dropped his sandwich and his coffee to the asphalt. Reaching into his left pocket, he grabbed the phone and looked at the unregistered caller message. With his other hand he took his FBI issued phone out his right pocket and pressed the record button. Only then did he press the speaker button on his old phone.

He listened and recorded the message.

Before he could say a word, with a click, the caller was gone.

"Captain, this is Detective Jones. He called again. We need to look for a Dr. L.H. Langston. We have four hours."

"Do I trust him, hell no! This is some sort of game to him. But I do think he will somewhat follow his own rules. Bottom line, yes, I think we have four hours,".

After a pause, Jojo agreed with his captain. "I know, could be anywhere in the country, maybe the world. However, he started his little game in Reidsville; I think he is from there. That still makes it our problem. I'm on the way to Washington D.C. I have a contact at the FBI I need to talk to." Jojo listened for a moment.

"Yes, Washington, sir. I can't explain why. This phone, your phone, could be compromised. I must go. Good luck."

Jojo looked at the ground at his now-empty coffee cup. A dog had already found his dropped sandwich and was taking its stolen treasure to the side of the station.

Walking to his car, he leaned up against it and made a call to the FBI.

"Mike, this is Detective Jones out of Reidsville. I'm fine, but I just got a call from the killer. I did like you told me. if it worked, I have the conversation recorded. Not much of a conversation really, just him talking. I'll email it to you, but get your guys looking for a doctor. L.H. Langston. No, I don't know what L.H.

stands for or what kind of doctor. All I know is we have four hours to find him, warn him, and somehow try to save his life. Yes, I'm still on my way, probably two hours out. See you soon."

Las Vegas, Nevada:

After a bit more time wasted, Chelle finally located the construction manager's office. Getting this far had taken all her talents in cajoling, sweet talking, and sometimes a veiled threat.

Her time waiting told her that the reception she would get in the back lot of Caesars Palace was not going to be the same friendly reception she had received inside. There were many, many cars; she didn't spot McConally's. His car could be anywhere over the huge work site. Or it was entirely possible that he wasn't even here any longer.

A big man in dirty blue jeans and dusty construction boots came out of a job trailer that was held off the ground by huge concrete blocks. He walked down worn and dirty wooden steps to greet her.

She handed him her card. He glanced at it. Reading her name off the card, "Detective Saltarie, I'm damn busy. What's this about?"

Chelle heard a workman yell loudly, "Hey, Klay, where do you want me to put the back-up generator?"

The big man replied, "Up your ass, idiot. I said I wanted it next to the main water supply station. Next time, f'n listen."

The forklift truck's engine roared, and the driver gave Klay the finger and he drove off.

"Geez, you think it was rocket science."

"Klay, I'm with the FBI."

Klay held up the card, "I can f'n read. Tell me something I don't know."

"I'm on official FBI business, it's very important for me to find a Mr. James McConally. he drives a blue Buick."

"Oh sure, James, blue Buick, sure, I'll call him right over." Klay laughed. "Look lady, I don't know any James, or Jim McConally. Hell, I don't know most of these guys' names. We need help, the union hall sends bodies over. As long as they do their jobs, I don't want to know their names."

Klay's phone rang. He answered, "What? No, it's delayed? No, I don't know why. I don't know, work around it. Well, figure it out."

Klay hung up his phone and picked up the radio slung against his belt.

"Broomsdale, do you copy?"

Chelle heard a few loud squelches on the radio and a reply.

"Hey Klay, what do you need?"

"I just found out the compressor is delayed. Go find something else for the electricians to do. If we're paying them, I don't want them playing cards on our dime."

"No problem, Klay, I have just the job."

"Look, lady...."

Chelle interrupted loudly, "Agent Saltarie, you call me lady one more time and I will throw you to the ground and cuff you for obstructing an investigation."

"Geez La.., I mean Agent, don't get your panties in a bundle. I don't know any James, what's his name."

"McConnally. I saw him drive his car onto this job site."

Klay's phone rang again. As Klay reached for it, Chelle held her hand on his forcefully and gave him a threatening look.

Klay left it ring.

"Agent, I am sorry, I don't know. He could be working right under our noses and I still wouldn't know."

"Who would?"

"What trade?"

"What?"

"What trade? Electrician, plumber, boilers workers union, Operating engineers?"

"You have heavy security. I had a hard time getting to you, and I'm FBI. Somebody must be keeping track of who comes and goes."

"You know, you bring up a good point. I can tell you it ain't me."

Klay's phone rang again. He almost reached for it and then looked at Chelle with pleading eyes.

"They want this f'n show to open in a couple of months. And it's my job to do that, not keep track of who wanders on and off the premises."

"What time is quitting time?"

"La.., I mean agent, we're working twenty-four, seven. Without knowing what your guy is doing here, I have no idea where to find him."

Chelle stared at Klay for a moment with daggers coming from her eyes, "I would like to thank you for your help. But I won't. Do you have a business card I can attach to my report?"

Klay hesitated, and said, "You look like a real sweetheart. I don't want no problem with the FBI, I got no beef with you guys. I'm just trying to do my job here. Can't you keep my name out of it?"

"I'm not your sweetheart and I will go to your supervisor if I have to."

"Yeah, yeah, I got a card. Why do you have to be such a hard-ass? Here it is."

Klay took out his wallet and handed over a beat-up business card.

Klay's radio blared once again.

Chelle turned and walked off. She could feel Klay staring at her backside and it made her even more angry.

Washington D.C.:

It was late afternoon by the time Jojo was admitted into the FBI building in Washington D.C.. Mike Turner was waiting for him by the elevator as he got off.

"Hi Detective Jones, I'm Mike Turner, welcome to Washington."

"Agent Turner, great to meet you in person." The two shook hands.

Jojo asked, "Any luck finding L.H. Langston?"

"Yes, as a matter of fact, twenty that are doctors."

"Twenty?"

"Big country. For now, we're only looking at US citizens. We are notifying them all, starting with anyone with a doctorate in computer sciences on the assumption these deaths are all IT related. I assume you have the memory card"

Jojo reached into his pocket and held up a wafer-thin card. "This is it. Might be garbage."

"Only one way to find out."

Stepping into the elevator, Mike said, "Let's stop off at the second floor. Jeff in the IT department has been waiting for it."

It didn't take long before they were walking through a department filled with banks of open cubicles with agents typing and examining computer screens in front of them, most with two or three screens going simultaneously.

Jojo saw Jeff coming towards them. "Detective Jones." Jeff stepped up and shook his hand.

"Hi, Agent Planter. Good to see you again."

"I forgot, you two have been already introduced."

Jojo pulled out a phone from his pocket. "Compliments of the FBI and Agent Planter. A secure phone for me to use until we get this all sorted out.

Jojo held up the memory stick. "Here's hoping that you can get some decent info off of this."

Jeff took the memory stick from Jojo and examined it. "These things hold up remarkably well. Even under water. It doesn't look too damaged. Follow me."

Jeff sat down at what to Jojo looked like a work bench. It was filled with small tools, soldering equipment, and electronics in various states of repair and in many cases, unrepair.

He watched nervously as Jeff took a dainty needle-nose pliers and applied it to the end of the memory card.

"I just need to straighten this insertion point out a bit."

Jeff delicately moved the end. After each small adjustment, he examined it under a desk mounted magnifying glass.

"That should do it," he announced with a degree of certainty.

"We should have our answer in a minute."

Jeff carefully slid the card into what he described as a universal card reader. Between working the mouse and keyboard, a video popped up on screen.

"Got it!" Jeff said excitedly

There was no doubt it was from the drone. There were several files all marked with consecutive numbers. They were watching the first of the files.

"That's where the kid lived. I was there talking with his parents. I went through his room. That is positively his parents' house from the air.

"Go to file eight, that's the last one. Has to be the one we want," Jojo suggested.

With a few clicks of the mouse, they were watching a high-definition view of a sailboat race from the air.

Jeff paused the video.

"What's the matter?" An anxious Jojo asked.

"I'm not taking any chances. I'm recording this on my machine, on the off chance we only get one shot at this."

Jojo patted his back slightly, "Good thinking."

With dire anticipation of seeing a murder take place, the three watched silently. The footage was remarkably clear.

"That is the reservoir lake. It's where I recovered the drone."

The video zoomed in on individual boats and zoomed out again focusing on different aspects of the race.

"The kid had talent," Jeff said softly.

When the video zoomed back out, it was plain that the videographer was giving his viewers a bird's eye view of the lake area as it turned slowly.

"The jogging path should be coming into view if it keeps turning. It's at the top of the ridge looking down at the lake.

"There, there!" Jojo said excitedly. "Oh my God!"

Jeff froze the video.

"It's her on the ground, top of the ridge. And look, there's somebody jogging away on the same path. It must be him. Can't you zoom in or something? I can't make out his face."

Jeff started up the video again. Unfortunately, the drone kept slowly turning past the jogging path until it was focusing on the boat race once again.

Jeff stopped the footage, turned around and looked at Detective Jones. "If you two have business, this might be a good time. I am going to get on this right away. I know it has priority. I promise you, detective, I will squeeze as much out of the footage as possible. But it will take time."

Jojo grabbed a nearby chair and sat down. He rubbed his tired eyes. "She was a mother of three small children. They will never know their mother. I went to her funeral. I saw her in the morgue, met her husband, saw her home.

"I, we, just watched her die all over again. Damn! Suddenly I feel so helpless." Jojo looked at the two agents and pleaded with his eyes as he said. "Help me catch this asshole."

Mike grabbed Detective Jones by the arm. "Come on, let's get a Coke or something. You look like shit."

"Yeah, I need a walk right now."

Jojo started feeling better after drinking a Coke in the break room down the hall.

"Anything new on the attempted murder of the guy in Vegas?" Jojo asked Mike.

"The doctors are keeping us posted. Last I heard, it was still touch and go, in intensive care and unresponsive."

"Any word from Carnegie Melon on the Professor's computer?"

"That we do. It didn't take long for them to confirm the email dump was cycled through the professor's office computer. It positively came from an outside source. We have sent computer forensic guys there to secure the equipment, take statements, etc..."

Jojo sat back against the break room countertop, "Which further confirms our guess that this guy is a computer nerd."

Mike laughed, "Careful what you say on this floor. We are surrounded by computer nerds. And this guy is seriously good. The Carnegie Melon people still can't believe they were hacked."

Jojo nodded. "No offense to your guys, you know what I mean."

"I do, and I agree, too many coincidences, has to be IT-related."

"Any other loose ends I should know about?" Jojo asked.

"Some. Let's go to my office."

Mike was still filling in Jojo about the search for anyone named L.H. Langston when his phone rang.

"OK, thanks." Mike hung up his phone.

To Jojo he said, "Jeff did his best. But all his technology stuff can't erase a baseball cap that conceals a face."

"You mean we got nothing?"

"Height, build, clothing. That's it."

"Shit!"

"Not much but more than we had before thanks to you. Because your email could be compromised, I'll give you the video on a mini-drive. Use it only on a computer not connected to the internet."

Jojo said, "Sounds like we are reverting back to the stone age."

Las Vegas, Nevada:

Chelle stationed her car across from James McConally's home. Her reasoning was that whatever he was up to, he would eventually come back to his home and family. At least that was her hope. She also realized that if he had caught wind that the FBI was looking for him, which at this point was a possibility, he might never come back home.

Her car was running and had been for the last hour. The constant blowing of the air conditioner was the only thing keeping her from baking in the afternoon Las Vegas sun, though the sun was beginning to set.

Chelle looked at her watch for the hundredth time. It was two hours past the four-hour deadline of finding and warning a particular Dr. L.H. Langston. One piece of good news: Agent

Fordham had told her that there were no Dr. L.H. Langstons in the Las Vegas area.

Chelle was eighty percent sure that James McConally was the killer. If he was here in Las Vegas and his next victim wasn't, she felt confident that a murder had been avoided. Still, she would feel much better with him in custody. Her plan was simple.

Ask a few questions, establish proof of identity. Stake out the house until the local police could assist her with an arrest on suspicion of murder.

Her phone rang. Chelle pressed the hands-free speaker system to answer. "Hi Mike, did you make an ID on the video yet?

Chelle felt the blood drain from her face when she heard what Mike had to tell her.

"Detroit? How?"

"This is all we've learned so far, a team is on the way. This Dr. L.H. Langston is a cryogenicist. His business is freezing the bodies of dead people. You know, rich people that think somebody, someday, will figure out a way to bring them back to life and cure them of whatever was killing them."

Mike continued, "I know this will sound crazy, but he froze to death. Some sort of equipment malfunction."

Chelle tried to understand, "What kind of an equipment malfunction could possibly freeze someone to death?"

"He works with super-cold water."

"That's called ice, Mike."

Mike laughed, "Yeah, that's what I thought, too. I was told, if done right, you can super cool water to minus fifty degrees Fahrenheit without it turning to ice."

"You're kidding."

"Apparently the doctor was next to a tank of this super-cold water when a safety valve burst. He was saturated with the water, and it turned him to ice instantly."

"Wrong place wrong time." Chelle mused.

"Precisely the wrong place and wrong time."

"I assume you are not buying into the accident thing."

"Not unless our killer is also a psychic."

"Does Jojo know yet?"

"You were my first call. We just learned of his death, even though Dr. Langston died hours ago. We were doing a follow up call to give him an all clear, because it was two hours after the four-hour window. A distraught assistant told us what happened. The local police sent to guard him were outside his office when it happened. They didn't call us because it was an accident, not a murder attempt."

"That means the death happened within the time frame given us to save him?"

"Almost to the minute. He's playing by his rules."

"What a stand-up kind of guy," Chelle said sarcastically.

Mike asked, "You want me to fill in Detective Jones? He's taking a rental back to Reidsville. He left his SUV here to see if we can find something of use in its computer."

"No, let me call him. Bye."

Chelle turned down the fan of the air conditioner. The sun was behind a mountain in the distance and no longer beating on her car.

Chelle tapped a button on her phone, "Hi Jojo, bad news. He somehow did it again. A doctor of science in Detroit, nothing to do with computers. It does sort of ruin our theory that only people in the IT field are his victims. This guy specialized in cryogenics."

"Freezing dead people?"

"Apparently there is a center in Detroit that does that."

"How did he get to him? You had police protecting every Doctor Langston in the country?"

"We did. The police were right outside his laboratory when he died due to an equipment malfunction. Their initial assessment is it was an industrial accident."

Over the car speakers she heard Jojo's voice boom, "Accident my ass! If he could take over a car and make it stop in the middle of a freeway, he can take over other equipment as well. How exactly did he die?"

Chelle saw a flash of headlights in her rearview mirror and watched it closely.

"Jojo, I'll fill you in later, I gotta go. James McConally just pulled up. I have a few simple questions for him."

"Chelle, be careful, I mean very careful. If he's our guy, he is dangerous as hell."

"I won't let him get anywhere near a computer keyboard. Besides, I don't think he's a match for my nine-millimeter."

The late fall sun was down when James drove past her car. Without so much as glancing at her, he pulled into his drive and into the garage. By that time Chelle was already out her car and approaching the still open garage door as James stepped out of his car.

Chelle greeted him. "James McConally?"

James turned and greeted Chelle, not particularly surprised by a person standing by his garage and knowing his name.

He asked her, "Can I help you with something?"

By this time Chelle had her one hand showing her badge; the other was prepared to draw her gun if needed.

"FBI? My security clearance has already been renewed for the year. I was specifically told. 'You are all cleared' by Agent Jones."

"Agent Jones? That's interesting." Among the FBI, the wording Agent Jones meant an assumed alias. God help the real Agent Jones's, of which she was sure there were many.

"I'm not here for your security clearance. But I do have a few questions for you if you don't mind?"

James looked at his watch, "I'm late already and a bit hungry. Can you make it quick?"

Chelle handed James a photo of Freddy Farly.

She asked, "Do you know this man?"

James took it and said, "Sure, it's Fat Freddy. Is that what this is about? I heard he took a bad fall. How's Freddy doing?"

He handed the photo back to Chelle.

"Can I ask how you know him?"

"No, you can't. And you should know that if they sent you here."

"I am here investigating Freddy's fall. It may not have been an accident. Unfortunately, he's still in a coma."

"Look, agent, I don't think we should be talking. You might get in trouble."

"I might get in trouble. Usually when the FBI is questioning someone about a possible murder, it's the other way around."

"You need to talk to your superiors. All I know is, with my security clearance, I can't talk to anybody about my work, my co-workers, employer, or most of anything else. If this is a trap of some sort, just fuck off!"

"Prove it!"

"I'll prove it all right."

Chelle tensed when he suddenly reached into his pocket. Her gun hand became instantly ready to draw.

"Relax, I'm just getting my wallet. You totally don't know, do you?"

"Know what?"

James opened his wallet and took out an identification card.

Chelle looked at it. It looked official, though not like anything she had ever seen before. It was more or less a universal get out of jail free card. This one didn't come from a game of Monopoly. She had heard of them, but this was the first time she had seen one.

James saw the look of surprise on her face, "There is a number you can call on the back. But basically, it says you can't ask me shit about anything without my attorneys present. And trust me, you don't want to mess with the agency's attorneys."

Chelle was stunned. Her prime murder suspect seemed to have some sort of immunity. She wasn't giving up that fast.

"I think I will try that number. You know, just for kicks. Don't move; we have more talking to do."

Chelle called the number. A male voice answered. She said. "My name is..."

She was abruptly interrupted, "We know who you are, Agent Saltarie. You are on thin ice. Go back to Washington ASAP. We got this."

Whoever was on the other end hung up.

Chelle couldn't contain her shock.

James said, "I told you so. I'm late for dinner. My family is waiting for me. Goodbye, agent."

Chelle took one last gamble. She asked,"What do you know about the Lake Lerna Project?"

This time her gamble paid off. James didn't have to say a word. The look of disbelief on his face was unmistakable. She could see that he knew about the Lake Lerna project; it was real, and he was part of it. Somehow it was all tied together.

"Fuck off!" James said angrily. He knew his facial expression had given him away.

Out of nowhere the quiet residential street became busy, Chelle heard cars coming to a stop all around them. Five cars surrounded them. Men and women all dressed in dark suits, shot out of the cars with guns drawn.

"Agent Saltarie, stand down," a booming voice said as he walked up displaying his own badge.

We will take it from here. James, you are coming with us. We have some talking to do."

"Shit, now look at what you've done. Shit!" he said again as an agent took his arm and led him to one of the identical black sedans.

The agent in charge turned to Chelle, "You are not to discuss what happened here with anyone. If you do, you will be arrested and charged with treason. Good night, agent."

Chelle was so stunned it took her a moment to consider what was happening. By the time she was ready to ask some of her own questions. All the agents were back in their cars and driving away. The whole thing must have taken less than a minute. If a neighbor wasn't watching the street at exactly that time, they wouldn't know a thing had happened. Chelle witnessed it and wasn't sure if she knew what happened.

Her phone ringing startled her back to reality. She looked at the caller ID. It was her partner, Mike.

"Mike, you won't believe what just happened here," Chelle said as she started walking towards her car. "What do you mean it's over?" Chelle didn't think anything else could shock her more, she was wrong. Into the phone she asked, "Just like that, the investigation is over? No, I don't know what the fuck is going on. I'll get a flight out first thing tomorrow."

Chelle hung up. Her head was spinning with the quick change of things. She looked up and down the street which was as peaceful as could be. She could even hear some kids splashing in a pool behind one of the houses.

Her partner Mike had been assured by higher ups that the serial killer was caught. They were to turn over all their files immediately. Case closed.

Chelle was standing at the end of the drive when she heard someone calling for Jim from the garage. It was a woman's voice, probably Mrs. McConally.

Chelle wanted to reach out, to tell her what had happened to her husband. Chelle turned towards the home for a moment then changed her mind and walked across the street to her car. The truth was, she didn't know what had happened and certainly couldn't calm the woman in any way. Guiltily she walked away.

Chapter 18

Reidsville, NC:

Chelle, Steven, Jojo, and Tamara were sharing a pitcher of sweetened ice tea on the Jones's patio. It was about seventy-five degrees, a bit warmer than an average day in October for North Carolina, but certainly not unusual.

Tamara was recounting the incident with the SUV. "I'm telling you, to this day I can't drive that car. And I don't trust any car anymore. Tamara sat her half-drunk glass of ice tea down on the glass tabletop, smiled mischievously at Jojo and sad, "Jojo, you know that 1965 GTO you have been talking about buying? I might be more open to it now. It has no electronics."

Jojo stood up and high-fived Steven, "Now you're talking, girl! All it has is a six-pack for a carburetor, four on the floor baby, and three hundred and sixty horses. All ready to go. The only electronics is an A.M. radio. And when I'm driving it, it will only play sixties music."

Chelle stood up and poured herself another glass of ice tea. She said, "I can imagine how scary it was for you and the girls, but the odds of somebody doing that to you again are astronomical.

"The FBI hot shots that took over the case claim they have a full confession from McConally."

"It all makes sense," Jojo said. "Apparently, he was some sort of high-level computer geek. He would have had the skill set to kill all those people, and after he was arrested, the calls from the killer stopped."

Chelle sat back down in the over padded deck chair. "I certainly don't like the way it was handled. I still don't know who the agent was that threatened me. It was my case; I mean our case. And just like that, a bunch of black sedans from the 'Men in Black' pull up and take my guy away."

Jojo nodded in agreement, "My chief wasn't impressed either. He was just happy they let him run an article in the paper stating that the FBI had caught the killer. What he didn't like was the press pushing him for more information, because he had nothing more. All he could tell them was that because the suspect was engaged in multi-state killing, his name was being withheld until all the charges were issued."

Chelle said, "Now that is total bullshit."

Steven was just sipping on his ice tea. He wasn't that fond of the sweetened version, but when in Rome. He stood and placed his glass down on the table. Walked to the rail and looked out past the porch at the houses up and down the street.

When he turned around, he said, "I still have a feeling this is all somehow connected to the 'Lake Lerna Project'. I received my own set of threats. I wouldn't doubt we are being spied on right now. I've been warned to drop my investigation. You've been warned to stop yours. Your suspect disappears right before your eyes. After that, an information black out. The only thing more we have learned is that Caesars Palace is building a 'Lake Lerna' water show, a construction project where Chelle saw her suspect go just before he was kidnapped by the FBI. That is too big a coincidence for me."

Chelle added, "I saw the look in his eyes when I asked him about it. He knew something, and it didn't have anything to do with a water show."

Jojo stood up and gave Tamara a hug and said, "Big corporations like to keep secrets too. Maybe he signed a confidentiality agreement on the show? It's likely Caesars wants to keep the show a secret until it's ready. You know, doesn't want anyone to steal their ideas for the show or their stars.

"You two can keep on chasing your ghosts. As far as we are concerned, we are happy to have our sleepy little town back. It could be years before his trial comes up. To everybody but the families of the victims, it will be a distant memory."

Coming down the stairs with back pack stuffed with clothes, two excited young ladies appeared. "I'm all packed," announced Kristal. "I can't believe we are finally going to see the Dancing Chickens."

"OK, let's get going." Steven said. "We have a long drive back to Washington. Tomorrow we jet off to Las Vegas. I have two adjoining rooms at Paris. You girls are going to be blown away;

the hotel is amazing. It has a huge rooftop swimming pool with shade trees and everything."

"Can we gamble?" Tracy asked.

Steven looked surprised, "NO! However, there is an amazing arcade station. I mean amazing."

"Really good?" Tracy asked.

"I'm told it is the best in the entire country."

Tracy and Kristal looked at each other, giggled, and gave each other a jumping high five.

Tamara gave Kristal a big hug.

Tamara warned, "You do exactly as you are told. If we don't get a good report, you will be grounded to your room until you are eighteen. Remember, Chelle is FBI, don't even think about fooling her. And not a single school assignment can be missed."

"Mom, my dad is a cop and my mom an ex-cop, I get it. And we can easily do our homework on the plane. No problem."

Jojo folded his arms against his chest and looked as menacing as he could and said, "And don't forget it." He smiled and gave his daughter a hug and said, "Have a good time, after what you went through, you deserve a little R & R."

"Thanks Dad," Kristal said as she broke off the hug.

Steven clapped his hands together and said, "Daylight is burning, let's saddle up."

Jojo kidded, "Better get going, that's your uncle Cowboy talking."

Las Vegas, Nevada:

The next day, with Steven driving, the four of them turned into the Paris Hotel.

"Oh my God!" Tracy exclaimed. "It's the Eiffel Tower."

Steven smiled at Chelle who was seated next to him in the rental he was driving. The girls in back had their heads on swivels. He enjoyed showing them the town and amazing hotels.

Steven answered, "It is a real, half-size replica. We can go all the way to the top later. Right now, we are driving through a two-thirds replica of the Arc de Triomphe. The Arc is an exact replica of the world war one memorial in France."

The girls' heads swiveled upward as they scanned the height of the hotel.

"Wow!" Kristal said, "Tracy, check this out. What floor are we staying on?"

"Don't know yet. But we'll be finding out real soon."

Steven turned into the multi-story parking structure.

Before long, Steven and Chelle walking hand in hand and pulling their small roller bags to the elevator for their room. They enjoyed watching the girls in front of them, who were pulling their own roller bags. It seemed with every step they took, there was a new discovery. From the cobblestone indoor road, they were walking, to them pointing at the streetlamps and the faux Paris street and residence looking out of the windows looking down at them.

Chelle settled her head on Steven's shoulder and snuggled her arm around Steven's. Steven turned his head slightly and kissed the top of Chelle's hair and enjoyed its smell.

They entered a large rotunda that had three different elevator banks serving the huge hotel.

"This is the way to our floor, ladies." Steven pointed. "We are on the 30th floor."

At their rooms, Chelle looked at Steven slyly and asked, "A suite?"

"With an adjoining room for the girls." Steven smiled. "I managed to pull a few strings. You know that VIP card I got last time? Let's just say it came in handy."

It didn't take long for the girls made themselves at home. Steven peeked into their room through the common door. "Family meeting in fifteen minutes. When I checked in, I learned something you two might be interested in."

Fifteen minutes later the girls came into the larger suite. Tracy said, "Dad, right out our window is the Eiffel Tower, and we can see the pool from here, can we go down to it?"

"We came in a day early so that you would have plenty of time to enjoy all the amenities. But first..." Steven held up two tickets. "I was told that as a VIP guest, my daughter and her friend are invited to a nightclub experience tonight."

"Dad, you know we aren't old enough." Tracy said sadly.

"For this night club you are. You see, there are so many young people here to see the Dancing Chickens concert, that the hotel is sponsoring a special, non-alcoholic nightclub experience for those under eighteen. It goes from six o'clock to ten, tonight at the Chateau Rooftop Nightclub. Are you interested or not?"

Steven moved the tickets over a trash can. Tracy ran up and took them out of his hands. "Very funny, Dad."

"Next stop, the pool." Steven laughed.

"Can you believe it, Tracy, we are going to be suntanning in the middle of October. Awesome!"

The girls high-fived each other again.

While the girls were swimming, Chelle and Steven lounged next to each other and soaked up some sun, both reading a book, and both sipping on a Mai Tai.

Chelle asked, "Steven, would you mind terribly if I slipped away for an hour or so this evening while the girls are at the night club?"

Steven lowered his sunglasses low enough on his nose so he could peak over them. "A little unfinished FBI business?"

"Even though the case is officially closed, I would be negligent in my duties if I didn't interview one of the potential victims, Mr. Freddy Farly."

"The guy that fell down the stairs?" Steven asked.

"I got a call from my office. He is out of his coma. The doctors said I could talk to him for a few minutes. I would like to pay him a visit."

Steven grinned, "I certainly wouldn't want you to be negligent in your duties."

Chelle added, "This whole thing isn't passing the smell test. In fact, being told to stand down stinks to high heaven."

"Any idea what time you will be back from Mr. Farly's?"

"I don't know how cooperative he'll be. Might be a real short trip."

"Tell you what, Call when you're on your way back. Either way, I'm going to be at the bottom of the stairs of the Chateau nightclub entrance at ten tonight to collect the girls."

"I can't imagine being gone that long. Worst case, I'll meet you there."

"Don't eat, after we collect the girls, we can go out for pizza."

"That sounds like a great plan."

Reidsville, NC:

At his home's kitchen table, Wade was typing furiously on his laptop. He couldn't believe his bad luck or Freddy's good. The son of a bitch was still alive and in a hospital. It was hard to get any information on Freddy, until he hacked into the hospital computer. Now he had everything.

Freddy was out of his coma but still couldn't communicate. At first it was considered a blessing because of his injuries. Now the hospital was concerned that he wouldn't ever come out of it. And the hospital staff was worried about the long-term effects of being in a coma.

Wade's problem was that he needed to make sure he never got better. Because if he did, and he remembered how he got his injuries. Fats would no doubt implicate him as the perpetrator.

Wade felt the pressure of his current hack. Of course, there was no way to prove that he did anything to hurt or kill Fats. But it could lead to more and more close looks between him and the other suspicious deaths. That kind of attention Wade didn't want.

The problem for Wade was he might not have that time. The hospital staff believed it was only a matter of time for Freddy to regain communicative abilities. If they were right, the police could be at his door shortly after. Wade couldn't take that chance. Freddy had to die.

Every hack had its challenges; tonight was no different. Cracking into the hospital was relatively easy. Even learning Freddy's room number came from a simple document search of Freddy's name. Now he was searching through a sea of peripheral devices connected to the hospital's Wi-Fi. Freddy was undoubtedly connected to monitoring devices. Determining which devices were Freddy's was the problem.

Each device was registered with a unique number, but as he had learned. The number had nothing to do with the patient's room number. Inadvertently or not, the hospital had used randomization to prevent any individual patient from being hacked.

Wade sat back in his chair. He calmed his mind. There had to be a way to find the machines connected to Freddy Farly.

Las Vegas, NV:

Chelle turned off the Strip and away from the giant hotels and bright lights advertising shows of any flavor you might want. She turned on to highway fifteen north towards the hospital.

Chelle showed her ID and was led to the intensive care floor.

A female nurse in a blue smock cautioned. "He's still adapting to being awake. Freddy is weak and I'm afraid I can't let you stay more than a couple of minutes."

Chelle nodded her head, "I understand. I just need to talk to him about his accident. It shouldn't take long but it is important."

"Follow me. He's on pain meds among others. But he seems lucid, though a bit gruff."

"Mr. Farly, there is an FBI agent here to see you."

"I already told them to go away."

Chelle interrupted, "Mr. Farly, this is my first time here."

"Not you, the others."

Chelle could only assume it was the 'Men in Black' that had insisted she stand down.

"Mr. Farly, I'm here to find the man who did this to you. We were warned you were targeted. Unfortunately, we didn't get to you in time to stop the attack."

"Attack! You know?"

Chelle stepped into the room, nodded a dismissal to the nurse. Chelle stepped closer to the bed. Freddy's head was bandaged, his legs in a cast along with one of his arms. He face looked warn with pain.

"I didn't think anyone was believing me. They all assumed I was just a big clumsy oaf."

"We, the FBI, believe we have the perpetrator in custody. I just need a bit more information."

"You have Wade? That son of a bitch."

"Wade? No, we arrested a Mr. James McConally."

Freddy looked at Chelle in disbelief. "Jim? Oh Jesus Christ! You didn't?"

"Actually, I didn't, I was approaching him to ask some questions when he was arrested by another division."

"Another division? I'll bet, bunch of guys, black cars. In and out like super quick."

It was Chelle's turn to be surprised. "Why yes!"

"Apparently you aren't one of them."

"One of them?"

"Yeah, I've had the opportunity to see them work before." Freddy laughed a bit, then regretted it. "Damn, that hurt. You gotta help Jim, he didn't do it. Wade did. I know it was Wade. I was the dumbass that taught him to fly the drone."

"Who is Wade, and what drone?"

"Wade Sullivan. The drone that knocked me down the stairs. I'm sure the son of a bitch figured I was dead. What do you mean you were warned?"

"The perpetrator gave us notice that a Freddy Farly was going to die. It took us a while to find the right Freddy Farly. Luckily, we found you when we did."

"The doctors told me it was pretty close call. Somebody jacked up my insulin pump on top of it all. The doctors think it happened during the fall. I know it was intentional and it was that son-of-a-bitch Wade. He fucking hates me."

"Where can we find Wade Sullivan?"

"I don't have a fucking clue, wait, maybe I do. He took a job on the East Coast. The Carolinas someplace. Jim told me, I can't remember exactly."

"Reidsville, North Carolina?"

"Yeah, yeah, that's it. How did you know?"

"There has been a string of murders in the area. In fact, that's what led me to Las Vegas and James McConally."

"I'm sorry miss, what is your name?"

"I'm sorry Mr. Farly, here is my card."

There was a knock at the door. It was the nurse again. "I'm sorry, I truly must limit your time."

"How are you doing, Mr. Farly?" the nurse asked with a smile on her face.

"I'm not fucking tired. Buzz off."

The nurse gave Chelle a curt wink when she turned. "Two more minutes, if he makes it that long."

Chelle agreed to the terms. Looked back at Freddy and saw his eyes closed though he was still awake.

"How did the accident happen?"

"Wade was over for a party at my place. I taught him how to fly my drone. It's a real trick, it gets beers out the cooler. A night after, the son-of-a-bitch flies the drone into my bedroom. I went out to see what was going on, he flew it right into me on the stairs, I took a tumble, like big time bad."

Freddy's eyes dropped shut again. He yawned a bit. "I know it was the son-of-a-bitch. Ever since I fired him from the project, he's hated me. You know, maybe the nurse was right. I think I have to sleep a bit."

"One more question, Mr. Farly."

"Hmmph, Oh, yeah, OK, a question, sure."

"What project?"

Freddy tried to get comfortable as he began to fall asleep. That seemed impossible because he could hardly move in any given direction.

"Project? Oh yeah, I fired him. Lake Lerna project. It's a computer thing, big fucking computer."

Suddenly Freddy's eyes opened wide. "Shit! Does he know I'm not dead?"

Chelle was shocked at his sudden lucidity."

"I, I don't know."

Tiredly Freddy said as his eyes slowly dropped shut again. "Don't let him kill me."

The nurse came back in the room.

Chelle offered, "I think he's asleep."

"It's all the medication. The pain is tiring. We are trying to keep him as comfortable as possible."

"Has he had any visitors?"

"The other FBI agents. He didn't stay awake long. Nobody else that I know of."

Chelle reached out and touched her arm gently, "Here's my card, I'll be in town for a couple of days. I would like to talk with Mr. Farly again before I leave if that is possible. Could you ask him when he wakes?"

"I will ask. He can be a bit uncooperative."

Chelle laughed at the nurse's patience. "I can only imagine."

****

On her way back to the Paris, traffic was heavy and the sun was setting. Chelle made two important calls over the hands-free system of the car. "Hi Jojo, it's Chelle. I know it's late in Reidsville, this is important. I have good reasons to think James McConally is not the killer. I met with Freddy Farly."

Jojo asked over the car's speaker, "The dude that was almost killed by falling down some stairs?"

"Yes. Freddy believes the killer is a man called Wade Sullivan. Wade used to work for him and is holding a grudge for firing him. Get this, Wade lives in Reidsville."

"If he's right, that means he could still be after my family."

"Exactly, don't worry about Kristal, she'll be safe here. Turns out it was a good time to get her out of town.

"Locate Wade Sullivan and surveil him for a while until we figure out what to charge him with. I'm afraid that Freddy's hunch that Wade is the killer is not enough to get an arrest warrant on him."

"If he's in Reidsville, I'll find him."

"I will call Mike to see if he can find Wade's name on any flight manifest to Las Vegas the last couple of months. If we can prove he was in Las Vegas during Freddy's accident, we might have enough to bring him in for questioning."

"Goodnight Jojo, and good luck."

That night at Paris, Las Vegas:

Chelle looked for Steven at the bottom of the winding open staircase that led up to the Chateau Rooftop Nightclub. There was a mob of young people, the over twenty-one crowd waiting for their turn. Many voicing disdains that they were being forced to wait while children attended their nightclub.

Chelle saw Steven in a corner trying to keep an eye on the stairway for his daughter. A loud band was playing not far away. The casino was a confluence of sounds and people. She came up to him and they gave each other a quick kiss.

"Any word?" She asked.

Steven said, almost yelling to be heard above the band playing in the casino, "Just a text. Apparently, it's as crowded upstairs as down here. They should be along shortly. Hungry?"

"Sure am. I'm sorry I'm late, traffic was heavy."

"No problem, you are right on time. The girls should be down shortly, and we can all get something to eat."

"Get this, the man that was nearly killed by the fall down the steps works at a project called, 'The Lake Lerna project.'"

Steven sounding astonished said, "It's real?"

Chelle looked around and decided that the crowd and noise provided ample security to their discussion. She was sure nobody would overhear anything she was saying.

Moving close to Steven's ear she said, "He was highly medicated, but he said he fired a man called Wade Sullivan from the project and that was why this Wade person tried to kill him.

"I asked him what project and he said the Lake Lerna project, just before he dozed off. He said it was a computer thing, a big fucking computer.

Steven's face turned white. "I was hoping I was wrong. And you're telling me my worst nightmare is true?"

"He said it just as he was dozing off. I hadn't mentioned the name and he didn't pull it out of thin air, so I believe him. In fact, he seemed terrified that the person would be back to finish the job."

"Now what?" Steven asked as he scanned the stairway for the girls.

"I called Jojo. Get this, the guy Freddy is worried about lives in Reidsville."

"The serial killer." Steven put two and two together.

"Very possible."

Out the corner of his eye he saw his daughter and Kristal coming down the stairs. He tried to get their attention to no avail.

Steven said as he pointed, "There they are, we better start fighting our way towards them or we might lose them in this crowd."

Hand in hand, Chelle and Steven shimmied their way through the crowd, Steven asked loud enough that Chelle could hear him and certain that nobody else could possibly hear, "Are you saying your serial killer and the government's Lake Lerna project are connected somehow?"

"It's beginning to look that way."

Steven nodded with his head towards a back wall, "Look who's here. Back by the band. I would recognize those three amigos anywhere."

Chelle stole a look and agreed. "What they told us appears to be true. It's not a surprise to see them hanging out here waiting to get into the night club, considering they work not far from here."

Steven asked, "Do you think their lives are in danger?"

"Don't know, I haven't put all the pieces together yet. I want to ask if they know Freddy or this Wade guy. Maybe they will shed some light on the situation if I share some information with them."

"Good luck. I'll find the girls and we'll wait outside for you."

DIGITAL SECRETS

Chelle disappeared into the crowd and circled around so she wouldn't be seen by the trio. She was nearly upon the trio when she saw that Marvin recognize her. He was still clutching his computer against his chest. Marvin was about to try and warn his friends when Chelle stepped up to them.

"Don't run. I'm here to warn you, your lives might be in danger."

The girl with the Mohawk said, "If we are, it's because of you."

Nearly shouting over the music, Chelle asked, "Does the name Wade Sullivan mean anything to you?"

She answered, "No, should it?"

She had the attention of Rodger and the girl. Marvin, who had been distracted by the noise and crowd, suddenly focused on Chelle.

Chelle explained, "He worked on the Lake Lerna project too." Chelle saw the surprise in their eyes and added. "We know it's part of the Caesars Palace complex right across the road from here."

Rodger said. "OK, so you know about it. But what does that have to do with this Wade guy and us?"

Marvin said as his eyes darted around. "Wade bad. He hurt me."

Chelle could see that the dark-skinned girl and Rodger were surprised at the short statement.

Rodger asked, "Marvin, did you know Wade?"

"Wade bad. He hurt me. Got mad, pushed me. I fell."

"At work?" Rodger asked.

"At work, Wade pushed me. My computer didn't break."

Marvin's eyes continued to dart from person to person in the crowded casino, much more agitated than normal.

Chelle maneuvered as best she could into the middle of the three.

"Do you know a Mr. Freddy Farly?"

"Yeah, we call him Fat Freddy, I mean, not to his face," Rodger said.

"Freddy Farly is in the hospital; he believes Wade Sullivan put him there. Only he meant to kill him. And there have been other suspicious deaths. I believe he is taking revenge against people he knew worked on the project by killing them because they all worked in the computer sciences except one person a Dr. L.H. Langston"

"Wade bad, Wade bad," Marvin repeated.

The girl with the Mohawk said, "I met Dr. Lagston. He worked on the cooling system for the project. I had to write some code for him. Did you say he's dead?"

Chelle realized all the pieces of the puzzle were falling into place. "Let's step outside; we need to talk. I believe your lives are in danger assuming you are part of the Lake Lerna project."

"Wade bad man. Wade bad man." Marvin repeated.

Chapter 19

The four hustled outside. The air was refreshing; the lack of bass pounding in her ears was even better. Chelle saw Steven and the girls by one of the feet of the Eiffel Tower watching the water show going on across the street at the Bellagio hotel.

Rodger said, "I, we know Freddy, he's lead, we're just contractors, but we don't know Wade. The dark-skinned girl just shook her head in agreement.

She looked at her friend and said, "Rodger, we shouldn't be talking about this."

Chelle said, "Maybe it's just as well you don't know him. If he doesn't know you work on the project, you might not be in danger. I don't know if he would mess with your friend if he was just an annoyance. Just the same, six people have already died that we know of, seven if you count the attempted murder of Freddy. I don't know who else is on this guy's list or why. I was hoping you could tell me."

The girl said, "We are bound by a strict non-disclosure agreement. The strictest. We could be sent to jail just for talking to you."

Chelle looked into the girl's eyes. "I understand, but something has gone terribly wrong. A man called James McConally has been arrested for the murders. The FBI thinks they have their guy. I'm beginning to think they are wrong. Many more lives could be in danger. I'm sorry but I desperately need your help. In fact, I don't know anybody else who could help."

Chelle glanced at Marvin and added, "It could be your lives or a friend's life you save. I beg you to help me."

The girl relented, "The project is huge, I can't even guess at how many people work on it. This Wade guy certainly can't kill everyone who works or worked on it."

"We don't know how the killer picks his victims."

Rodger looked at his female companion, then back at Chelle. "I can assure you, it's not Jim, he wouldn't, couldn't hurt a fly."

The girl looked down and nodded her head in agreement and added. "Him and Fats were friends."

"You know James McConally?"

"Well enough, he's no murderer," the girl insisted.

Rodger asked, "Who are the people he killed, their names, tell us their names."

Chelle listed each and said how they died.

The girl and Rodger nodded to each other a few times. He said, "Some of the names we recognize. We kind of did our own thing. We didn't work with many other people. They liked it that way, you know, compartmentalized."

Chelle took out a card and handed it to Rodger and one to the girl with the dark Mohawk; she refused it. When she tried to hand one to Marvin, he wouldn't release his clutch on his computer long enough to accept it. "I want you to be aware and be careful. I wouldn't be doing my job if I didn't warn you. If you want to contact me about anything, just call, day or night."

Chelle started walking away towards Steven. Steven and the group locked eyes and Steven waved but made no attempt to approach.

Chelle turned back towards them with a finial request when her phone rang.

"Hi Jojo, did you learn anything?"

After a moment on the phone with Jojo, Chelle looked at Marvin specifically and asked, "Marvin, a detective thinks he is outside of Wade Sullivan's condo unit. He can see somebody typing at a computer.

"My friend took a photo through the window and sent it to me. He needs to know if it is Wade or not."

Chelle turned her phone towards Marvin. "Is this Wade?"

Marvin stammered a bit and said, "Wade bad, friend should leave." Marvin repeated, "Wade very bad, he hurt me." Marvin turned away and hugged his computer even more tightly.

Chelle interrupted, "Jojo, I have someone here visibly upset at the photo. I believe you found him."

Jojo said over the speaker. "Only one way to know for sure, I'll just knock on the door and ask him."

"Be careful Jojo, if he suspects you're there to arrest him he could become dangerous."

DIGITAL SECRETS

"Not my first rodeo, Chelle, I sort of hope he does. Don't worry, I'll be ready."

Chelle's phone rang with another call. "Jojo, I gotta go. Text me the address you're at. If I don't hear from you in ten minutes, I'm calling your chief."

"You got it, bye."

Chelle answered her next call, "Nurse Nelson, is everything OK?"

The three amigos were not even thinking of leaving. Things were changing by the minute. They listened to the Agent on the phone.

"Is Freddy OK?"

"Oh my God no." Chelle felt her face flush.

After a brief discussion Chelle hung up and looked at the three who she could see sensed the direction of her conversation.

"It was Freddy's nurse. He's dead."

Chelle looked across the small mall at Steven. He must have detected the concern in her eyes because soon he and the girls were soon by her side.

He asked, "Chelle, what's wrong?"

She turned towards Steven and said, "The man I visited today in the hospital died."

Steven said, "I'm so sorry. You said he was critically injured."

Chelle looked at the girls, trying to decide how much information she should divulge. "Steven, would you and the girls mind going for pizza without me. I need to follow up on some things. Make some calls, you know."

Chelle could tell that Steven understood the dodge. "Sure, call when you're done."

As Steven and the two girls walked off, Chelle said to the three amigos, "I don't think Freddy's death was accidental. I think he was murdered."

The girl looked at Rodger, "Maybe she's right. Our lives might be in danger, Especially Marvin's."

The girl took the card from out of Rodger's hand and examined it for a moment, she said, "Marvin is special."

"Yes I know, a bit shy," Chelle agreed.

"I mean to the project. He's one of the few that knows how to talk to the computers. These are quantum computers. It's a whole new language being invented to talk to them. If this guy is trying to sabotage the project, Marvin would be a target. And he knows Marvin."

"Wade bad, very bad." Marvin repeated.

The girl extended her hand, "I'm Tesia." She said to Chelle. Whatever we can do to help. How did Freddy die?"

"Apparently his pain killer machine malfunctioned. He got overdosed."

Marvin said, "Wade bad, Wade bad."

Tesia said, "Marvin, can you track his hack?"

Marvin nodded his head and without saying a word sat down on a street curb, crossed his legs, opened his computer, and started typing furiously.

Reidsville, NC:

Wade heard the doorbell ring. He clicked an icon on his laptop and saw on the front door camera the detective standing at his door.

"Shit!" Wade said as he closed his laptop.

He got up from the kitchen table and walked to the door. After opening it he said, "Hello, detective."

"Wade Sullivan?" Jojo asked.

"Why yes, I'm surprised you know me.

"Same here."

"Don't be so modest, detective, everybody in Reidsville knows you. With the string of murders on your hands, you have been on the local news fairly often."

"May I come in for a moment?"

"Sorry, detective, I'm just ready to go to bed. Is there something I can quickly help you with?"

"I see you are a biker, a speed biker."

"Now how would you know that?"

"When I walked up, I saw your bike hanging in the garage."

"That's incredible, all dark and everything. And you could see that, amazingly observant. And of all the bikers in Reidsville, you decided I was the one biker you needed to talk to at this late hour."

"Were you biking in the vicinity of Reservoir Park on the day of July 8th?"

"Detective, that is a rather blunt question. How could I possibly remember that?"

"Because it was the day Sue Witting was murdered. I hoped you might remember that day. Certainly, you would remember if you were or weren't in a park on the same day as somebody was murdered in it."

"Indeed, I would. Didn't connect the date. I wasn't. Can I go to bed now?"

"Thank you, Mr. Sullivan. I just needed you on record as stating you were not in the park that day."

"Detective?" Wade asked slyly, "Should I be contacting an attorney?"

"Mr. Sullivan, I'm sure you understand that I cannot give legal advice. Good night. Maybe we'll get the chance to talk again soon."

Wade slowly closed the door as the detective walked away. Wade made no attempt to hide himself as he watched as Jojo got back in his car a drove away."

"Damn!" Wade said loudly. "How in the hell?" He remembered the unfinished business on his computer.

Las Vegas, NV

Rodger asked Chelle, "What hospital is Freddy at?"

"Valley Hospital. What is Marvin doing?"

"He might be able to track the hack. If it was Wade manipulating the machines, he might be able to track it."

"Do you mean he could prove that it was done by Wade?"

"Wade's computer, but yes. There are many ways to cover your tracks when hacking. If Wade was working on the Lake Lerna project, I'm sure he knows them all."

"What is Marvin trying to do?"

"Marvin is the best, the very best. Covering your tracks takes time. Marvin might be able to follow the hack all the way back to Wade's computer. It's worth a shot."

"Wade was here," Marvin said excitedly. "He was at the hospital. He hacked into unit 23 and unit 56."

"What does that mean?" Chelle asked.

Tesia answered, "In the internet of things, or IoT. In the hospital, many things are connected to it's LAN."

Chelle said, "That I know, it's a local area network."

"Right, and it is connected to the internet, which is connected to everything. Unit 23 and 56 could be anything at all, but they are electronic and connected to the hospital's LAN. And once somebody hacks into the LAN, any electronics connected to it are also exposed to hacking."

Rodger typed furiously, he said, "He used multiple access points, but the hack is coming from east of the Mississippi. The trail is shutting down behind me. He's doesn't know I'm in front."

"That's it, Marvin, you can do it." Tesia said.

"He's fast," Rodger said as he looked at the computer over Marvin's shoulder. He added, "Now he's routing through Canada; it's just a trick. You've got it. You can do this, my man."

Marvin's face instantly went from a satisfied smile to an ominous grimace.

"What's wrong, Marvin?" Tesai asked.

Marvin twirled his open laptop towards her. She bent down and read it.

"Shit! He's on to you. Wow, he doesn't mess around."

Rodger squeezed in close to Tesia and read the screen. "Shut it down. Turn it off. Make sure he doesn't get into your computer."

Marvin hit the power switch; within twenty seconds the machine was dark.

Tesia looked at Chelle, "He knows it was Marvin."

Marvin stuffed his computer back into its case and clutched it hard as he stood. He said, "Wade bad, Wade wants to hurt me."

"How do you know it was Wade?" Chelle asked Marvin.

Marvin looked away scanning the people around them.

Rodger offered, "Kind of like fingerprints. Certain hackers do things a certain way, and always the same. If Marvin says it was Wade, it was."

"How can I prove to my bosses who it was?"

Marvin spoke haltingly, "Wade used a VPN. I searched the VPN, it is Wade. He's bad. He lives in Reidsville."

She asked again, "Did you track his IP to Reidsville?"

"Wade is in Reidsville; he wants to kill me."

Tesia and Rodger took their attention away from Marvin and looked at Chelle. Rodger pushed up his glasses; they were no longer broken. He explained, "Wade routed his computer through a VPN network."

Chelle filled in the blanks to let them know she was following the explanation, "You mean a Virtual Private Network."

"Yes, considered by experts to be un-hackable, and that is mostly right. Marvin has an in with most of the VPN providers. He can search their databases, and he found Wade's account. That automatically gave him his IP address. IP addresses are assigned geographically, so Marvin could trace it to Reidsville. An exact address is possible to find now if Marvin hacks into the local providers servers and locates the IP physical address."

Chelle added, "And all of that is strictly illegal."

Tesia added, "Maybe illegal, but it doesn't make the information wrong. The person who hacked into the hospital and killed Freddy lives in Reidsville. Wade lives in Reidsville."

Chelle's phone rang. "Hi Jojo, what did you learn?"

"It is Wade Sullivan, he admitted it. Cocky little bastard. I wouldn't be surprised if it's the same guy calling me with the death threats. He was working on his computer, but he wouldn't let me into his house."

"Jojo, I think your timing was perfect. Can't explain now. What next?"

"I'm going home to get some sleep. Maybe I'll come up with something by morning."

"Good idea, let's talk tomorrow."

Chelle hung up.

Tesia asked Marvin, "Marvin, can you hack into the local provider and get an exact address on the IP address you tracked?"

"It's Wade," Marvin said dejectedly.

"I know, but the detective needs an address."

Chelle said, "No I don't, we know where he lives. Besides, it would be illegally obtained. For now, I'm convinced the real killer we are after is in Reidsville and is Wade Sullivan. If we got his computer from him, would it give us the evidence we need?"

Rodger answered, "It might, I mean if Wade didn't have time to secure erase everything on it. I'm sure he has a self-destruct mechanism in place. All black-hat hackers do."

"We must get to that computer legally somehow," Chelle mused out loud. "We can't do any more hanging out on the street. Let's find my friend and get something to eat." Chelle rested her arm gently on Marvin's shoulder and asked. "Are you hungry for pizza, Marvin?"

Marvin smiled and nodded a yes.

"Good, please fill me in on whatever you are comfortable telling me as we walk. Anything at all could help me catch this guy. It may be the only way to keep Marvin safe. I don't think the cavalry is coming to help us until we can prove a link.

Paris Hotel, Las Vegas:

Later that night, while in their own room and with the girls safely in theirs, Chelle and Steven talked. They kept the television on a bit louder than they otherwise would have as a precaution against any eavesdroppers.

Chelle suggested, "With what we have learned lately, we had better have our phones off."

Steven said, "It's a pretty sad state of affairs when two reasonable adults have to be worried about being monitored twenty-four, seven? By their own government."

Alan D Schmitz
DIGITAL SECRETS

Steven went to his phone pushed a button and showed Chelle as it shut down.

Chelle said, "China has been doing it for years. If you get on the wrong side of the Chineese government your travel, job, apartment can all be restricted."

He set his phone down on the counter and walked over to a large print on the wall opposite where Chelle was sitting that depicted the Eiffel tower being constructed.

He studied it for a minute then asked, "How in the world did you get the three amigos to join us for pizza?"

"They were hungry." Chelle laughed. "I didn't know a whole evening of conversation could be made about the Dancing Chickens and the upcoming concert."

Steven turned towards Chelle, "I know, they almost have me wishing I was going."

"We did have an interesting discussion on the way to dinner. I warned them not to talk business in front of the girls. They are well intentioned."

Chelle's eyes focused on the smart watch on Steven's wrist. She said, "I know I'm sounding very paranoid, but your watch, you can make calls with it."

"In a pinch, yes I can."

"That means it has a microphone in it. Could you turn it off too?"

Without saying a word, Steven slid it off his wrist and turned it off.

After it was also turned off, Steven said, "You're not the first to remind me of that fact. So back to the three amigos. You mean they're well intentioned when they're not stealing from the casinos."

"Let's say we didn't catch them at their best. But they were there to warn you."

Steven walked over to the wet bar in their suite and popped open a bottle of Cabernet. "Care for a glass?"

"Sure, we might be up for a while. I have quite a story to tell."

Steven poured the two glasses. Handed one to Chelle sat down next to her on the plush couch. They clinked a small toast.

Steven said, "I'm all ears."

"I'm not sure where to begin. Might as well start with Freddy being killed."

"What? You said he died; you didn't mention he was killed."

"Another accidental death. His medication devices mysteriously went into overdrive and killed him."

"And you're not buying it."

"It seems that Marvin, the nervous one, is some sort of computer savant. Right there, on the side of the Eiffel Tower, he traced Wade's hack into the hospital and back to Reidsville."

"This is the guy that Freddy told you about before he died."

"It is. Jojo happened to be at his home in Reidsville when Freddy died."

Steven nodded slowly, "The perfect alibi. But why was Jojo there?"

Based on the tip from Freddy, Jojo tracked down where Wade lives. Jojo saw a hat hanging in his garage that was identical to the only identifiable image from the drone footage he retrieved, so Jojo decided he should talk to him.

"It just so happens; this was just after I got the call about Freddy dying. He was working on his computer during the time the machines at the hospital went haywire."

"Not hardly hard evidence."

"The hat either, all circumstantial, just the same, it all makes sense."

"Not to me."

"Our three friends think that Wade is on some sort of revenge kick for getting dismissed from the program. Some of the names I mentioned they knew, and worked on the same project. My guess is all of them besides the young student are connected to it somehow.

Chelle sat her wine glass down on the Napoleon III-styled coffee table in front of them. The couch they were sitting on, the coffee table, and the other furniture in the room were all obviously a matched set.

She turned towards Steven and explained, "There are two quantum computers. They are called Iphicles and Hercules."

Steven looked a little puzzled, "Hercules I know and can guess it's meaning for a supercomputer, what or who is Iphicles?"

"Hercules had a twin brother, Iphicles."

"No kidding! I didn't know that. Now it makes sense, two identical computers."

Chelle took a taste of her wine, she corrected Steven, "Just like Hercules and Iphicles, twin brothers, but not identical. It's all housed under Caesars Palace."

"The new addition, the Lake Lerna wing," Steven suggested.

"Hence the Lake Lerna project."

"And our three new friends shared this with you?"

"They are afraid that Marvin is on Wade's list. Why, you ask?"

"Do tell."

"Everything is compartmentalized. They have never seen the computers but have put two and two together because Marvin is one of the few that can communicate with the Lake Lerna quantum computers. Marvin is apparently key to the project, and they think that would make him a target.

"Dr. L.H. Langston, who we were warned by the killer was going to die and did die in a freak industrial accident, was part of it. He was an expert on using super cooled water. I'm talking water that at minus-fifty Fahrenheit isn't frozen; it's still liquid. Dr. Langston was the brains behind the heat transfer technology used to cool the quantum computers.

"Freddy oversaw getting the information securely to the quantum computers. He mentioned that it's hacker proof. That was where a guy called Wade Sullivan came in, He is an expert at computer security. That tidbit came from Marvin. He doesn't say much, but when he does, I listen."

Steven took a long sip of his wine contemplating the new information. "That would explain where the billions of dollars went. Did they say what it's being used for?"

"That's it. It's not being used yet. They think Wade is doing whatever he can to slow its operation."

"Why?"

"Just out of spite, they guess."

"Interesting turn of events. Your serial killer and my missing funds are all related. This is a lot of information to digest."

Chelle said, "It is, and it explains why our investigation was closed down so rapidly."

Steven finished the logic, "Higher powers don't want their super computers being exposed, even if it means letting a serial killer go free."

Chelle stood, "I'm so tired right now I can't think straight."

Steven stood and gave her a big hug and said, "That makes two of us."

Steven was the first into bed as they both prepared for sleep. He was already resting his head on his pillow with eyes closed.

Chelle slipped under the covers wearing nothing but an old t-shirt of Steven's, which was oversized on her. It had become her favorite night slip.

Chelle asked, "Who else warned you about being spied on using your electronic watch?"

"The President," Steven sleepily answered as he rolled his body over. "when he warned my about a possible grand jury investigation against me."

"What? A grand jury investigating you? For what?"

Just like that, Chelle heard snoring. Chelle said to herself with a smile, "I can't say you are not full of surprises, Senator. So much for a romantic getaway to Las Vegas." She bent over and gave Steven a kiss on his cheek as he let out a loud snore.

****

Chelle woke up to the sound of the hotel phone ringing. Still half-asleep, she glanced at the time; it was six am. The receiver was wireless so she grabbed it and walked out the bedroom of their suite.

"Hello." Chelle said sleepily. Chelle's eyes suddenly became wide open. "Jojo?"

"I'm sorry," Chelle explained, "we both turned off our phones."

Chelle listened for a minute then said, "I can't believe he called again after your visit. If it's Wade, and I believe it is, he got a lot of balls. Let me get a pen and paper. If there's a silver lining, after this call the FBI can't ignore the implication that they have the wrong guy."

"OK, give me the name. I'll call it in to my team as soon as we hang up."

"Jojo, oh my God, I think we can stop this one. I know a Melbourne Winston, or rather Steven does."

"I think so. This particular Melbourne Winston works in the computer industry, in fact some sort of computer genius."

"I agree, I'm waking Steven. He should be able to get me a telephone and address. I will be getting my team on it as soon as I can. Talk later."

Chelle sat on the side of the bed and gently she rubbed Stevens bare shoulder until he woke.

"Morning love," Steven whispered out as he squinted the sleep from his eyes.

Chelle gave Steven a kiss on his cheek. "Sorry for waking you. I need your help. Or rather your friend Melbourne Winston does. He's the next target."

Chelle knew that would wake Steven fully and she wasn't wrong. Steven swung his legs off the bed and said, "What?"

"I just talked to Jojo. He got another call from the killer. A Melbourne Winston is his next victim. I'm thinking it's your friend Melbourne, Winnie's husband."

"Whether it is or not, we certainly can't take that chance. I'll call Shannon immediately for his contact info. I'm sure it's in our database somewhere. She'll find it."

"I have to call this in. There is no way my team and I are sitting this one out, despite what the top brass says."

Chelle called her team in Washington. While she did that, Steven called Shannon, who already had a few hours of work time in for the day. Chelle heard Steven say, "Great, text me the info the second you find it. And please text it to Chelle's phone too."

Steven rushed to get ready. The second Chelle was off the phone, she was doing the same thing. Steven was tucking in his red polo shirt into his khaki trousers when he asked, "I know we are rushing, but, to what end? I mean, where are we going?"

Chelle was finishing brushing her teeth. She swished some water around in her mouth and spit it out. "Either my team or Shannon are going to come up with the number for Melbourne. We'll get someone from the FBI on task to find him wherever he is."

Steven turned Chelle around from the sink, he took a dry washcloth and dapped her mouth dry. He gently held her cheeks in his hand and kissed her. "My point is, let's slow down a bit. We are on vacation; you and I aren't going to save the day, at least not today. Besides what we've already done, there is nothing else left for us to do but pass on the information Shannon gets us."

"I guess you're right. Jojo is on his way to Wade's house. He doesn't know exactly what he's going to do either, but for now his plan is to at least disrupt whatever he's doing."

Just then both of their phones dinged. After scanning their respective phones, they said to each other. "Shannon."

Steven's phone rang. "It's Shannon. Hi, Shannon just got your text. Do you have more info?"

"Sit tight for a moment, I'm putting you on speaker so Chelle can hear."

"Melbourne doesn't have a phone, or at least any that I can find. The number I texted you is his wife's phone, Winnie. The good news is I do have their address on file, I'll text that to you too, they live in Newport Beach, California."

"Good work Shannon, if I need more, I'll call."

Chelle said, "Steven, I think you need to make the call to Winnie; she'll believe you."

As he was dialing the number, he mumbled, "Please answer, Winnie."

"Hello?"

"Hi Mrs. Winston, this is Senator Westcott."

"Hi, Senator, how are you?"

"I'm fine, but I'm afraid I have some upsetting news and time is of the essence. Winnie, Chelle is with me. You remember, my FBI friend, you met her in Las Vegas. I'm going to put the phone on speaker so you can hear her too."

Whinnie asked sounding a little sleepy, "Senator, what is the problem and how can I possibly help you?" Chelle and Steven heard over the speaker.

Chelle spoke first, "Winnie, this is Agent Saltarie, there have been a series of murders that the FBI has been tracking. This person taunts the police with a name, daring the FBI to find them before he kills them."

"Oh my, he sounds terrible. But how does that concern me? Don't tell me he wants to kill me?"

"No Winnie, we believe you are perfectly safe. But the name he gave to us as his next victim is called Melbourne Winston. Winnie, I don't have time to go into detail, however, we have reason to believe he means your husband. You need to warn him."

After a period of silence, Winnie responded, "I'm not with him, I'm upstate, Melbourne doesn't carry a phone. I don't have any way to contact him. I believe he is home but I'm hours away. I don't know what to do."

"Winnie, Steven and I are in Las Vegas; we can't help either."

A text came through on Chelle's phone. She looked at it. Chelle asked, "Winnie, do you still live at Cathem Court, Newport Beach?"

"We do."

"I'm calling my office and I'll try to get someone from the FBI to warn him."

"I'm afraid even if they do, he won't believe them. He has some history with the FBI and doesn't trust them. You and Steven have to go; he'll believe the Senator."

Steven looked at Chelle with a frown and said, "I'm afraid that won't work, Winnie, By the time we get there it'll be too late. The killer gave us three hours, and that was fifteen minutes ago. Our best bet is the local FBI."

"I can get you there in a few hours, you have to try."

"Winnie, it's a five-hour drive or more."

"You start driving to Las Vegas International; go to the light jet center. Leave the rest to me."

Before Steven and Chelle could say a word, the line went dead.

Steven said, "The girls!"

Chelle said, "We sure as hell can't leave them in Las Vegas while we go to California."

Steven agreed, "I guess they're going with us. How fast can two teenage girls get ready? They are not going to be too happy about this."

Chelle said, "You deal with the girls. I'll get our car and meet you out front ASAP."

****

Steven knocked hard on the door connecting the rooms.

Finally, a sleepy, "What?" was heard.

"Girls, I need you ready in ten minutes. We are going on a private jet ride to California. I'll explain in the car. I'm serious, ten minutes max."

It was Tracy. "Dad, you're not making any sense. I'm going back to bed."

"Tracy, I'll come in with a bucket of cold water if I have to. Nine minutes, life, and death. Yours, if you're not ready."

Somehow the girls did it. Both were dressed in jeans and their favorite Dancing Chickens t-shirts. Steven rushed them out the door, down the elevator and through the casino to the bank of glass doors welcoming patrons into Paris.

"Dad, what's going on?"

"Look, there's Chelle. In the car. I promise I'll explain on the way to the airport."

"We can't leave, the concert is tonight."

"I'll get you back in time, I promise."

Inside the car everybody buckled up. Chelle said, "Winnie texted me the address. It's ten minutes away, tops."

"Dad, what's going on?"

Steven used the ten minutes to get the girls up to date.

It was Kristal who said proudly, "You mean we are going to try to catch the serial killer my dad has been trying to catch?"

"You two are going along so we can keep an eye on you. You will have nothing to do with catching any killer."

Chelle pulled up to the parking for executive jets. A man dressed in a dark suit was standing outside with a white board with Steven's and Chelle's names on it.

Steven and the girls ran up to him, "I'm Senator Westcott."

"I was told time was of the essence. The plane is waiting on the other side of the building. Walk this way please."

Steven, Chelle and the girls soon saw the large jet waiting for them. Painted across the side and the tail were the words, Caesars Palace.

Kristal said, "This is our plane, just for us?"

Chelle took a moment to admire the sleek aircraft, "Winnie wasn't kidding when she said she had connections."

The four hustled up the stairs into the aircraft. A flight attendant was on duty waiting atop the short stairway into the plane. He welcomed them aboard one by one. Steven waited on the tarmac by the bottom of the stairs as first Chelle walked up the stairs, followed by Tracy. When Kristal was on the second step Steven followed closely behind.

"Sit wherever you like; I understand we won't be on the ground for long, so I'll serve refreshments once we are airborne." The flight attendant assured everyone.

The two girls high fived each other, forgiving Steven instantly for dragging them out of bed as they looked at the plush accommodations. Deciding which leather chair or couch to sit on was their next challenge.

The plane was soon rolling down the taxiway.

Steven texted Winnie to assure her they were on their way. Chelle was working her phone alerting the Califirnia FBI of the threat.

In the air the pilot said over the intercom that they would be landing in about a half-hour. Touchdown was smooth, Steven felt the pressure of the seatbelt as it held him back from flinging forward as the plane decelerated.

Steven and Chelle were both checking their phones to see if anything had changed during the last forty-five minutes.

Steven said, "Winnie has a car and driver standing by. She said depending on traffic, we're fifteen to twenty minutes out."

Chelle read a message on her phone. "My team in Washington is back in gear. They've been contacted by the FBI office out here and confirmed the threat. It'll be a race between us or them to get to the house first."

"What if Melbourne isn't home?"

"Let's hope he is and is alive and well."

The plane came to a halt and the four disembarked as fast as they had embarked. True to her word a car and driver was waiting.

The driver announced as he closed the back door of the limo, "I have the address; it's not far."

Steven said to the two young girls in the most authoritarian voice he could, "When we get there, you two stay in the car. I mean it. We do not know what we are up against. Stay in the car. No excuses."

The girls' eyes opened wide when they saw Chelle take her weapon from her purse and made sure a bullet was chambered. "Girls, Steven is right. Stay in the car."

Chelle's phone rang, "It's Jojo."

"Put dad on speaker, I want to tell him about our cool airplane ride," Kristal said.

Chelle did, more for Steven's sake and wondering how he was going to explain that they were all in California now.

Jojo spoke first and fast, "I'm in Wade's house, he's not here. His car is gone. I've searched the house. The only computer I found was a big one. In the basement. It's the biggest computer

Alan D Schmitz
DIGITAL SECRETS

I ever saw. It's inside some sort of plexiglass cage that's big enough for a person to fit into. It's cooled by a window air-conditioner running right into it. It looks like a fire hazard to me, I'm unplugging it."

"I wouldn't do that if I were you."

Jojo's heart skipped a beat. He whipped around towards the sound with his gun at the ready.

"Wade? Is that you?" Jojo spoke to the walls.

"Yes it's me. What are you doing in my home?"

"You know why I'm here."

"No I don't. I think my attorney would be interested too. Did you honestly think I wouldn't have security cameras?"

Everybody in the car was silent as a mouse, including the driver.

"You know, you're right. Let's meet up and talk about this. Where are you? I'll come to you."

"I would recommend you do not touch a thing. I will sue the police department and the city for millions of damages if you ruin my computer and the work it is doing."

"What work is it doing?"

"That would be none of your business."

"Who are you speaking to on the phone?" Wade asked.

"And that would be none of your business," Jojo said.

"I'm sure it's that cute little FBI agent your friend Senator Westcott hangs with. Hi Chelle, can you hear me? So nice to talk with you."

Jojo started to hear sirens outside even though he was in the basement.

"Oh, oh, detective. Looks like the police are on their way to investigate a break-in. By everybody, I must go now."

They all heard the conversation end.

Jojo said, "I have to go up and explain things. We will talk later."

"Shit!" Chelle said.

Kristal asked, "Is dad going to get into trouble?"

The driver said, "We're here."

Chelle said, "Park on the street. Don't go up the drive."

DIGITAL SECRETS

"Look." Steven said, "A package is being delivered. I guess we'll see in a moment if Melbourne is home."

Chelle and Steven hurried out the car. They wanted to intercept Melbourne when he answered the door.

The delivery woman rang the doorbell and patiently waited as she set the small square package down. Chelle was immediately suspicious of the package. The brown box looked to be about two-foot square; it could be holding just about anything. The box was normal enough; it was the timing Chelle was suspicious about.

Chapter 20

Las Vegas:

Wade looked out at the Vegas strip from his tenth-floor hotel room. The strip was busy today, he could see massive crowds flooding the sidewalk along Las Vegas Boulevard in both directions. He had just said good-bye to the detective who had broken into his home. After the detective's visit the night before, he had decided that the detective and thus the FBI had somehow pulled on a string that led to him. Staying home waiting to be arrested didn't sound like a good plan to him, so he had used a fake I.D. and flown to Vegas.

Wade wasn't sure how a connection to him had been made, just that it obviously was. He was certain there was no direct evidence connecting him with the murders. Still, it was undeniable that the authorities had come up with a link. Undoubtedly a minor one or the detective wouldn't have left his home without him in handcuffs.

Wade genuinely did have to attend to other business when he hung up with the detective. The delivery company had just sent him a text announcing his package was at the intended address.

Inside the package was a small computer, along with a portable hotspot and a spare battery backup to make sure the system didn't run out of power.

His computer dinged, confirming it was at the right coordinates. Wade went back to his laptop and clicked a few keys and a small security camera came on. Only this time it wasn't from a home security system; it was mounted inside the box that had just been delivered to the Winstons' home.

The small black hole the pin-hole camera made wouldn't even be noticed.

Wade watched the impatient delivery driver ring the doorbell once again. Wade celebrated his plan. This was his most ingenious murder so far. The package had been sent by a fictitious client, with messaging sent to a burner phone connected through a VPN network. The computer was made from spare parts, the mobile hotspot was purchased with cash.

The bomb inside the package would obliterate any evidence traceable to him. Though upon an examination of the remnants, there would be no doubt it was a sophisticated bomb.

Because the package had to be signed for, Wade felt that it would be a fifty-fifty proposition that Melbourne would claim it. Either way, eventually Melbourne's face would appear on the camera, and one simple key press and ka-boom, no more Melbourne.

"Come on Melbourne, I don't have all day. Answer the damn door."

Newport Beach, CA:

Chelle and Steven were walking up the brick, paved walk to the Winston home. Chelle turned to Steven and said, "I'm suspicious about that package, I'm going to check it out. Please stay back until I call an all clear."

"If it's that dangerous, you shouldn't be going either."

"One of us has to. It's a small percentage hunch. Either way, I must warn Melbourne to stay clear of it until it's been inspected. Under the circumstances we just can't take the chance."

"Chelle, no dice."

"What? Both of us should take a risk when only one of us will do? You're a Senator and father. I'm a trained FBI agent; you lose. Don't make me shoot you in the leg or something stupid like that."

"Damnit Chelle."

Chelle smiled at Steven, knowing how hard it was for him to agree. The front door opened, just as Chelle was approaching the front door.

"I have a package that needs to be signed for. It's for a Mr. Melbourne Winston," the delivery woman said.

A woman, clearly of Mexican decent said, "I can sign, Mr. Winston is inside."

Chelle stepped forward, "Señorita? I know this sounds strange, but I must ask you to not touch that package." She showed her gun and badge.

The delivery woman backed off. "Can I go?"

Chelle asked, "Does the delivery paperwork say who or where this was shipped from?"

Nervously the delivery person scanned her electronic information. "It's from a Mercury Electronics Company. Taped to the box should be the same information."

Chelle took note of the delivery company's name. "That should be good for now. By the way, what is your name?"

"Caitlin, Caitlin Winsor."

"Thank you, Caitlin. You can go now."

Caitlin back away and hurriedly backed her vehicle out the drive.

Chelle looked back at whom she assumed was the housekeeper by the duster in her hand. "I am Agent Chelle Saltarie of the FBI. Is Melbourne home?"

"Sí Señorita. He is inside."

"Could I ask you to let me inside, without moving this box? I have reason to believe it could be dangerous."

The maid stared at the box with fear.

Chelle said, "Please, señorita, we need to move fast."

"Sí, yes, sí, come in, come in."

Chelle turned to Steven and gave him a sign with her hand to stand back as she hustled inside the door with the maid.

Las Vegas:

Wade watched the maid sign for the package. That was a good sign. Then something strange happened. She suddenly had a frightened look on her face and was talking to someone.

Wade cursed. A microphone wouldn't have been that hard to install, but he had made the conscious decision that it wasn't necessary. Why wasn't she picking up the package?

"No, no, shit! I can't fucking believe it," Wade said as he saw Chelle face for just an instant as she rushed past the package and into the house.

"Damnit bitch! And how the fuck did you know which Melbourne Winston to protect and how did you get to California so fast? What the fuck?"

Wade looked at his watch, talking to himself he whispered, "I only told the detective two and a half hours ago. What did I miss?"

Wade kept his eyes on the computer in front of him. The front of the home looked like a still photograph. Nothing moved.

Wade sat down and tried to calm himself. "OK," Wade said calmly, "Just a small setback. The bomb will go off, whoever opens that door next. Ka-boom." Wade paused his finger over the two keys that would set off the bomb instantly when pressed simultaneously.

Newport Beach, CA

Steven had walked back to the car to explain to the girls what Chelle was up to. He was still bent over and talking through an open window when a black SUV pulled up behind their car.

Both men got out and approached him.

"Senator Westcott." The closest addressed him.

"Yes."

"We had a call for a murder threat against a Mr. Melbourne Winston. This is his address?"

"Yes it is, that is why I'm here."

"With two young ladies?"

"My daughter and a friend. There is an agent inside trying to warn Mr. Winston that his life has been threatened."

One of the agents took a hard long look at the two girls in the back seat.

"It wouldn't be Agent Saltarie by any chance?"

"It is."

The taller agent said, "She was told to stand down. Stay here while I clean up this mess."

Alan D Schmitz
DIGITAL SECRETS

Senator Westcott said forcefully, "Don't approach the house."

Both agents turned towards Steven with their hands threateningly on their weapons.

"Are you giving us orders, Senator?"

Steven, tempted to let them go, decided to explain. "Chelle said she was suspicious of that package that was just delivered. She's afraid it could be a bomb."

"You mean Agent Saltarie, who shouldn't even be here, thinks it might be a bomb. No shit? Come on, Jones, time to kick Saltarie's ass back to Washington D.C. They can deal with her there."

Inside the Winstons' home:

"What is all the commotion Maria?" a man's voice gruffly growled because Maria was calling his name loudly over and over.

They found Melbourne at his desk.

"Señor, señor, I am sorry. This señorita insist on seeing you. She has a gun."

That got Mr. Winston's attention. He looked up.

"My name is Agent Chelle Saltarie, I'm with the FBI."

"Yeah, you and everybody else. Get the hell out of my house."

"I'm with Senator Westcott, he's waiting out by the car."

"Why?"

"Why what sir?"

"Why is he out by the car? I know him, I don't know you. Wait, yes I do. You were with him in Vegas. Now I remember, Winnie told me about you. You're Westcott's girlfriend."

"Yes sir, but that's not why we are here. We believe your life is in danger."

Calmly, Melbourne placed the pen he was using back into a round leather pen and letter opener holder. And equally as calm asked, "Is that so?"

"There is an active serial killer. He has already killed a few of your associates. It seems all but one worked on the Lake Lerna project. I believe it's Wade Sullivan."

Winston looked at Maria, smiled a bit and said, "Maria, muchas gracias. You can go now."

"But the package, what about the package?"

"It's OK, Maria, I will take care of the package."

Melbourne changed his focus to Chelle, "About the package. What do you know?"

"Were you expecting a delivery today?"

"Can't say I was. Then again, Winnie has something delivered almost every day from somewhere or another."

"There is a big box on the front stoop that had to be signed for. It is marked specifically for you, from a company called Mercury Electronics."

Melbourne scratched his chin whiskers that looked like a few days' growth to Chelle.

"Nothing I remember. Let's take a look."

"I don't recommend that sir. The killer has been diabolically creative. Most deaths were made to look like suicides."

"I see. So, what do you propose we do with the box on the front stoop?"

"We need to call in the bomb squad, sir."

Melbourne laughed, said indignantly, "I would be the laughingstock of the neighborhood if it turned out to be some computer parts I forgot I ordered. Can you imagine, bomb sniffing dogs, robots crawling around, people in padded bomb suits. All because I forgot I ordered something through the mail. I don't think so."

They all heard a car door slam.

"Ahh, that's Winnie now, I'd know that door slam anywhere. Let's see what she has to say."

"NO! She can't go near the box. Chelle turned and ran towards the door."

****

DIGITAL SECRETS

Steven watched the two FBI agents ignore his warning as they kept walking towards the home. He was in the process of calling Chelle when he saw a car approach from the other direction. It turned into the drive.

In another second, he saw it was Winnie.

Steven shouted at the girls, no matter what. Stay in the car. Steven started running towards the driveway.

The two agents, hearing Steven's warning, turned and drew their weapons at the advancing senator.

Steven saw them and ignored their warnings for him to stop. He yelled, "Winnie, Winnie, stay in your car. Get back in your car."

Winnie looked around confused, she saw the two men in black suits drawing their guns towards the Senator.

Winnie shouted in a panic, "It's Melbourne, is he alright? I have to see him."

"Stop, Senator, stop now!" the two agents shouted.

"Winnie," Steven shouted while he ran towards her, "we think the package is a bomb, stay away."

"What?" Winnie shouted back as she approached the doorway.

The agents took up a firm shooting stance not far from the front stoop. "Stop Senator. Stop, stay away from her and the house."

Las Vegas, Caesars Palace:

Wade held his fingers over the two keys that would detonate the bomb. One way or another, he would have to detonate the bomb, if for no other reason than to destroy whatever evidence the FBI could glean from an intact bomb.

His plan was simple. The first face he saw in the camera, ka-boom. He was oblivious to all the commotion outside and inside the house. As far as he could see it was the same calm photo of the front door looking at him.

Then he saw her, the FBI agent opened the door. She would make a fine target. She came closer to the box. "Goodbye Agent Saltarie."

Winston residence:

Chelle opened the door; she heard Steven scream. "No Chelle, stay inside."

Two men Chelle didn't know were aiming their guns at Steven who was clearly on a run towards the house.

In an instant she saw everything going wrong. Mrs. Winston was nearly to the front door and the package. Chelle knew that if it was a bomb, something had to trigger it. She could feel in her stomach this was to be it.

Chelle recognized the FBI shooting stance, she screamed. "Steven no, drop to the ground. Now! Or they'll shoot. I'll stop Winnie."

"Steven stopped running; Chelle gently walked past the package towards Winnie."

Las Vegas, Caesars Palace:

The screen went blank as Wade pressed the K and the B keys simultaneously. The screen in front of him went instantly dark. The bomb had worked. The female agent and anyone remotely near her were gone, along with the front of the house.

Chapter 21

Newport Beach, CA:

Steven dropped to the ground; hands outstretched. He looked up and saw Chelle rush Winnie around the back of the house. The agents had their guns pointed at him.

He saw something peculiar. It was Melbourne stepping through the front door and closely examining the box. The agents approached Steven and looked back at what Melbourne was doing.

He picked up the box and cautiously walked it towards where Steven was laying on the grass. "Get up," he said to Steven. "This is a bomb, and I'm placing it in the middle of the yard, precisely where you are lying."

Steven looked at the two FBI agents, who still had their guns drawn.

Melbourne said to them, "Bug off you two. This man and his friend saved my life, and my wife's. That's a hundred times more than you have ever done. "Do something useful and get a bomb squad out here. It is possible for this thing to re-arm itself."

Steven got up and saw the agents holster their weapons. "We thought he might be the danger," one of them said.

"Right, and his FBI girlfriend, bullshit. Now do what I said. Call the bomb squad, you morons. And get some black and whites here. And turn off your phones; he could use the damn things to re-arm this thing."

Melbourne carefully placed the package down. He placed a small black box on top of the box. "Make yourselves busy and block off traffic and keep everyone at least a half-block away."

By this time Steven was back down to the car and checking on the girls. Melbourne ran away from the bomb and towards Steven and the girls. He asked, "Friends of yours?"

"My daughter and her friend."

"Drive around the back side of the house. It'll be safest there."

"Steven nodded and said, "Thank you."

"I'll go find that brave girlfriend of yours and my wife. Ladies, could you please turn off your phones. It's entirely possible that they could be used to re-arm the bomb."

With mouths ajar they both managed to nod in affirmation. Steven, the girls, and the driver all hurriedly depowered their phones.

Inside the house things were mostly calm. Melbourne worked hard to keep it that way as he slowly prepared some refreshments for all six of them as sirens wailed outside.

"I gave strict orders for no cell phones. I hope those fools out there actually pay attention. You see, Wade may have set up the bomb to scan for cell phones. They could provide a temporary connection to the internet, giving Wade time to re-arm it. That is, if he figures out it didn't go off. My timing may have been off a hair. Oh well, I can't control everything."

Winnie said, "No you can't, but you certainly do try."

"Compliment accepted," Melbourne said. "As soon as Wade discovers his bomb didn't go off, he will start trying desperately to reconnect so he can destroy the evidence. He might have planned for some sort of back-up contingency, though I doubt it. He's pretty sure of himself, that one. Probably never anticipated that his bomb might not work."

Steven said, "It was certainly brave to examine the box as you did to determine it was indeed a bomb."

"Nonsense, I'm sure you mean exceedingly foolish. But not as much as you think. You see, when this brave woman dashed out the front door to stop my dear wife from going near the implement, I analyzed the predicament for a brief moment.

"If it was me building a bomb to kill, well, me, I would want to make sure it didn't go off until my intended victim was near it. How would I do that? Not with a timer, that wouldn't work. One way would to be physically near with a detonator in hand. But the killer didn't know when I would be home or even exactly when the package would be delivered. No, not probable; he would have to hide nearby for a day or two, and if the package was inside the house, he would have no way to know when or if I was near.

DIGITAL SECRETS

"I reasoned it must be done remotely. But if you're going to do it remotely, why not do it from anywhere you want? Simple, all you would need is an internet connection. But you would also need to know when the intended target is nearby. Hence a camera, which I detected when I examined it, thus, knowing it indeed was, is, a bomb.

Chelle asked, "But how did you know it wouldn't go off as you approached it?"

Melbourne looked at the two young girls, who were mesmerized by the story. He winked at them. "Because in a sense, I disarmed it. You see, when you ran for the door, I deduced what I had to do. I always, I mean always, have a cell phone jammer near me. Not legal in the United States, but I feel completely naked without one nearby. Though there are other ways the bomb could have been communicating with the web, none were more likely than a portable hot spot inside the box. If I know Wade, and I do, it would be what he would do. It is brilliant you know.

"I assumed Wade had seen you go into the house to warn me. At that point, killing me with the bomb was statistically out of the equation. Killing you, though, was a reasonable second choice. When you ran for the door to warn my wife, I was right behind you with the cell signal jammer in hand and with the hope my assumptions were correct."

Melbourne looked back at the two teens, "Obviously, I was correct, and it disrupted his signal to the bomb to detonate. Now that you saved my life, it's time to get these young ladies to their concert tonight. I'm a huge fan you know. I love 'Time to Reboot'."

Steven quizzed, "How did you know that was our plan?"

Melbourne pointed at Kristal's shirt, "The t-shirt says it all, and you came from Las Vegas. It's obvious."

Winnie said, "Caesars's jet is waiting to take me to Las Vegas. That's why they brought you here. To pick me up. I told you I was a high roller."

Melbourne looked at his watch. "In an hour-and-a-half, we can have you back to Las Vegas girls. More than enough time to still get a tan and see the concert tonight. Do you girls like their latest hit, 'Old Sneakers'?"

Tracy gushed, "It's one of my favorites."

Melbourne agreed, "The sound reminds me of old sneakers. I don't know how they do it. You can feel the comfort of old sneakers when they sing it, it's awesome."

Steven asked, "What about the bomb?"

"We'll sneak out the back, not our problem anymore."

Winnie said, "I have a go-bag mostly ready. Let me finish packing and we're off."

Chelle said, "I'm sure the FBI is going to have questions."

"I'm sure they will," Melbourne answered. He looked at the girls and winked again. "So, the sooner we get going the better."

****

Steven waited at the bottom of the plane's stairs as all climbed aboard. He couldn't help but scan the tarmac to see if they were being watched. Winnie and Melbourne were next to last. Steven as the last passenger assured the flight attendant, "Our group is all on board."

"Welcome back on board," the flight attendant said, "I have sandwiches all ready to serve as soon as we are off the ground."

The two teens found their favorite seats near the back of the aircraft, two leather recliners across from each other. The four adults found comfortable seating for four around an oak table.

Steven looked out the window of the aircraft as it smoothly left the ground.

Melbourne said over the roar of the engine and the thump of the wheels retracting into the fuselage. "Is everybody's phone still turned off? I would not want our conversation to be overheard."

Steven and Chelle nodded an affirmative, Winnie double checked hers.

She said, "Melbourne, you can be so melodramatic."

"If you recall, I was forced to leave my cell signal jammer at the house."

Melbourne pointed to Steven's watch. "May I see your watch, sir?"

Steven slipped it off and handed it to him. "It's one of the newer models," he said.

Melbourne pressed the appropriate buttons and it turned off. "Yes, I recognized it. It's a great listening device. Always close, in the open. It reminds me of an outdated term. Remember the old spy movies when they would 'bug' a room?" Melbourne laughed a bit. "Those devices are so passé now. We wear our own spy devices now. Telling anyone who might care, 'listen to my conversations.' At any rate, now we can talk. At thirty-five thousand feet and moving at four-hundred plus knots we should be about as safe from listening devices as possible, however the airplane does have Wi-Fi so the added precautions.

"You two saved my life. Let me repay the debt by telling you, Senator, what you have been working so hard to learn. Of course, you didn't hear it from me, and make no mistake, if you say you did, I will deny it vehemently. Let's start by telling me what you know or think you know."

Chelle started, "Our information tells us that there are two quantum computers. They are called Iphicles and Hercules. They are being built under the new addition to Caesars Palace and cooled by a process using supercooled water being engineered by a Dr. Langston. He is now dead through a laboratory accident that I believe Wade Sullivan masterminded. Why I believe that, is because just like you, we were told he would die next before his fatal accident."

Melbourne nodded knowingly but didn't comment.

"Steven added, "I estimate that over a billion dollars have gone into this project, possibly up to two billion. It is called the Lake Lerna Project."

Winnie looked at her husband, "Mel, I think it's time you tell them and me about this project. I know it's top secret, but your life has been threatened. I have a right to know."

Melbourne smiled, "I agree, though I know certain FBI agents, if that's who they truly are, who would disagree. I can start with the fact that your information isn't wrong. Your two billion estimate is not far off. Funding hasn't been a problem. It's not just under the new addition, it's under all of Caesars Palace, the whole eighty-five acres. The lake used for the show is a huge cooling facility for the computers, and you're right about the super cooled water and Dr. Langston.

"They are collecting the smallest of details on everybody. They collect free data roaming the internet and data stored in its own third-party data center. That is part of its strength, it's a third-party cloud storage system. The government rents data storage and fast retrieval to anyone who needs it. They claim it is competitively priced. Which means, many institutions are sending their data directly to the government without even knowing it."

"And that is where the quantum computers come in," Steven supposed.

"Think of Iphicles as the collector. It collects such things like grocery store information, medical prescriptions, phone records, bank transactions, credit card transactions, texts sent, emails sent, voice mail, and on and on. It collects all government information, everything, even security video and traffic cam video.

"Iphicles scans the internet for information. but it needs someplace to keep all that information. It stores that in a state-of-the-art computer farm, built of mostly conventional type computing power. In fact, it contains so much data, that it would be useless unless there was a way to sort and manage it. The information is enormous and that is a big problem. But Hercules is the solution.

"And fortunately, or unfortunately, that is where I come in. These are quantum computers that are connected on a quantum realm that is way freakier in reality than any science fiction movie. It's a particle world were everything has to balance out, even if they're not physically connected, and that is called entanglement."

Steven added, "We had a subcommittee lecture on quantum physics once. I was highly motivated to learn about it; still, it made no sense."

"I have a hard time wrapping my head around quantum mechanics too, everyone does. But even if I don't understand it, I do know how to make it work. God it was, is, exciting. The point is, Hercules is exceptionally good at matching all the pieces to the puzzle together nearly instantly with Iphicles' help. The science got the best of me. To have unlimited funding to create the finest working quantum computers, it's past exhilarating. Then I saw where my work was going. Whoever has access to the computer will control the country, probably the world."

"Well, it's not the President."

Chelle asked, "Not the President? What's not the President?"

"Who has control of the computer. He wanted me to find out more about it and tell him, because he knows something suspicious is going on in the Justice Department."

Chelle asked, "You talked to the President about Lake Lerna? When? Why didn't you tell me? Is that when he told you that you might be under a grand jury investigation?"

Steven confirmed as he loosened his tie some more. "It was. And our discussion was top secret. So top secret it didn't even happen. However, it's time to put all our cards on the table."

Chelle asked, "He doesn't know about it either?"

"He had an inkling that something big is going on. He knew I was getting close because certain people were starting to target me. That's when he said that there is a group that want to brand me as a traitor. Might even start a grand jury investigation into me."

"That's absurd," Chelle said, upset over the allegations.

"The President suggested I walk away from the whole thing. And since that meeting, I pretty much have. He suggested that it might be the only way to stop them from coming after me."

Melbourne said, "Even if the President does know about it, he doesn't control it or them. That I can assure you. I didn't understand or maybe I didn't want to understand the depth of what I was inventing. Now I do, and I'm afraid it's too late to stop it."

Winnie came to her husband's defense, "If it's illegal, you couldn't have known what they were going to do with it. I mean, it doesn't make you complicit."

Melbourne took his wife's hand in his, "I don't think it's illegal, or what it does is illegal. How can there be a law against something that nobody even knew was possible. Though, once I learned its true objective, I disagreed with its usage on more ethical grounds."

The flight attendant came by to inquire about any drink requests and reminded everyone that landing would be in about a half hour.

Bottled water was all the adult guests wanted.

The flight attendant asked, "I have a selection of prepared sandwiches if anyone is interested."

Steven smiled. "I am famished. We haven't eaten all day."

Chelle agreed, "A sandwich sounds wonderful right now."

The flight attendant looked towards the two girls in the back of the plane. "The young ladies are also taking advantage of a light snack. I'll be back in a moment with the refreshments."

As soon as the flight attendant was out of listening range Steven asked, "Who is controlling the project and the computers?"

"It's the fourth arm of government."

"The fourth arm?" Steven questioned.

Melbourne explained, "The federal government employs over nine million people. That counts contract workers like me, the military, post office, and on and on. These workers outlast administration after administration. It doesn't matter what party is in control; these millions of workers don't change.

"They are not voted in and out of their jobs by the winds of change. Some call them the deep state. I call them the fourth arm of government because they run things on a day-to-day basis. And mostly do it their way, regardless of which party is in control. Basically, it's the bureaucracy in general.

"Part of that group is the huge intelligence arm of the government. All the seventeen agencies, maybe more, depending on who you want to count. They are the ones in control of this mega spying apparatus. The most directly involved is James Mitchell."

Steven whispered, though everyone heard him, "The Director of National Intelligence. I suspected as much."

The flight attendant returned with the water and a plate of sandwiches. The conversation abruptly stopped with everyone giving a hardy 'thank you' before he left again to check on the teens in back.

Winnie asked, "Who are they spying on and why?"

Melbourne looked a bit surprised that they hadn't assumed that part out yet. "Who? Why, everyone, of course. It collects metadata on everyone."

Winnie asked, "What's metadata?"

Melbourne patiently explained to his wife, "Say you take a picture of a cat and you send it to me. I will then have a picture of a cat. The photo might be cute and all, but I know nothing about it. If you also send me or I somehow attain the metadata on the picture, I would know the size of the photo, where the picture was taken, and at what time and date, and so on.

"Imagine your name and a photo of you is the cover of the book. The metadata of your life is the contents. These computers excel at writing the book on every detail of a person's life. The implication of that is beyond measure."

"Our files," Steven said to Chelle.

"Exactly," Melbourne agreed, "a file on everybody, and all perfectly legally obtained. What you can't imagine is the detail. It has your eating habits by obtaining what groceries you buy, and what restaurants you go to and even what you ordered, how many drinks, what wine. It knows where you have been by the minute and how long you were there. It knows what television shows you watch, how late you stay up at night by what time your cable television was turned off. The information is unbelievably detailed. And how can anyone challenge the government's right to collect it, if they don't even know it exist?"

Steven or Chelle didn't explain their glimpse into their own files, but they certainly understood the broader implications.

Chelle asked, "Are these people capable of murder to keep the Lake Lerna Project a secret? Do you buy into the dark government side of things?"

Without hesitation Melbourne said, "Without a doubt."

"Our source thinks that this group is letting Wade Sullivan kill. They believe whoever they are, arrested a friend of theirs for the murders with the intent of throwing the authorities, namely myself and my team off the trail of the real killer.

"The fact of how my team and I were ordered to immediately shut down our investigation after the arrest of James McConally is suspicious to say the least."

Melbourne's face showed shock, "James, arrested. They didn't tell me, nor ask me about him. Ridiculous, I tell you."

Steven asked Chelle, "Wouldn't that be normal operational procedures? I mean, if the FBI captures and puts into custody the person they believe is the killer? Isn't it by definition, case closed?"

"To call the end to an investigation without proof such as the suspect giving us motive, possibly a confession, along with positive information on how he did the killings, or other positive evidence, is not normal ops."

"Maybe they got that and just didn't tell you."

"We were shut down immediately after they arrested him. There was no time for interrogation. I was told to stand down and my office in Washington was told to stand down immediately. And nothing was shared with us, that is odd."

Melbourne said, "You're suggesting your digging was coming close to exposing a top-secret government project. They, whoever they are, wanted the digging to stop, immediately."

Chelle picked up a mini sandwich but before she bit into it, she said, "Yes, exactly."

Melbourne answered, "You don't have to convince me."

Chelle finished a few bites and washed it down with some water.

Melbourne continued. "The government is working desperately hard at keeping exactly what the project is designed to do a secret. Everything is compartmentalized. Purposely not letting any of the teams know what the other teams' objectives are. The problem was they needed me to coordinate things. And eventually, I learned the real value of what they were building, what I was building for them.

"This is a powerful group we are talking about. All with top secret authorization. Heads of the most clandestine arms of the government. I call them the fourth arm because most the time they don't care who is elected. It doesn't matter to them. They see themselves as the great invisible regulator on the country. If they don't like a policy, they just don't implement it, or drag their feet until a new administration come to power."

Steven agreed, "I get that, I've seen it in action over and over again. But where does Hercules come in?"

"Now they can take it one step further. If you as a politician don't fit into the bureaucracy's ideology, they wipe you out, make you unelectable."

"And how would they do that?"

"Without it costing them a cent, they press a button and ruin your image. They can have photos of you buying alcohol at your local liquor store and use social media platforms to make you appear an alcoholic. Or find a compromising picture of you in any number of unflattering situations and post it to back up whatever argument they want. Maybe even control the election itself through electronic manipulation of voting machines. Of course, nothing has to be true. Just undeniable and unexplainable in the two seconds the media might give you to try. It'll be like the Matrix."

"The movie?" Winnie asked.

"Yes, exactly, except we won't be hooked up to some giant mind machine, but our lives will be make-believe all the same. Social media will only tell us what they want us to know. Step out of line and your life will be debased. Even reporters who get out of line will find their lives upside down in a hurry.

"A few might learn the truth, even try to expose it. But the overwhelming disinformation campaign will more than wash their efforts away like an ocean wave sweeps away a castle of sand."

"Honey, I love you, but this sound like the rantings of a madman, maybe a genius madman but just the same, a madman."

Melbourne nodded in agreement, "Don't think I don't know that. They have already done it. Small test, small cases. Some people have already lost their jobs because of a tweet that went viral."

Steven agreed, "I have seen plenty of that. Didn't know it was fake."

Melbourne shrugged his shoulders a bit, "It may have been true, or not. Knowing what I do, I suspect anything I haven't seen with my own eyes to be untrue."

Melbourne laughed, "I guess I don't even believe my own eyes anymore. Photos, videos, audio, can all be expertly faked. At any rate they have the capability to make tweets go viral and toxic at the same time."

Looking at Steven he added, "This group can create enough disinformation to make you look like a traitor. Don't think they can't. They can do it to anybody, they made a point of showing us, that's how they keep us in line.

Steven asked, "How far is the project? When will it be done?"

Melborne dropped his head and shook back and forth slowly. "It is finished; that's why I was home. Tonight is the official turn over to the government. I wanted nothing to do with it.

"Everything up to now were mere tests, always restricted by non-intelligence type contractors looking on and over the shoulders of whoever was pushing the buttons. I'm afraid that after tonight, they will all be gone. The intelligence community will no longer be bound by, well, anything."

The flight attendant came back and cleaned up the table he advised, "We will be landing in ten minutes. Please stay in your seats with seat belts on."

"Love," Melbourne looked at his wife, "where are we staying while here?"

"We have a suite at Caesars Palace. As a matter of fact, it's in the new Lake Lerna wing."

"Poetic justice I suppose. The one place I didn't want to be tonight. If asked, all I told you was that I have no idea why anyone would want to kill me. The rest of our discussion was centered around the concert tonight."

****

Chelle was driving back to their hotel. Steven, in the front seat beside Chelle, heard a ring tone come from someone's phone in the back seat. He chuckled, he recognized it as a tune from the Dancing Chickens.

From the back seat, Kristal said, "It's Dad, I can't wait to tell him we stopped a bombing and flew in a private jet to California."

Chelle looked at Steven and laughed. "He's not going to trust either of us after this."

Steven replied, "And I wouldn't blame him one bit."

Kristal said, "Hi dad, you won't believe what we just did."

Chelle took out her phone and turned it on. "I had better let my team in on our escapades too."

Steven asked, "What about this Wade fella?"

"Hopefully, my team has found some probable cause."

Tracy said from the back seat, "Dad, you're all over 'The Little Bird Says'."

"What?"

"The social media app, 'The Little Bird Says'. You and Kristal are on it."

"I know what it is, I have an account, remember." Steven said sounding a little exasperated. "Why are Kristal and I mentioned?"

"Your picture, it's when we got on the jet. Ohh my God...it says 'Senator Steven Westcott is caught going on a Las Vegas fling with underage hooker.'"

Steven said, "Chelle, pull over in that drug store parking lot."

Kristal leaned over and looked at the photo on Tracy's phone. "Oh my god, Dad, I gotta go. I'll call back soon." Kristal abruptly ended her call and held her breath as she read the caption beneath the photo of her and Steven getting onto the stairs of the jet.

The car came to a stop. Tracy handed her dad her phone. Steven looked at and read the caption. He muttered, "Those 'son's-a-bitches'" He handed the phone to Chelle. "They started ruining me already. I guess it's game on."

Steven took out his phone. "Two can play at this game. I need a group photo. Right now. I need to respond to this post immediately with a counter message. To clear our names."

Steven opened the app. "Everybody out of the car. One family photo coming up. SHIT! My account has been shut down. I've been canceled."

All four exited the car, deciding where to merge for a group photo with the plan of getting as much of the Las Vegas strip on the photo with them.

"I can post it, Dad." Then just as suddenly, she said, "My, my app isn't working anymore. Just a second ago it was working fine. I can't get it anymore either. Let me try PhotoBook."

After a few seconds Tracy said, "It's closed too."

Kristal said, "Mine too."

Chelle offered, "The papers will be all over this. Steven, you will have your time to explain it. The truth will come out."

Steven said to Kristal who was in tears. "Kristal, Chelle's right, the truth will come out."

Kristal blurted out, "But, it's not true."

Steven held her as she cried. "Of course, it's not. We all know that. As soon as we get back to Washington, I will go on television and explain the truth."

Steven got the girls resettled into the back of the car. "Let's forget this for now. There is nothing we can do about this today. Tonight is the Dancing Chickens concert, let's think about that.

Steven glanced at the door of the pharmacy, "I feel a headache coming on, I'll be right back. I need to get some aspirin."

Soon Steven was back in the car. Tears seemed to by drying, Steven was glad Kristal's apps weren't working. Dwelling on what was said or exposed on the social media sites was best not seen or heard.

Chelle's phone rang, "Hi Jojo, everybody's fine. We are almost to the hotel. I will call you back, I promise. I just can't talk now. I know, ten minutes, I promise."

Chelle looked sadly at Steven, "I think I feel a headache coming on too."

They headed north up Las Vegas boulevard and soon they turned into the drop-off area for Paris Hotel. The day seemed ruined as they crawled out the cab, it was only noon though it seemed as if a whole day had passed.

Steven feeling dejected whispered into Chelle's ear as they walked to the elevator. "Welcome to the Matrix."

Chapter 21

Las Vegas, Caesars Palace:

Wade stared at the blank screen of his laptop. He had expected to see nothing after the bomb he had delivered to the Winston's went off. The small computer transmitting the video images to him via the Winston's Wi-Fi hotspot interceptor would have been instantly destroyed.

Instead of celebrating his success, something nagged at him. It was small, almost un-noticeable, but he did notice it. He wasn't entirely sure; it had happened so fast. He saw the front door move. He waited an instant to see who was near the bomb.

He saw Chelle's face as she peeked out the door. That was the instant Wade simultaneously pressed the K and B on his keyboard. The K and B stood for Ka-Boom! That's when his screen went blank. It was too fast. A second or two would have had to pass for his digital instructions to travel through the internet and give the instruction to the waiting computer to blow itself up.

A pit in his stomach grew. He slowly closed the laptop. If his bomb didn't go off, there would be repercussions. He had tracked his bomb all the way from Charlotte, where he had shipped it from. It's also where he caught a late-night flight from the Charlotte/Douglas International Airport direct to Vegas.

It was possible that the unexploded bomb could, in time, give up evidence to link him to it. The computer had too many parts, each marked, stamped. He had counted on it being disintegrated or at least ninety-nine percent of it.

Wade stood up and stared at the view of the strip from his window high above Las Vegas. If an explosion wasn't reported on a Cathem Court, Newport Beach within the next two hours he would have to assume it didn't go off.

Wade smiled; his smile reflected at him from the glass of the window. If the agent had somehow foiled his attempt to kill Melbourne, it would only be fair to put her on his list of three final kills.

Wade glanced at his watch. Two hours from now, he would scan for news articles mentioning a bombing in Newport Beach.

If the bomb did not go off as planned, it didn't mean Melbourne was off the hook. His death was critical to his plan. Melbourne Winston had to die; another way would be found.

For now, he was hungry and there should be time to pick up some cash from a single-deck blackjack game somewhere in town. The odds were of course on the side of the casino, all casino games were. Blackjack was the fairest game in town, though still in favor of the casino, unless you knew all the tricks to turn the odds. Wade did, it would be an easy source of cash.

****

Steven, Chelle, and girls were getting some pool time in before the concert. The girls were spending time in the huge rooftop octagon pool, taking turns pushing each other off an air-filled mat. A couple of boys their age had somehow managed to join in their game.

Steven looked at Chelle through his sunglasses. "The girls are having fun, as it should be. Tell me, how did it go with Jojo?"

"He understands, sort of. Tamara and he saw the postings on the social media sites. I would expect it to hit the news by tonight. They're angry of course. Not at you, at the press and whoever is promoting this nightmare."

"The more I think about it the more I want them to keep it up."

"What, you're kidding?"

"Somebody is going to have a great deal of egg on their face when the truth comes out. The bigger the story, the bigger the egg they laid. I have contacts, the truth will come out. Kristal and I will get our due justice, trust me."

"Who? Who will have egg on their faces?"

"That will come out." Steven went back to his book and whispered to himself, "I hope."

Steven couldn't concentrate on his book, he asked, "Honey, would you mind watching the girls for a few minutes while I step away to make a phone call?"

"Of course not. Take your time. Say hi to the President for me, will you?" Chelle kidded.

"He calls me, remember."

"Oh, that's right. It's a one-way relationship between you two."

"Funny, funny girl. Bye, and you're in charge."

Steven found a corner away from the pool that was unused and unlikely to be coveted by other guest near a double door work entrance that was relatively un-used.

Steven dialed a number on the burner phone he had bought at the Walgreens store they had stopped at earlier. The phone rang once and went silent. Steven checked the number he had dialed. It was a number he had committed to memory; it was correct.

He tried one more time, same results. He started walking back towards Chelle when a text message came through. "Call again five minutes."

Steven glanced at his watch. He peeked around the corner and saw the girls actively splashing. A cocktail waitress walked by in a swimming suit carrying a tray of drinks. She smiled at him from a distance. Steven gave the universal sign for signaling he was OK. She walked by. Another two minutes passed; Steven made the call.

"Yes, Mr. President. I have that information you wanted."

After listening to a brief conversation, Steven said, "Yes sir, that's right. Confirmed. "Two quantum computers, called Iphicles and Hercules"

Steven listened to his phone pressed up against his ear, as he watched the girls playing in the pool a distance away, he heard the President say, "Steven, I am the President of the United States, and I'm literally talking to you through a bootlegged telephone while I'm hiding in the Presidential bathroom off the Oval Office. You bet I'm serious."

Steven said, "Your data confirms mine. At least seventeen spy agencies are involved."

The President asked a question Steven answered, "James Mitchell?"

Alan D Schmitz
DIGITAL SECRETS

The President said in a whisper over the phone, "Yes, of course. It all makes sense. Is it online yet?"

"I don't believe it is, but it will be soon."

"Steven, thank you. Destroy that phone. And Steven,"

"Yes sir?"

"Things are spinning out of control, you appear to be target number one."

Steven said, "I'm suspecting you're right. My goddaughter and I have been all over social media, and not in a good way. None of it true of course."

"Yes, I saw the photos. Of course, I don't believe them. In my opinion I think you need to get back to Washington as soon as possible and start doing some serious damage control."

Steven agreed, "First thing tomorrow.

"I can't stay in the bathroom much longer or my personal surgeon will bust in. Politically speaking, it would be bad for me and you to be seen as collaborators right now. So don't tell anybody, especially that cute FBI agent you hang around with, you talked to me."

Steven turned off the cheap burner phone. He laid it on the concrete besides an oversized potted planter. After a careful look around, he tipped the planter and brought its edge down on the phone repeatedly. Soon the phone was in pieces.

He picked up the pieces and with a hard yank, he disconnected the thin wires connecting what was left of the phone to the battery. On his way back to Chelle, he disposed of pieces of the phone in various refuse containers scattered about.

Steven slid back down into his recliner lounge chair noticing the girls not tiring out one bit, nor the now three boys they attracted.

Chelle asked sarcastically without looking up from her magazine article, "What did the President know?"

Steven nonchalantly answered, "Oh, nothing special, he sends his regards."

"How nice."

"I think it's time we get the girls back to the room. By the time we get a bite and they get ready for the concert, it'll be time for them to catch the hotel shuttle to the arena."

Chelle glanced at the girls again. "Good luck with getting their attention."

Steven laughed, "Yeah, that might take an hour on its own."

Caesars Palace, Las Vegas:

Wade sat back on the small chair next to the ultra-small desk in his hotel room. A thorough scan of the internet left no mention of a bomb going off in Newport Beach, or anywhere else for that matter.

Even stranger, there were no reports of a bomb scare of any kind. That meant to Wade, the powers-that-be that watched over the Lake Lerna project were containing the incident. He didn't know for sure, but he had to assume the bomb didn't go off. Containing a bomb scare is one thing but containing a bomb blast in a suburban neighborhood was another. The computer inside the delivery box had been silent ever since he pressed the detonation keys.

A smile came over his face. Working literally under Caesars Palace for years had given Wade many chances to crack into the main servers for Caesars Entertainment Corporation. It started as just a hobby, a distraction from the many hours of secluded work. It also served to keep his skills sharp. Casinos had a history of using cutting-edge computer security measures.

Caesars was no exception. Of course, eventually Wade found a way. He had even installed a back door into the system. Wade leaned forward and started typing. He was already logged into the guest Wi-Fi system.

There it was, 'Winnie and Melbourne Winston'. As of today, at 1:00 P.M., they were guests at Caesars Palace, Augustus Tower, room 25148. That meant the bomb had failed. Somehow the FBI agent had prevented it.

Wade sat back and contemplated all the implications, and there were many. Undoubtedly, the FBI would reverse engineer his bomb, unless they detonated it on purpose. That was unlikely, somehow, they had learned how to disarm it.

Wade envisioned a robot on tracks cutting at certain wires. The explosives wouldn't be that difficult to isolate. He hadn't built in a failsafe. Wade shook his head and scoffed a bit at himself for that mistake.

Wade jumped up from his chair and admonished himself, "Of course, you dumb shit, the FBI agent is here, they're all here. Wade old boy you're slipping, you even saw a picture of the Dancing Chickens tickets on his daughter's message board."

Wade sat down and worked his computer some more. "Son of a bitch. Two suites, how convenient. You and the Senator his daughter and a friend. The detective's daughter no less. My we are one big happy family, aren't we.

"But that still doesn't explain how you knew which Melbourne Winston and how did you get to California so fast."

He looked at his watch. Melbourne's death was key to his plan. Now that Melbourne knew he was a target, following through on the promise to kill him would be more difficult. The question Wade pondered was, how do you kill somebody who is expecting it?

Another bomb was out of the question, he had neither the time nor the materials to make another one. And killing Melbourne quickly, as in before the day ended, was critical. Wade went over the mental list of murder techniques. Of course, death by poison, a favorite through the ages. And, he was prepared. No self-respecting assassin would leave home without some, and he hadn't.

He chuckled, "Thank you, Mrs. Murphy," Wade said to himself, addressing his next-door neighbor. "Did you know your beautiful monkshood was deadly? In fact, the queen of poisons."

North entrance of Paris, Las Vegas:

Steven checked his airline app for the third time that afternoon. The President's warning was weighing heavy on him, making him re-think his decision to let the girls see the Dancing

Chickens concert. One more day in Vegas shouldn't hurt, he reasoned. Denying the girls their chance to see the Dancing Chickens didn't seem fair. Besides he had no plausible explanation about why they would all have to leave Vegas immediately. He had made his decision, now he hoped it was the right one.

"What's the matter, Dad?" Tracy asked.

"Why do you ask? Nothing is the matter."

"You keep checking your phone, and you look worried."

Chelle looked at Steven with knowing eyes, letting Steven know it wasn't just his daughter who noticed.

"I checked us all in on our flights tomorrow. I'm making sure everything is a go. If I don't have you two both back home when I promised, I will lose a best friend and your mother will never let us do something like this again. Steven smiled at his daughter. "Everything is fine. Our flight is still scheduled to be on time."

Steven slipped his phone in his pocket. He glanced at Chelle and could tell by the concern on her face that she wasn't buying it.

"Why the tux, Dad? Are you and Chelle going someplace special? You're a little overdressed for Vegas, but you know, you sort of pull it off."

"If you must know, we have an elegant dinner at Joe's Steak House, then," Steven paused for effect and produced two tickets from inside his tuxedo, "The Lake Lerna Experience. And I want to go in style. What's wrong with that?"

Steven added, "Besides, look at my date, anything less than a tux and I would look like a bum next to her."

Chelle blushed just a bit, she had on a red dress. Two narrow straps held up a low-cut top that displayed ample cleavage. The dress further wrapped around her mid-section and thighs with a revealing slit that showed off her shapely left leg when she walked.

Tracy kidded, "Get a room, you two."

DIGITAL SECRETS

Steven said, "Never mind us; the shuttle should be here soon. Some last-minute instructions. Always keep your phones handy."

"Dad, when you bought the tickets, you signed a release that agreed to having your phone cell phone's signal blocked during the concert."[9]

Tracy held out her ticket, "It's right here."

"Son of a gun, I forgot they can do that now."

Steven explained to Chelle, "The entertainment industry lobbied for this right. Their argument is that when buying the ticket, the concert goer is entering into a contract with the production company and or entertainer. If the ticket owner agrees to having their cell reception blocked for a specific time or reason such as during a concert, it should be legal to do so.

"Listen girls," Steven added as he spoke to them specifically, "We may not be back here until midnight, our show starts at ten. I'm guessing that by the time your show ends, you get back on the shuttle and with the heavy traffic expected after the show, you won't be here until midnight either. However, if you don't see us for some reason, you go straight to the room. The concert has security all over, same for the hotel when you get off the shuttle. If you go straight to your room, you will be perfectly safe."

"Dad!" Tracy rolled her eyes. "We're not little children. Kristal, look, it's Jack and Tom from the pool."

Steven and Chelle glanced over too. "I guess that shouldn't be a surprise." He said to Chelle. "Strange, I feel better they know someone even if they just met them a few hours ago."

Kristal said excitedly, "The shuttle is here."

Steven looked at his watch; it was six p.m. "Don't get nervous, you have plenty of time. The doors don't open until seven. Text us when you are on the way back. And girls?"

---

[9] In the U.S., at the time of this writing, it is illegal to electronically block cell phone reception. However, collecting, locking up, or forbidding phone use during concerts is becoming more and more acceptable.

"Yes, Dad?" Tracy asked with another roll of her teenage eyes.

"Have fun. Do you have money for souvenirs, snacks, you know stuff?"

"Dad!! You already gave us some."

Kristal pulled on Tracy's arm, "We have to go, I want to make sure we can sit with Tom and Jack."

In an instant the girls were gone. They waved from the bus window.

After the shuttle went down the road, Chelle took Steven's arm. "They'll be fine."

Steven patted her hand on his arm. "I know, I know."

"What time is dinner?" Chelle asked.

"We have 7:30 reservations. I was thinking we could gamble a bit, have a drink or two at the bar."

Chelle smiled warmly, wrapped her arm around Steven's and cozied up against it. She said, "A handsome man in a tuxedo can talk me into anything I guess."

They strolled down Las Vegas Boulevard on their way to Caesars Palace. The evening air was refreshing as the sun went down.

Steven pointed to the outside escalator that would take them to the bridge over the boulevard. "Your chariot awaits," he said graciously as they stepped on to the moving stairs.

As they stepped off, Steven's phone buzzed; he checked it, "I got a text from Melbourne inviting us to their suite for a drink. What do you think? It's on our way and we have plenty of time before dinner to say hi."

"That sounds like it could be interesting."

"I'll let them know we are just down the street and gratefully accept their offer."

"Perfect, that'll give me time to check in with my team. I'm officially on vacation so I'm sure they are trying not to bother me."

Steven chuckled, "So you are going to bother them?"

"I know you are worried about this Wade guy, and so am I. It would be a great relief to both of us if we knew he was at the very least being monitored, at the best, maybe my team has found enough links to bring him in for questioning."

"You do that, and I'll give Jojo and Tamara a call to let them know the girls are safely on their way."

Chapter 22

Caesars Palace:

Wade spoke into the phone. "I would like to order a box of nuts, chocolate covered. Yes, exactly. Could you send them up to my room immediately? Wonderful, thank you."

The small vial of poison and a small syringe were in his luggage. Poisoning the bait would be easy. Delivering the Trojan Horse without suspicion would be the trick, but he had a plan.

Wade smiled crookedly, thinking, I always have a plan.

There was a knock on his door. He looked at his watch. It was only 5:30; time was on his side. He didn't need to be at the arena until just before seven. He answered the door.

"Hello."

A young man smiled, "Did you order a gift box of a selection of chocolate covered nuts?"

"I certainly did." Wade smiled back, took the box of nuts. he handed the delivery person a five and said, "Thank you."

Wade made sure his do-not-disturb sign was displayed and latched the door. He carefully opened the box making sure to keep the gift wrapping and red bow intact. Inside the box, the delights were further sealed in cellophane. That wasn't going to be a problem; the fact that the nuts were sealed would give the recipient of the box a bit of confidence in their being untampered with.

Wade handled the syringe carefully with his gloved hands. Creating a suction with the plunger of the syringe he sucked it full of poison. Refining the Aconitine from the flowers and roots from his neighbor's garden was relatively easy, though dangerous. The woman next door loved her tall monkshood plant, though she had no idea of its deadly nature. Merely touching the plant can cause numbness and mild toxicity. Wade took the small syringe, pierced the cellophane, and injected the poison directly into the chocolates. In the years working with Melbourne, he had learned of his sweet tooth. Chocolate-covered almonds were irresistible to him.

The poison caused paralysis of the lungs and heart when ingested. The dosses he was injecting into the chocolate covered treats was more than enough to cause nearly instant death. And the best part was, there was no known antidote.

The toxicology report would undoubtedly show exactly how Melbourne died. Wade knew that after Melbourne was found poisoned to death, the entirety of the Department of Justice would be after him. That revelation wasn't particularly concerning. He had intended to leave Wade Sullivan behind anyways. In fact, in many ways, he had already. For instance, when he checked into this room, he used one of his many fake identities. He used cash whenever possible, and if it wasn't, stolen and altered charge cards bought off the dark web worked.

The irony that Wade Sullivan was a victim in his vendetta wasn't lost on him. He pondered a question of fairness. If Wade Sullivan's life was over, and it was, at least as he had known it, did that, or should that count as one of his remaining three victims?

A smile came over his face, no, that wouldn't be fair. As he had already admitted to himself, Wade was already in effect dead as soon as he started his little crusade. Three more victims it was, his mind made up. And Melbourne Winston would still be one of them.

In fact, Wade felt more excited than ever. At this point, the FBI was on his trail, they had to be, he reasoned. Also, Melbourne was on alert that he was a target. Killing people unsuspecting was one thing; this would take more cunning. But first he had a delivery to make.

Caesars Palace, Augustus Tower, twenty fifth floor.:

Wade kept his head down; a sports cap shielded his face from hallway cameras. He saw the floor maid and approached her with a wide smile. "I'm so happy you're here."

The maid, who was no more the five-foot tall, if that, smiled back from behind her stainless-steel wheeled cart that towered over her and contained everything she might need to clean and prepare a room.

"Is there something I can help you with sir?"

"Me? Oh no, sorry, I don't need anything. My room is just down the hall. But this was delivered to my room by accident."

Wade held out the box of candies, holding it with a clear plastic bag under his fingertips. "I think I know what happened. The sticker on top says complimentary for room 25148. My room is 25048. A simple mistake; I don't want anybody to get into trouble."

The maid looked at the box of chocolates, not sure what to do. Wade continued, "I was getting some ice and was going to leave it by their door. But I was afraid somebody would steal it before they noticed it. If you could deliver it personally, I'm sure it will save another employee some embarrassment."

"Yes, of course, it is just down the hall. I will try."

The maid took the chocolates in her hand and Wade made a point of using the plastic bag he was holding the chocolates with to line the ice bucket he was carrying.

"That's all one can ask. Thank you, miss."

"Oh no sir, thank you!"

Wade walked to the small room that contained an ice machine and two vending machines, one for snacks, the other for liquid refreshments. He filled his bucket with ice and peeked around the corner of the open doorway, watching to make sure the package was delivered.

He heard laughter coming from the direction of the elevators. A man wearing a dark suite and white shirt and blue tie, and two women, one in a red curvy formal dress with thin shoulder straps and another older woman with a 1960s-looking hairdo and casually dressed. The three came down the hallway laughing. They met up with the maid who was knocking on door 25148. Melbourne answered the door.

Wade kept himself hidden inside the small room. He listened intently on what was happening down the hall.

The maid explained her purpose first. "Sir, these chocolates are for you, compliments of the hotel."

"Thank you so much. And timely," Melbourne answered as he smiled at his wife, Steven, and Chelle.

Awkwardly the maid stood looking at Melbourne for a moment.

"Oh..., pardon me. Steven if you would?" Melbourne handed the chocolates to Steven to hold. He searched his pocket and pulled out his wallet.

"Thank you again." He gave the maid a generous tip.

"Thank you sir."

The maid walked away and Melbourne said, "I can see you found each other OK."

Chelle answered, "We spotted Winnie right outside the elevator lobby.

"Did you win, my dear?"

Winnie produced a printed voucher. "I did, fifteen-thousand."

Melbourne took the chocolates back from Steven and said, "Joe sent a box of chocolates. Let's eat them quick before he finds out you were a big winner and wants them back."

They all laughed as Melbourne ushered them all into the large suite.

Wade walked out of the room with a bucket full of ice. The maid couldn't see the wide grin on his face as he walked away taking the long route back to the elevator. Wade was ecstatic. With just a bit of luck, there would be three deaths and aside from one last task. His work would be done, and Wade Sullivan would evaporate to the world and a new soul would take his place.

What Wade didn't know and didn't suspect was that someone was watching his every move intently.

****

Steven and Chelle and Winnie stepped into the large suite; Melbourne set the box of cholates down on the white, marble-topped coffee table.

"You are dressed formally and divinely; I hope we are not keeping you from an important date."

"Not at all, this is perfect. We have tickets for the ten o'clock show tonight."

"The Lake Lerna Experience, I assume."

"You got it," Steven smiled. "And dinner reservations at Joe's Steak House."

"Well done, Senator, well done. Care for some wine? I happen to have a lovely Napa Cabernet."

Chelle said, "Perfect for me." As she dropped her purse on top of a counter near the door.

"And me," Steven agreed.

Winnie said, "There is a bottle of white in the fridge. I was enjoying that earlier. I think I'll stick with that."

Melbourne asked, "I trust the girls are on their way to the concert?"

Steven glanced at his watch, "That's right; they should be there by now."

His phone beeped; Steven laughed. "I should say, they are there. Tracy just sent a selfie of them in front of a sign advertising the concert. She says, 'We are early, the doors won't open for another forty-five minutes. We are hanging out with Jeff, Mitch, and Mike.'"

"Wonderful!" Melbourne smiled wide as he twisted the cork out of the bottle. "And who are those lucky gentlemen?"

Steven chuckled, "Friends the girls met at, more appropriately, in the pool today."

Melbourne poured a few glasses of wine. "Technology is nice I suppose, especially for a parent in today's world. For security reasons, I would suggest you turn off that damn thing, but with a daughter under your protection I know that would be a losing argument. I guess we will have to do things the old-fashioned way." Melbourne clicked the remote control and the television sprang to life." A little background noise may be the best we can do for now to try to prevent our being listened to."

Winnie said, "You can be so dramatic, Melbourne. I seriously doubt anybody is listening to us. Why would they even want to?"

"Merely a precaution, I'm sure you are right."

Alan D Schmitz
DIGITAL SECRETS

Melbourne served the three glasses of wine as Winnie helped herself to a glass of the white.

"So nice of our host to send us this chocolate-covered assortment of nuts. Should go well with the wine," Melbourne said as he took off the gift bow from around the box.

As he unwrapped the box he said over the sound of a commercial advertising a cure for foot pain, "The reason I asked you here tonight is I'm afraid a bit intrusive. I feel guilty about my part in creating these computers. Now that you know all about the Lake Lerna project, what are you going to do about it when you get back to Washington?"

Winnie scolded, "Melbourne, is that any of your business?"

Steven tasted a sip of wine from his long-stemmed wine glass he said, "Excellent wine, and I don't know. Personally, it sounds like something I would never support if it came to a vote. I can assure you it's nothing congress has voted on. But we don't approve every single project the military or the various intelligence agencies authorize, that would be impossible."

Steven looked around the ultra-modern room, detailed in square backed furniture, glass and stainless polished steel tables. With a slight flair of Roman influence. Different from their own Parisian-themed suite at Paris Hotel.

The television was an annoyance which they all tried to ignore to satisfy Melbourne's paranoia.

Melbourne interjected, "Meaning it probably isn't illegal."

"Probably not. As a member of the Gang of Eight, I will bring it up and demand some answers. Doesn't mean I'll get any. In fact, the way it sounds I will probably be run out of Washington one way or the other as an example."

"How's that?" Winnie asked as she looked over the selection of chocolates. "I see chocolate-covered cashews, Melbourne." She smiled at Chelle, "They're Melbourne's favorite."

"Impossible to resist." Melbourne smiled back.

Winnie opened the plastic wrap around the chocolate covered cashews and poured them into the tray it had come in.

Chelle explained, "After we left the plane, the girls noticed on their social platforms that Steven was pictured with Kristal as they were getting onto the plane this morning. The caption said, Steven was having an affair with an underage prostitute."

"Oh my!" Winnie said.

Melbourne, who was just about to taste a handful of chocolates, stopped to ponder the information. "It has to be from the project. Nobody else would have access to that photo that fast. It was most likely pilfered from a security camera at the airport. I wish I never heard of the damn project. I'm sorry Steven, I'm as much at fault as anybody. It also means you're probably right; they believe you already know too much, that makes you a threat to them."

Steven said sullenly, "Kristal's my goddaughter, in time I can undo the damage."

Melbourne agreed, "This time, but Chelle's right, it won't stop there. As of tomorrow, they will have the means to cause you much more trouble. They are intent on destroying your reputation and therefore your ability to cause harm to the project.

"I'd destroy those damn computers if I could. I mean it. It sounded like a good idea at the time. It was so exciting, I just became enthralled with the challenge, I didn't ponder the ultimate consequences. It's just too powerful, it will be like an opioid to anyone who has control of it; it will give ultimate power. And that kind of power corrupts whoever has it."

Steven looked at Chelle and said, "The President warned me to stay away, I guess it's too late."

"He knows about it?" Melbourne asked.

"He had his suspicions, but yes, he knows about it now. The only thing I can do is bring it up to the attention of the entire Gang of Eight and hope sanity prevails."

"Damn!" Melbourne said as he sat down deep in thought, the chocolates resting in his hand.

Steven picked up some of the snacks from the tray resting on the glass top of the sofa table. He placed the small handful of chocolates on a napkin resting on the coffee table to check his phone for messages.

DIGITAL SECRETS

Melbourne took one of the chocolates out of his hand and lifted it to his mouth. Instead of eating the chocolate, he smelled it. He looked at his hand, the one containing a fistful of the chocolates and lifted it to his nostrils and said, "That's odd."

The Winston's room, Caesars Palace:

There was a knock on the door. Melbourne set down his chocolates once again, smiled and said, "No doubt the maid wondering if we want turn down service."

Melbourne walked over to the door and opened it widely. The smile came off his face when he saw a man dressed all in white pointing a gun at him. The man in white stepped inside. Melbourne stepped back to keep his distance from the gun as the man in white entered the room and closed the door with a slight push off his foot.

Winnie, Chelle, and Steven all had their eyes on Winston when he opened the door. They were stunned into silence as the man entered with gun drawn and leaning slightly on a white cane with an eagle-head topper.

Steven immediately recognized the visitor and said with surprise and hatred in his voice, "Alphonso Lucas."

Alphonso, using the same hand as was gripping his cane, lifted it to his white fedora and tipped his hat in a gentlemanly fashion. As he did, he glanced at the television that was now discussing tomorrow's weather. "Good evening, Senator, Agent Saltarie, Mr. and Mrs. Winston. I apologize for the intrusion. But I'm sure you'll forgive me once I have a chance to explain."

Steven said with a sneer, "The President promised me I would never see you again."

"This wasn't his idea. He told you to leave Las Vegas, didn't he?"

"How do you know about that?"

"We have obviously communicated. I'm afraid it's too late now, you are here at an unfortunate time. You will most likely be implicated and that is something the President and I both wanted to avoid."

"Implicated? Implicated in what?"

The gun in Alphonso's hand didn't waver, he said. "Please, I insist that everyone sit." He looked at the open box of chocolates.

The man in white asked, "Has anyone tasted the chocolates yet?"

Melbourne said, "I was just about to indulge. Why do you ask?"

Motioning with the gun, Alphonso coaxed everyone into a chair.

Melbourne said, "There poisoned, aren't they?"

The man in white smiled, impressed. "Yes, they are. How did you know?"

"I didn't, until now. I handled some, my hands didn't smell like chocolate. I couldn't place the smell, but something was off. I almost ate one."

Alphonso said, "If you had, I would expect you would be dead by now."

Chelle, Steven, Melbourne, and Winnie all looked at each other for a moment then at the dish of chocolates in front of them.

"Again, my apologies for the intrusion. I was following a Mr. Wade Sullivan, curious as to what he was up to. He handed a box of chocolates to the maid. Shortly after, she delivered them to your room. Luckily, I recognized your face, Mr. Winston, and surmised what Wade was up to, seeing as how his first attempt to kill you with a bomb failed."

Chelle spoke up. "Now that we know why you are here; there is no need for the gun."

Alphonso said, "I wish I had your same conviction. I understand the bad blood between us. Please forgive me if I don't let down my guard quite yet."

Steven thundered, "Bad blood? I'll say it's bad blood. You killed my daughter. You admitted it! You tried to kill me."

Calmly Alphonso said, "Times change, conditions change. Now you understand why the gun is a necessity at this time, even though I saved your lives just now. Before I leave, I do have a bit of advice for you, Senator. Go down to the casino and keep yourself on camera. You might need to prove your exact whereabouts in the near future."

Steven interjected, "Why did you warn us? Why not let Wade do your dirty work?"

"Let's just say that I owed you and the President a favor in return for mistakes on my part. Besides, the United States, the world, will be going through a difficult adjustment. Worldwide, bold new leaders will be needed. You are such a man; the United States will need you. The President can't run for another term, and he thinks you might be the right man for the job.

"As for Mr. Winston, his wife, and Agent Saltarie, you're right. I had no desire to interfere with their fate one way or the other. They were mere beneficiaries of my warning to you. In fact, Mr. Winston's death has a certain appeal to it. No offense, Melbourne." The man in white gave a slight nod of the white fedora.

Melbourne asked, "I can guess Wade's incentive to have me dead, but why you? I don't even know you."

"Let's just say your skills could become inconvenient for me in the future. But please don't worry, I will take care of that problem when and if it arises."

Melbourne deadpanned, "I appreciate your candor. Let's pray that doesn't happen."

Steven forcefully demanded, "What difficult adjustment? From what? What does IRENE have planned?"

"Soon enough, all will know."

Steven reaffirmed his speculation, "So IRENE is behind it all and the President knows?"

"Of course we are. But do not trouble yourself with some sort of altruistic vision of saving the world from whatever we have planned. At this point it is unstoppable. Make no mistake, the world will shortly become even more volatile than it already is, one could say apocalyptic. Only then will your heroics be effective, if you choose to accept the challenge at that time.

The President knows a reawakening is at hand. He doesn't know how, but he is smart enough to know he can't stop it and neither can you.

Alphonso started backing his way out the room.

Chelle asked, "Why were you following Wade? What does he have to do with your plan?"

"I'm sorry, that I can't divulge. And Senator, consider my debt repaid."

Steven sneered, "I will never consider your debt repaid."

Alphonso opened the hotel door and checked the hall for other guests; there were none. He stepped back into the hall, keeping the gun steady on the group. He grabbed the brass door handle and closed the door.

Steven started for the door. Chelle held his arm.

She said, "Let him go. If you chase him, he might intentionally shoot you or somebody else by accident."

Steven felt the gentle tug on his arm. He looked into Chelle's eyes and realized she was right.

"Damn it," Steven said, "Why do we always have to play by his rules?"

Melbourne spoke up, "Obviously an acquaintance of yours. Not a friend, I take it."

Steven looked at Melbourne and chuckled a bit at his ability to neutrally sum up a situation. With a slight grin he said, "You can say that again."

Melbourne looked to his wife, "Winnie my dear, are you all right? You look a bit peaky."

"I'm fine, I think, I'm so confused. Can somebody please tell me what is going on?"

Melbourne said, "First, I think it wise we all wash our hands thoroughly. The poison doesn't seem to be transmitted via touch, but let's not take any chances."

They all carefully washed their hands. Melbourne sat down on the couch in front of the coffee table and examined the remaining packages closely, using a napkin to protect his hands.

"There is a pinhole in this bag." He picked up a single chocolate with the napkin and examined it. "It's discolored, I smell something and it's not chocolate."

Chelle carefully collected the chocolates and put the box they came in into a plastic bag. She said, "Attempted poisoning is an FBI matter, especially when an FBI agent is one of the targets. I'm calling the local bureau. This is all critical evidence to be used against Wade. I need to talk with the maid to get a statement."

Winnie walked to the television and turned it off, she said forcefully, "Can somebody please tell me what is going on? Melbourne, why does everyone want you killed? This can't be happening."

Melbourne sat down next to his wife on the sofa, he took her hand in his and with two hands held it gently. He looked at Chelle and Steven, who were now also seated on two identical square backed cushioned chairs, then back at his wife's eyes.

"Everyone, I hope, doesn't want me dead. Only Wade Sullivan, though that is most certainly one to many. I can only guess, but here it is. Wade is here to destroy the quantum computers. He wants me dead so I can't help rebuild them. I suspect that was why he killed the others. It is all an effort to thwart the rebuilding of Lake Lerna."

Melbourne brought both of his hands together as if praying, he lifted them to his lips deep in thought, his eyes closed.

Chelle said, "Regardless, I must notify the bureau that your life was threatened again. We now know he's here. According to Alphonso, he personally delivered these poisoned chocolates. Maybe the maid saw him; we could get a positive ID. We have a lead; we can stop him from trying to kill you or anybody again."

Melbourne with his eyes still closed and his hands still pressed together touching his lip, said, "Let's think this through. Would tipping our hand that his plan didn't work be the right play? He will only try again."

Melbourne's eyes opened, and he looked at Steven with a revelation in his expression and exclaimed, "Steven!" his hands went to his knees. He got up and paced the room a bit."

Finally, Steven asked, "What are you thinking, Melbourne?"

"I believe, in fact I'm entirely sure, Wade is the solution to our problem."

Chelle said, "He isn't the solution to the problem, he is the problem."

Melbourne chuckled, "Yes of course, to your problem of finding the murderer of all those fine people. "

Steven asked, "What do you mean the solution to our problem?"

"Don't you see? If I'm right, and I'm certain I am, Wade will destroy Lake Lerna for us."

Steven sat down contemplating what Melbourne was suggesting.

"What are you proposing?" He asked,

"I'm proposing we don't tell anybody anything, not yet, at least."

Shocked, Chelle asked, "What?"

"We let Wade go for now. My guess is sometime before midnight he will try to destroy Lake Lerna. Let's let him."

Chelle looked at Steven, "You aren't seriously considering it?"

Steven asked, "You said it couldn't be destroyed."

"Not by me, I never had intentions to do so. But Wade, you have seen, he can be devious. And mark my word, he is intelligent, highly intelligent. His mind has probably been working out that problem for the last year. With that kind of time, and his brilliance, trust me, he has a plan. He was hired to make sure it couldn't be hacked, but a master hacker like him may have some sort of back door in it already. Never trust a hacker not to hack."

Melbourne was quiet for a while as he turned toward a wall with a large, framed painting of some of the ruins of ancient Rome. It seemed as if he was studying the artwork when he said, "He must have a portal somewhere on site. That has to be how he's going to destroy it."

Chelle asked, "Why on site? It seems like he can hack into any system he wants pretty much at will from anywhere in the world."

"Yes, it certainly appears that way to a non-hacker. In truth, it takes a lot of planning and effort and knowledge. But the quantum computers are different. They are not connected to the internet. That turned out to be the only way to assure they couldn't be hacked. It's the failsafe. Anything collected off the internet by the conventual search robot is sealed off and quarantined offline. It is scanned and scanned again before being passed on to Iphicles, which is only connected to Hercules quantumly speaking.

"Wade has to hack into the computers on site at Caesars."

Steven said, "You're suggesting we knowingly let Wade destroy a couple billion dollars' worth of Uncle Sam's equipment?"

Melbourne interrupted, "I doubt that we could stop him if we wanted to. I am proposing we may not want to. Let's have some more wine and friendly conversation, let the next few hours take care of themselves. Chelle, I know it's a small dilemma for you, but only the four of us know exactly when we realized the chocolates were poisoned. You can report things in due time. After all, you are on vacation."

Steven reminded everybody, "Alphonso knows, and he warned me to stay visible in fact to make sure I'm on camera." He added, "Melbourne, this isn't our decision to make. It cost the government billions to build it. It could prevent the next terrorist attack, or worse? It could gleam enough information off the internet to pick up a planned attack by a foreign power. It could prevent war. Think about knowing about the attack on Pearl Harbor weeks or months before it was to happen. Or the attack on the pentagon and the twin towers. Hundreds of thousand, perhaps millions of lives could be saved by that kind of knowledge."

Melbourne agreed, "I'm sure those are the exact arguments made to convince the seventeen intelligence agencies to build it. It also collects everything on everybody and has the intelligence to connect all the dots. And not just on U.S. citizens, anybody who does anything electronically in the world can be tracked and spied on.

"Steven," Melbourne admonished, "you have already seen an exceedingly small sample of what it can do. Whoever controls it will forever stay in power, no political rival could survive an information attack from Lake Lerna. Listen to me," Melbourne stayed deceptively calm trying his best to persuade the group to his thinking, "Wade didn't know I was going to be in Las Vegas tonight. He is here for a different reason.

"Your other foe, the man in white. At first, I assumed he was here to stop Wade. Now I realize it's not that, not it at all. When he said that my death has a certain appeal to it, I asked myself why. Of course, it's for the same reason. He wants the computers destroyed too and sees me as an avenue for the government to rebuild. And I believe the President may have sent him on the mission."

"What!" Steven said incredulously.

"He suggested that he talked to the President. How else would he know that the President warned you to leave Las Vegas, something nobody but you and the President supposedly knew."

Steven sat in silence thinking for a moment. He said, "The President said, and I quote, 'You should come back to Washington ASAP.'"

Melbourne said, "Essentially the same thing."

Steven argued, "As we know, nothing can be taken as being private anymore. Somebody could have been listening to our conversation. I have found that IRENE has eyes and ears everywhere."

Melbourne asked, "Who is IRENE and why would they want the computers destroyed? I understand Wade's sense of revenge, but what does this IRENE have to gain?"

Steven explained, "They believe the United States is too powerful for the world's good. They want to give the current world order a reset. Chelle and I have learned the hard way they are a dangerous organization."

Melbourne pursued, "Yet he saved your life, and ours. Why?"

"You heard as much as I did. He thinks I could be important after some sort of cataclysmic event they are planning."

"Strange," Melbourne said as he put his hands together and gazed at the evening lights of Las Vegas.

Melbourne continued, "He may be right about the President. You did admit that the President warned you to be away from Las Vegas. When did he want you gone?"

"It was when we were at the swimming pool this afternoon."

"What did he say? Exactly." Melbourne insisted.

"Things are spinning out of control, you appear to be target number one. In my opinion I think you need to get back to Washington as soon as possible and start doing some serious damage control.

"He said he was calling me from the Oval Office bathroom. The only place he could find privacy."

Chelle asked, "You mean you weren't kidding when you said you were talking to the President."

"He instructed me not to tell anybody, not even you. I didn't want to lie, when you teased me about talking to the President I agreed with your joke."

Melbourne interjected. "I think the President should have been a bit more blunt with you. My guess is that he wanted you out ASAP, As in before midnight tonight.

"The President is trying to protect you from the fallout. I'm telling you, he's behind this Alphonso guy being here. They both want Wade to destroy this thing. I'm begging you; we need to let this play out."

Chelle got up. She said, "Melbourne, there were two attempts on your life, one on ours. We know Wade is a merciless killer. He must be stopped. That means I must get the FBI this information."

Melbourne calmly said, "I have something in the next room that might convince you I am right."

Melbourne got up and went into the side bedroom of the suite.

When he came back, he took everyone's breath away.

"Melbourne, put that gun away, you're scaring everyone," Winnie admonished.

"Not my intent, my dear. But nonetheless, nobody is calling anybody. We are waiting this out until after the concert, which is hours from now. If I'm right, the damage will be done by then.

DIGITAL SECRETS

Certain protocols will happen at the turnover to make it more difficult to destroy. Wade will make his attempt before that time, starting at eleven this evening about the same time the concert is set to finish.

"We need to wait here until after the concert. Steven, you will be allowed to meet your daughter and goddaughter as planned. My actions relieve you of any moral responsibility to stop him. Same goes for you, Chelle. What befalls me after tonight is not of concern. If I go to jail for stopping you and drawing a weapon against you, so be it. I helped create the monster, it is my responsibility, my duty, to see it destroyed if I can. For now, we wait to give Wade time to do what he will."

Chelle said, "What if he decides to kill someone else and we could have stopped him?"

"Again, my responsibility, not yours."

Winnie couldn't believe what she was seeing, "Melbourne, these are our friends."

"I know my dear. And I am so sorry I brought this predicament upon us. I have made up my mind. The monster must be destroyed. If I can't do it, I must help whoever can, including a cold-blooded murderer. Do not test my resolve. I will try not to shoot to kill, but I will stop any of you in any way I can. In the scheme of things, our lives," he looked at his wife sorrowfully, "sadly, our happiness is outweighed by the seriousness of this matter."

"Trust me, I don't want anybody hurt tonight, I detest violence. Everyone, place your phones on the table. Enjoy the wine."

Chapter 23

Wade exited the taxi in front of the arena, keeping his baseball cap pulled down as much as he dared to shield his face. He looked at his watch, the thirty minutes it had taken him to get here he hoped had been enough time for the chocolates to kill Melbourne and hopefully the others back at Caesars Palace.

There were several entrances. He walked to the VIP entrance for Caesars' Entertainment guests, which would include anyone from the Paris hotel shuttles. The V.I.P. entrance was starting to open.

Wade didn't see the two particular people he was waiting for. He knew they hadn't already gone in, so he waited in a recessed alcove until he saw them. They were with three boys, all young teens excited for the concert to begin. They stood in line together. Wade knew that soon their flirting would come to a sudden stop. The five were next to be security checked and to have their tickets scanned. The look on the two teen girls' face was priceless when they were told their tickets were fraudulent. All five stepped out of line.

Wade slowly shuffled himself a little closer to hear their conversation. The girls were near tears. Tracy insisted that there had to be an error, and her father would sort it out after she called him. After a short discussion the girls insisted that the boys go inside and promised they would call them after the concert. Wade waited as the two girls bid their new friends goodbye as they were allowed into the arena and disappeared behind the open doors.

That was when Tracy and Kristal could hold back their tears no more. A sobbing Tracy removed her phone from her purse just as Wade stepped up. He lowered his hoodie and asked, "Ladies, what seems to be the problem?" Wade said, sounding as concerned as he possibly could be. Tracy wiped some of the tears from her eyes. "They said our tickets are fakes. We know they're not. My father bought them at Paris months ago."

Wade asked, "May I see them?" Tracy and Kristal looked at each other not sure if they should trust the man. Wade smiled and pulled out a badge that he had on a lanyard around his neck. He showed it to them.

"I'm with the band. I'm part of the stage crew for the Dancing Chickens." The girls looked at the official-looking backstage pass. Their jaws dropped in awe.

"You're...you're with the Dancing Chickens?" Kristal asked.

"You bet. My name is Kenneth Kieth." Wade looked around, tilting his head one side, then the other. "Not too loud, I don't want to be rushed by our fans. Please, let me check your ticket, I can tell if it's a fake or not."

"Yes, sure, here it is." Tracy handed her ticket to Wade.

"Do you want to see mine too?" Kristal offered.

"One ticket should be all I need." Wade examined the ticket front and back. He held it up to the setting sun.

"I'm so sorry girls, I'm afraid they are right. These tickets are complete fakes. I mean they are somewhat convincing. But fakes nonetheless." Wade handed the ticket back.

The girls started to tear up again, "What are we going to do? We came all the way from Washington D.C.," Tracy said.

Wade swiveled his head, taking a quick glance side to side. He said, "I shouldn't do this, but I have a plan." Wade smiled a crooked smile at Kristal.

Wade pulled out a hotel key card out of his pocket. "I have a key for a side door. If you want, you can watch the concert behind the stage with me. If you would like autographs from the band, I can probably arrange for that after the show."

Kristal and Tracy looked at each other not believing their luck.

Tracy asked, "You mean it?"

"Sure, I know I can slip you two in with me. Nobody will care, we do it all the time. But until we get to the backstage area, you must do exactly as I say. Sometimes the locals get a little fat-headed with their authority. They might want to see your stage pass." Wade looked at his watch. "But we have to get going, I need to be inside when the show starts in case they need me. Are you in?"

Kristal and Tracy looked at each other and giggled. "Of course, we're in," Tracy said.

"Follow me, we have to move fast."

Keeping his head down, Wade went around the side of the Arena where he found a fire exit door. Using his key card, he slipped it into the electronic security key system. The door clicked open.

Wade whispered, "Quick, and stay out of sight."

Wade held the door open as the girls scurried inside the side hall.

"This way, we have to go down these stairs, through the basement and we will come up behind the stage."

The building was huge and cavernous. Wade promised the girls he knew exactly where he was going. Soon, the girls and Wade had made so many twists and turns, going up stairs and down that the girls were hopelessly lost.

Around one bend, Wade whispered loudly. "I hear footsteps, quick hide in this room."

Wade held open a door that accessed a small room. The room was concrete on three walls. The fourth held multiple electrical sub-panels. The girls joined him as he slid into the room and quietly closed the door behind him. It clicked itself closed and locked.

Inside the room it was noisy from the sound of huge air-conditioning fans. Wade pulled out a gun from the small of his back, hidden until now by his hoodie.

"Sorry girls, you won't be seeing the Dancing Chickens after all."

Wade gave the girls a crocked smile. He saw a flicker of recognition in Kristal's eyes. Kristal said, "You're that killer my dad is after, aren't you? I saw you when you passed us in your car. You caused our accident on the freeway."

"Bravo, young lady. And you know what else, your tickets are perfectly legit. I hacked into the computer and changed the UPC code on them just so we could have this quality time together." Wade laughed, "I wish you could have seen your faces when you were told your tickets were fraudulent. It was hilarious. Turn around, both of you."

Kristal and Tracy looked at each other, neither moving. Wade yelled, "NOW!"

That scared both and they turned, fighting back tears.

"Hands behind your back."

It didn't take long before Wade had their hands secured with wide, thick zip-ties.

With the girls secured, he unlatched a small steel access door. He opened it to reveal another small room. It wasn't a real room; it was more of a hall. It was intended as walk-in access to the back side of huge electrical switches. The opening was large enough for an adult male to climb through on his hands and knees.

"Get in," he said.

"In there?" Kristal protested.

He grabbed her roughly by the arm. She fell to the floor, and he pushed her through the small opening.

Kristal struggled onto her knees. With her hands still tied behind her back it was no small task,

"You too!" He shouted to Tracy

Tracy dropped to her knees so as not to hit it against the access door as she entered the small room struggling with her ballance. Both girls were soon tied hand and foot. Wade also secured their hands to pipes, keeping the girls sitting on the concrete floor feet apart from each other. As a last measure, he took a wide roll of duct tape and covered their mouths with it.

"Don't be frightened. I'm not going to kill you. At least, not right now. It's only fair that I give your dad time to find and save you. It wouldn't be much of a game if I didn't." Wade smiled at the girls, he looked directly at Tracy. "And it's entirely possible I won't have to kill you at all. You see, by the rules, if your father, the esteemed Senator, died tonight along with his girlfriend and your new friend Mr. Winston, from the poison I planted, you two young ladies don't have to die tonight. My target will have been met. I guess you could say you two are just my back-up plan. Call it an insurance policy."

Wade pointed to a small container already on the floor. "It's perfectly safe, just some bleach and vinegar. Unfortunately, if I, or someone else, doesn't reach you by one AM, this little battery timer will cause them to mix. That is a problem. It will create deadly chlorine gas. I'm afraid in this enclosed area, there will be no escaping it. I understand it's a painful way to die." Wade took a stick and pushed the chemical bomb under a panel. "No sense taking chances. The hatch can't be opened from inside. If somehow you do get loose, you still can't stop the gas. All you have to do is pray that somebody finds you before, well, before it is too late. Though I wouldn't count on it. Not tucked back here. Hell, I had copies of the building's schematics and barely found this access panel."

Wade looked at Kristal, "I wouldn't count on your father. Last I heard, he was still in Reidsville looking for me."

Wade crawled out of the small room. He found their purses and, after taking their cell phones, he tossed them into the small room. Sticking his head in through the opening, he said, "For your sakes, let's hope we don't meet again."

Wade sealed the access panel. On his way out of the arena, he kept to the shadows with his hood up covering his face as he tried to avoid the cameras. Outside, he cracked the girls' cell phones in half and tossed them into the garbage.

A glance at his watch let him know that he still had a few hours to kill before he could begin his hack of the quantum computers. He made a phone call.

"Chardonnay, my sweet little wine, did you keep yourself available for me like I asked?"

Wade smiled at the answer he heard.

"That is wonderful, I'll meet you at the Nobu bar, Caesars Palace, in a half-hour."

A half hour later Wade found Chardonnay waiting for him. He didn't order a drink for himself. Instead he paid for her drink and said, "Time to go."

Chardonnay asked, "Is there a hurry, cowboy?"

"No, but there is a bottle of champagne waiting for us in my room."

Chardonnay beamed, "That sounds lovely."

Ten minutes later, Wade opened the door to his small room. He was in a great mood. He felt more than alive, and it wasn't Chardonnay or her marvelous body that had him excited. Wade wondered who he would be in his next life. The options were boundless. With his skills and dark contacts, his next identity was a peach to be plucked from a ripe tree. He dwelled on the possibilities.

With a laugh, Wade popped the cork on the champagne.

Chardonnay asked, "What's the special occasion, sweetheart?"

"Your arrival, of course, and my new promotion."

"How exciting, what is it?"

"I haven't decided yet." Wade chuckled and clinked his glass against hers. "I have a few things to do on my computer. Why don't you take a quick bath? I'll come in and get you when I'm done."

"That sound lovely." Chardonnay made a point of undressing in front of him and tossing her clothes one by one across the floor. She said as she picked up the bottle of Champagne and a glass, "Don't be too shy to visit if you want some."

Wade swatted her backside playfully with a loud slap. He said, "Don't get too comfortable, this shouldn't take me long. And I guarantee you, I will want some."

He had been right; it hadn't taken him long at all to delete the security footage from the arena's cameras. He had already hacked into its security system to create a universal access key and to delete the two girls' tickets from the computer system. It was the same electronic key he had used to gain access into the side door at the arena.

Wade looked at the clock on his computer. It was time to make a phone call. He didn't bother to turn on his voice changing software, it didn't matter anymore. The phone rang and rang. Strange, the detective wouldn't dare not answer.

After a few more seconds the voicemail took over. As he had promised the girls, he left a message promising the detective that his daughters would be safe until midnight.

Wade finished his Champagne and closed his laptop. He walked into the bathroom and saw parts of the naked beauty of Chardonnay through the volume of bubbles in her bath.

The Winstons' room, Caesars Palace;

Steven kept his eye on Melbourne, hoping for an opportunity to jump him, though it didn't seem prudent to take any chances. He didn't feel any of them were in imminent danger. Melbourne had been clear that sometime after ten-thirty, the concert would be over and he would let them go. To that point, he told Chelle she would be free to arrest him at that time. Steven peeked at his watch. It was nearly eight; two and a half hours to go.

The room was oddly quiet, except for every few minutes when Winnie would plead to Melbourne to come to his senses and let them go. At first Melbourne had felt obligated to explain the seriousness of the situation and the consequences if he did as she asked. Though he apologized profusely, nothing changed. The last time she pleaded he ignored her question. Thus, they all sat quietly waiting for ten-thirty.

Steven's phone rang. They all looked towards Melbourne for guidance.

"Who's it from?" Melbourne asked, making sure he kept his distance and his gun at the ready.

Steven leaned forward a bit and looked at the phone on the tabletop in front of him. "It's Kristal's father. Let me answer. All I will do is assure him that his daughter is safely at the concert. Maybe send him the photo of the girls they sent me. If I don't answer, it will cause him to be suspicious, I can guarantee you, my phone and Chelle's will keep on ringing until one of us answers it."

"Senator, I hope you understand that you are in no danger unless you challenge me. I trust you not to change the equation. Go ahead, answer, keep it short."

Steven picked up the phone, "Hi Jojo, the girls are at the concert. I have a picture...What?"

Steven's face turned instantly white. "Lord no, no. I'll get them Jojo, I promise. Chelle and I will get them right now. We won't let anything happen to them. No time to talk, we'll call as soon as the girls are with us."

Steven looked up at Melbourne with fire in his eyes. "Wade called Jojo, the girls are his next victims. He hasn't lied yet. He told Jojo that now he knows what it's like to have skin in the game. Melbourne, for the love of God, let me go get our daughters."

Melbourne looked equally ashen face, though he didn't drop the gun. "I didn't know, I couldn't. Trust me, I didn't want anyone else hurt, that's the last thing I wanted."

Chelle spoke calmly, "We know, Melbourne, you were doing what you reasoned was right, but now we have to leave and save the girls. That is our top priority, not stopping Wade from whatever he has planned for the computers. We just want to get the girls before it is too late. Your plan, his plan, whatever it is will still go on. We just want the girls back."

Melbourne looked at his wife, his eyes suddenly looking worn. I'm so sorry Winnie. He lowered the gun, turned it in his hand and gave it to Steven. "Take this; you might need it. I might be able to help if I can make a few calls of my own. Keep your phones on. Remember, there is jamming technology going on inside the arena. Do you know where their seats are?"

Steven felt panic, "No, I didn't think it mattered; they were thrilled with the tickets. I never looked."

Chelle said, "When you bought them, you took a photo and sent it to Tracy. Do you have that photo yet?"

"Yes, yes, I'm sure I do. Let's get a taxi to the arena. I'll search for it on our way."

Steven tucked the gun into the small of his back under his tuxedo jacket. Chelle lifted her purse, weighed down with her gun and both darted down the hallway. It took the taxi ten minutes to make the one and one-half mile ride from Caesars Palace to the arena. Traffic to the arena had dwindled as the concert was well into its two-and-a-half-hour run. Still the drive seemed an eternity to Steven. He had found the photo taken of the tickets months ago.

"Should I text the girls to meet us somewhere? They might get it somehow." Steven suggested.

Chelle deliberated for a moment. "We must assume they won't get it. And if they did by chance, it would be better to not scare them and to keep them in their seats. That would be the safest place and easiest for us to find."

"How are we going to get in?" Steven asked.

Chelle flashed her FBI badge at him. "This should do it. And my escort being a U.S. Senator whose daughter just received a death threat shouldn't hurt. Trust me, we'll get in."

They rushed from the cab to the main entrance. True to Chelle's word, they were soon welcomed in.

A minute or two later, a man and a woman in security uniforms greeted them.

Chelle wasted no time on formalities, "I'm Chelle Saltarie of the FBI, this is United States Senator Steven Westcott."

The female guard said, "Welcome Senator, I recognized you immediately."

Steven said, "We got a threating call. Someone knows my daughter is at this concert and has threatened her life. Look, here is a picture of her tickets. We need to find her and her friend immediately."

The older male guard said, "Intermission is just over. They should be back in their seats by now. Follow us, it's this way."

The arena lights were still on as the guards led the way down the steep steps to Tracy's and Kristal's seats. The lights of the arena slowly dimmed.

Steven said, "Are you sure these are their seats?"

Chelle said, "It checks. These are the seats."

Steven frantically asked the couple sitting behind the empty seats. "Has anyone been in these seats?"

"Sorry sir, those seats were empty for the entire time."

Chapter 24

Steven said to Chelle, "He has them already."

Chelle looked at the guards. "We need somebody posted here. If the girls come back, don't let them out of your sight, and it is critical that you contact me immediately. Chelle gave them one of her FBI cards.

The lights went dark, Steven recognized the beginning of "Time to Reboot," which signaled the beginning of the second half of the show.

Steven stared at the empty seats for a moment longer. He said to Chelle, "There is no way they would miss this. We must find them."

Steven, Chelle and one of the guards walked up the steep stairs and out into the lobby which was now like a ghost town.

Chelle said, "I'm calling my team in Washington. This is the work of Wade. It's time for all-hands-on-deck."

Steven was deep in thought. He reached up and put his hand on Chelle's shoulder and said "Thanks." he added, "I have a feeling it won't be enough. I need to talk to Jojo."

Steven looked at his phone and realized it was blocked. "We're not doing any good here. Let's go outside."

Caesars Palace, Wade's room:

Lying in bed, Chardonnay and Wade finished off the bottle of champagne.

Chardonnay looked at her watch and asked, "Sugar, do you want another hour? I'm in no hurry."

Wade glanced at the table clock; it was only nine. He smiled; he didn't need to be in position until eleven tonight. He pulled down the sheet that was just barely covering up Chardonnay. Gazing over her body he asked, "Do I get the replay special? After all, you're already here."

The door to the small hotel room opened. Chardonnay and Wade both looked up. Wade said, "Shit!"

He turned towards the nightstand and started to fumble through it for the gun he had hidden there.

Alan D Schmitz
DIGITAL SECRETS

A man dressed in a white suit paused calmly and pointed a pistol at Wade and said, "Please stop. I will shoot if you don't, even though I am not here to harm you."

Wade stopped rifling through the nightstand drawer and looked at the man to ponder his choices. The man was older with a neatly trimmed white beard, and a small white mustache. He was leaning on a simple white cane with an eagle grasp. The gun looked steady in his hand. Wade noticed the silencer screwed into the end of the pistol. That meant the man was prepared to use the gun inside the small room.

"Please slowly take your hand away from the drawer. We have business to discuss."

Chardonnay pulled up the sheet, but it came short of covering her breasts. Wade's nakedness was covered from his waist down.

Wade slowly did as asked. He felt obliged to raise both his hands slightly.

The man in white said, "Chardonnay, my dear, or should I say Mariam Steiner. I'm afraid I must ask you to leave."

Chardonnay was stunned, "How do you know my name?"

"I do my homework. I know all about you. In fact, did you know your mother is critically ill?"

"My mother? I haven't seen her for years."

The man in white held the gun steady, pointed at Wade's midsection. "Yes, in fact over seven years. I have a suggestion for you. A rather strong suggestion. Leave town tonight and visit your mother."

The man in white took out a small slip of paper from his inside suit jacket pocket.

"Here is the hospital she is at."

"Mom's in the hospital?"

"Yes, cancer. Her last wish is to see you one more time."

"Can I get dressed?" Chardonnay asked the man in white.

"I would highly recommend it."

Wade said, "Can I get dressed too?"

"Please stay as you are. When Miss Steiner is gone, you will have an opportunity."

Chardonnay got out of bed hastily and picked up each item of clothing that was scattered around the room. She walked towards the bathroom.

"I'm sorry, Miss Steiner. I prefer to keep you in my sight."

Chardonnay froze, she turned towards the man in white slowly.

"You said I could get dressed."

"And you may. But not in the bathroom. Quickly, my dear, you don't want me changing my mind. Do you?"

Chardonnay dressed unabashedly in front of them as fast as she could. As she was buckling the thin leather belt around her red skirt she asked, "Is my mom going to die?"

"I'm afraid so my dear. I suggest you do not hesitate. There is a flight to Memphis leaving tonight at ten-twenty. I strongly suggest you are on it."

"I left a note to your roommate that you were leaving town for good."

"For good?" Chardonnay asked. "You know my roommate?"

"I know where you lived, yes. It would be bad for your health to come back here. Or to say anything about this young man or myself to anybody. And I do mean anybody. Do you understand me?"

"Yes sir, but I can go see my mother?"

"Yes, time to run along. Remember!" the man in white put his finger up to his lips. "Not a word or you will meet up with one of my friends and I'm afraid he won't be so accommodating. And one more thing, Miss. Steiner. Your phone won't work until you are in Memphis. Do yourself and your mother a favor and be on that plane."

Chardonnay grabbed her purse and rushed out the door.

Wade Watched Chardonnay step out the door. The man in the white suit stepped back and turned the dead bolt while never taking eyes off him. Wade was particularly interested in the gun which never wavered.

"Mr. Sullivan, please do get dressed. I am here to help you, but I warn you, any sudden movements could turn out badly for you."

****

The outside of the arena was nearly empty of pedestrians. The large sign advertising the Dancing Chickens illuminated Steven and Chelle.

Chelle was on her phone organizing her team around the latest threat. Steven tried in vain to contact Jojo.

He said to Chelle, "Jojo's not answering. I tried Tamara too. I don't get it. I'm sure they're waiting for my call."

"Jojo recorded the call from Wade. He sent it to me, and I just sent it to my team. I didn't get it until we stepped outside. I think you should hear it."

"I feel like I could reach through your phone and strangle the son-of-a-bitch."

"You won't feel much better after I play his message. He didn't even bother to disguise his voice this time."

Chelle pulled up the audio file and touched the play button, "Hello Detective, and anybody else listening. Detective, I promised you that you would have to have skin in the game. I'm giving you fair notice, four hours' notice in fact. I needed two more kills before I can quit this game. Anyway, your daughter and your friend the Senator's daughter should do the trick. There is hope I won't need to kill them. You see, I planted deadly poison at a little get together that your friend the Senator and his lovely FBI girlfriend attended. Pray I was successful, because if I can confirm their deaths before one AM, game ends, quota met.

"Anyway, you understand, rules are rules. Try not to forget, you have until one AM tomorrow, Vegas time. And no complaining, that's more than fair. You have the advantage. You know exactly who my target is this time, and you know where they are or at least where they are supposed to be. Should be a piece of cake to stop me. Good luck!"

Steven was shaking, his rage boiling inside of him, his fists in a ball ready to hit something or someone.

Despite his anger, he noticed Chelle calmly looking over the arena entrance area. "Chelle, tell me you have an idea how to find them."

"You have a picture of them standing right about here where we are now. May I have your phone for a moment?"

Chelle found the picture and examined the meta data on it and made a note of the exact time. She sent the picture to her phone. She handed Steven's phone back to him.

"They had V.I.P. passes, so they should have gone to that door. There are cameras all over. Keep trying Jojo and Tamara, I'm going back inside to get my hands on those videos. First ,I want your picture."

"My picture?"

"Say cheese." Chelle snapped a photo of Steven in about the same place she placed the two girls.

"In case I need some leverage, I can say I have Senator Westcott just outside the arena and can prove it."

"Please hurry, Chelle. Steven looked at his watch, it was almost nine. We only have three hours."

Chelle had been gone only minutes when his phone rang. "Melbourne, I can't be talking to you right now...No, the girls weren't in their seats nor were they all night...Kidnapped most likely, Wade gave us until one AM tonight to find them alive...Help? What kind of help?...OK, OK, I promise, I'll answer when you call back...Yes, thank you. We need all the help we can get."

Steven's phone rang again. "Jojo I've been trying to call you."

Steven listened to Jojo for a minute then said, "Chelle and I are fine, we discovered the poison in time...I know, we heard his threat...I'm sorry Jojo, we got to the arena, they weren't in their seats, nor had they been all night. Chelle is inside the arena looking at security video. We know the girls were here, we have a picture of them smiling in front of the marquee... I'm afraid we have to assume Wade has them. One AM, I know...Where are you?...Vegas? How the hell! Never mind, tell me when you get here. Come right to the arena. I'll be waiting by the large marquee."

Wade's room Caesars Palace:

Wade stepped out of bed slowly. His clothes were as equally strewn about as Chardonnay's. Soon he had his pants on and was buttoning up his shirt when he felt brave enough to ask. "You said you want to help me. Help me with what?"

"My information has it that you are going to destroy the twin quantum computers underneath Caesars Palace, and you're doing it tonight. I am here to help you."

"Look, Colonel Sanders, you have the wrong guy. I'm just here to have a little fun. I don't know anything about quantum computers."

"Wade, I know about the murders. All, well, mostly all, except the young man, had something to do with the Lake Lerna Project. Let me demonstrate my sincerity. Open your laptop."

With the gun firmly pointed at him Wade didn't think it wise to argue. He took his computer off the nightstand and sat on the bed. His lifted the screen top and the laptop came to life. He tried to initiate the screen.

"What the fuck? What did you do to my computer?"

"The master hacker was hacked. Is that such a surprise? We've been watching you for some time. Sometimes literally."

"You've been spying on me?"

"A common fallacy among hackers. They assume they won't or can't be hacked."

"You changed my password?"

"We did. Not important, or is it?

Wade felt violated, he became angry.

"Give me the password! You have no right."

"No, we don't, at least we don't have any more rights than you."

"You think that will stop me? Do you think I can't hack into my own computer?"

"Not in time." The man in white leaned a bit against his cane that had a golden eagle top. "Of course I will give you the password. As I said, I want to help you."

"I don't need or want any help. If you really want to help, leave me alone."

"Your back door. It was found."

"What!"

"The electronic back door you created into Lake Lerna. They found it. Did you believe they trusted you?"

"I don't know what you are talking about."

"They went over every millimeter of your code; they found the back door you installed."

"I still don't have a clue what you are talking about, Colonel."

"I want Lake Lerna destroyed. And I want you to help me do it."

"Look, mister, I don't know you and I certainly don't trust you. So why don't you just go back to your fried chicken and leave me alone."

"Hashtag, two, zero, two, four, IRENE, ten, three, one, asterisk."

"What?"

"That's the password. Open your computer. We disabled your program, the worm you were going to use to destroy the computers. It was useless anyway."

Wade typed in the password.

"Your password worked, big deal. I would have eventually hacked it."

Wade for the first time ignored the gun pointed at him. He typed methodically on his computer. Clearly something wasn't right, as he angrily tried different patterns of keystrokes. After fifteen minutes, he said, "Son of a bitch. You're right. It's gone."

"A little mutual trust is in order. We both want the same thing. You need me, we need you."

Wade looked at the man in white incredulously and asked, "You have a way in? How? Nobody knows what I know. And what is this we thing? We who?"

"You are obviously not as infallible as you believe. We created another worm. It's a one-time use and will probably be picked up on nearly immediately. To use it, we need your secret portal. Once you initiate our program from your portal, you'll have access to the system, my guess is it'll take fifteen or twenty minutes to stop your hack. Can you get it done by then?"

"Depends on if the worm works and where takes me. I don't know how long it'll take to hack my way to where I need to go. How do I know I can trust you?"

"Look for a file named IRENE. Inside it is a specialized hacking software. It's yours to keep."

Outside the arena:

"Jojo, Tamara, thank God you're both here," Steven said, as he gave both Jojo and Tamara a hug.

Steven couldn't look Tamara in the eyes and instead focused on Jojo's. Steven said, "After we got your message, Chelle and I headed right over here. We know the girls were here. I have a picture they sent me of them standing right here in front of the sign. When we got to their seats they weren't there. The people around their seats said they had been unoccupied all night.

"Chelle is going over security footage right now. The FBI has been notified. We're doing everything we can."

Jojo gave his sobbing wife a hug. Looking over her shoulder at Steven, he said, "We know you are doing everything you can. Wade doesn't bluff. He said we have until one AM. That doesn't give us much time."

Steven looked past Jojo, coming out the doors of the arena he recognized some familiar faces. The three amigos approached.

"Mr. Senator," Rodger spoke first, "Melbourne Winston texted us at intermission. He said he needed our help immediately. We just talked to him and he explained everything."

Tesia said, "We would have come sooner, but bonehead wouldn't miss 'Time to Reboot.'"

Rodger attempted to explain, "I didn't know why Melbourne wanted us; I didn't know the girls were in trouble until we talked to him a few minutes ago." Give me a break."

"Wade bad man." Marvin chimed.

Jojo and Tamara looked at Steven confused. "Guys, these are Kristal's parents. Wade told their father in a recorded message that he was going to kill the girls, and we have until one AM to find them and save them."

The three looked at the couple and glanced away, not sure what to say or do.

Steven asked, "Why did Melbourne think you could help?"

"Hercules knows." Marvin said monotoned.

Jojo and Tamara looked at Steven and the three eclectic young people.

With a confused sound in his voice Jojo asked, "Who's Hercules?"

Steven answered, "Not a who, a what." He asked Marvin, "Can you ask Hercules where they are?"

"Can't talk to Hercules no more. Hercules my friend."

Steven turned toward Tesia and Rodger. "If he can't talk to Hercules, why did Melbourne think you could help?"

Rodger looked at his watch, "Technically, he still can until midnight."

Steven said, "Because at midnight, the government officially takes over. Does Melbourne think he can get Marvin into the complex before midnight?"

Marvin clutched his computer bag tight against his chest. "Wade must be stopped. Wade bad, don't let him kill my friend."

Tamara insisted, "Who or what is Hercules? If he can help us find the girls, we must contact him."

Steven asked, "Is there a way?"

Tesia and Rodger looked at each other. Tesia explained, "Melbourne thinks there might be a way. It's a long shot. Our security clearances should still be in effect until midnight. After that, we can't get near Hercules anymore."

"How, what is Melbourne's idea?" Steven asked.

"Wade is somehow going to communicate with Hercules. He needs to talk to it to destroy it. If we can trace his hack, we might be able to find him."

"At Lake Lerna?" Steven asked.

Rodger nodded his head, "He must be close. His access must be hardwired, theoretically impossible, but the only way."

Chelle approached the group as she came out the arena's main doors. "Jojo, Tamara, how did you get here?"

Steven said, "I'm wondering the same thing, but first things first. Any luck?"

Chelle said sadly, "Amazing, all the surveillance videos were deleted, exterior and interior."

"Wade," said Tesia and Rodger in unison.

A car at the drop off zone for the arena started honking its horn continuously.

Rodger said, "That's Melbourne, he's taking us back to the project." Rodger tried to sound optimistic, "It is worth a shot."

Melbourne yelled out an open window, "Hurry, people, we don't have much time. Steven, I promise I will call the instant we learn anything useful."

Rodger and Tesia hurried to the car. Marvin pressed his computer bag against his chest and waddled as fast as he could, following them.

Jojo demanded, "Cowboy, don't keep us in the dark any longer, what the fuck is going on? There seem to be a lot of moving pieces. And none of them are making sense. For starters who or what is Hercules?"

Steven said, "Sorry Jojo, Tamara, I'm trying to not waste a second here, but you deserve to know. Chelle and I stumbled upon something the government is building under Caesars Palace. It's called the Lake Lerna Project. It's a supercomputer, two, called Iphicles and Hercules."

Chelle said, "Wade isn't randomly killing. Every one of his victims, except the young boy, were working on this project, along with Wade himself."

She continued, "We believe, and we were told by Melbourne Winston, that Wade is going to attempt to destroy the computers tonight. He was fired from the project two years ago and is still carrying a grudge. We think the murders are an attempt to slow down or stop another from being built."

Tamara asked, "Why are our daughters caught up in this?"

Chelle answered, "Our profilers have the killer tagged as exceptionally intelligent. In fact, without the challenge of the Lake Lerna Project he's bored. So bored, he created a game out of killing people. Kristal and Tracy are meant as added incentive to keep your head in the game we guess. Or, because of me or because of Steven's association with the project because he didn't expose it to the public. We can't know his motives for sure."

"What about those other three? And that guy that picked them up?" Jojo asked.

Chelle continued, "That's Melbourne Winston. He also worked on the project, as did the other three. They believe that Marvin may be targeted by Wade as well and are helping us."

Steven asked, "What I want to know is why are you two here, and how did you get here so fast?"

Tamara answered, "I felt so sorry for Kristal. I can't imagine what she is going through. Being called a prostitute by the news media and the social networking sites must be terrible for her. Sooner or later, the press is going to be right on top of her. We both felt she needed us to be with her when that happened. We went to the airport and got on the first flight to Vegas."

Jojo added, "The second we landed, I saw the voice message from Wade and forwarded it to you. The rest you know."

Steven said, "According to the people who should know, Wade must take down the computers from inside Caesars. I suggest we go there and do our best to find him ourselves."

Chelle agreed, "Maybe I can get the local FBI involved." Chelle stepped away to make a call.

Jojo turned towards his wife and said, "Something that Chelle said is bothering me. She said that Wade deleted the video files of both inside and outside the arena. I can understand the outside cameras; you can't get inside without first being outside. But if he deleted the inside footage, it must mean he was worried about it showing him inside. My instincts tell me he didn't want us to see him inside the arena or who he was with."

"The girls!" Tamara said.

Steven considered the logic, he said, "We know they were at the arena waiting to enter. I can't believe our daughters would have left the area. Not willingly anyways. Getting them into a car without creating a scene would have been a big risk. A risk Wade couldn't afford. It's possible he tricked them once they got inside the arena. I can't argue with your logic."

In a low voice, he added, "You and Tamara do what you can here. I promise you, if I find Wade, he will tell me where the girls are. That's why I must find him before Chelle does. What I'm going to do to him might not be considered ethical by the FBI. Good luck."

Steven flagged down a cab. Chelle and he climbed in, Chelle still on her phone.

"Caesars Palace," Steven said.

Chelle showed her badge and said, "The fastest way. Lives are in danger."

Steven handed two twenties to the driver."

The male cab driver said, "Yes ma'am, you got it. Traffic is dead until the concert lets out. I can have you there in five minutes tops."

Deep inside the arena:

     Kristal had finally worked the duct-tap off her mouth. "You can do it, Tracy, just keep wiping the tape against your sleeve, get a corner started, use the sticky side of the tape to loosen it.

Kristal kept up her encouragement until eventually Tracy had her mouth free.

Fighting back tears Tracy asked, "What are we going to do?"

The giant control panel in front of them was loaded with small LED lights. They didn't give off much light but there were enough of them for them to see each other.

"We got the tape off. Maybe we can break our hands free too. Don't stop trying."

Tracy sobbed, "Dad doesn't know where we are, nobody does. That man said he's going to poison Dad and Chelle."

"My dad said that if you know how, you can break the plastic zip ties. Keep trying, Tracy, we must get free to warn them."

Both girls struggled and wiggled their thin wrists against the ties in the hope they could somehow dislodge them.

Caesars Palace:

The cab stopped at the main lobby.

They rushed into the main reception area, they stopped in front of the statue of the three goddesses of love. The water of the fountain splashed behind him. Steven asked, "Now that we're here, what's the plan? How are we going to find the girls?"

Chelle said, "We need to find Wade. He's the key. I'm going to start flashing my badge and try to get into the security section. Maybe I can convince them to use their facial recognition program to locate Wade. There isn't any place in the world with more security cameras. Somewhere there is a video of him, there must be."

Steven looked at Chelle and said, "While you do that, I'm going to go to the show."

"What?" Chelle looked shocked.

Steven took his two tickets out his pocket, "Not kidding. Everything is circling around the Lake Lerna Project. If I can get into the show, maybe I can get behind the scenes. Wade can't just waltz into one of the most secure buildings in the country. According to our new friends, the computer can only be accessed through a direct hard wire connection. That would mean he must have a way to communicate with the computers from outside the secured area.

"We do know the water of Lake Lerna is used to cool the computers. If I can follow the water to the computers, we might stumble upon Wade and his secret portal."

Chelle left for the security center. Steven walked through the noisy casino towards the main entrance to the Lake Lerna show; it was already a bit late, he hoped he would still be allowed in.

Steven approached the usher with his two VIP passes in his hand. It was almost ten and the show was about to begin. A sign posted in the lobby warned that all cell phone coverage would be suspended during the show.

The usher asked, "Is your guest nearby?"

Steven answered, "She became indisposed. I'm afraid I'm all alone, but I have heard so much about the show I don't want to miss it."

"Follow me, your tickets are right up front. I must warn you, your seats are close to the stage; there is a possibility you might get a bit wet. I have a rain poncho for you to protect your suit from the worst of it."

Steven slipped the rain poncho over his clothes and followed to his seat. The lights were already dimmed, and the usher used a small flashlight to direct him to his seat. Immediately after he sat down a young girl holding a tray asked if Steven wanted a refreshment.

"A scotch, top shelf, two fingers, and one ice cube," he whispered.

Steven knew he wouldn't be around long enough to drink it, but he didn't want to look out of place among the other V.I.P. guests. He kept his head down in the dim light, hoping not to be recognized."

The show started. The lights went even darker as spotlights concentrated on the performers. The unexpected was to be expected as the show began with performers appearing overhead and around the audience. A huge waterfall bounced off rocks and descended into Lake Lerna. A multi-headed dragon produced itself from the depths of the lake.

Steven found it hard not to be mesmerized by the show. He focused on the side curtains performers snuck in and out of when the focus of the lights wasn't on them. The cocktail waitress came back with a trayful of drinks. Somehow, she managed to serve them all with a minimal amount of disruption.

Steven hardly ever took his eyes off the side stage. Timing would be critical, but aside from a possible guard preventing a non-performer from entering backstage he didn't see any barrier.

With a small amount of distraction, he slipped off the thin plastic poncho. His dark tuxedo acted as camouflage. The lights went dark for the next scene to begin. Steven stood and walked away.

He remembered some of his special forces' advice. If you must infiltrate past unfriendlies, act like you belong. That's what he did, he walked confidently in the dark towards the side stage. His VIP seats left the distance he had to cover minimal. The high curtain that cut the backstage area off from the audience was heavier than he imagined as he pushed it aside. He found the opening and disappeared behind it.

There were no guards, only a strange glow from the red lighting to get the performers used to the darkness before they emerged. Luckily, he had picked his timing well; no one was around, Steven had no idea exactly where he was going. But it didn't take much deduction to know that the direction he needed to go was down.

The deeper into the bowels of the stage area he could go, the more likely his success. He envisioned an architecture where the entertainment giants, hotel, stage, and gaming areas had to intersect with the government-controlled secret computer complex.

If he was right, there had to be some common walls. Those walls were certainly heavily reinforced and protected in myriads of ways, but the water used in the show was also used to cool the computers, which meant the two had to be connected somehow.

Wade had no more chance at breaching those walls then he did. But, Steven surmised, he didn't have to. In fact, he would have planned a way not to. Per Melbourne, Wade only needed one wire out of millions. An extra wire running along the maze of pipes to move the water, perhaps even piggybacking over a legitimate wire that could have an alternative use if needed.

The backstage area was a maze all its own. Away from the wing, or in Steven's case stage right, the lighting was subdued, though brighter. He kept looking for an exit sign. He was sure a staircase existed, he just had to find it.

"Hello, sir. You had better step to the side or you're likely to be trampled. In a few minutes all hell is going to break loose with acrobatic performers racing to the pool."

Steven tried not to act surprised, though he was. He never saw the performer walk up to him. Steven said, "Thank you, I was told to watch from here, just wanted to see how my money is being spent."

Immediately the young man stood a bit more at attention though it wasn't easy in the skimpy body suite he was wearing. "Just press yourself to the wall. The devils of Hades are setting up to attack Hercules."

Steven asked, "What's your job?"

"I'm a high dive expert, and I must go. I can't be late to the high platform."

Steven asked, "I'm supposed to find the stairs, are they near?"

"Very. The stampede I'm telling you about comes from the dressing room below. But don't go now, wait until things quiet down."

The young man ran towards a small ladder and started climbing.

True to his word, a stampede of young people ran past, all dressed in various mysterious and colorful costumes, all had a set of what he guessed were devil horns. Steven pressed himself against the wall. The performers were focused, and he doubted most even noticed him.

With the stampede over, Steven peered around the corner and for the time being the hall looked clear. Steven casually walked on, hoping his tuxedo was enough to gain him entry. He saw the stairs going down, he took a deep breath and exhaled and walked down them as if he personally owned all of Caesars Palace.

The walk down the winding stairs was uneventful, though he could hear voices and what sounded like a commotion of some sort going on past the open doorway. At the landing a level down, he peeked around the corner and his suspicions were confirmed.

It was pandemonium, perhaps planned pandemonium, but pandemonium nonetheless People were rushing about to-and-fro. It did seem like one person was taking point. She was pointing, calling out names, swearing a bit.

The stairs continued down at least another level. When he suspected nobody was glancing his way, Steven stepped past the door and skirted down another level. It appeared he had left the din behind him. Another level down the exit door was closed, yet the staircase continued down. He decided that lower was better and continued down.

At the third level, the stairway stopped. The door was locked. The only tool Steven had was a nine-millimeter Glock. He looked up the spiraling staircase; the distance and the craziness above would probably camouflage the shot, he reasoned.

He stepped back, to a steady aim at the lock and made a careful shot. The noise of the shot reverberated around him, hurting his ears. He stuck the gun back under his jacket and into the small of his back. It took a bit of jostling, but the door finally opened.

Steven looked at his watch. Another half hour had passed. He only had two-and-a-half hours left to find his daughter and Kristal. Pulling his phone out his pocket, as suspected, this deep into the building he had no reception.

In the distance he heard machinery running. There had to be pipes and pumps somewhere. His goal was to follow the water. Steven looked overhead and left and right. He saw no piping, just a long concrete corridor. He ran down it, hoping he would know what he was looking at when he saw it.

Chapter 25

Wade's room, Caesars Palace:

Wade did as he was instructed. He examined the hacking code in complete concentration and silence for an hour. Wade finally looked up. "This is genius, I don't recognize the coding, who did it?"

"That is not important."

Wade demanded, "I need the rest of it to initiate the self-destruct program."

The normally unflappable man in white repeated, "What self-destruct program? We know of no such thing."

"Yeah, you wouldn't or couldn't. It was a last-minute add-on. Dumbasses, totally unnecessary. They were thinking this thing could become aware or something like that, you know artificial intelligence and all.

"Not going to happen. These two computers, this generation anyhow, is not self-aware or ever will be. Still, they were thinking that somehow if these computers started acting towards their own self-interest, with the push of a button they would be destroyed. Won't work anyhow."

"If it won't work, why do you want access to it?"

Wade sounded disgusted, "Because obviously, if the computers became self-aware, the first thing they would do would be to disarm a self-destruct system. Think about it. If these computers became self-aware, they would instantly know everything about everything.

"If, and this is a huge if, they became self-aware, that would mean the quantum computers would know more about quantum computing than any person on the planet. But don't worry, it won't happen. It can't happen."

"I appreciate your confidence. Why?"

"They aren't that smart, that's why. The coding to make them work is unbelievably basic. Remember, the software is first generation. It was built from scratch. Frankly I'm surprised it works at all."

From across the room, Wade saw the man in white slip his gun into its holster on the inside of his white coat jacket. He pretended not to notice or care.

"Please indulge me," the man in white said. "If it won't work, how do you plan on using it to destroy the machines?"

Wade looking disgusted at the ignorance of the question. He typed on his computer as he answered. "I said, if they became self-aware. That isn't going to happen, soooo...that means the mechanism will work. The problem is, after tonight, the military will install protocols that I might not be able to work around. That's why it must be tonight."

"When?" The man in white was clearly anxious and Wade sensed a weakness to be exploited.

Still sitting on his bed, Wade closed his computer. "Soon, at eleven. That's when the handoff begins. It's a series of final computer checks, the best time to hack in. I must be in position by then, but not before."

The man in white pulled out a thinly padded chair from a small desk. "We will wait until it's time to leave."

Wade stood up with his closed laptop in hand. "I'm afraid I can't. I need to check up on some sick friends, possibly fatally sick."

The man in white patted his suit jacket where his gun was holstered. "I strongly suggest we wait here until it's time to leave. And about your sick friends, I'm afraid they are all fairly well."

Wade shrugged his shoulders in disappointment. "Oh crap, you warned them."

"I saw your exchange with the maid. I had immediate suspicions about the chocolates. I had to warn them even though my visit wasn't appreciated at first. You see, I may need the services of Senator Westcott in the future."

"Damn it, Colonel, that makes my life considerably more complicated. I made promises I need to keep. Especially concerning Melbourne Winston." Wade chuckled, looking at ease. "Look Colonel, I get it, you need me, and apparently, I need you. But I have a busy evening ahead of me, I'm sorry, I can't dawdle here any longer."

The man in white reached back into his open suit coat for his gun, he said, "I'm sorry, our mission is too important to take any risks by having you roaming the streets of Las Vegas. Nor for you to risk committing another murder."

He looked at his watch, "We don't have long to wait."

As the man in white began to pull out his gun, Wade turned back towards his bed, feigning resignation. An instant later he spun and tossed his laptop at the sitting man like it was a giant, heavy Frisbee. The man in white instinctively raised his arms to protect himself from the flying laptop. The gun came loose from his hands. At the same time, Wade flung himself the short distance and was on top of the man in white almost as fast as his laptop, which had cut through the man's defensive blocks and into his neck.

Wade landed a series of blows against the man in white's unprotected head. Soon he was on the ground with Wade on top. Wade grabbed the gun and used it to pistol whip the man repeatedly.

The man in white's face was bloodied. Wade pointed the gun between his eyes.

"Before I leave, you have some information I need. You said you know a back way into the computers. What is it?"

"If I tell you, you will kill me."

"You're not on my list. You might get lucky and live. I don't give a fuck about you one way or the other. You said you want the project shut down and destroyed, so do I. I can tell you this, if you don't give me the information, it won't be rhetorical anymore. I will kill you by pounding the information out of you."

The man in white gave a slight nod of his head to say he understood.

After the man in white shared what he knew, Wade took the butt of the gun and hit him hard across the head. Wade slipped his laptop into his carry bag; it was a modified travelers backpack. He searched the man in white's pockets and was surprised there was no wallet or identification, only a money clip. He tossed the money clip and the gun still inside the nightstand into his carry bag. He carefully used a bed sheet to wipe down the man in white's gun and dropped it near his dead body.

Wade tucked his head inside the hood of his hoodie and walked out the door of his room, making sure he had the do not disturb sign visible, though he had no intentions of ever returning. He assumed the body would be found in a day or two, by then he would be far away, using one of the new identities he had lined up. The only thing he needed was time to create past histories compatible with his new goals.

He looked at his watch and said to the bloodied body of the man in white, "Well Colonel, I'm still going to kill that son of a bitch, Melbourne. Just not right now. I have an appointment at a certain computer terminal only I know about."

After an elevator ride down to the main floor of the casino, he walked back into the lobby and past the statue of the three goddesses of love. Next, he passed the eighteen-foot high replica of Michelangelo's masterpiece, the statue of David. Wade considered it appropriate, for just as David was contemplating how he would slay Goliath, Wade was contemplating the same thing.

He casually strode up an arched marble stairway. Patrons on either side of him were busy feeding slot machines, each hoping they would be the next jackpot winner. The noise of ringing machines announcing a payout, or music and enticements from unused machines, surrounded him. He glanced at his watch; it was 10:45, time to find his backdoor into the computers.

His scheme of destroying billions of dollars' worth of computers and capping it off with the deaths of the two young women was exciting him. He smiled as patrons of the hotel passed him in the hallway. If only they could know why he was smiling and what the images in his mind were, they wouldn't be smiling back. Wade chuckled. He hoped he would have time to circle back to the arena and confirm their deaths, nothing would give him greater pleasure. Tonight was going to be the night of nights.

Under his hoodie he wore a lanyard with an oversized laminated I.D. badge, announcing to the staff of Caesars that he was one of them. With it and the fake access card in his hand he would be able to sneak away from the noise of the public access areas and into the bowels of the huge casino. He untucked the lanyard and dropped his hood to be less suspicious. He made sure the badge was clearly visible to the overhead cameras.

With a swipe of his access card, he opened a side door. Wade smiled at the other workers as they passed by him as he began his journey through the maze of hallways that spanned the eighty-five acres that made up the entirety of Caesars. Wade checked his watch again. He had twenty minutes to navigate the huge facility. It had been a few years since his last visit, but he had memorized the route. By his calculations, he had a five-to-ten-minute margin of error.

Caesars Palace Security Room:

The people inside the main security unit were as helpful as they could be. Chelle's badge and ID, along with more than a few who remembered her and Steven from newspaper and online articles, gave her story credibility.

Duke, the head of that particular shift, said, "I took the picture you gave me of Wade. I uploaded it to the facial recognition software. I must warn you; this could take hours. We have a tremendous amount of surveillance video to filter through."

Chelle said, "We know exactly where he was around six. That should help."

"It does. We only have four elevators going to that floor. The elevators have cameras, so that will confirm he was here, but it doesn't help us to know where he is now. We video every square inch of the casino, every second. That is a lot of videos. If he is here, or was here, we will find him. But to find him in real time before midnight. I hope you have a plan B."

Four suits, all dressed in black, including one woman came through the door flashing their badges. The leader said, "Agent Saltarie, you have a problem following orders, don't you?"

Chelle immediately recognized the leader; it was the same man who had arrested James McConally.

Chelle said, "Agent, I'm sorry I didn't get your name."

"I didn't give it. You're coming with us."

"Agent, you don't understand, I believe two young girls have been kidnapped and are being threatened with their lives. I believe it's the real serial killer, Wade Sullivan, who has them."

"Just because some hayseed detective got threatened, you think you can turn all of Las Vegas upside down. I told you to stand down. Your own office said you were off this case. In fact, the case is closed."

"You still don't get it. A United States Senator's daughter is one of the girls missing."

"A teenager missing for a few hours. Hardly a federal problem. And you believe the kidnapper is the nut from Reidsville. I'm sure he's back in Reidsville right now, laughing his ass off at your gullibility."

"Agent Saltarie," Duke said, "We've got our first match, in the elevator going up to Mr. Winston's floor."

Chelle looked at the unknown agent with anger in her eyes, "Reidsville, right."

The lead agent asked Duke, "Did you say Mr. Winston?"

Duke answered as he kept his eyes scanning the multitude of security screens in front of him but froze one image on screen. "Yes, we suspect that this man tried to poison Melbourne Winston tonight."

Chelle added, "It's the second attempt on his life today."

The agent responded as he pushed himself towards the video display, "I am well aware of the bomb threat earlier today." The agent looked at the frozen image on the display screen, he said to his team. "It's him, he is here. Take Agent Saltarie to the cars; she speaks to no one."

The other agents produced guns aimed at Chelle and the female agent pulled out a pair of handcuffs.

The lead agent said, "Agent Saltarie, you are in enough trouble as it is. I suggest you go along quietly. This is not your case, this is not your jurisdiction, and we are not under your direction. Far from it."

The agents surrounded her and roughly yanked her arms behind her and handcuffed her.

Chelle glanced at the clock on the wall. There was only a half-hour left. She didn't resist, realizing it was fruitless. Nevertheless, she threatened, "Do you have any idea what Senator Wescott is going to do to you when he finds out you stopped me from finding his daughter?"

The same agent replied, "Nothing, he won't be doing nothing to me. Senator Westcott is washed up after tonight. A nothing, a has been. In fact, he'll probably be rotting in a cell soon. And you will be in a cell of your own a thousand miles away in an opposite direction, if I have any say in the matter."

The three agents took Chelle away.

Deep inside the Arena:

Tracy said, "Kristal, I finally did it, I can breathe. I thought I was going to suffocate with that tape over my mouth."

"I knew you could do it. Any luck with your hands?"

"No, I think they're bleeding. I feel something slipperyI think it's blood."

Kristal said, "I think mine are too. That's OK, maybe it'll help our hands slip through, keep trying."

"Do you think my dad is dead?"

"Don't think that, but we can't wait for someone to save us. I don't think I can break the plastic ties. We have to try to slip out of them."

"I've been trying, Kristal, real hard. Mine are too tight. I can hardly move my hands."

"I know, I can hardly feel mine anymore. Just don't give up. We must keep trying."

Deep under Caesars Palace:

Wade was three stories down inside Caesars Palace. There was a three-foot thick, reinforced concrete wall between him and the government-owned side. No wires connected one side to the other. The government run-side was autonomous from the public side of Caesars Palace. Autonomous, except for the two twelve-inch pipes that circulated the computer cooling water from Lake Lerna, stories above.

The quantum computers needed to stay a few degrees above absolute zero, so around -450 Fahrenheit. Wade knew the system well. It was designed by Dr. Langston.

On the government-run side, the water was super-cooled by a system ingeniously designed by the late doctor. He had discovered a way to keep ultra-pure water in liquid form even at those insanely low temperatures. It took a series of heat exchangers, but by the time the water had cooled the quantum computers, and circulated around the giant server farm, the water was pumped back up warm enough to give the performers a comfortable environment in which to conduct the water show.

Deep inside the bowels of the concrete behemoth, it was starkly quiet, though in the background was the constant hum of pumps and mechanicals working. Wade worked silently, even though the odds of someone finding him were slim to none, he didn't want to attract attention. He set his laptop computer on top of a ledge made by intersecting piping. He took two magnet-operated clamps and placed them carefully on each of the two huge steel water pipes.

Out of his backpack, he pulled out another electronic device. On the other side of the wall was an identical set of magnets and a signal scrambling device hidden in a wall that was sealed up two years ago. It was time to wake that device up.

Once connected to his computers, he gave a series of commands. The two signal scrambling devices needed to talk to each other through the steel pipe. It took another minute for the device on the other side to wake up and reply. He now had his direct connection into the government side.

If the worm worked the way the man in white said it would, he should be able to circumvent the quantum computers, get into the security protocols and initiate the self-destruct program. Wade typed in the security password he had beaten out of Colonel Sanders. He turned the worm on.

His job was to make the decisions on what to instruct the worm to do as it encountered electronic roadblocks. The information it collected on the way was fed back to him to help make those decisions. The man in white was right about one thing: it wouldn't take long for the sophisticated machinery on the other side of the wall to realize it was being hacked.

Deep under Caesars Palace, government side:

James Mitchell, Director of the National Security Agency, was pacing nervously. He asked Melbourne for the third time. "I still don't understand why you and these three misfits are here."

"I can't make it any simpler for you. Up until midnight, these computers are still under our authority. If something goes wrong with your test, it'll be our asses, not yours in a sling. We are here to make sure you don't screw up our computers. What you do with them after midnight is your problem."

"Technically you're right. But you and your three..." Director Mitchell looked visibly annoyed at the group as he emphasized, "associates, had better not get in the way."

"Sir!" It was Peter, the computer tech in charge of the final tests. "Something isn't right. If I didn't know better, I would think we are being hacked. But that's impossible."

Director Mitchell looked at Melbourne, "You knew something was up. Who is it?"

"I didn't know, but we suspected an attack tonight was possible."

"Why now?"

"This is the most vulnerable time. The hacker would know this. We might be able to stop it. That's why we're here."

The Director looked back at Peter, whose back was towards them, and asked, "Well, are we or are we not being hacked?"

"We are, and I can't stop it. I don't know what or where it's trying to go in the system."

He looked back at Melbourne. "Can you stop it?"

"We can try, if you'll let us."

"What is their objective?"

"If I'm right, it's to destroy the entire system."

Director Mitchell's face turned white. "Destroy it? How?"

"We need access to it immediately. Every moment we delay increases his odds of success."

Chapter 26

Director Mitchell shouted nervously, "Do it, do it now. Like you said, this project is still yours. You had better stop him."

Melbourne whispered instructions to the three amigos. "See if Hercules can find Steven's daughter, then get out of the system as fast as you can. We must find the girls before midnight, that is our mission tonight, nothing more. Understand?"

Marvin hurried to a workstation and plugged in his laptop into a docking port.

Director Mitchell suspiciously asked, "Who is the hacker?"

"I can't know for sure, but if I had to guess, I would say a former employee. I believe you personally fired him. His name is Wade Sullivan."

"I do remember him, cocky little bastard. He thought he oversaw the whole project. Just couldn't follow instructions."

Marvin was doing the typing, while Rodger and Tesia gave technical advice.

Director Mitchell asked Peter, "What are they doing? Is it working?"

"I don't know, sir. They are asking Hercules some sort of encrypted questions."

Melbourne calmly explained, "Hercules is the best source of what the hacker is doing. If Hercules can identify how it's being hacked, we can try to stop it."

Director Mitchell looked at a big digital clock on the wall, it was ten to midnight.

Rodger typed frantically for the next ten minutes. It was just after midnight, he mumbled, "Hercules is safe."

Peter confirmed, "It looks like the hack was stopped. Did you put up a firewall?"

Tesia said, "He did. Once we knew the path of greatest weakness, Marvin plugged the hole."

Everyone looked at the clock; it was now five minutes after midnight.

Marvin had already unplugged his computer.

Peter announced, "The security protocols are all online, sir. I believe the system is safe."

Director Mitchell turned to Melbourne and shook his hand heartily. "Great job people, all of you. I assure you, we will find the hacker, but you all have done your country a great service."

Marvin nervously said, "I'm done, must go now. My friend is safe." Marvin shuffled out of the room.

Director Mitchell asked of no one in particular, "What does he mean, his friend is safe?"

Rodger shrugged his shoulders, "I don't understand him most the time. But I gotta go find him before he gets lost."

Rodger left the room along with Tesia.

The Director turned to ask Melbourne what was up with his three associates but when he didn't see Melbourne, he assumed he had left, too.

****

Wade's faced turned furious. His hack was stopped. His entry port was useless, the terminal was dead. He took his laptop, closed it with a slam, he tossed it at the concrete wall across from him. It hit the wall; there was a crash and pieces scattered.

Instantly, Wade regretted what he had done. The computer was replaceable, but some of the software on it wasn't.

"Dammit!" Wade cursed. He realized he had to pick up the pieces to his computer and hope he hadn't damaged the hard drive beyond repair. "Don't worry old boy." He said to himself. "The night isn't over yet. A new life awaits, after a promise is kept."

****

Steven heard a crash. A loud voice cursed. He had been in the basement looking for something or someone for over an hour. He was in the process of tracing some water pipes through the cavernous sub-basement when he heard the noise.

He assumed that the only other person down in the belly of the beast was Wade. Steven walked cautiously towards the sounds. Small grains of sand crunched under his hard-soled dress shoes. He slipped them off, Drew the gun from the small of his back; the sounds were coming from beyond the next turn in the tunnel.

Steven turned the corner and saw Wade putting his computer or what was left of it in his leather computer case. "Freeze," he shouted.

Wade looked up and smiled. "Why is everyone pointing guns at me tonight? It's starting to get annoying. And especially you. I was hoping you might be dead. It is too bad for your daughter that you're not. I did warn her, if her father didn't die tonight, she would have to."

"Put the bag down, slowly. Make no mistake, I want to kill you," Steven said calmly, but with anger. "Where is my daughter and her friend?"

"Come now," Wade said as he lowered his computer bag full of computer parts down to the ground, "you don't expect me to just give away my trump card when you have already said you want to kill me. Not so easy Senator."

Steven pressed the trigger; in the cavernous empty basement the sound of the shot was loud. The bullet splintered the concrete behind Wade. The fragments lashed back at Wade, causing him to instinctively raise his hands to protect his face.

"You don't understand," Steven said. "I'm not going to kill you right away. Think about it. I only care about saving my daughter and her friend. I don't care about you, and I don't care what they do to me after. The only thing that matters is saving my daughter. That puts you in a deadly position.

"This is my last polite request. Where is my daughter?"

Steven heard a click behind him. "Don't turn around, Senator. Drop your weapon."

"Alphonso Lucas." Steven recognized the voice. "Are you here to take another daughter from me?"

"Senator, I made the mistake of letting my guard down once today. I won't do it again. Drop your weapon," he said forcefully. "Your daughter is not yet lost. Do not make her situation worse."

Steven dropped the gun. "How do you know my daughter is alright? Where is she?"

Alphonso said, "Move to the wall, by Mr. Sullivan. I don't know where she is; I just know that Mr. Sullivan hasn't killed them yet. Isn't that so Mr. Sullivan?"

"So true, so true. That's why it would be a shitty idea to kill me."

Alphonso asked. "Were you successful in destroying the computers?"

"Fuck you. None of your god damn business."

Another gunshot rang loudly through the basement as a bullet whizzed past Wade's ear and spit concrete fragments at him for the second time in minutes.

Loudly, Alphonso demanded. "Were you successful?"

"Look mister, I don't know who you are, but I do know you have important contacts, so you'll find out soon enough anyway. No, somebody with exceptional skills detected my hack and stopped it."

"I guss that would make your usefulness to me over." Alphonso pointed the gun at Wade's forehead.

"Wait, Alphonso, wait," Steven shouted. "He's the only one who knows where my daughter is. You can't kill him until he tells me where she is."

"And what good will that do? You are assuming that I will let you live."

"You said you need me," Steven said as he stepped toward the wall opposite Alphonso.

"No, I said the United States will need a strong statesman. I think you are that man. Right now, I think everyone would be better served by concentrating on what I need. What I need is the computers destroyed. Your failure is disappointing to say the least, Mr. Sullivan. You know this complex and the computers, how can they be destroyed? And I remind you, your use to me is marginal at this point."

"Easy," Wade said. "All we must do is break through about two feet of reinforced concrete. Once we get to the other side, undetected of course, we can do some real damage. The other side is basically unprotected because nobody believes anybody that would be capable of doing any damage would be able to get even close to it. My plan to have the computer attack itself is now a moot point.

"Look Mr. Alphonso, or whatever your name is. I'm sure there is a weakness to be exploited. Right now, with a gun pointed at me, strangely, I not thinking clearly enough."

Alphonso took a step back. Steven was now looking at the man and saw his white shirt and coat were covered in drying blood. His face and nose looked like it had been hit by a bus.

Alphonso reached into his white suit jacket inside pocket, he pulled out a wide plastic zip tie and tossed it towards Steven.

"Tie his hands behind him."

Steven roughly grabbed Wade's arms and hands, pulled them behind his back, and gladly tugged the zip tie as tight as he could.

"Mr. Sullivan will be coming with me. He is right, with his knowledge of this place, killing him now would be premature. With the right incentives, over time, with only one objective to think about, it's possible Mr. Sullivan can come up with an alternate plan."

"Why?" Steven asked, "Why is the destruction of this installation so important to you?"

"Too bad you won't be around to see the apocalypse yourself. Imagine a world in which no computer, nothing with an electronic chip needed to run it will work. Unfortunately, the architecture of these computers is too unique to be affected by our plans. It's knowledge to complete. It could be used to not just rebuild society but recreate it. That is the opposite of our goal."

Steven said, "You're talking about cars, phones, planes, hospitals, medical equipment, all not working. That is impossible. You're insane."

"Insane or a visionary? Most visionaries are not understood in their own time."

"Look, Alphonso, I'm stepping down from being a Senator. You leave me and my family alone, I will never mention you or IRENE again. And I don't care what you do to those damn machines. As you know, I'm not sure they have been legally built anyways."

"Unfortunately, I can't take even a small chance that leaving you alive might cause a premature exposure to our plan. As any gambler would agree, leaving you dead, here in the basement of Caesars, is the best bet. Nobody will discover you for days or weeks. At any rate, I will be long gone, and I can guarantee you will never mention me or IRENE."

Steven said, "What you are proposing is a massive EMP blast around the entire world at the same instant. You do realize that is impossible."

Alphonso picked up Wade's computer bag and draped it over Wade's shoulder. All the while keeping the gun pointed at Steven. He answered, "You're right, it would be. Think of this, on the bright side, your daughter will not be distressed over your death."

****

Melbourne hid among the series upon series of racks holding computer components. It was easy to dodge the security cameras. First, there weren't that many inside the secure facility; second, he knew exactly where each and every one was.

He looked around, trying to anticipate exactly what Wade was going to do next. Melbourne was upset that Marvin stopped the hack. He had been exceedingly specific to the three. Locate the girls but don't stop the hack.

That was unfortunate for the girls he hadn't listened. They seemed like nice young ladies. There was no doubt in his mind that Wade had been behind the attempted hack of the computers. If it hadn't been for the need to find Steven's daughter, he could have left Marvin and his friends happily at the concert.

Marvin had muttered something about his friend being safe now. At first, Melbourne assumed it meant he had located his new friends, the young girls, and they were safe. Now Melbourne realized that it hadn't meant that at all. Unfortunately, his problem at the moment, was greater than saving the lives of two young girls.

Melbourne turned his analytical mind to the task at hand. It was up to him to destroy the most personally evasive computer ever designed by man. The question was how one man could destroy acres and acres of computers.

****

Steven argued, "My career, my reputation, it's going to be attacked by those in the deep state. Even if I wanted to expose these computers, expose you, it will just sound like the rambling of a desperate man.

"Take Wade, I don't give a shit about what you do with him. I just want my daughter. Give me that, and I promise I am out of your hair. If you kill me, you know that when my body is eventually found there will be an investigation, it could expose you and your plan."

The man in white responded, "An investigation that will undoubtedly be compromised. Powers that you don't understand will see to it that your body was found miles from here. The people who built this place have way too much invested to let your death interfere."

Steven knew he was fighting for his and his daughter's life, said, "Who's side are you on, aren't my enemies your enemies at this point?"

"Ah, the adage, 'The enemy of my enemy is my friend.' Sorry Senator, you are neither my enemy nor my friend, but merely a loose end at this point."

Chapter 27

Caesars Palace, government side:

Melbourne had an idea; heat was the nemesis of all computers. If he could turn off the cooling system, the computers would automatically go into shut down mode. The problem was that a temporary shutdown wouldn't solve the problem. The change would have to be quick and extreme; the computers couldn't be given the opportunity to shut themselves off.

The circulation pipes of the ultra-cold water were scattered throughout the complex. Each section had its own heat exchange system designed to specifically prevent a catastrophic failure. Melbourne understood the basics of the system; however, it hadn't been his expertise that designed it.

Melbourne cautiously crawled towards the closest heat exchanger. It was a huge machine of pumps and transfer coils. If there was a weakness to exploit, he reasoned it would be his best chance. It was soon obvious which of the two big circulation pipes carried the ultra-cold water coming from the chiller, and which carried away the cold exchanged water, which was now warm, back up to Lake Lerna. Melbourne didn't know what would happen when minus four hundred degree Fahrenheit water instantly mixed with plus ninety-degree water, but he assumed it would be catastrophic.

****

Chelle was sitting in the back of a black sedan. Her hands were growing numb from the cuffs. She was locked alone in the car, her hands cuffed behind her, she sat helpless. She was still at Caesars Palace. The knowledge that Wade Sullivan was spotted on the property had changed everybody's plans. Whatever they were going to do with her was on hold as all agents were tasked with finding Wade.

****

Alan D Schmitz
DIGITAL SECRETS

Melbourne spent long minutes studying the myriad of pipes and valves trying to understand the system as best as possible. He could see no way to divert either pipe into the other. However a plan came to light. He started crawling forward when out the corner of his eye he spotted movement.

He crept silently. A technician walked past, focused on making notes and reading gauges. Melbourne felt his heart beating and tried to will it to calm. He closed his eyes and meditated taking small breaths as he hid between two equipment racks.

The facility was an ultra-clean environment, so the special static free boots the tech wore, were silent on the floor as she moved. The technician's toolbox was on the floor not far from him. He crawled to the box. A hammer was visible. The trick would be to get the hammer without the tech noticing.

There were several tools on top of it. He lifted out a wrench with the utmost care. He glanced toward the tech still occupied with taking notes. Gently he lifted out a screwdriver, and a set of pliers.

Setting the other tools softly on the floor next to the case, he reached in and lifted out the hammer. After another glance at the tech, he replaced the pliers, and the wrench.

He had the screwdriver in hand when he noticed a shadow come over the toolbox. He glanced up at the technician dressed in a white throwaway coverall.

"Mr. Winston!" She said shocked to see the man on his hands and knees with a screwdriver in his hands.

"Jean, I thought I recognized you." Melbourne stood up slowly.

"Are you supposed to be here?"

"I was just wrapping up some details when I noticed an open terminal cover. You know me, I just can't stand even small details out of place." He looked at the screwdriver in his hand and added, "I saw your toolbox and needed to borrow this to fix it. Shouldn't take more than a minute or two."

"If you show it to me, I would be more than happy to fix it. I was told that after tonight you would no longer have access to the computers."

"Just taking care of some final details. I'm sure you understand."

"Hell, I don't care," said the young tech. "But I'm afraid I will have to escort you out, sir. You understand, orders, strict rules are in effect."

Melbourne smiled, "Of course." With a sudden thrust of his hand the screwdriver pierced the white coverall, the girl's mouth opened in a gasp from the sudden pain. A growing spot of blood appeared on her white covering at heart level.

Melbourne held her collapsing body with the screwdriver sticking out of her chest in his arm and cried, "I'm sorry Jean, I'm so sorry." He lowered her down next to the toolbox, her blood now covering the white tiled floor. He said to the dying woman choking on her own blood. "You have to understand, if I'm successful, you would have died anyway tonight. This might be the preferred way."

Melbourne wasted no time. He picked up the hammer and went to the spider distributer, where the larger volume of super cold water was circulated to a series of heat exchanging coils. It was these coils that cooled the heat absorbing liquid mix that ultimately cooled the computers.

If he could damage the spider distributer, the super cold water would pour out onto the machine, instantly freezing the unit and any and all moving parts and pumps. The hot water coming back from being circulated wouldn't be cooled and the computer components would quickly overheat.

Melbourne took a giant swing of the hammer, hitting the device square. He bent some of the spider tubes, but the mixer stood solid. He took another swing; this time there were no tubes to absorb the energy. The component metal was brittle from the severe cold. It shattered.

Super cold water under high pressure poured out as expected. Unfortunately, as it hit component after component, it splashed back at Melbourne and instantly super froze any exposed skin. Melbourne's saw his hands turn instantly frosty white. He felt nothing, but he knew the pain would soon be excruciating.

He stepped back to admire his work. In a surreal way, the liquid water was instantly becoming ice. First the water froze where it hit the equipment, he watched in amazement as the ice climbed up from the equipment towards the valve.

The freezing water was overtaking the liquid water. It climbed against gravity towards the main pipe. It kept climbing making it look like the flow of the water was reversing itself until it reached the valve and climbed inside the pipe.

Melbourne's heart sunk when the pipe froze solid, effectively blocking the flow of water.

"No, no, this can't be happening," Melbourne shouted to the pipe.

With hammer in hand, he ran. He had to find another one of the heat exchanging mechanisms. There were numerous scattered about. He needed to destroy more of them for his plan to work.

He found another station and repeated his motions, this time remembering to step back immediately. He avoided the worst of the spray back. His face was starting to sting. He assumed real pain would eventually follow.

He ran to the next station, working his way back deep into the labyrinth. The brittlely cold metal shattered just as before. Alarms were starting to blare. He recognized the alarms as a high heat warning. The system was built on fail-safes; if one unit went down others were designed to take over. He was ruining too many for the system to compensate. Nobody had envisioned so many going down at the same time. his plan was working. He ran to the next.

His face was burning now and the skin on his hands had turned black. The pain was becoming debilitating. As he approached yet another heat transfer station, he passed a component cabinet with a glass front. Inside were numerous routers and switches and the corresponding blinking and flashing red, green, and yellow lights indicating the performance of the equipment.

As he passed the glass, he also saw his reflection. It was no wonder he felt pain around his face. His black skin was sagging off his face. He didn't recognize the person reflected. He needed immediate medical help if he were to survive, and he knew that wasn't going to happen. Melbourne looked at his reflection and prayed he died soon and without too much pain.

At yet another heat transfer station he pounded on the same spider valve assembly. It wasn't as brittle, yet he eventually broke it, but no water spilled, it was already solid ice. Strange, Melbourne pondered the paradox.

He was now at the back of the complex. The concrete wall behind him was a common two-foot wall separating the government facility from the privately owned Caesars Palace. He wondered what would happen when the computers and components all overheated at the same time.

"Melbourne, what the fuck are do you think you are doing? Your face, my God?" It was the director, and he had a gun pointing right at him, but his eyes were focused on his face.

He heard a screeching sound, like metal on metal. He looked up towards the sound. The pipes sounded like they were screaming in pain. What Melbourne didn't count on was a curious phenomenon of super cold water. It stayed liquid if it was pure H_2O, but once contaminated, it instantly froze, each molecule taking its cue from the molecule before it. The pipes above him were freezing and expanding.

The director took his eyes off Melbourne for a second to look to where the sound of the screeching metal was coming from.

****

The man in white aimed his gun at Steven and said calmly, "Your reputation is undeniably ruined. In fact, your political career is over whether you want it to be or not. Still, I can't take the chance that you make a desperate attempt to stop us, you do have allies, of that we are aware."

Alan D Schmitz
DIGITAL SECRETS

All three heard a rumbling like distant thunder. They felt the concrete under their feet vibrate. An instant later the concrete wall blasted towards them.

Steven instinctively closed his eyes, raising his arms to cover his face from concrete fragments that were exploding like hand grenades all over the place. A force of some sort gave him a mighty push. His military instinct immediately kicked in and he curled himself into a ball in the air. When he opened them again, he was half-buried. The room he had been in was gone, or at least not recognizable. He felt oddly cold. The air was full of dust, cold, wet, sharp dust. He coughed; his lungs hurt. Only feet away he saw the man in white's arm sticking out through a pile of frozen rubble.

The frozen concrete was covering him too, but the trillions of micro explosions had so thoroughly disintegrated the concrete that the pieces of concrete covering him were small enough that he could push them off.

Wearily Steven stood. His black tuxedo was torn, his right leg was bleeding and exposed through his torn dress pants. His bare stocking feet were bleeding.

Steven searched the area for another body. Wade had his hands tied behind him. He was helpless and certainly under the ruble.

Steven said, "fuck!"

****

Melbourne saw the director look away for an instant. In that instant he ducked behind some equipment. A glass protective case acted like a mirror when he hid behind it. Melbourne saw his face; his skin was black and sagging off him. Melbourne looked at his blackened hand and realized the excruciating pain already in his arms and hand would soon be over his ruined face.

The steel-on-steel screeching continued. He looked up. The pipe above him was about to burst he could see it growing bigger than it was ever intended. Melbourne peaked around the corner and saw that the director realized something disastrous was about to happen right over his head. The director holstered his gun and began running.

Melbourne stood up and walked forward. The pipe burst and gallons and gallons of super cold water gushed out. It sprayed over the floor, over the equipment, onto the back wall, and onto Melbourne.

Within the concrete, on a microscopic level, were water molecules. They were the remnants from when the concrete was placed in a more liquid state. When the super cold water sprayed onto the concrete, it caused any water molecules still trapped in the concrete to instantly freeze and expand with exploding force. The combined effect was one massive explosion and disintegration of the concrete. Anything with moisture was instantly frozen, including Melbourne.

****

Steven looked around through the swirling dust. Where there had been a solid wall was now an opening into another world, a noisy world with continuing explosions coming from deep in its bowels. The area was lit in an eerie red emergency light.

Steven limped a bit, coughed a bit, and spit out the dust in his mouth. He had to find Wade and pray that he was still alive. He spied the pouch of the leather computer bag that was draped over Wade's shoulder. He dropped to his knees and started to dig frantically with his hands.

He followed the wide leather strap hoping it would lead him to Wade. He soon found a head. With bloody hands he revealed more and more of his face.

Wade gave a mighty cough and inhaled deeply. "I couldn't breathe," He gasped.

"Tell me where my daughter is," Steven demanded.

"Dig me out, then I'll talk."

Steven stood, "I think we'll do it my way." Steven dropped a handful of pulverized concrete onto Wade's face. "I can just as easily bury you again."

Steven took another handful of debris and dropped it.

"OK, OK!" Wade said as he spit out the debris dropped on him. "She and her friend are locked inside the arena. But you'll never find them, certainly not in time anyway. You need me. Dig me out and I'll show you."

"I tell you what. If you tell me exactly where they are, I will send someone down to rescue you after they are safe and sound."

"If I tell you, you will let me here to rot. Not going to happen. If you torture me, I will give you an answer. Only problem is, you will never know if I am telling the truth or not. Another little detail, you need me to save them. If we don't get their before one AM, game over, they're dead, I've seen to that. Only one way: you take me with."

Steven turned away, "Let me think about it for a moment."

While coughing, Wade laughed. "If you don't take me with you out this hell hole, I'm assuming I'm a dead man. So, fuck you.

Steven got down on his hands and knees, he started to dig out the body of the man in white. When he had the man in white dug out sufficiently, he turned his body from on its stomach to on its back. He appeared dead to Steven. Finally, he found what he was looking for, the gun that he had been forced to drop.

Steven tuned away from the man in white's body and placed his knee on Wade's neck. He pointed the gun at Wade's head.

"I'll spare your life, for my daughter and her friend's life. But one wrong move and I will kill you."

Steven tucked the gun into the small of his back. Digging with his bare hands it took another precious ten minutes. Finally, he believed he had Wade dug out enough to lift him out of the debris pile. Assuming his hands were still securely tied behind him Steven reached forward and began pulling on Wade's arms to free him.

Behind his back Steven felt the gun being removed. He twirled around and heard the safety being turned off. Alphonso had stolen his gun back. "It appears I no longer need your services, Mr. Sullivan."

There was a shot, Wade instantly had a hole in the middle of his forehead.

Steven screamed as he turned towards the man in white, "No, no, he was the only one who knows where my daughter is."

The gun was now pointed at him, Steven kicked at the gun; it flew out the man's hand. He had barely any strength to resist. Steven fell on him and started to pound his already bloody face.

"No more, no more," Steven screamed as he pummeled him over and over again. He fell back in exhaustion.

He stared at the lifeless bodies around him. He watched carefully the man in white's body. It wasn't breathing, he had seen dead men before, this time there was no doubt. Alphonso Lucas was dead; he had killed him with his bare fists.

Out of habit, he checked for his phone. It wasn't in his ripped pants pocket. He saw it under some debris, cracked and bent, useless. Still, he picked it up, bent it as straight as he could and slipped it into his pocket. Though he was mentally and physically fatigued, Steven found his shoes and started the long climb back out the way he had come.

Arena after Dancing Chickens concert:

Tamara was trying to maintain her composure, knowing it was after midnight. She knew from her time on the police force that a hysterical woman, a hysterical mother, was not taken as seriously as a stoic one. It was hard for her to appear calm because she was panicking on the inside.

They were standing just outside the main entrance. The sun had long set and the desert air was cooling rapidly. They were outside the row of forty or so doors into the arena.

Jojo had his badge in hand and pleaded for the tenth time, "I'm a detective, this isn't just some cockamamie story. We, all of us, and more, need to search every inch of this building for my daughter and the daughter of Senator Steven Westcott."

Mack, the head of security was patiently listening. He had on his security uniform and Jojo guessed he was ex-cop. He was wearing all the standard issue cop attire on his belt, aside from carrying a gun. Mack said for the tenth time, "This building is on sixteen acres, the arena itself has 650,000 square feet, the loading dock another 75,000. I don't even know how many rooms, suites, equipment areas. If we had the security footage, it would help, I agree with you, but we don't. I don't have a clue what happened to it. I'm sorry, just the way it is."

Jojo argued, "It's big, I get it. So, let's get started. Do you want this building to get the reputation that it was where a Senator's daughter was murdered?"

Tamara said through tears, "We don't need to search ninety percent of the building. He would have avoided the common areas. We believe the killer hid them somewhere non-descript, private."

Mack agreed, "Yes of course, but that is what I'm trying to tell you, even the non-common area is huge. And I must repeat one more time, this is all a guess on your part. We have a hockey game tomorrow we must get ready for. If we were to search every inch of this building, it would take a small army of people to get it done in time.

"Everyone but us has gone home to get some rest before tomorrow's event. I can't even think about calling them back in to work all night and all day again tomorrow based on a hunch."

Jojo's frustration was showing. Tamara thought he was going to hit something or someone at any moment.

Tamara stepped between Mack and Jojo. Looking Mack in the eyes she said, "You must have a night shift, a few people, that's all we ask, someone to guide us through the building. We will search all night, we might get lucky, we must try. What would you do if it was your daughter or son?"

"Dammit!" He said, "I guess I don't need to sleep tonight. Nobody knows this place like me. We need to come up with a plan. I have drawings up in my office, let's try to come up with the most likely areas and start there.

A taxi stopped near the concrete expanse of the main gate. It was Mack who spotted the three characters walking towards the closed arena.

"Now what?" he said.

Jojo and Tamara looked in the direction he was staring. "Thank God," Tamara said.

Jojo added, "They're with us; they might have more information."

Jojo ran to them. Tamara and Mack just behind him. "Did you get it? Do you know where our daughters are?"

Rodger shook his head, "Marvin got into the computer. He had to stop the hack first. But he didn't have time to run a query through the computer."

"You have nothing?"

Marvin spoke up, "Hercules is alive. I saved it."

Jojo looked with disgust at Marvin, "I think my daughter is a bit more important than your fucking computer."

Marvin pressed his laptop case tightly against his chest and looked away.

He looked at Tesia and Rodger, "Any word from Senator Westcott?"

Tesia answered, "No, we haven't seen him. Where's Melbourne? We waited around for him outside of Caesars, but he never came out. We decided he must have come straight here."

Tamara said, "It's just us. We haven't heard from Steven or Chelle either."

Mack interrupted, "It's getting late, do you still need to search the arena?"

Tamara, touched Mack's arm lightly, "Oh, yes, please we must try. They were our last hope, unless Senator Westcott somehow gets more information."

Mack said, "You would think a US Senator and his daughter would have some protection from the Secret Service or something."

Jojo said, "Afraid not. We're on our own."

Tamara asked Tesia and Rodger, "Will you help? Please!" Tamara couldn't contain herself any longer and cried. Jojo held her for just a moment.

"Sweetheart, we don't have much time."

"I know," she sobbed. "Let's get on with it."

The six walked into the first of forty entrance doors. They had a huge task ahead of them.

****

Steven dragged himself up the seemingly never-ending series of stairs. The level the actors had staged from was oddly quiet. It was lit by a stray incandescent bulb here and there.

He pushed himself up the last set of stairs. The seating area for the show was illuminated by red exit lights. It was silent as if he was the last person on earth. He was tempted to rest for a while on one of the thousand seats that were available in the darkness. He pushed on.

When he emerged through the main entrance doors to exit the theater, he expected pandemonium as workers and patrons of Caesars Palace raced to empty the four thousand rooms and casino.

Steven emerged into the brightly lit casino area in front of the main doors. He was bloodied, filthy from cement dust, his tuxedo ripped in various places. His shoes were filthy and untied. The normal activities of the casino and hotel were in full swing, even considering it was 12:30 AM.

All appeared oblivious to the destruction happening four stories below. Steven stumbled through the crowd getting strange stares for his condition and lost look of confusion on his face.

When he passed the fountain of the three goddesses, he used some of the water to splash his face clean. He staggered out the main entrance doors. He needed to find Chelle and Jojo and Tamara. He was sure they were at the arena, and he wasn't going to waste a moment getting there.

Outside the great hall of the main reception area, cars and cabs were still dropping off passengers and picking up smiling and laughing patrons. He flagged down a cab and noticed flashing police lights a block away, though still on the Caesars property. He studies the scene and saw more than one ambulance standing by.

Curious, he walked towards the commotion. As he got closer, he became more curious and suspicious, so he stayed in the shadows. There were paramedics from the ambulances rushing into the building, men in black suits, and people dressed in military attire directing the activity.

People were being carried out on stretchers; it was clear that something major had happened on the military side of the underground structure. Somebody had caused serious damage. He wondered who, because clearly Wade and Alphonso were under the impression they had failed to destroy the complex.

He was on the south side of the Caesars complex, there was a side entrance into the casino and he saw an opportunity to pick up a cab there. As he walked trying not to get noticed, he saw through the flashing lights what looked like a familiar hair style and a lady in a red dress in the back of a black sedan.

He crept up on it slowly. He picked his head up from his crouched position and peaked in the window, he wrapped on it.

"Chelle, is that you?"

"Steven, thank God," Chelle said loudly through the closed window. "What happened to you?"

Steven looked around to make sure nobody saw or heard him. "Wade is dead. But he didn't tell me where the girls are, they're still in danger. Why are you in the back of this car?"

Chelle turned slightly and showed him the handcuffs securing her hands behind her back. "I'm under arrest."

"By who?"

"Not sure, wouldn't tell me. Maybe the FBI, or CIA."

"Fuck them." Steven cursed as he tested the locked doors.

"Look away, I'm getting you out."

"No Steven, it'll only get us in more trouble."

A big rock appeared in Steven's hand. "Fuck em. Look away."

Chapter 28

Before Chelle could object, the rock smashed the window. Steven hit it repeatedly. The glass spider cracked into a thousand pieces. He used the rock to brush away any glass pieces still in the frame.

Steven reached in, grabbed Chelle by her underarms, and pulled her out of the car through the opening ripping her dress.

"They have their hands full," Steven said. "Somebody has severely crippled the computer system."

Steven took off his filthy black jacket and wrapped it over Chelle's hands to hide the handcuffs.

"Let's get out of here."

Steven blocked Chelle from view by placing himself between the rescue operation and her. They rushed to the taxi stand and were soon on their way to the arena.

In the cab, Steven took Chelle's hair pin and started to work on the handcuffs.

"Give me the hair pin," Chelle said as Steven fumbled with the lock. "I've been trained to open them with various tools."

There was a click, one of the cuffs sprung open. "I have skills," Steven said and handed the hair pin to Chelle's now-free hand.

"I would never question your skills," Chelle smiled. With a click, the other cuff was opened.

They were soon at the arena and Steven handed the taxi driver a twenty, they ran up the deserted square in front of the main gates. They ran with hands laced together up to the main entrance. Steven ran down the row of forty doors and pulled on each, all were locked.

"Do you have your phone?" Steven asked.

"No, they took it."

Steven pulled his from his pocket and showed the destroyed device. He saw a grouping of landscape blocks used to protect the base of a tree.

"I should be able to loosen one of these," he said.

"What is it with you and rocks going through windows?"

Steven was working to loosen the big block when Chelle noticed someone at one of the doors.

It was Mack, the arena security chief. "I recognized you two from earlier. I don't mind saying that this is the strangest night I have ever experienced, and that is saying something.

"Your friends are inside starting a search of arena with a couple of my men that I could spare. We have been trying with no success to restore the security videos." He looked at the Senator's bloody face and filthy ripped clothes.

"What happened to you?"

"No word on the girls yet?" Steven asked, ignoring the question.

"No, as I've explained to your friends, searching sixteen acres will take forever."

Steven looked up slowly, his face drawn. "If you think I'm quitting now, you grossly underestimate me."

"Your friends already convinced me that wasn't an option, which is why I'm still here. I'm just saying, it'll be a herculean task without knowing exactly where they are. Come inside, let's locate your friends and see how their search is going."

Mack locked the doors behind them and ushered them to the security room. He led them into a room full of television monitors, one other person besides Mack was on duty in the room.

Chelle glanced at the bank of video monitors all displaying a different scene, she asked, "I thought the cameras were down."

"They were, this is live, which is fixed now, but the earlier recordings are still missing. So, this doesn't help us discover what happened to the two young ladies. It is my understanding that we do not even know if they are here or not."

Steven said, "The kidnapper confirmed that they are here somewhere. I was also told that they would never be found in time to save them. Unfortunately, he will not be able to help us."

Mack asked suspiciously, "Would the kidnapper have access to construction details, like mechanical drawings, air conditioning specs, electrical routing, plumbing? You know, diagrams of the non-public areas."

Steven answered, "You can bet on it. Why?"

"That's a problem, a huge one. There are miles of subterranean tunnels and such that carry water, electrical, and air-handling duct work. We need more people to search, many more." Mack pointed to a video screen, "Your friends started their search in the lowest level and will work their way up. That alone will take them all night, and they are searching only the most obvious of places. My fear is, after what you said, if the girls are hidden here somewhere, it won't be in the obvious places."

Mack pointed to another screen, "Here are three more of your friends with one of my guards checking out the same floor at the opposite area of the arena. They could walk right by where the girls are hidden and never know it."

Steven glanced at the screen, in camera view he only saw Tesia and Rodger. Marvin wasn't on screen, but he knew wherever his friends were, he wasn't far behind.

Steven remembered Wade's last words of warning, he asked Mack, "Can you contact them? They must stop looking immediately."

"What?" Chelle asked incredulously as Mack looked confused.

"The kidnapper warned me, there was some sort of device set to go off at one AM. It might also be detonated by an unauthorized entry."

Mack got on his radio, "Sam, Kurtis, immediately stop the search. There may be a bomb, a booby-trap. Stand by for more information."

Jojo was soon on the radio himself demanding more information.

Steven took the radio, "Jojo, it's Cowboy. I talked to Wade, he told me that if we didn't find the girls by one AM, they would die. He said I needed him to save them. We must assume some sort of bomb; we also must assume he rigged it to go off if anyone but him went to the girls."

"Where is he? I'll beat it out of him."

"He's dead Jojo, I'm sorry, I'm so sorry. I tried to bring him here. It's a long story, but trust me, he's dead."

Jojo came back on the radio and asked, "What are we going to do? We can't just wait until one AM, and hope he was bluffing."

Chelle answered, "We must assume he wasn't bluffing. Bluffing wasn't his M.O."

Steven looked at his watch, in fifteen minutes it would be 1:00 AM. His stomach turned. His daughter and Kristal only had minutes left to live.

Mack made a decision. He took back the radio, "Sam, Kurtis, get back up to the main control center with our guest. By force if you must. I need everybody back here pronto."

Mack looked at the Senator, "I'm sorry Senator, if there is going to be an explosion somewhere in this building, I need everybody here. It's probably the safest spot for now."

Ten minutes later, everyone was gathered in the control room. As soon as Jojo saw Steven he asked, "Are you OK? What the hell happened? You look like you just crawled out the ground."

Steven said, "You don't know how right you are. I'm OK." He looked at Tamara. "Tamara, I had him. He wouldn't tell me where the girls unless I took him with me. I was going to bring him here."

"What happened?" Tamara demanded.

"He was shot. I was next, but managed to kick the gun out of Alphonso's hand before he could pull the trigger."

"Alphonso?" Tamara asked.

Steven looked at Chelle, who now understood. She whispered, "IRENE was behind all of this?"

"Involved, yes," Steven said.

Jojo asked, "Who is IRENE, what does this have to do with our daughters? Cowboy what aren't you telling us? We only have minutes left to find them."

Just then, all the security video feeds went blank.

Rodger looked around, "Hey, where's Marvin?"

The screens came back to life, all at the same time.

Mack looked at the screens examining them for a clue. "Hey, these aren't live, these are all from earlier today. These are the missing recordings. Look at the time stamp, it's just before the concert."

Tamara said, "Everybody take a screen, look for the girls."

Chelle saw something, "Look it's them outside, they're taking the picture they sent us."

Steven pointed to his screen, "It's Wade. I recognize the hoodie he's wearing. He's talking to them."

Another screen flashed, Jojo said, "He's taking them into a side door."

Mack looked, and said, "That's the side security door; it shouldn't be open. Somebody is feeding this to us, these are all different areas at different times. It's a map of sorts. Here they are going down hallway B. They're just following him."

Mack said, "Keep your eyes on all the screens, we need to know where they go next."

Chelle said, "Here they are, it's a minute later, where are they?"

Mack looked at the screen, "Down a level. Camera says, hall Q. This is crazy, it would have taken my team at least a day to put this all together."

Tesia saw them again, "OK, I've got em."

Mack looked, "Another level down, in the basement, lowest level."

Steven was scanning all the screens from two steps back, he said, "Look, they're going into a room. The door is marked."

All the screens froze at the same time. Each with a different still shot of the time and place. All leading to the three going into the door, with one last still shot. It was Wade leaving the same door, alone.

Steven said, "That must be it. Take me there now."

Mack looked at his watch, "It'll be close. Everybody else stay here."

Mack ran out the door, with Steven, Jojo, Tamara, Chelle, behind him.

Tesia said to Rodger as she looked at the series of still photos in each of the many monitors, "Marvin."

Rodger smiled and said back, "Marvin, you son of a bitch," he said admiringly.

Tesia, still staring at the row of monitors whispered to herself, "But how?"

****

At the lowest level of the arena the group ran up towards the door, it was marked B3-5elec. They all stopped. Steven said, "Jojo and I have had some bomb training. I need you all to step back. Anything could happen when I open this door."

Steven looked at his watch; it was five minutes to one. Steven added, "Jojo, if this thing goes south, you rush in after and do what you can to save the girls. It's critical that we all not be incapacitated if there is a bomb, so back up."

He could see the look on everyone's faces showed the urgency of the situation was lost on no one. Jojo backed the group up to what they hoped would be a safe distance far down the hall.

Steven turned the handle slowly. He could feel the latch release. He stopped and took a breath. Very, very slowly he opened the door until there was a sliver of light he could look through.

Steven looked carefully and felt softly around the door. He noticed nothing out of the ordinary. He opened the door a sliver further. He could now see inside the room and around the door. Again, he saw or felt nothing. He cracked it open a bit more and became confident the door itself wasn't booby trapped.

He motioned for the group to stay back as he opened the door even more. With a clear view, he knew it was safe and opened it enough for him to enter. Now he scanned the room for the girls and any other possible traps. The room was open and empty.

Steven looked at his watch, it was a minute to one AM. He motioned the group forward.

"The room is empty; the girls aren't in it. Mack, check with the control room. Are they sure this it the right room?"

Mack picked up his radio, "Sam, precisely what room did the kidnapper lock the girls in?"

Over the radio the call came back, "I'm looking at the freeze frame right now. The sign on the door says, B3-5elec."

Everybody looked at the door and confirmed it was the right door.

Jojo asked, "Any chance there is more than one door marked like this?"

Mack said, "No, impossible."

Chelle ran down the hall looking at other doors in one direction, Tamara ran in the other.

Chelle came back first, she said. "Every door in that direction is in ascending order."

Tamara said, "Every door goes down from here."

Steven looked at his watch again, it was 1:00 AM.

****

Jojo had a hunch and went back into the room. He said to Steven as he scanned the room. "They came in and didn't come out. Where are they?" Suddenly he saw it and pointed, "That panel. It's big enough for a person to squeeze through."

Steven and Jojo ran up to it and loosened the latches. It was too late to worry about a trap; they removed the cover and heard excited shouts. "Dad, dad."

"Are you two all right?" Jojo shouted.

"Dad, over there, its poison, we heard it start up, he said it was chlorine gas."

Jojo and Steven looked in the direction the girls were staring. A yellow green gas was coming out from under the equipment housings.

Steven and Jojo realized that they needed a knife to cut through the heavy-duty zip ties. A knife they didn't have.

Jojo yelled, "I'll try to break them free. See if you can find a knife."

Steven said as he rushed out the small room, "Girls, take a couple deep breaths, hold your breaths for as long as you can and close your eyes."

Steven poked his head out the hatch opening, and yelled to the small group just outside and in the bigger room. "I need a knife, scissors, anything sharp. The girls are OK, but we must get them out ASAP. He booby trapped the area with deadly chlorine gas."

Mack said, "I have a knife." He took it out of its leather pouch and handed it to Steven.

Steven held his breath and ran back in. Jojo was struggling to break the ties with his bare hands without injuring the girls. The thick ties wouldn't break.

Jojo said, "Sorry girls, I'm going to have to break your wrist to get you out of here, there is no other choice." The gas was starting to burn his eyes.

Steven rushed back with the knife. The two men worked against time, their eyes burning. Jojo had to take a breath, he couldn't hold his any longer. Despite his coughing fit, which caused him to inhale even more gas, they got the girls loose.

"Keep holding your breath for a moment longer, girls, it's still not safe." Steven warned to the girls. "Keep your eyes closed. We'll get you out."

Each man dragged their respective daughter to the opening. From there, Chelle and Tamara, with the help of Mack, got the girls past the opening and dragged them out into the hall away from the deadly gas.

Steven climbed out and dragged out his gagging and coughing friend. Steven took a deep breath, replaced the steel cover containing the gas on the other side.

Jojo winced in pain as he coughed and gagged. Jojo looked up at Steven and smiled and gave a thumbs up sign. Talking was impossible.

Chapter 29

Las Vegas, NV:

T he small group was standing outside the 'Little White Chapel'. Kristal, Tracy, Tamara, and Jojo playfully threw rice at Chelle and Steven as they came out of the church.

They all laughed. Steven stopped Chelle long enough to give her a long kiss. He had found another black tuxedo, Chelle wore a white dress that came down mid-calf, and she had also found a short white veil.

Both Kristal and Tracy had bows and a small flower on each of their wrists. It had been Tamar's way of dressing up the bandages from where the zip ties had cut into them.

The moment was festive, though everyone, including the young girls knew the reason for the spontaneous marriage was because dark times were coming to the newly minted couple.

Jojo coughed a bit. Steven asked, "Are you sure you're up to this? You just got out of the hospital yesterday."

"Hell yeah, there was no way I was going to miss this." He coughed again. "The docs said my lungs would be sore for at least another week, but they're healing up fine."

Tracy gave her dad a big hug. "Congratulations, Dad."

"Thanks honey. You do know your mother is going to kill me when I finally get you back home."

"We talked," Tracy reminded him. "She understands that we couldn't go home until Uncle Jojo got out of the hospital."

"Uncle Jojo," Jojo said with a laugh. "I don't think I'll ever get used to hearing that."

"I'm sorry," Tracy said, looking sheepish.

Jojo gave a big smile, "Sorry? Hell no, I love it. I will always be your Uncle Jojo and don't you ever forget it."

Everyone laughed, including Kristal. Steven reminded, "Fun and games are over. Tomorrow it's back to the real world for you."

"For all of us," Chelle added.

Five black sedans pulled up to the chapel. The six of them knew it was coming, they just didn't know when. Steven had assumed the shit wouldn't hit the fan officially until they got back to D.C.

The same agent that had originally arrested Chelle walked towards them. Men and women all dressed conservatively emptied from the cars with guns at the ready. Behind those cars was a parade of news vehicles, all tipped off by the Department of Justice about the impending arrest.

"Senator Westcott," he said, "you are under arrest for traitorous actions against the United States."

Steven ignored the man and looked at his new bride and gave her a big hug. "As we suspected, I guess the honeymoon is going to have to wait."

They hugged tenderly as the rest of the arresting agents came forward.

Chelle said, "I'm so happy we got married, I may never be able to hold you again, but I am so proud to be Mrs. Steven Westcott. Even if the rest of the country is misled to hate you, I will always know the truth."

Steven looked back at the team of black suites who seemed to be waiting for some reason before arresting him. He saw why. It was James Mitchell, the Director of the National Security Agency walking towards them.

Steven knew why. He clearly wanted his time in the sun to be personally associated on national TV with the arrest of a traitor to the country. A traitor he had caught red-handed.

Steven looked at his daughter and gave her a smile and a wink. He had prepared her. He knew the five people he loved the most knew what had actually happened.

He turned to Jojo and said, "Get her home to her mother safely, that's all I ask."

"You know I will, buddy."

When he knew the television cameras were rolling, Director Mitchell said, "Senator Steven Westcott, you are under arrest for traitorous actions against the United States. You are being charged with the destruction of federal property necessary for the national security of the United States. We have video of you fraternizing with factions that are known enemies of the United

States. Two accounts of murder, one for the life of Wade Sullivan, an important government contractor, the second was the murder of another know conspirator."

Mitchell stared at Kristal, "And," he added, "transporting a minor across state lines for sexual gratification."

Steven surveyed the surreal predicament he was in. He knew the President could not in any way come to his defense. He was officially a pariah. He couldn't argue with James Mitchell. The offending videos had already been widely scattered over the internet and all the social media platforms.

His reputation had been irreparably damaged by photos and videos he couldn't explain, even if given the chance. He now understood how Kristal must have felt and still felt, only his problems went past a handful of school friends.

"I've got you now, you traitor. I have a lot of other charges; I just haven't had the time to catalog them all yet."

The agents roughly swung his arms behind him and cuffed him.

Mitchell said, "Before you are locked up so tightly you will never see the light of day again, I want you to see one more thing."

The agent in charge and three other agents walked up to Chelle standing in her white wedding dress and holding on to a bouquet.

He said, "Chelle Saltarie, you are charged with aiding and abetting, resisting arrest, escape from an officer's custody."

A female agent took the bow from her hands and the two male agents roughly twisted her hands behind her back and cuffed her.

Steven eyes reddened, "I'm so sorry, Chelle."

She said loudly, looking into one of the cameras, "I'm not."

Jojo and Tamara held onto the girls; all were in tears as the arresting agents led both away. Tracy broke free of Jojo's light embrace and ran up to Mitchell and kicked him as hard as she could in the shins.

DIGITAL SECRETS

Mitchell in front of the cameras hopped up and down on one leg as he held the other. Forgetting he was on live national television, he shouted, "Ow, ow, damnit, get that little bitch!"

Tracy shouted as she was being restrained, "I know the truth, my dad is not a traitor, and you know it too."

Mitchell shouted back over his shoulder at Steven, "And your delinquent daughter is going to be locked up too."

Steven attempted to turn and help his daughter, but agents shoved him into one of the black sedans. Chelle was soon in another. Seconds later the black line of cars was gone. The parade of news vehicles hurried to catch up with them.

Jojo stepped up to the agent holding on to Tracy, he said forcefully, "She's a minor, I am her guardian, and you had better let her go this instant."

Jojo saw the look of confusion in the agent's eyes.

"I'm telling you, you are manhandling a female minor, a US senator's daughter, on national television. Is that something you want to be remembered for, dragging away a female minor whose father you just arrested?"

The agent released Tracy, who ran to Jojo's protection. The agent warned, "Don't think we don't know where to find you. This is not over."

****

Steven was still in his black tuxedo; his one hand was handcuffed to an airplane seat of the private DOJ jet taking him back to Washington D.C. Director Mitchell was near the front of the plane; Steven was back towards the small bathroom all alone.

Steven had seen most of the evidence against him on social media and television; they all had. It looked convincing, even to him. He closed his eyes and imagined Chelle was being paraded around a public airport getting on a commercial jet in a humiliating way.

He couldn't help but review the incriminating evidence against him. He had seen the video and photos and explanation of them over and over again. As had anyone who followed any of the social media systems or television and cable news.

Melbourne's body had been found and connected to the destruction of government property. Exactly what was never disclosed, only that it was of national security importance. There were numerous photos of Steven with him at various times all time stamped to paint a timeline of events.

The photos of him helping Kristal onto the private plane also were played time and time again. He understood that the director first wanted to try and convict him in the court of public opinion. It would make getting a sympathetic judge that much easier.

Steven knew his DNA was all over the basement where he did in fact kill Alphonso Lucas. His bloodied hands had left residual all over Alphonso's face.

He had befriended Melbourne Winston. He was sure there were plenty of video evidence to support that. If it wasn't Wade or Alphonso Lucas who destroyed the Lake Lerner project, it had been Melbourne; however, he could never prove it.

Even if Winnie Winston testified that her husband was the one who wanted to destroy Lake Lerner, he was sure that information would be suppressed as a national security state secret. Was the evidence against him being manipulated? Of course. Did he have a chance of defeating a determined bunch of lawyers with unlimited funds and the courts and public opinion against him? Absolutely not.

He would attest that it was he who broke Chelle out of the FBI sedan. And that he had done so against her will. However, her actions after would undoubtedly negate that argument.

In short, they were screwed. He was going to jail for a long time, maybe life, maybe even be the first execution of a saboteur since before the Civil War. Undoubtedly, Chelle wouldn't get such a severe consequence, however her career as a law officer was finished.

Steven felt the plane slowing down. Soon he would be paraded before a long line of television cameras. He was already marked as a saboteur and traitor who had infiltrated into one of the highest political positions possible.

The talking heads on television were already speculating on how much national security information he had learned from being one of the members as the 'Gang of Eight'. And they were speculating on who he sold that information to and when and why he had flipped from being a respected former military man to informant.

The plane landed and taxied up to the airports private access area. He was guided down the stairs by strong hands. His hands were securely locked behind his back. There was no way from hiding his face from the cameras.

The reporters started shouting questions, but, to his surprise, not to him, but rather, at James Mitchell.

"Director Mitchell, now that Senator Westcott can positively prove his alibis for nearly every moment he was in Las Vegas, are you still pursuing charges?"

Steven realized he must have looked perplexed, but he doubted that he looked anywhere near as perplexed as Director Mitchell.

Steven watched as the director motioned for one of his aides to have a private discussion with him. Steven noted the aide had not been on the plane with them.

Another reporter shouted out, "Director Mitchell, is it true, that not only is Senator Westcott not a traitor to his country but was instrumental in trying to save the mystery project that you claim he destroyed? And why is the Senator still handcuffed?"

Steven was ignoring the throng of reporters; he was more interested in the animated discussion Director Mitchell was having with the aide. Director Mitchell was clearly upset.

Finally, Director Mitchell stepped forward towards the camera with a huge smile on his face.

"Ladies and gentlemen of the press, it is with great pleasure and relief that I remand Senator Westcott into his own custody. Unfortunately, I had to be the one to publicly embarrass the good Senator. So, I wanted it to be me, in front of all of you, to release him.

"The charges against the Senator are grave, and technically he is still charged with them until we can substantiate the proof he has submitted. But, assuming the video documentation he provided is accurate, he is not a flight risk."

Another reporter asked, "When will the charges against him be formally dropped?"

Director Mitchell with a wide smile assured, "As soon as possible. Though I suspect it could take weeks to verify."

"Are you suggesting that Senator Westcott may have falsified all these videos and phone records? How would he have done that?"

Steven had no idea what was going on, only that the handcuffs were being taken off him. He looked at Director Mitchell, whose red face couldn't conceal his embarrassment at not knowing what was going on either.

Mitchell answered, I am not proposing any such thing. But these are recent developments and need to be cataloged. I'm sorry, it has been a long day and I cannot take any more questions."

Director Mitchell turned away and walked down the tarmac towards a group of waiting black sedans, followed by his aids and other agents. The reporters turned their attention towards Senator Westcott, who suddenly found himself standing by himself in the middle of the tarmac.

Soon he was surrounded by reporters. One female reporter shouted, "Senator Westcott, you are obviously innocent of everything the Justice Department was charging you with. Are you going to sue the government?"

Steven smiled at the cameras and said, "First, no comment. Second, could somebody give me a ride back to my office?"

Chapter 30

President Julius Walker was sitting behind the Resolute Desk and his Chief of Staff was standing nearby. The only other person in the room was Director Mitchell.

The President asked, "Jim, are you incompetent or a liar?"

"Sir, I am neither."

"Senator Westcott, on his own, proved his innocence. He didn't have millions of dollars, and teams of government lawyers or FBI agents to help him, yet he blew your case against him out of the water by posting videos and getting the meta-data of his phone records to prove his whereabouts every minute he was in Las Vegas. Either you lied about everything you were charging him with or somehow you were clueless about what he was doing in Las Vegas. Which is it?"

"Sir, I had him followed, I don't know how he falsified those videos and documents. I have agent reports that say otherwise."

President Walker nodded his head at his Chief of Staff, who dropped a stack of papers on the Resolute Desk.

"Yes, I went through the reports."

Director Mitchell was clearly upset and surprised, "Those are Department of Justice confidential files. How did you get them?"

"A whistleblower in the department figured I should have them. They were right. What's the problem? You didn't have time to falsify them yet to make the senator look guilty? What do you have to say for yourself?"

Director Mitchell was clearly flustered. He said, "Senator Westcott is a traitor. He and his friends tried to destroy the computers. They did destroy them."

President Walker calmly asked, "The computers? What computers? You mean the ones you secretly built under Caesars Palace? A secret project even the Gang of Eight didn't know about, a project I didn't know about, called Lake Lerna?"

The President, who was watching Director Mitchell's reaction carefully, spotted a look of sudden epiphany on his face, "Son of bitch." Mitchell said, "That's how he did it. He used

Hercules; it must be. He used the computer to falsify his whereabouts."

The President said, "You mean as in your top-secret, impossible-to-be-hacked, hundred-million-dollar supercomputer? Let me get this straight. Steven Westcott, while you were spying on him, while he was vacationing with his daughter and an FBI agent, in-between playing blackjack and slot machines and going to shows, and getting married, still had time to destroy your heavily guarded, top-secret computer?

"Not only that, but somehow after he destroyed it, he hacked into the un-hackable computer, which is now in shambles, and rewired it to exonerate himself. Do I have your theory correct, Jim?"

Director Mitchell opened his mouth, but no words came out.

The President said, "Jim, you're fired. You tried to frame Senator Westcott and it backfired badly. To answer my previous question, you are a liar and an incompetent. I hope Senator Westcott's committee drags you so far through the mud that you will never be able to wash it off. Now get out of here."

Steven's apartment two weeks later:

Chelle was naked in Steven's arms; he was naked as well. They were enjoying a Sunday morning lounging in bed as husband and wife.

Chelle asked, "Now that you had time to think about it, any theories on what happened to clear our names?"

Steven looked at the television that was dark. He knew it was offline because he unplugged the power cord and the cable line to it. He still felt like it was watching them.

Chelle saw his glance, "I know, I'm paranoid too."

"I don't think of it as being paranoid anymore."

"Do we have to keep wrapping our watches and phones up in aluminum foil?" Chelle asked as she looked at the aluminum foil bundle on top the dresser top.

Steven chuckled, "Only if we don't want our pillow talk to end up on the internet. I'm going to buy a nicer looking Faraday case for eavesdropping protection at night."

"I guess Melbourne was right."

"I'm afraid he was right about a lot of things."

Chelle kissed Steven's chest, "I ask again, what happened?"

"My best guess?"

"Exactly."

"My guess is Melbourne was responsible for the destruction of Hercules. He is confirmed dead, found inside the complex under Caesars Palace. In a way he saved my life. The explosion that knocked Wade and Alphonso out, must have been caused by him. I was privy to photos of what was left of the Lake Lerna project. The damage looked extensive."

"Rebuildable?"

"Anything is rebuildable, and in truth it might be, but at least this time we'll know about it."

Steven ran his fingers lazily up and down Chelle's arm. She asked, "What about all the video evidence that cleared our names?"

"It had to be our three new friends. You and I, and a few others, know that things didn't exactly go down like the video evidence showed. Our names were cleared by fictitious facts."

"Fictitious facts? I like that. Everything looks so real."

"We know the time-stamped videos of us playing blackjack as part of our alibi were fake. Somebody got real video footage and inserted us into it somehow. It was so well done, it was accepted as real by the DOJ experts.

"The video of us outside the arena was real enough, but the meta data on the security recording was changed to prove we were there at a different time then in reality.

"Adding the footage of the girls to it made it look like we were the ones who dropped them off. Combined, they proved we were never with Melbourne or Winnie at all that night. In fact, the amount of video recordings and the time stamps proved we were with the girls at the pool, or at a restaurant with them, or in a hallway or elevator at a specific time. All backed up by the meta data of our phones proving we were where the videos said we were.

"The girls' kidnapping was never acknowledged by anyone. I guess if a tree falls in the forest and nobody hears it, it didn't fall. As far as your being charged with escaping from custody, there is no record of you being arrested in the first place. And besides, you were always with me, the videos proved it."

"But how?"

"I know, sophisticated stuff, the kind of stuff only Hercules could do that rapidly. Only Hercules couldn't, so it had to be Rodger, Tasia, and Marvin."

"And you haven't heard from them?"

"No, and I don't want to. I don't want to be tied to them and they don't want to be tied to us. It's no mystery that their images never appeared anywhere."

Chelle added, "I know we were both being framed, so the turnaround in my book is fair play. I just wish we could thank them. The publicity also cleared the accusations against Kristal. At least her friends got a lesson on not believing what is said on social media."

"I promise you this. In four years, my term is up and I'm not running again."

"Never say never, Senator. After what the Department of Justice tried to do to you, the country is in an anti-government mood right now. That is, except for the Senator that beat the Washington swamp at their own game. You know your poll numbers better than me. You would be a shoo-in."

"Doesn't matter. I've had it with the swamp and all the swamp creatures, and I certainly don't want to be one of them. Time to walk away while I can still hold my head high."

The End